Staplewood Park

MICHELLE GRAHAME

authorHOUSE®

AuthorHouse™ UK
1663 Liberty Drive
Bloomington, IN 47403 USA
www.authorhouse.co.uk
Phone: UK TFN: 0800 0148641 (Toll Free inside the UK)
UK Local: (02) 0369 56322 (+44 20 3695 6322 from outside the UK)

Published by AuthorHouse 01/09/2023

ISBN: 978-1-7283-7549-6 (sc)
ISBN: 978-1-7283-7550-2 (hc)
ISBN: 978-1-7283-7551-9 (e)

Print information available on the last page.

Any people depicted in stock imagery provided by Getty Images are models, and such images are being used for illustrative purposes only.
Certain stock imagery © *Getty Images.*

This book is printed on acid-free paper.

By the same author:

Love Will Have to Wait
Lord of Hades
Rhapsody in Black
The Yellow Diamond

Dedication

To my children: Katie, Richard and Alex.

About the Author

Michelle Grahame lives in Northwest Kent, and enjoys visits from her family, reading and taking part in local activities. "I love creating characters and plots for my novels." Says Michelle. As an avid collector, she likes attending boot and antique fairs, where a random purchase can become an inspiration for her writing. A qualified Art Historian and lecturer, now retired, she has had many opportunities to engage with people who share her interest. The YELLOW DIAMOMD, and its sequel, STAPLEWOOD PARK, are her first historical novels.

Chapter 1

Thunder and lightning rolled and flashed across the sky, and torrential rain drenched the young man standing in the middle of the lane. He was looking up at a three-fingered signpost situated on a grassy island, trying to shield a scrap of paper from the downpour. A streak of lightning forked to earth, and the peal of thunder that followed deafened him to the sound of a horse-drawn vehicle racing towards him at top speed, until it was almost too late. He just managed to jump to one side, but a wheel clipped his shoulder and spun him into a ditch, his head striking a stone wall that rose above it.

The vehicle careered on. The seventeen-year-old driver, having completely lost control of the galloping horse, was aware he had hit someone but was powerless to do anything about it. With reins torn from his hands, all he could do was cling, terrified, to the side of the carriage and hope it didn't overturn. Eventually the horse slowed and, within a few strides, came to a complete stop, totally exhausted. It stood, sides heaving, legs trembling, head down, unable to take another step. The driver got down cautiously and retrieved the reins. He had no idea where he was, but he knew he must have travelled several miles from the signpost. The rain had eased somewhat, and the storm was moving away. He was concerned about the tall dark figure he had nearly run over. He needed to report it to someone, if only he knew where he was. The horse was in no condition to continue, so he hitched the reins to the side of the kicking board and set off on foot.

It wasn't long before he recognised a lane leading off to the right and knew he was only about a mile away from his new home. With immense relief, he reached the iron gates of his house, Staplewood Park, and he was soon inside the building, calling for his father.

1

Lord Hargreaves came out of his study, newspaper in hand, and took one look at his white-faced mud-bespattered son. 'What in God's name has happened to you!?' he exclaimed.

'Horse bolted, frightened by thunder and a tree falling.'

His father looked out of a hall window but could see neither horse nor vehicle. 'Where is it now?'

'Dunno, but it's worse than that. I think I hit someone. He was standing in the middle of the road and didn't have time to get out of the way.'

The baron noticed his son begin to tremble with shock. 'You'd better come in to the study. I'll pour you a brandy, and you can tell me more. Better get rid of that wet coat, though.' He raised his voice. 'Parsons!'

Through a door, at the back of the spacious hall, a black-clad figure emerged. 'Yes, My Lord?'

'Please take Mr Nicholas's coat to be dried, Parsons.' Hargreaves looked at his son's rain-flattened blond curls. . 'Did you have a hat?'

'It fell off somewhere along the way,' his son replied, allowing the butler to remove his rain-soaked garment.

Once seated by the fire in his father's study and fortified by a small brandy, Nicholas was able to tell his father more clearly what had happened. But he still had little idea where the accident had occurred, or where exactly his horse and vehicle had ended up.

'Well, we'll have to do something. We can't leave a probably injured man lying in a ditch. It's a pity we don't know the area well.'

'There's hardly been time, Papa. We've only been here less than a month.'

'Ring for Parsons. He may know the place you describe.' Moments later, the butler arrived.

'Are you a local man, Parsons?'

'No, M'lord. I am a Londoner, sir.'

'Send someone in who knows the area. I want to talk to them.'

'Yes, My Lord.'

'I also want Hampton to bring my carriage to the front door. And send a groom out to find Mr Nicholas's gig. Where did you say you think it is, son?'

'About a mile or so along the road to the left of the main gate.'

'Have you got that, Parsons?'

'Yes M'lord.'

'Very well, then. Get to it.' The butler bowed and retreated. 'And you, son, had better go upstairs and change. Get out of the rest of those wet things. Get Joseph to help you. Then be ready when Hampton brings the carriage round.'

'Right away, Papa.'

There was a discreet tap on the door, and a young maidservant entered nervously, smoothing down the creases in her apron and dropping a curtsey.

'Don't be scared. What is your name, girl?' said his lordship, moving over to a desk.

'Maisie, sir.'

'Well, Maisie, Mr Parsons says you know the area round here well. Is that so?'

'Born and bred, sir.'

'Perhaps you can tell me where I might find a three-fingered signpost on a road somewhere on the left as you leave the drive?'

'I think so, sir.'

'Good.' Hargreaves pushed a piece of paper and a pencil towards the girl. 'Can you write down the names on the post for me?'

The girl said nothing, and the apron smoothing began again.

'Well, Maisie?'

'I can't rightly read nor write, sir, beggin' your Lordship's pardon.'

'I see. Well, never mind.' Hargreaves made a mental note to find out how many of his newly acquired staff were illiterate. 'Perhaps you can draw me a map of the roads or lanes I need to take to get there?'

With some difficulty and much licking of lips, Maisie produced a diagram of sorts, which they could probably follow.

'Thank you, Maisie. That will be all. You've been very helpful. You may go.' He followed her into the hall, just as his son was descending the stairs. 'That's better, less like a drowned rat. I can hear the coach coming.' He noticed that Nicholas was carrying a pillow and a couple of blankets. 'Good thinking, son. Your idea?'

'No, sir, Joseph's. I told him what had happened, and he thought we might need them if someone was injured.'

'That man is very thoughtful. I don't really know what to do with him. But nevertheless, I'm glad Royston and his wife decided to come with us from Ludlow. Now, the sooner we can find the casualty, the better. It must be well over an hour since it happened.'

The coachman was able to follow Maisie's diagram without difficulty, and although the rain had stopped, and a watery sun had appeared, progress was slow. The torrential downpour had softened the road's surface, and the lanes were narrow, making the possibility of getting bogged down very real.

Sticking his head out of the carriage window, Nicholas exclaimed: 'There it is, I'm sure that's the one.'

'Pull up along here, Hampton.' Hargreaves, despite his forty-eight years, jumped agilely down from the vehicle, followed by his son.

Nicholas rushed forward, pointing to the grassy mound. 'The man was standing just here, Papa.' He took up the position. 'He jumped a little to one side, but I was coming too fast, and something—a wheel, probably—caught him. He must have fallen to the side, into that ditch perhaps. But I passed so quickly—'

Hargreaves went over to the spot his son was indicating. There was certainly no one lying in the ditch now. 'I'll walk down this way and keep looking. You go up the hill and see if you can find anything.' As he was speaking, he was examining the rough stone wall that rose up immediately above the ditch, for any signs that it had been hit, but the heavy rain would probably have washed away any blood.

Then something caught his eye. A small scrap of wet paper that looked as if it had been torn from a larger sheet was sticking between two stones in the wall. He carefully removed it. There certainly was—or had been—writing on it, but water had all but obliterated the lettering. Not wanting to smudge it still further, Hargreaves took it back to the coach, telling Hampton to look after it.

Nicholas had disappeared round a bend in the road but soon came back into view, shaking his head. 'No sign of anybody this way, Pa. But the road is blocked by a huge branch from an oak tree.'

'Could someone on foot, get past?'

'Just about, but it would be a quite a scramble.'

'There's nothing here, son. If we go home the way you went, we can look as we go. You're positive you hit him?'

'Yes, I just caught a glimpse of him falling. I feel awful about it.'

'Well, we've done what we can, and just hope he got up and went on his way.'

But all they found on the way home was Nicholas's hat—rather the worse for wear. And when they arrived, they received the news that his horse and gig had suffered no permanent harm. The wet piece of paper Hargreaves had found had only part of one word and a single capital "K", still readable.

Chapter 2

Eight-year-old Bethany St Maure jumped down from the window seat. 'Mama! Mama,' she exclaimed excitedly. 'Aunt Amanda's carriage is coming up the drive. I'm going to meet her.'

Before her mother, Rosalie, Lady Benedict St Maure, could remonstrate about unladylike behaviour, her daughter had fled the room, tugged open one half of the massive front door, and was running across the wooden bridge that spanned the moat, arriving at the other side just as the vehicle pulled up. She was followed by a butler, who managed to squeeze past and open the carriage door. The occupant, a tall middle-aged lady of athletic build and smiling brown eyes, descended without assistance and immediately bent down to kiss her eager niece.

'Oh, Aunt Amanda, what was it like? Did the Queen wear her crown all day? Did Uncle Justin kneel down before her? Did ...?' The questions tumbled out one after another. 'Will you draw me some pictures, please Aunt Amanda?'

'My darling Beth, I will tell you all about the Coronation later, but first I must say hello to your mother, and shake some of this travel dust off.'

They crossed the bridge together, and Amanda embraced Rosalie. 'I'm so glad to be here. Peace and quiet at last. London's been quite impossible for weeks.'

'I'm just as keen to hear all about the coronation as Beth is, after, that is, Mrs Soames has shown you and your maid to your rooms.'

Settled comfortably around a table, laden with refreshments, Rosalie and her daughter were eager to hear all about the coronation of the young Queen Victoria—an event at which Amanda, as the wife of the Marquis of Coverdale, had an excellent view of the entire proceedings.

'It was a very long service, over four and three quarters of an hour, and none of us could move. I was so stiff I could hardly walk to our carriage, and then there was a long procession all through London. The crowds were amazing. We were cheered all along the way.'

'Did you wear a crown, too, Aunt Amanda?'

'Yes, but it's called a coronet—not quite so grand or so heavy.' Beth's aunt laughed. 'The little queen bore up really well, even when poor old Lord Rolle fell down the steps. She actually got up and helped him. She is only nineteen, the same age as Julia and as you were when you married Benedict, so I hope we are in for a long and happy reign. At least, God willing, I shall never have to g through another coronation. Three in one lifetime is quite enough.'

Rosalie agreed. 'But you didn't actually go to George the Fourth's one, did you? If I remember correctly, you gave birth to James the very next day.'

Amanda gave a sigh. 'Yes, I can hardly believe he goes up to Oxford next year; it makes me feel old.'

'Nonsense, Amanda!' exclaimed her sister-in-law. 'You're not yet fifty.'

'Next year, my dear, next year,' she replied with a rueful expression. 'But I want to hear, what's been happening here, Ros, since my last visit?'

Before her mother could answer, Bethany said, 'Mama has found a man.'

Amanda's eyebrows rose questioningly.

'Not the sort of "found" you're thinking, Amanda. But Bethany's right; I did find a man.' Rosalie pointed through the window. 'He was lying right there, in the drive, in the middle of a thunderstorm.'

'My goodness! What did you do? Where is he now?'

'Soames and Darrow and I managed to get him back to the house. He was barely conscious.'

'Yes, Aunt Amanda, there was blood all over his face—'

'Bethany,' said her mother sharply, 'that's quite enough.'

'Where is he now?'

'Upstairs, in one of the guest bedchambers. I called the physician, of course, and he examined him and dressed a very nasty wound in his head. It was twelve hours before he came too properly. I only found him two days ago.'

Amanda was thoroughly intrigued. 'Do you know who he is?'

'I have no idea, and the strange thing is, he doesn't either.'

'What on earth do you mean?'

'He seems to have completely lost his memory. He doesn't know who he is; or where he has come from; or where he was going; or how old he is. But my guess is he's somewhere between twenty and thirty. The doctor said loss of memory is not uncommon with head injuries.'

Amanda, for whom mysteries of all sorts had been very much part of her life before her marriage, immediately said, 'What about his belongings? Did they give any sort of clue? Anything in his pockets that might tell us something?'

Rosalie shook her head. 'Not a thing—no money, no letters, no watch, absolutely nothing. He didn't have a valise or a cloak bag or luggage of any kind.'

'That almost sounds as if he had been robbed,' said Amanda, adding, 'What does he sound like? I mean, is he English?'

'He hasn't said much at all, and the doctor says we shouldn't ask too many questions until he's less confused. But he definitely speaks English.'

'Who is looking after him? I suppose you're doing your part, Rosalie, as you usually do.'

'Of course I am, with my faithful maid, Jenny, and Darrow, who is my only footman. Unlike our late mother-in-law.' Rosalie laughed. The Fifth Marchioness of Coverdale was famous in the family, for the number of footmen she employed at the Berkeley Square house and Coverdale Hall. The bracket clock struck four. 'It's time for the patient's warm milk. The doctor was very particular that he only have a light diet but given often. I ordered the yolk of an egg and some honey, beaten into it. Follow me, Amanda. Who knows? You might recognise him.'

They encountered Jenny carrying a tray, and Rosalie relieved her of it. 'Just open the door, quietly now.'

Amanda did so, not following Rosalie into the room. Rather, she stood watching from the doorway. The bed curtain on the side of the window was drawn, but there was enough light to see that the man's eyes were closed. One thin hand was clutching a fold in the coverlet; his hair seemed almost black; and his face, with a considerable growth of dark beard, was almost as white as the pillows his head was resting on. For a moment, something reminiscent in his appearance startled Amanda, and a cold shiver shot up her spine. Then he opened a pair of dark blue eyes, and the moment passed.

Rosalie advanced towards the bed and laid the tray on the bedside table. 'Are you feeling a bit better? I've brought you something to keep up your strength.' She poured some of the milk from a covered jug into an invalid cup, saying, 'Can you manage, or shall I hold it for you?'

'I can manage, thank you. I think I'm much better.' His thin face lit up with a smile. 'The trouble is, I can't remember how I felt before!'

At least he hasn't lost his sense of humour, thought Amanda.

'The lady in the doorway is my sister-in-law. She is very grand, the Marchioness of Coverdale, no less, but quite the kindest person I know in the whole world. Now she and I will adjust your pillows so you can raise up a little and drink your milk.'

'I am afraid I am putting you to a great deal of trouble.' He tried to raise himself, but the effort was too much, and the two ladies did it for him.

'No need to worry yourself on that score, I assure you,' Amanda said. 'Lady Benedict is in her element with someone to look after. She has brought me in here to see if I recognise you.'

'And do you?' the man said hopefully.

'I am afraid I do not.' Her brief moment of prescience, she kept to herself.

'You've not to worry about anything,' Rosalie reiterated. 'The doctor says it won't help. You must just rest and think of nice things you can remember. You have had a really nasty blow to your head. And since you can't remember your real name, we need to call you something. You can't just be Mr X. You have a gold signet ring on your right hand. It has an "M" engraved on it.'

The man raised his hand from the coverlet and examined it as though he had never seen it before. 'So I have. But it doesn't mean anything. Suppose you call me Matthew. Will that do?'

'Excellently. Now it's time you drank your milk.'

The sound of Bethany running along the passage made Amanda immediately decide that a strange man's sickbed was no place for an eight-year-old. 'Come on, darling,' she said. 'Let's go downstairs, and I will draw you pictures of the Queen in her coronation robes for your scrapbook.'

9

The newly christened Matthew drained the last of the milk, and Rosalie took the cup. 'Do you think you could manage a little chicken broth for supper?'

Matthew smiled rather weakly. 'That would be just dandy.' He added rather uncertainly, 'My Lady? Is that the proper form of address?'

Rosalie smiled. 'Just call me Lady B. That's more friendly. Now if you want anything—anything at all—just ring this bell.' She pointed to a silver bell beside the bed. 'And someone will come. You must not try to get out of bed. The doctor was adamant about that.'

'No, ma'am, I won't. As a matter of fact, I don't think I could.'

Rosalie carefully adjusted his pillows, so he was lying flatter, as the doctor had ordered. 'I'll come and see you later, Matthew. Now get some rest.'

When she had gone, he looked again at the gold ring and tried to remove it, but it wouldn't come off. Was Matthew his name? It seemed sort of right. But it could be Michael or Mark. The effort was too much. His head hurt, his side hurt, and his feet felt they were on fire. But despite the pain, he drifted off to sleep.

Back in the drawing room Rosalie said, 'Well, Amanda, what do you think?'

'I think whoever he is, he's a very sick man.'

'You're certainly right about that. And I haven't told you about his other injuries. The doctor says he has a massive bruise all down his right side, from shoulder to hip. He doesn't think his ribs are actually broken, but some may be cracked, and I can hardly bear to tell you about the state of his poor feet!'

'What about his feet?'

'There is hardly an inch of skin on them that wasn't blistered.'

'Poor man. What do you think caused that?'

'His boots were in a terrible state. On one the sole was completely worn through, and the uppers on the other were coming away. Walking far in them—and in the rain—would cause blisters.'

'Walking for a very long time, I should imagine,' Amanda said. 'So what do we know, or can deduce about him?'

Rosalie thought for a moment. 'Well, he can't remember who he is, but he knows ordinary things, like chicken broth. He speaks English, but nevertheless, there's a hint of an accent of some kind. But it's not one I can place, like Scottish or Irish. And that expression he used, "just dandy", I've never heard that before. If I send for his clothes. They should be clean and dry by now. And you can see what you think, Amanda.'

Soames came in with a bundle of clothes and put them on the sofa. Rosalie held up a long black coat, and Amanda went over to examine it.

'It's very shabby and threadbare, and this pocket's torn, too.' She picked up the trousers. 'These are different, fine worsted cloth by the feel of it and well-tailored. So is the waistcoat, and the shirt is a good quality linen one. It's very strange indeed. Do you think all his stuff has been stolen?'

'I think you're right,' said Rosalie. 'It definitely looks as if he's been robbed. They've taken everything of value, everything they could get off in a hurry and left him with an old coat and, judging by what you said about his feet, taken his boots and left him with ones that leaked and probably don't fit, either.'

'The question then, Ros, is where did all this take place?'

'The doctor said the deep wound in his head had been inflicted not long before I found him, because of all the blood. He said the poor man might not have survived without immediate attention.'

'Does that mean we have a band of robbers roaming our country lanes?'

'I hope not, indeed.'

'But that doesn't account for the blisters, though, does it? For his feet to get into the state you described, he must have walked for miles. So, what are you planning to do, Ros?'

'Nothing. What can I do, except look after him. There must surely be someone, somewhere, missing him. Perhaps they'll put a notice in the papers. I'll keep a lookout. I can send Darrow down to the village in case he was seen there.'

'That's a good idea. I could do a sketch of him. That might help.'

'Can you do it from memory? Or do you want to go up to his room?'

'I was doing some drawings of the Queen for Bethany. She left her drawing things on the bureau.' Amanda quickly got pencil and paper and drew a quick sketch of the man she had seen lying in bed. 'There.' She handed it to Rosalie. 'Is that good enough? I've given him fewer whiskers. You know, that's a sort of clue. He must have shaved at least not much more than ten days ago, so he must have had had the means to do so then. Whatever happened to him can't have been before that.'

'Now I come to think of it, the doctor said he didn't think he'd eaten for quite a long time. Are we getting a picture, Amanda?'

'Well now, let's see. A young man who has a name that probably begins with an "M", is robbed of all his possessions, walks for miles in ill-fitting boots, is then hit over the head and severely bruised, and then ends up half-dead on your doorstep. We also know he speaks English, with a slight but unknown accent, has some good clothes and some awful ones, and likes chicken soup.'

'That seems to cover everything.'

'Except his looks,' added Amanda. 'What age do you think he is? I should say mid-twenties.'

Rosalie nodded agreement.

'How tall?'

'At least six foot but not heavily built and very thin. Soames and Darrow carried him quite easily between them, and he's dark-haired with blue eyes. I suppose it's not a lot to go on, but I can send Darrow down to the village with your sketch and the description. There's plenty of light still. Then I must go to Bethany. I always have supper with her, and we read before she goes to bed.'

'May I come, too?'

'Of course. She'll be delighted. I thought perhaps you'd want to rest before dinner after your journey.'

'Amanda gave Rosalie a withering look. 'I'm not in my dotage yet, young lady.'

Rosalie laughed. 'I don't know any other lady approaching fifty who looks half as good as you do, Amanda.'

The two ladies were having their after-dinner tea when Soames tapped on the door and came in. 'My apologies for the intrusion, My Lady. But Darrow has returned from the village and has something he wishes to impart to Your Ladyship.'

'Send him in, Soames.'

'Very good, M'lady.'

The footman duly arrived and stood nervously, wondering if he should speak before he was spoken to.

'Tell us if you have discovered anything, Darrow,' said Rosalie eagerly.

'There wasn't many folks about, the shop and mail-office being closed, M'lady. But the two people I arst, din't know nothing. When I showed them the picture, I thought someone in the Three Tuns might know somethin', it getting busy like, so I goes in—'

'It is a warm evening, Darrow. I hope you had a tankard of ale while you were there.'

Relieved of a worry, Darrow smiled. 'Yes, thankee, M'lady. But no one in there could 'elp me neither. Then Mr Tibbs, 'im being the landlord, said, "Show me that picture again." So I gives it to 'im, and then 'e arsts, "Did the gentleman 'ave a long black coat?" An' I says yes.' Darrow looked at Rosalie. 'I knows that, M'lady, cos 'e was wearin' it like when we carried the gentlemen into the 'ouse.'

'Very good, Darrow. Please carry on.'

'Well, then, Mr Tibbs, 'e said, "A man was makin' enquiries about a gent in a long black coat, and 'ad 'e seen 'im, like, but 'e din't 'ave no picture. But 'e says to Mr Tibbs, if 'e sees or 'ears anything about this cove, 'e's to send word to this address.' Darrow fished around in a pocket—he was not wearing livery—and produced a scrap of paper, which he handed to Rosalie.

'Any other information, Darrow?'

'No, M'lady.'

'You've done very well, Thank you. You may go now.'

As soon as the servant had left, Amanda and Rosalie sat together on the sofa to read the note.

'There's not much information, just a name, "Lord Hargreaves", and the address "Staplewood Park, Staplewood." What are you going to do, Ros? Do you know this Lord Hargreaves? Is Staplewood far from here?'

'Which of those questions do you want me to answer first?' Rosalie laughed. 'I can't do anything until tomorrow anyway. Staplewood is a village about five or six miles from here. It depends which way you go. We have so many little lanes in Kent. As to your third question, I know very little about Lord Hargreaves, and I have certainly never met him. But what I do know is quite interesting.' She paused.

'Go on, tell me. Don't be a tease.'

'He inherited the title and the estate about four or five months ago, I think, and has only been in residence at Staplewood House for a few weeks. That is all I know, and that only from local gossip—'

'What about the previous Lord Hargreaves, his father?'

'Oh no, that's the interesting part. *That* Baron Hargreaves was only a very distant cousin. There were at least three closer relatives. But apparently, they all predeceased him. And the new lord was a solicitor in Ludlow and certainly not born with expectations, or so the vicar told me.'

'How amazing. I wonder what he's like? You have a chance to find out now. It's all rather exciting, isn't it?' Amanda glanced over at the harp case standing in the corner and couldn't help letting a little sigh escape. Ever since Rosalie's husband, Lord Benedict St Maure, had died, nearly five years earlier, she had withdrawn from society, and Amanda worried about her. She was barely forty—too young to be buried in the depths of the country for the rest of her life, however much she busied herself with local affairs.

Benedict and Rosalie's marriage had been perfect. Devoted to each other and to music, they had been acclaimed in the highest musical circles when they'd performed in private salons throughout Europe. Since Benedict's tragic death at the age of forty-one, the harp, her favourite instrument and the one that had brought them together, had remained silent. Perhaps a new neighbour and the presence of the young man upstairs would open another chapter in Rosalie's life. Amanda sincerely hoped so.

'Will you pay Lord Hargreaves a visit?'

'No, Amanda, I shall write a note, saying that a person who may be the one he is looking for is currently resident in this house, and that I should be obliged to him for any further information he can give me.'

'That's a bit stiff, isn't it—for a new neighbour?'

'I don't want to get involved in anything, but I need to know more.'

'You're probably right.' Amanda sounded a little disappointed.

'You will stay until it gets sorted out, won't you? Whoever Matthew is, he certainly can't be moved for some time.'

'Of course I'll stay. Justin is fixed in town with the aftermath of the coronation and finishing up business in the Lords. He won't be going to Coverdale for at least two weeks. I'm to join him there. Now, before you go and see that Matthew is settled for the night, as I know you will, could you play one of those delightful piano pieces written by Frederic Chopin?'

Chapter 3

The message to Lord Hargreaves was despatched with the groom at nine o'clock. And by eleven he had returned with a letter from his lordship. Rosalie broke the seal and read it aloud to Amanda:

My Dear Lady Benedict,

I was very pleased to receive your note. The welfare of the man I believe to be the same person my servant was inquiring about, has been of concern to me for the past few days. On the day of the severe thunderstorm, my son unfortunately lost control of his horse and gig, and, regrettably, nearly ran over a man answering your description. My son was convinced that he saw him fall but was unable to stop. On his eventual return home, he described what had happened, and together we scoured the area of concern but could find no sign of the man. The accident happened at the junction of three lanes, where a signpost stands on a grassy mound. Eventually we found the spot, but again there was no indication of an accident, only wheel marks where the gig had swerved onto the grass.

I am aware, Lady Benedict, that we have not been formally introduced, but I would consider it a great honour if you would allow me to call so that I can apologise to your visitor on behalf of my son, who has returned to school following the coronation holiday.

If this is not too much of an impertinence, I will wait
upon you at three o' clock, this afternoon, unless I hear to the
contrary.

Your most obedient servant,
Charles Hargreaves.

'Well, Rosalie, what do you think of that?'

'It gets us nowhere really. He obviously has no idea who the man is any more than we do, just a stranger.'

Will you allow Lord Hargreaves to visit?'

'Certainly, I shall, Amanda. He seems to be a man with a conscience. I wonder what he will say when he finds out what has happened?'

'I imagine he will be quite upset. It's hardly the start to a new life he would want. However, he will get to meet you, Rosalie, and that must be good.'

Just before three o'clock, Rosalie saw two horsemen approaching, and summoned Soames. 'Lord Hargreaves has arrived. Please admit him and tell his groom where to take the horses and then bring some ale and prepare the tea tray.'

'Yes, My Lady, at once.'

Rosalie and Amanda had not long to wait before Soames announced in his most sepulchral voice, 'The Lord Hargreaves, Your Ladyship,' and stood aside to admit a man of middle-age, just above medium height, with abundant mid-brown hair just showing signs of silver, and steady grey eyes. He was clad neatly but not extravagantly in well-tailored riding dress.

He bowed deeply, and Rosalie came forward and curtsied. 'You are welcome, My Lord. May I introduce Lady Coverdale, to you?' With the formalities over, she begged him to be seated. 'I have asked for a jug of ale to be brought. You must be thirsty; it is such a hot day. How are you enjoying your new home, Lord Hargreaves? I have never seen it; your predecessor was hardly ever there.' Rosalie endeavoured to put him at his ease.

'Everything is very new to me, Lady Benedict. I have no doubt you have heard that, until a few months ago, I had no expectations of inheriting either the estate or the title.'

Amanda nodded. 'I know well enough what a change it can be in one's life. I went from being the widow of a clergyman to becoming a marchioness,' she smiled.

At that moment, Bethany bounced in, saw a strange man in the room, dipped a curtsy, and said, 'Mama! Mama! Jenny says, Can you come? She thinks the man you found has taken a turn for the worse!'

Amanda and Rosalie looked at each other. 'I'm afraid, Lord Hargreaves, that I shall have to leave you for a while. Amanda, perhaps you could put his lordship into the picture concerning our visitor.' She whisked out of the room, barely giving Hargreaves time to stand.

'That was Lady Benedict's daughter. And it is true, my sister-in-law, did indeed find a man. He had collapsed on the driveway. I'm afraid he was in a very bad way, with a severe head wound and much bruising, possibly cracked ribs, too, to say nothing about being on the point of starvation.'

Their visitor had gone quite pale. 'It is worse than I had feared, though we could find no trace of the man when Nicholas showed me the place where the accident occurred. But then it had been raining so heavily any blood would have been washed away. This is terrible.'

'We—Lady Benedict and I—are doing everything we can for the poor man. We must hope for the best.'

'Do you know who he is? Can you get in touch with his people?'

'That is the problem, My Lord. It seems that he has completely lost his memory. He does not know his name or where he came from or, indeed, where he was going.'

At that moment Rosalie returned, a smile on her face. 'It is not as bad as I feared. He just became too hot and tried to throw off his bedcovers. I have instructed Jenny to bathe his forehead with lavender water. I don't think it is the brain fever that the doctor warned us about.'

'That is a relief,' said Amanda. 'I have just been telling Lord Hargreaves about Matthew's loss of memory.'

Rosalie took her seat, so Hargreaves could sit down again. 'I expect you wonder why Lady Coverdale called him Matthew.' She went on to describe what he had been wearing and their theory that he had probably been robbed of all his belongings, except the gold ring with the initial 'M'. 'So we call him Matthew,' she finished.

'Ah, yes, I nearly forgot.' Hargreaves took a small piece of paper from his waistcoat pocket. 'I don't suppose this will be of much help, but Nicholas and I found it near the site of the accident.' He handed it to Rosalie. Apart from now being dry. Of the two words on it, the only legible one, was "Kent", the other, possibly had an "s", in it.

'Thank you. I shall keep it safe. But at the moment, I don't think it will be much help.' She laid it on the sofa table.

'I'm sure you must be wondering what my son was doing driving about in a thunderstorm. And I can only say his intention was to explore the surroundings of his new home. It was the first time he'd had an opportunity to do so. But had I known, I would have advised against it, with a storm impending.'

'Please, My Lord, I do not hold your son to blame. A bolting horse is almost unstoppable. It was fortunate that your son was not hurt also.'

'Well,' put in Amanda, 'I think he is to be congratulated for admitting what had happened and insisting on a search. Some young men would simply have said nothing. He has clearly been brought up to have a conscience.'

'It is kind of you to say so, My Lady. My late wife and I endeavoured to instil moral values, although I admit, since her death I can sometimes be accused of spoiling him. He misses her very much, as indeed, do I.'

Amanda glanced at Rosalie, whose expression was one of sympathy and understanding. 'Would you like to see Matthew? You never know; you might recognise him.'

The three of them went upstairs. 'Wait here. I'll see if he's asleep first.' She opened the door and then beckoned Lord Hargreaves in. Matthew was lying against his pillows, his damaged feet in linen bags protruding from the light covers. 'Here is someone who might know you,' Rosalie said, hopefully. But looking at both men, she could see that there was no recognition in either face.

Hargreaves looked shocked, faced with the reality of the young man's condition. Eventually he said, 'I have also come to apologise on behalf of my son, who was responsible for the unfortunate position in which you now find yourself. I'm afraid he lost control of the horse he was driving, due to the thunderstorm and, regrettably, was unable to avoid hitting you. We are so sorry you have been so badly hurt.'

Matthew managed a smile. 'I'm afraid I have no memory of what happened—or, indeed, of any of my life—until I woke up in this bed, being looked after by these two kind ladies.'

Amanda spoke from the doorway. 'Perhaps, Lord Hargreaves, your son gave some indication what Matthew was doing just before the accident. Any little bit of information could be helpful.'

His Lordship scratched his head. 'I'm trying to remember exactly what Nicholas told me. He said he was travelling quite fast because the horse didn't like the thunder. They were going downhill, when there was a terrific streak of lightning and the sound of a tree crashing quite close behind them, and the horse just took off. Nick lost the reins, and the gig careered round a corner, and there was this chap standing in the middle of the road. Nick couldn't remember if he shouted a warning, but even if he did, the next clap of thunder would have drowned his voice. The horse swerved to the right, and the man jumped to the left but not quickly enough to prevent part of the gig hitting him—probably a wheel,' Lord Hargreaves concluded.

The man in the bed said wryly. 'People who stand in the middle of roads are quite likely to get run over. Your son can hardly be blamed for hitting me.'

Amanda said, 'The only reason I can think of, for someone standing by a road junction is to read the signpost—'

'The paper!' Rosalie exclaimed. 'That bit of paper you found, Lord Hargreaves. Matthew must have been looking for directions. I'm sure of it. I'll go and get it. Matthew might recognise it.'

But when she returned with it, he did not. And she could see that so many people in his room was beginning to tire him. She suggested they should all leave him to rest. Once downstairs again, Hargreaves asked if he might see the clothes Matthew had been wearing when he collapsed.

'I'm afraid that, although they've been dried out, their condition is not good. But you may be able to tell something from them that we have not.' Rosalie smiled as she summoned Soames with her request.

He returned carrying the garments over his arm and the boots held by finger and thumb. with an expression of deep disapproval, laid them on a chair. 'Will that be all, My Lady?'

'Yes, thank you, Soames. No just a minute.' Rosalie turned to Lord Hargreaves. 'Can I persuade you to stay to dinner, My Lord? You won't be late home. We keep country hours here and dine at six thirty.'

'That is very kind, Lady Benedict. I shall be delighted, if it's not too much trouble.'

'I shall inform Mrs Soames,' said the butler as he withdrew.

'Now then, Amanda. Let us see what Lord Hargreaves can deduce from these somewhat unsavoury garments.'

He picked up the overcoat first, felt the material, and checked the pockets. 'This is very poor quality. It has worn threadbare but not through age.' He turned to the waistcoat and repeated his examination. 'This is quite different. It is of excellent quality and relatively new. But do you see this pocket?'

Both women looked at it but could see nothing special.

'It is where Matthew, or at least someone, kept a rather large watch. There is wear on the inside where it has repeatedly been taken out and replaced, and one of the buttons is missing.'

The trousers were of a similar quality but yielded no further information. Hargreaves turned his attention to the boots. He looked at each one and quickly laid the left one down. 'Someone has put newspaper inside, probably to alleviate the pain of walking with a hole in the sole. It has turned to nothing more than papier mâché. But in the heel of the other boot, writing is still discernible. It could be an important clue if I can lever it out.'

Rosalie looked delighted. 'We didn't think of that, did we, Amanda?' She immediately went over to a small bureau and came back with an ivory-handled paperknife, and handed it to Hargreaves.

He ripped the remains of the sole from the upper and levered out a wodge of newsprint, dried out but stuck together. However, some letters were discernible—part of a title banner, "OL … MER" but little else.

Chapter 4

Rosalie put her hand out towards the paper. 'Look,' she said excitedly. 'Surely that must be part of the name of a town?'

Lord Hargreaves gently put his hand on her sleeve. 'I believe, Lady Benedict, that it would be better to soak the paper first, so you can separate the pages. To try and do so now might destroy what the legend could tell us.'

'He's right, Rosalie,' said Amanda. 'Soames is going to be even more surprised when you send for a bowl of warm water!'

If he was, he gave no outward sign of it as he placed the bowl on a side table. Finally, he was asked to bring several huckaback towels. When all was ready, Amanda carefully placed the dried-up stack of paper in the bowl. 'How long do you think it will take, Lord Hargreaves?'

'I think we might peel the first layer in about five minutes. Too long and it will go to mush. Too soon and it will tear.'

'While we wait, I do have another problem you might be able to help me with, although I hesitate to impose.'

'You could never impose, Lady Benedict. I am so delighted to make your acquaintance—and yours, too, Lady Coverdale—even if under quite unusual circumstances. I admit that I have spoken to no one except my son, the vicar and my staff since my arrival at Staplewood. How can I be of assistance?'

Rosalie immediately responded. 'Oh, that's terrible. I'm sure you are going to be a great asset to the community and to the House of Lords. Don't you think so, Amanda?'

'That's very kind,' Hargreaves said. 'But perhaps we should address your problem first.'

'Well, My Lord, it's this. I think Matthew would very much like to be clean-shaven. He keeps rubbing his chin and seems surprised to find over a week's growth of hair. However, there is no one in this establishment who can perform such a task—especially on one who is bedridden. Since my husband ...' Rosalie hesitated and then continued. 'Since my husband died, there has been no need for a valet, and Soames, excellent though he is as a butler, has never trained as a personal servant. And,' she added, 'I certainly wouldn't trust Darrow, however willing, to perform the task. So that is the problem, My Lord.'

'This is very fortuitous, Lady Benedict. I believe that I can solve not only your problem but also one of mine!'

'Yours, Lord Hargreaves?' put in Amanda.

'Indeed, so. When I came down from Ludlow, I brought my own man and his wife, who had been my cook/housekeeper. But the previous Lord Hargreaves also had his man, and I felt it would be wrong to dismiss him out of hand, so he is staying on with me until the next quarter day. I am sure he will be delighted to have a gentleman of his own to look after. I will, of course, continue to pay his wages and his board here.'

'My Dear Lord Hargreaves, I couldn't consider that for one moment,' exclaimed Rosalie.

'Please, Lady Benedict, consider this. It is my family that has brought this young man to the condition he is in now. Supplying his needs, is not only my pleasure but also my duty. However, I will withdraw my offer of board, which I now fear you found offensive, and apologise for it.'

'Oh, fiddlesticks!' Rosalie raised her eyebrows. 'Of course I wasn't offended. You offered it with the best of intentions. A good compromise is that you pay his wages, and I'll look after the rest. But I must ask if your man—what's his name, by the way?—understands that Matthew is an invalid and likely to remain that way for some time?'

'Goode—Joseph Goode—is his name, Lady Benedict. And I believe that my predecessor also suffered from ill health, so I do not think that will be a problem.' Hargreaves looked at the paper soaking in the bowl. 'I think it may be ready to try and peel off the top layer. May I have your permission to try?' He went over to the bowl, and carefully, with thumb and forefinger, eased the first layer of newsprint from the rest, placing it gently onto a towel. 'I don't think we should touch it yet, but it's worth a try to get some more off.' One by one, the layers came away, until the lower ones were too badly damaged to extract. 'I believe that is all we are usefully going to get, Lady Benedict.'

A mantel clock chimed six. 'I must go and see to Bethany. Jenny is looking after her, but I always read to her before she goes to bed. Amanda, will you ask Soames to show Lord Hargreaves where he can freshen up before dinner?'

During the meal, his lordship described his utter amazement when he received notification of his predecessor's death—and the news that he was now Baron Hargreaves of Staplewood, a title he had never expected, a place he had never seen, and in a county he had never visited. 'I also understand that the late lord was not in the habit of spending much time here. But I would very much like to get to know the neighbourhood and its people.'

'Well, you've got to know us.' Rosalie smiled.

'But not under the most auspicious of circumstances, I'm afraid.'

'Nevertheless,' said Amanda, 'without those circumstances, we could not have met at all, since etiquette prevents you calling on single females or either of us calling on you—unless you could persuade a female relative to stay with you. Do you have such a relative, My Lord?'

'I have a married daughter, but she lives in Bradford, with numerous offspring, so she would certainly not be suitable. But I have an older sister in Bath. She lived with my mother until her death, eighteen months ago.'

'She sounds perfect,' said Rosalie. 'Write to her at once. Then we can all visit, and so can you.'

'Really, Rosalie, you must not start ordering Lord Hargreaves's life.'

'But she is right, Lady Coverdale. I shall put the matter in hand soon and see what she says.'

As soon as the meal was over, everyone was keen to return to the drawing room to find what light, if any, the scraps of newsprint could throw on Matthew's situation. Amanda removed the towel to reveal that the six pieces had curled up somewhat but were, nevertheless, readable. And each person took one of them to examine.

On Amanda's piece, there was part of a list of livestock prices on one side and mention of the forthcoming coronation festivities on the other, neither of which was of much use. But Rosalie's fragment had the word

'Bristol' quite clearly legible. 'That makes it certain it's a Bristol newspaper,' she exclaimed. 'I wonder what the "MER" means?'

'If I may suggest, Lady Benedict, papers often use "Mercury" in the title. I think, therefore, we are possibly looking at the remains of the *Bristol Mercury*. Do you both agree?'

'Yes, I certainly do, Lord Hargreaves,' said Amanda. 'Now all we really need is a date. If we can find that, we will know that the paper cannot have been put into the boot before that date.'

All three of them searched through the scraps of paper, with no definite result, until Lord Hargreaves said, 'This bit has part of a death notice. It's not very clear, but the person seems to have died on the twelfth. The paper's torn here, but I can just make out a "J". That must mean June, since today is only the second of July. This edition of the *Mercury* must have been printed between June 12 and June 28.'

'How did you work that out? And what does that mean for Matthew?' Rosalie asked.

'I think one of you mentioned coronation festivities. That means it must have been published before that event. But as to Matthew, not a lot, I'm afraid, Lady Benedict. If we put together all that is known so far, what does it amount to?'

'I do believe that the disparity of his clothes, together with the total lack of money or valuables, strongly suggest he has been the victim of robbery,' Amanda stated.

'And the terrible condition of his feet, that he has walked a long way,' added Rosalie.

'Could it really be from as far away as Bristol? Let me speculate for a moment, ladies, if I may?'

'Go ahead, My Lord,' said Rosalie and Amanda in unison.

'Well, you have a young man who was probably robbed of all his possessions about a week ago. Before that he would have been in possession of his belongings—including razors. He could not have put—or at least the boots he was wearing could not have had the newspaper put in them before the twelfth of June. From what I could see, his hands were not those of a labourer, and he has a gold ring and some good quality clothes. That suggests to me that he is a gentleman. Would you agree with me so far?'

Both ladies nodded enthusiastically.

'His language is English, but his accent is different but not common. And the only thing I can think of is that he could possibly be an American.'

Rosalie clapped her hands. 'That's brilliant, My Lord. Neither of us thought of that.'

'Which ties in with coming from Bristol,' Amanda added. 'Lots of ships arrive there from America.'

'It still doesn't answer the question, Why or how did he get *here*, though, does it?' said Hargreaves. 'But now I must take my leave, with many thanks for your hospitality and for relieving my mind of the whereabouts of the young man my son knocked over. I will send Joseph—he prefers to be called that—to you tomorrow morning.'

As Rosalie and Amanda waved him across the moat to where his horse and groom were waiting, Amanda turned to Rosalie. 'Well, my dear what are you thinking?'

'About what?'

'Don't be obtuse, Ros. You know perfectly well what I mean.'

'I think he seems very nice, but rather like a fish out of water, wouldn't you agree?'

'I do. And I think it is up to you to create a nice pond for him here in Kent. I will ask Justin to do the same for him in town. He seems just the sort to be an asset to the House of Lords—whatever his political leanings. You and I will call on him in a few days' time. That will give him your seal of approval. Even although he's a single man, I think our standing in society will survive the breach of etiquette. He's nice-looking, too, this new Lord Hargreaves,' Amanda said with a twinkle in her eye.

'Amanda, really!' said Rosalie in mock astonishment.

Chapter 5

Lord Hargreaves approached his massive lodge gates in better spirits. He really didn't like Staplewood House much. It had been built in the mid-eighteenth century by the first Lord Hargreaves, who had little idea of what was required by an English gentleman, having spent half his life abroad, amassing a huge fortune. To that end, he had employed a fashionable architect and a firm of furnishers and designers and told them how much he wanted to spend, and then left them to it. The result was a cream-stuccoed mansion with an impressive eight-bay façade, a Portland stone-pillared portico. Inside was a magnificent entrance hall and grand staircase, four large, and two smaller reception rooms. At that point, so rumour had it at the time, his money had run out. Consequently, the rest of the house had been finished in the cheapest possible way, with poor quality materials and maximum inconvenience.

During the previous Lord Hargreaves's absence, the place had not been neglected, but neither had it been loved. Essential repairs to the fabric of the building had been attended to. But when trees had died or fallen, saplings had not been planted. Nor had rose bushes been replaced. And what had once been topiarised yews were now amorphous lumps. Regrettably, the title and estate had not been accompanied by a fortune.

Hargreaves' relative had resided in a hotel and had lived up to his income. The estate just about paid for itself. But as he trotted up the drive, these depressing thoughts seemed farther away than usual. It was not hard to put this down to an afternoon and evening spent with two charming ladies, and a problem to solve that he could get his teeth into. It was too late to start on the mystery of Mr Matthew, but Lady Benedict's problem could be addressed immediately. He summoned Joseph to his study, the only room he felt at home in.

'You wished to speak to me, My Lord,' said the manservant, standing tentatively in the doorway.

'Yes, Joseph. Please do sit. I have rather a lot to say.' Hargreaves indicated the chair on the other side of the desk behind which he himself was seated. 'You have no need to worry, Joseph. It is just that a position as a valet has become available, and I hope you will be able to see your way to accepting. You will, however, still be in my employ.' Lord Hargreaves unfolded his plan for Joseph to join Lady Benedict's household in the capacity of valet to Matthew. 'Do you think this position would be to your liking?'

'Oh, indeed it would, Your Lordship. I have spent nearly all my working life as a gentleman's personal gentleman, and I take great pride in my work. I have references, if you would care to see them, sir.'

'That won't be necessary, but I must emphasise that Mr Matthew has suffered a severe injury and is currently bedridden, and likely to remain so for some time. That will not present a problem for you?'

'Not at all, My Lord, I can assure you.'

'Good, but please understand that, although I will be paying your wages, which I intend to increase by three shillings a week, you will take all your orders from Lady Benedict. Finally, I will give you a sum of money to be spent, as required, on the needs of Mr Matthew, such things as toiletries, small-clothes, and so on. I put my trust in you absolutely, Joseph. Do not let me down.'

'No, My Lord. I will give my very best endeavours.'

'Very well. Gather all your things together. I will send you to Mairsford tomorrow morning. Report to me before you leave. I hope you will be pleased to be able to exercise your skills once more.'

Lord Hargreaves performed one further task, before pouring himself a brandy and taking himself off to bed. He wrote a letter to his sister.

Amanda, Rosalie, and Beth had just finished breakfast when Soames announced, 'The Mr Joseph Goode of whom you spoke to me yesterday, your Ladyship, has just arrived.'

'Ask him to wait in the morning room, Soames. I shall be with him presently.'

The figure Rosalie and Amanda saw standing in the small room was barely above medium height. But although slender, the man looked as though he possessed a wiry strength. He was pale complexioned, with very dark eyes, that gave the impression of being quick and intelligent. He bowed deeply to the two ladies. 'Welcome to Mairsford, Joseph. I am Lady Benedict St Maure, and it is into my household that you have come to be valet to Mr Matthew. How much has Lord Hargreaves told you about the position?'

'That the gentleman in question is currently bedridden and will require me to see to his comfort and care, My Lady.'

'And you are experienced in these matters, Joseph?'

'Indeed, yes, My Lady. I have been trained in all aspects of a valet's duties, including those of attending to an invalid.'

Amanda glanced out of the window.' I think I see the doctor's gig coming up the drive, Rosalie.'

'In that case, Joseph, I will ask Soames to show you to your quarters. We will speak again later, when the doctor has gone and you have settled in.'

Soames entered to announce the doctor's arrival, and ushered Joseph out.

'I expect that you would like to examine your patient alone, Doctor. But I can tell you that he passed a reasonable night and has partaken of some gruel—although Jenny tells me that he does not like it.' Amanda smiled. 'But we have followed your orders regarding solid food.'

It was some considerable time before the doctor reappeared. 'Tell me,' Rosalie said eagerly, 'how do you think Matthew is doing?'

The doctor drew in his breath. 'In some respects,,Lady Benedict, his general condition has greatly improved, and it is time to change his regimen. I now believe that all danger of brain fever has passed, and he may now be allowed to sit up—for no longer than half an hour at a time but several times a day.'

'That is good news. I'm sure he was pleased.'

'I have also said he can read for a short period each day. It is time that his mind was subject to some stimulation. His head wound is healing, and his ribs are less painful.'

'I feel a "but",coming, Doctor,' said Amanda.

The doctor looked at her from under bushy eyebrows. 'Quite right, Lady Coverdale, quite a big but. I am not at all happy with the progress of his feet. The right one is healing slowly but satisfactorily. However, the left is giving me cause for concern and giving him considerable pain. The skin on the ball of his foot was worn away right down, deeply into the flesh and had become ingrained with dirt.'

Rosalie gave a gasp.

'It will be very slow to heal, and there is a constant danger of infection. It must be cleaned out and lightly dressed twice a day, I'm afraid.'

'Oh, dear, poor Matthew. But we can manage that, can't we, Amanda? And perhaps Joseph can help, too. We've engaged a valet to look after him. There was no one in this household, Doctor, who could perform those duties.'

'There is one thing, Lady Benedict, that is somewhat of a mystery to me as a medical man. Perhaps you can throw some light on it.'

'Lady Coverdale and I know very little. We have not questioned Matthew, as you said not to, about his past—'

'No, it's more about the young man's condition. You suggested, I believe, that he may have been robbed. But he must have had access to a razor not more than ten days ago at most, at which time I presume he could also have eaten. He is so emaciated, though, I fear he may have starved for much longer. But I can find no underlying cause for it. Is his appetite for the light diet satisfactory?'

'Yes. indeed it is. He takes everything he is given'—she smiled—'even the gruel.'

'Then I can't account for it. However, he's making good progress on all accounts except his foot, so there is probably nothing to worry about. I will return in two days' time, Lady Benedict.'

As soon as the doctor had departed, Rosalie summoned Joseph to the morning room. If you are ready. I will take you to see Mr Matthew. We call him that, but we do not know his real name, as his head injury appears to have caused complete loss of memory. The doctor has asked us not to question him, and hopefully, his memory will return in due course. However, you should encourage him to talk, as he may give clues to his identity. Lord Hargreaves is working to try and discover anything he can about the gentleman.

'I understand, My Lady.'

'Good. Now I will take you up to his room.'

Matthew was looking a little pale. The doctor's ministrations had been painfully unpleasant, but the bed curtain on the window side had now been drawn back, allowing in full daylight. He smiled as Lady Benedict entered. 'I have brought someone to look after you, Matthew. A highly qualified valet, who comes with Lord Hargreaves's recommendation.'

'Who?'

'Lord Hargreaves. Do you remember he visited you to offer his apologies on behalf of his son, whose gig knocked you over and caused the injury to your head.'

'Ah, yes, I do remember his visit. He said I was standing in the middle of the road!'

'Well, now he has sent Joseph to care for your needs.' She turned towards the door, saying, 'You may come in.' Rosalie stood aside and allowed the manservant to enter.

Joseph bowed deeply to his new master. 'I am come to do your bidding, Mr Matthew, but I am subject to doctor's orders, too.'

Matthew grinned. 'That is a great pity. No chance of a good broiled steak and some red wine, then.'

'No, sir. But Mrs Soames is preparing breast of chicken in a white sauce for your luncheon, or so she tells me.'

Rosalie, seeing that relations seemed to have been established, started to leave, saying, 'If you require anything, Joseph, ring that bell, and Darrow will come.'

As she went downstairs, she felt sure that, when his identity was discovered, Matthew would prove to be a most interesting young man.

Chapter 6

'**I** hope I'm not going to be too much trouble for you.' The man in the bed smiled.

'It is not for you to be a trouble, sir, but for me to see that you do not have any troubles. I understand that you are to be allowed to sit up for a time each day. Perhaps that is where we ought to begin.' Joseph approached the bed. 'This is your uninjured side, sir?'

Matthew nodded.

'Now, sir, if you grip my arm just above the elbow, and I hold yours, thus—don't try to raise yourself; let me take the strain.' Joseph pulled the young man forwards, and with a deft rearrangement of the pillows with his left hand, Matthew found himself in a sitting position, his back fully supported. 'You may find that you feel a little light-headed. It often comes from lying down for a long time. I will give you some minutes to get used to it before I proceed with the shave I understand you wish for, sir.'

Matthew rubbed a hand over his chin. 'Yes, it is. I shall be damned glad to get rid of these whiskers, Joseph. I don't think I can ever have had a beard.'

'If you have no objection, sir, I will use my own razors, as I believe your own ones are temporarily absent.'

'Yes, I suppose they must be. But I have no recollection of even owning any. I am sure yours are excellent, Joseph.'

'Do you feel ready for me to perform the office, sir?'

'I think so. The room did swim a little, but it seems to have settled down now. Go ahead.'

Joseph pulled the bell rope by the bed, and within minutes, Darrow appeared with a can of hot water and some warmed towels, together with a shaving bowl and a wooden case. There was no doubt about Joseph's expertise with a razor. Swiftly but with great care, Matthew found himself bereft of the hated beard and his face soothed with a mildly astringent lemon-scented lotion. 'I have not performed as close a shave as possible, sir. The skin needs to settle down first; tomorrow will be soon enough.' He produced a small hand mirror from the tray. 'Is that satisfactory, sir?'

'Good God!' exclaimed Matthew. 'Is that what I look like? I can't remember.' He gingerly touched the bandage round his head. I think it's getting better.' Suddenly he seemed exhausted by the effort.

And immediately, Joseph said, 'I think you should rest for a little while before luncheon.' He rearranged the pillows and drew the bed curtain forward slightly, before slipping unobtrusively out of the room.

An hour later, Jenny entered bearing a tray with folding legs, followed by Joseph carrying a bolster. 'Put the tray over there, Miss Jenny. I will see to it. You may bring Mr Matthew's luncheon in fifteen minutes, if you please.' Joseph pulled back the bedcovers and slid the bolster under Matthew's knees. 'This will stop you from sliding down the bed while you are eating.'

'You think of everything, don't you, Joseph?'

'That is my purpose and my pleasure, sir,' he replied, setting the tray on Matthew's lap.

'Have you always been a valet?'

'No, sir. I entered His Grace, the Duke of Alloa's, service at the age of thirteen as a scullery boy. Then I became a kitchen assistant. But my heart was not in the preparation of food—although I am able to cook simple meals.'

'So, what happened next?'

'I asked the head butler if I could work above stairs, and I became an under footman. By then I was sixteen, and I taught myself to read and write, with the help of the linen keeper. She was—'

'So many servants in one house,' interrupted Matthew.

Joseph pursed his lips. 'Their Graces' establishment is one of the finest in London, in Europe, I don't hesitate to say.'

'I'm sorry, Joseph. I didn't mean to imply ... It's just that I don't think I know about such places.'

'No, sir, of course not, sir. but I have every reason to be grateful that it was such a household.

'Why?'

'There were constant visits from the most important people in England and abroad. And when royalty came, extra valets were required to service minor members of their staff. I was delegated to look after one such, and I knew I had found my vocation. Of course, I was very green, but I quickly learned from older valets, and I always kept a notebook.' He dug into his waistcoat pocket and produced a small leather-covered book with a pencil attached. 'Once I get to know my gentleman, I do not require this.' He slipped it back into his pocket.

A tap on the door announced the arrival of Matthew's luncheon. To his surprise, it was not Miss Jenny or a maid who entered but, rather, Lady Benedict herself, who was carrying a tray with covered dishes, silver cutlery, and a snow-white damask napkin.

'I hope you're feeling hungry.' She smiled, releasing the tray to Joseph, who placed it on the bed table. Whipping off the covers, he revealed a plate with a small portion of chicken breast in a white sauce, two new, mint-freckled potatoes, and a small portion of buttered peas.

Matthew eyed the feast. And for a moment he didn't recognise any of the food set before him. Then the delicious aroma kicked his memory into life. 'I really think I am in heaven,' he said, picking up the knife and fork and transferring the knife to his left hand.

Joseph made a mental note, and, having left the room, took out his notebook and wrot: *"Query—left-handed?"*

Rosalie, who had been looking down at the slow movement of water in the moat from the bedchamber window turned back to face the bed. 'Would you rather I left you alone to eat your meal, Matthew? I won't try to make you talk while you are eating, but I thought you might like to learn more about the place you arrived at so unexpectedly.' She smiled.

Matthew paused his fork on the way to his mouth and returned the smile. 'Please do, Lady B.'

Rosalie sat on the upholstered chest at the foot of the bed. 'Well,' she began, 'you are in England, in the county of Kent, which is south-east of London. This house is called Mairsford, and it has a moat.'

Matthew paused from eating. 'I think, from the look of it, it must be very old.' He gestured with his fork towards the heavy oak beams that surrounded him on every side.

'Quite right. Parts of the building date from the fifteenth century. When you are able to get about again, you will be able to see all of it.

'When is that likely to be?'

'When the doctor says so. And no, I have no idea. He hasn't said, but I'm afraid you'll have to put up with this room for the time being.'

'It's a very nice room, but I'm putting your household to a great deal of trouble, not to say expense—'

'Fiddlesticks! I am grateful to have something to do that is different from our usual routine, and Lord Hargreaves and Lady Coverdale are trying to unravel the mystery of who you are, and why you are here. This is such an out-of-the-way place. I'm sure it can't be just chance.'

Matthew had put his knife and fork down, but there was still food on the plate. 'You know, Lady B, I really felt hungry. But I just can't manage it all. Will your cook be very upset? It was delicious.'

'No, of course she won't be. Everyone understands an invalid's appetite can be difficult. But there is a small bowl of strawberries for you. could you manage a few, do you think?' Rosalie went out and returned with a glass bowl of ripe fruit, a small silver jug of cream, and a sugar sifter.

Matthew ate three strawberries before leaning back against his pillows. Rosalie recognised the sign of exhaustion. 'I will send for Joseph. It is time for you to have some rest. This morning has been quite tiring for you.'

By the end of the week, three things occurred almost simultaneously. Lord Hargreaves received a letter from his sister, Emily, to say she would be delighted to come and see the new family home, but she would be bringing her companion, as well as her maid, and to expect her in four days' time. Hargreaves was unaware she had a companion. But since his ennoblement, there had been no time for family matters, so it wasn't a great surprise. And the house was big enough to accommodate them.

On the same day, Amanda received a letter from her husband, Justin, saying how much he missed her and enclosing a note for Rosalie to be so kind as to put him up at Mairsford for a few days and that he would be bringing Julia. Rosalie was delighted. Julia, the Coverdale's eldest child, was also Rosalie's god-daughter and a great favourite of hers and Bethany's. In Justin's letter to Amanda, he had underlined, 'Julia is being difficult'. This was no surprise to her mother. Julia was both intelligent and wayward, but Amanda decided to keep the information to herself for the time being.

That same evening, just as Rosalie and Amanda were enjoying their after-dinner tea, there was a knock on the door. And on being asked to come in, Joseph entered. 'I have no wish to disturb you, Lady Benedict, but I believe there is a matter of some urgency concerning Mr Matthew.'

'Not worse!' exclaimed Rosalie, putting aside her teacup.

'I'm afraid so, My Lady. I was dressing his foot, and I think it has developed an abscess, and—'

'We must summon the doctor immediately,' exclaimed Rosalie.

'That may not be possible. Darrow has the evening off and has gone down to the village. It will take some time for me to walk there and for us to return before he can ride for the doctor. And ... er,' he added, 'it may not be safe for Darrow to—'

'I understand what you mean, Joseph. Can it wait until tomorrow?' put in Amanda.

'Tomorrow is Sunday, My Lady. The doctor may not be at home, and I fear that Monday will be too late.'

Rosalie looked horrified. 'Too late for what?'

'To save Mr Matthew's foot, My Lady.'

'But that's awful. What can we do?'

'If you will permit me, and with Mr Matthew's consent, I can treat the abscess myself, Your Ladyship.'

'You have that sort of skill, Joseph?'

''I believe so, My Lady. I have travelled extensively and have had to undertake the treatment of wounds and illnesses in places where there was no other help at hand.'

There was a twofold sigh of relief. 'Well, Joseph, we are going to rely on you completely. And since that is the case, I want you to take control. No "Yes, My Lady, no, My Lady". Just tell us what you want, and we will do it. Is that understood?'

'Yes, thank you. I have all the instruments I shall need in my room, but there must be plenty of hot water, clean towels, and a bucket. If you could put the contents, including the leaves of that teapot'—he pointed to the pot Rosalie and Amanda had just used—'into a large jug and fill it with boiling water. If you have a piece of muslin and a sponge, they would be useful. I cannot treat Mr Matthew in bed. Mr Soames will have to help me get him into a chair—'

Rosalie interrupted. 'Amanda, will you see to the things Joseph needs? Jenny will help you. I will go to Matthew. He has to agree to the procedure. And send Soames to Matthew's room.' She turned to Joseph. 'Come with me, Joseph. Amanda will see to everything,' she said, forgetting to use her title.

Chapter 7

With everything in place, Matthew was seated in an armchair and supported by cushions. A small cloth-covered table set with instruments was at Joseph's side. It was time for Rosalie to retire from the room, as he had requested. 'Jenny will remain by the door,' she said. 'Just call for anything you want, Joseph.'

She and Amanda had both been shocked by Matthew's appearance; his pale brow was beaded by sweat and he was clearly in pain. The reason was all too obvious when Joseph exposed his patient's red and swollen left foot.

'I'm sorry, Mr Matthew,' Joseph said as he poured hot water into a jug and the instruments into it. 'I'm afraid this is going to hurt rather a lot. But before I begin, I want you to dip your foot into this basin.' He placed it on the floor and poured out the contents of a large metal ewer. 'Don't be alarmed by the colour; it is only tea,' he reassured his patient.

'That's a strange thing to use. What good does it do?' queried Matthew.

'I'll tell you, sir, if you start dipping your foot now. Just the toes and only for as long as you can bear it. My travels in the East taught me many things that are unknown here. One of them was the beneficial effects of tea, other than drinking it.'

Matthew said, 'Ouch!' and withdrew his foot. 'That hurts!'

'Yes, sir. But the more you persevere, the quicker and less painful the next part will be.'

Matthew gripped the arms of his chair and continued dipping. 'Tell me about your travels, Joseph. It may help to take my mind off this torture.' Matthew managed a wry smile. 'Last time you told me how you decided to become a valet.'

'Ah, yes, sir. After I left the duke's service, I obtained a post with a young gentleman, whose health, unfortunately, was of a consumptive nature. And despite everything his parents and the medical profession tried to do, after three years, sadly, he died. However, I learnt a great deal about looking after the sick, and all knowledge is useful, however obtained.'

Matthew continued dipping, now able to bear the heat more easily. 'Then what did you do?'

'Mr Andrew left me one hundred pounds in his will, and his parents gave me another fifty. So, I was a rich man.' He tested the water with his finger. 'Only a few more minutes, and then we will be ready for the next stage. Well, sir, I had become engaged to one of the housemaids, whose father was the head ostler at a coaching inn, and we both went to work there. But alas, neither the engagement nor the job worked out well.'

'Why was that, if it's not too personal a question?'

'Not at all, sir. The lady found someone more to her taste, and I found cleaning and pressing clothes for a succession of the inn's guests not to *my* taste. But the tips were very good, and I left better off than before.' He tested the water again and then examined Matthew's foot. 'I think it's ready for the next part now, sir.'

'It may be ready, Joseph, but am I?'

'I'm afraid you don't have a great deal of choice in the matter.' He pulled a chair towards him so he could sit facing Matthew, selected a small knife from the jug he had prepared previously, and spread a towel over his knees. 'I can promise you that you will feel much better after it's done, sir.'

'Well, I suppose that's something to look forward to,' Matthew observed with a rueful smile as he renewed his grip on the arms of the chair.

Joseph took Matthew's foot onto his knee and carefully inserted the point of the knife into the centre of the abscess, catching the resultant gush of bloodstained poison in a linen cloth, and then lowered the foot back into the basin.

'Is that it?' queried Matthew, pleasantly surprised by the relatively painless procedure.

'Not quite.' Joseph lifted Matthew's leg back onto his knee. 'I have to clean it out and see if I can find the source of the problem.'

Matthew used the arms of the chair to good effect, not to mention the gritting of teeth, while this was going on. Finally, Joseph took out a pair of tweezers. And after several seconds—Matthew was sure it was hours—he triumphantly held up a dark-coloured thorn, at least an inch long. 'There, sir, that's the cause of all the trouble. It was in very deep. You must have trodden on it, sir, and driven it deeper as you walked.'

'So, everything should be all right from now on then,' said a relieved Matthew.

'I hope so, sir. But don't count on a quick recovery. Healing of this sort of wound takes time. Rushing things can often delay recovery even more.' As he was speaking, he made a pad of clean linen and bound it lightly onto Matthew's foot. 'That is all for now, sir. I will ask Miss Jenny to call for Mr Soames, and we can get you back into bed.'

A little while later, Rosalie, herself, entered the room, with a bowl of chicken broth and some buttered toast. 'Joseph says you must keep your strength up. Was it very bad?'

'It wasn't good, Lady B, but Joseph was right when he said it would feel much better. Did he show you the thorn he took out?'

'He did, indeed,' she replied, setting the tray down. 'How could you not have known you had trodden on it?'

'Perhaps I did. I can't remember.

'No, I'm sorry, of course you can't. Has anything come back yet?'

'Not really. Now that I am allowed to read, I recognise things more, but not personally. I mean'—he pointed to the plate—'I know that's toast, and it comes from a loaf. But apart from eating it here, I have no idea where else I've seen or eaten it. I must have done, I suppose.'

Rosalie was sorry she had brought up the subject. 'The doctor says it will take time. And don't worry. We are happy to be able to look after you.'

On Monday morning, the doctor was being fully informed about the episode. Joseph had been invited to join the discussion, and he showed the doctor the thorn he had removed from Matthew's foot. 'It was in very deep, sir. And although it would have been better if you could have been called, I considered, having had experience of such things, that immediate treatment was desirable,' said Joseph tactfully.

'You did a good job. Leaving that thorn in could have led to a much more serious outcome.' The doctor was magnanimous; he had almost started to treat Joseph as a colleague.

'I don't know what we would have done without, Joseph, Doctor, we had no one to send for you,' Rosalie added. 'Have you anything more you want to instruct him about continued treatment?'

'No, Lady Benedict. He should carry on as before. I will return at the end of the week if that is convenient.'

Joseph cleared his throat in a significant way. 'Is there something you want to say, Joseph?' said Amanda from her seat on the sofa.

'If you will permit, My Lady.'

'Please, Joseph, is it about Mr Matthew's foot?'

'Not exactly. It's rather about his general condition. I understand that you, sir'—he turned to the doctor—'were puzzled about your patient's emaciated condition, and I may have learnt something that might explain it.'

'Please, tell us. We are all ears,' Rosalie exclaimed.

'It's like this. I have been in the habit of describing my past adventures while dressing Mr Matthew's foot; he says it takes his mind off it. I was telling of the many long sea voyages I had undertaken with a previous master. Mr Matthew expressed horror at the very idea, saying he suffered nausea just standing on a jetty—'

'Really?' interrupted the doctor.

'Indeed, he did, sir. And it occurred to me that, if he had recently undertaken a long sea voyage and had been unable to keep down food for a week—or even as long as ten days—that might, in part, account for his condition.'

Rosalie's eyes lit up. 'Of course,' she exclaimed excitedly, 'that could explain …' She caught a warning look from Amanda and finished lamely, 'Why he hadn't eaten for so long.'

When the doctor had gone and Joseph had left the room, Amanda explained why she thought it unwise to say too much—even about the little they knew about Matthew. 'After all, he may be hiding from someone. He may be in danger. Or, but somehow I don't think so, he may be wanted by the law.'

'I'm quite sure he's not,' replied Rosalie firmly. 'But you're right. We should say nothing until we know more. A sea voyage would be consistent with the Bristol connection, though, wouldn't it?'

Chapter 8

The forward-facing window in the chaise gave Mrs Emily Clayborne a full view of her brother's new abode as it approached Staplewood, the multitude of windows glinting in the late afternoon sun. *Well, well, well*, she thought to herself as the horses were pulled up beside the portico. As if by magic, the front door was opened, and a butler, accompanied by the familiar figure of Royston, came forward to open the carriage door and let down the steps. But this was barely accomplished when a very large dog charged out and galloped into the house, almost knocking Parsons over in the process. The dog slithered across the marble floor and nearly knocked itself out on one of the massive pillars guarding each side of the grand staircase.

Hargreaves, who was descending the stairs to welcome his sister, looked down at the dog, which seemed confused, and then at the plump little white-haired lady, whose concern was directed towards the animal.

'Welcome to Staplewood, Emily my dear.' He went forward and kissed his sister, eyeing the two servants over her shoulder, piling another trunk on top of the two already in the hall. 'I see you have not brought Precious the parrot, with you. But what is that?' he said, pointing to the dog, now sitting with about a foot of pink tongue hanging out.

By now, another woman had entered the hall and was busy checking the trunks, several bandboxes, a valise, and a canvas-covered dressing case.

'It's a dog, Charles.'

'Yes I can see that.'

'I did tell you I was bringing him—in my letter, Charles.'

'I think you were somewhat ingenuous, calling him a companion, though.'

'Well, he is my companion, and I am his—in a kind of way.'

'Does he have a name?'

'I call him Bedford,' Emily replied briefly, concentrating more on her surroundings. The enormous hall, stretching right up to the roof and capped with a stained-glass dome, the grand staircase leading up to a balustraded landing, and galleries on two sides. But it was the incredible amount of gilding that really stunned her senses. Gold vine leaves and bunches of grapes twined themselves up each side of the stairs, echoed in the four-tier, wrought-iron chandelier suspended from the dome. Four massive mahogany doors had fielded panels edged with gilded beading, as well as gilded door furniture, their pediments crammed with carvings appropriate to each room and, once again, covered in gold leaf. Even in such a large space the effect was quite overwhelming.

'Welcome to my little country cottage, sister dear,' Hargreaves said with a wry smile. 'It's a pity that *all that glisters is not gold.*'

'Does the rest of this monstrous house glister in the same way?'

'I'll show you round later, but here's Mrs Royston. She'll show you and Withers your rooms and see that your trunks are brought up.'

'I think I'd better take Bedford out first. He's been very well house-trained, but he's been shut up in a coach for a long time.' At the sound of his name the dog rose to his feet, and Hargreaves was able to see just how large he was. The dog charged towards his mistress but crashed into the table in the centre of the hall, letting out a yelp. 'Oh, darling. I'm sorry, I should have helped you,' she said as though speaking to a child. 'Did you hurt your poor little nose?'

'What!' said her brother in stentorian tones, 'have you not told me about your monster hound?'

'Well, Charles. I don't think he can see very well, at least not those things directly in front of him.' She caught the look in her brother's eye. 'But he's very good at finding his way about, once he's been shown where to go; I promise you.'

'Take him outside, Emily. We'll discuss what to do with him later.'

'What d'you mean, *do* with him?' she asked nervously.

'I mean how to organise my household round the requirements of a partially sighted dog the size of a small horse.' He smiled, seeing the relief on his sister's face. 'Now when you get back in and have seen your room, tea will be ready in the blue drawing room. You know, I'm really glad you've come, Emily. This is far too big a house to be outnumbered ten to one by servants.'

Over her shoulder and holding Bedford's collar, Emily informed her brother, 'I'm glad you're pleased, because I have let my house in Bath, for six months.'

The blue drawing room pleased Emily Clayborne much more than the over-gilded hall. The walls were covered in faded blue damask and hung with paintings of classical views of ancient Rome or pastoral scenes. The furniture was of walnut, upholstered with blue velvet. Gilt-framed pier-glass mirrors flanked either side of tall French windows, leading out to a large conservatory. Tea was laid out on a table in front of the fireplace.

'If you feel the cold, Em, I shall get the fire lit,' said her brother. 'But that dog will have to move off the hearthrug.'

'No, Charles, the day is still warm. But you are right. He needs somewhere he can go, so he knows where he is. How many rooms do you have?'

'A lot, but I will put the matter in hand. Now tell me how you acquired such an extraordinary hound, and why have you let your house.'

'The answer to your first question is, I found him tied up to the railings outside my house. He was soaking wet and half-starved—so what else could I do?'

'Being you, Emily, nothing else, I suppose.'

'Quite right. And as to the house, I got an offer to lease it that was so good I couldn't refuse. And besides the tenants had an African grey parrot called the Captain, and Precious fell in love at first sight. It would have been too cruel to separate them.'

'Of course it would; anyone could see that.'

Emily looked up at her brother to see if he was teasing, but his face was straight.

Later that evening, Hargreaves, after some cogitation, penned a note to be sent to Lady Benedict the following morning. His main purpose was to inform her ladyship of the arrival of his sister, Mrs Clayborn, at Staplewood. But he also wanted to enquire about the progress of Mr Matthew, whose well-being was of concern to his son as well. Nicholas had asked after him in his latest letter from school. He surprised himself by the eagerness he felt in hoping for an early response.

Emily stood in the middle of her bedchamber, wondering why it seemed so cheerless. There was nothing specific she could put her finger on. A fire burned brightly in the grate. The walls bore a green flock paper with a pattern of small leaves. The half-tester bed had drapes of red and green on a cream ground, likewise the curtains. The atmosphere wasn't damp. But somehow, the whole room seemed to depress her, and she was not, on the whole, a depressive personality. She went over to the window and looked out. Below her was the large conservatory that opened off the blue saloon. But what was in it was almost entirely obscured by filthy glass. And then she realised that the general air of gloom in the whole house was caused by the daylight being filtered through grime. Charles, she thought, must get the windows attended to immediately.

'Well, Bedford this will be our new home, so you'd better learn to find your way about.' Emily took hold of his collar, allowing him to sniff the bed and various pieces of furniture. To test his ability, she sat on the bed and called him.

Bedford made straight for it and took a flying leap onto it, which wasn't exactly what Emily had intended.

'I can see,' she said, 'that you, this house, and my brother all need a bit of order in their lives. Especially,' she added, 'if you are both going to impress the local ladies.'

Chapter 9

The man stood on the pavement, of a Bristol street. peering at the well-polished brass plate, confirming that the premises were indeed those of Pettigrew and Smith, Solicitors and Commissioners for Oaths. He tugged a knob, conveniently labelled, 'Pull', and waited, nervously running a finger inside his neckband.

Eventually a young lad opened the door. 'Yes, what do you want?' His tone was not exactly welcoming.

'I have come to see Mr Pettigrew.'

'Do you have an appointment?'

'No, but my business with him will not take long.'

'You had better come in. I dunno if he's available.' The lad led the man along a narrow passage, ending in a small room overlooking an ill-kempt garden and furnished with several hard wooden chairs. 'What name shall I say?'

'William Swinton, from the Atlantic and Maritime Shipping Company.'

'Wait here … sir.' He added, 'Please,' reluctantly.

It was not long before another, much older man entered, dressed all in black and with a pen lodged behind his ear. He bowed politely. 'Mr Pettigrew will see you now, sir, if you follow me.'

He led Swinton up steep stairs to a landing, on one side of which he could see, through glass-topped doors, a row of clerks seated on high stools, busily writing. A door on the other side was opened, and he was ushered into a long room with windows at both ends.

Seated behind a partners' desk was a middle-aged man, wearing two pairs of spectacles, one pair of which he removed before offering his hand. 'How can Pettigrew's be of service to you …er, Mr Swinton? Please take a seat.'

'It's like this, sir. Our company, Atlantic and Maritime, has in our warehouse a cabin trunk that bears a label addressed as "care of" this office. And since it has been in our possession for over a month and not been claimed, my principal would like it removed, as space is of a premium. He hopes you will understand, sir.'

Mr Pettigrew raised his eyebrows. 'Over a month, you say. From whence has it come?'

'From New York, sir. It was unloaded from the SS *Marianna*, on'— Swinton took a piece of paper from his pocket—'on June the eighteenth. She was over forty-eight hours overdue, on account of bad weather, sir.'

'I see. And is there a name attached to this trunk, other than ours, Mr Swinton?'

'Yes, sir.' He consulted his paper again. 'A Mr M Stuart, sir, and some rather faded lettering stencilled onto the surface that says, "Major W Stuart, RE".'

A spark of recognition flashed into Mr Pettigrew's eyes. 'And you have not seen this Mr Stuart since the ship docked?'

'No, sir.'

Pettigrew picked up the discarded spectacles and twiddled the arm between his fingers. 'Is that not very strange? He must have been on the ship for some considerable time. Did no one see him?'

'That's the problem, sir. Once we realised no one had collected the trunk, we made enquiries. But the *Marianna* is now halfway to New York, and there is no one from the ship to ask. It is my—our—opinion, sir, that, if I may use the expression, he must have "missed the boat".'

'Is it possible for his luggage to have sailed without him?'

'Oh, quite, sir. Heavy trunks and the like have to be loaded before the passangers come aboard.'

'I see. And what will happen to Mr Stuart's trunk if it is not claimed?'

'That is why I am here, sir. According to our terms, we will dispose of any goods left in our warehouse unclaimed for twenty-eight days, unless alternative arrangements are made.'

'In that case, then, you had better have it delivered here.' He sighed. 'Although God knows where we'll put it.' Pettigrew stood up and offered his hand. 'Thank you for coming to tell me. I will put enquiries in hand.'

He pressed a bell on the desk, and the head clerk reappeared. 'Please, will you show Mr Swinton out, Fitton, and then return to this office.'

When Fitton rejoined him, Pettigrew gave the head clerk a brief account of Mr Swinton's visit and ended, 'I am relying on you to throw some light on the matter.'

Fitton removed the pen from behind his ear and scratched his head. 'I can, and I can't, sir, in a manner of speaking. If you will excuse me for a moment.'

Pettigrew nodded, and the clerk left the room. He returned carrying a scroll of paper tied with green tape, which he slid off, and, laying the contents on the desk, said, 'This is correspondence from a Mr Matthew Stuart from New York City. Pettigrew smoothed out the sheets and picked up the first page, removing one pair of glasses and putting on the other ones. 'You will see, sir, that Mr Stuart first writes to us last year, explaining he found our name among his late father's papers, and since it is his intention to come to England next year—that is to say this year, he begs to come to this office—'

'Yes, yes. I can see that. Did we reply?'

'Yes, sir. You will see a copy of our reply attached, in which we said we would be happy to be of help.'

'Did I say that?'

'Yes, sir.'

'The third letter tells us of his intention to take a ship from New York in the early summer of this year.'

'What do you make of it, Fitton?'

'I suppose there are two possibilities, sir. One is that his trunk has come without him. Or, and this is more serious, something has happened to him, which I fear can only be bad.'

'I think you are right. Have you any suggestions?'

'Well, sir, if he had come by the next available ship sailing from New York, he should have been here by now. I could look in the shipping list in the *Bristol Mercury* and see when the latest one is due. And if he is not on that one, we could advertise in the personal column.'

A ship from New York docked four days after Mr Pettigrew and his clerk had made their decision. But on enquiry, there had been no passenger named Matthew Stuart on board, so the following notice was inserted in both Bristol newspapers:

> *If anyone has any information concerning the whereabouts of Mr Matthew Stuart, would they please convey it to Pettigrew and Smith, solicitors, where they may hear something to their advantage.*

This last sentence was queried by Mr Fitton, on the grounds that it might encourage fraudsters, but Mr Pettigrew felt it would be more likely to produce a result. In fact, neither event occurred, and the trunk remained as an inconvenient obstacle in the narrow passageway.

It was all of a fortnight later that a note was delivered to the office. It was an ill-written scrawl on rough paper, but the message was clear:

> *I got somethink you mite be ntrestsd in. Meet me at the Blue Anchor at seven.*

It was signed, *'A friend'*.

Mr Pettigrew rang for his clerk. 'What do you think of this, Fitton?' he asked.

'It seems we have had an answer to your advertisement, sir.'

'Yes, yes,' Pettigrew exclaimed impatiently, snatching off one pair of glasses and substituting them for the other pair. 'But what do you think we should do? It seems very irregular to me.'

'Yes, of course, sir. But do you not think it should be followed up? There has been no other reply.'

'Very well, Fitton, we shall go together.'

The Blue Anchor was not the most salubrious of establishments, but neither was it the least. It also had as a landlord an ex-prize fighter, who few wished to upset. So its reputation was not one of rowdiness; obstreperous drunks were soon shown the door. Nevertheless, two gentlemen in dark business suits were certainly an unusual sight.

The landlord leaned across the bar, displaying massive shoulders, and gnarled black fists, souvenirs of his boxing past. 'Can I help you, gentlemen?'

'We've ... er ...come to meet, a ...a ... friend,' replied Pettigrew, a trifle tentatively.

'You don't look like you have the sort of friends who come here. Are you the law?'

'No, we're not,' interjected Fitton, fearful that any such suggestion would prevent further information from being forthcoming. 'Is anyone here waiting for someone?'

The landlord pointed to a lone customer, seated in a dark corner. 'Maybe it's him.'

'What's he drinking?'

'Porter.'

'Another pint and two of ale, Landlord.'

A smile creased the landlord's black face, clearly deciding that customers were customers, whatever their business.

Pettigrew and Fitton carried the tankards over to the corner. 'I understand you're waiting for a friend.' He put the drinks down on the table.

'Maybe,' said the man cautiously, eyeing the porter. 'Just the one, though.'

'This is my associate,' said Pettigrew, 'Mr Fitton. I'm Mr Pettigrew.'

'All right, better sit down.'

They did so, pushing the porter towards the man. 'Well, Mr ...'

'No names.'

'Very well. What have you got for us. Do you know where Mr Stuart may be found?'

'Nah, but I got this.' He looked round nervously in case anyone was looking, before placing a grubby handkerchief on the table and carefully unfolding it and shielding it from view with his arm.

Pettigrew and Fitton peered at the object thus revealed—a gold pocket watch.

Fitton put his hand out as if to pick it up, but the man immediately covered it again. 'Not so fast, gentlemen. What's this watch to you? Valuable it is, see.'

'We are just trying to find the whereabouts of a Mr Matthew Stuart. If you believe that watch may belong to him, we are interested to know how you came by it.'

'Honest, sirs, I came by it honest, on my oath.'

Mr Pettigrew didn't have much faith in the man's oaths, but so far he was the only lead they had. 'What makes you think it may have belonged to the man we're looking for?'

The man unwrapped the watch again and picked it up. 'This, sir.' He held it out to show a monogram on the outer case, an entwined M and S. He flipped it open, and both Pettigrew and Fitton could see the name Matthew W Stuart, engraved inside the cover and, beneath it, a date. The two men looked at each other and nodded.

'I believe you are right, Mr … er.'

'No names. I already said.'

'Oh, very well, but can you tell us how you came by it?' Pettigrew repeated. 'Otherwise all this is a waste of time, yours and ours.' This wasn't entirely true, as it was now established for certain that Matthew Stuart had arrived in England.

'Pledged, that's how.'

'So you're a pawnbroker, then?' put in Mr Fitton.

'S'right, Honest Joe Meakins, that's me,' the man said proudly and then realised what he'd said.

Ignoring this slip of the tongue, Pettigrew asked, 'And when exactly did the watch come into your possession?'

''Tain't mine. Pledged, told yer.'

'Yes, so you did. Do you have the pawn ticket?'

The man fumbled in several greasy waistcoat pockets before producing a small card. ''Ere.' He handed it to Pettigrew, who read it carefully: 'Brass watch. Five shillings. 18/09/38' and another number. Below that were two sets of initials—JM and the other indecipherable.

Pettigrew showed it to Fitton, who said. 'Do you know who brought it in?'

'Nah.'

'Why the September date?'

'Arter that, it's mine to keep, If''n she doan' come back.'

'She? Can you describe her? Have you seen her before?'

'Nah. Face 'alf-covered up, like she 'ad the toothache. Bonnet pulled down.'

'Ah, well, never mind.' Pettigrew was of the opinion that, even if Honest Joe Meakin knew it was his own grandmother, he wasn't going to say. 'Now this is very important. If someone comes to collect the watch. Tell them you have a buyer who will give a good price, but you have to contact them first.'

'You wants to buy it, sir?'

'Let us just say there will be a reward for finding it. Meanwhile'—he dug into his pocket and produced a leather purse, and extracting half a crown, said, 'Take this for your trouble today.'

The man turned it over twice before saying, 'Thankee, sir.'

Pettigrew and Fitton rose to go. 'Now don't forget. I'll meet you here on the nineteenth of September— with or without the watch.'

As they passed the bar Pettigrew said, 'Give that man in the corner another pint of porter. He threw a few coins on the counter.

Glad to be out of the stuffy atmosphere of the pub, Fitton said to his employer. 'Are we not sailing a little close to the wind there, sir?'

Pettigrew smiled. 'Not yet, but we have gained some useful information. Now, at least we know Matthew Stuart arrived in England. The question is, What has happened to him since,? And what should I do about it?'

Chapter 10

Rosalie received Lord Hargreaves's note on the morning of the day that the doctor had given her good news. 'I am pleased to say, Lady Benedict, that Mr Matthew is well enough now to sit in a chair for a period each day. However, he must, on no account, be allowed to walk—or even stand—if that can be arranged. I am very pleased with his general progress.'

'And his feet?' asked Rosalie.

'Slow, My Lady, slow, but your man Joseph is doing excellent work, yes indeed.'

As soon as he had gone, Rosalie summoned Joseph. She gave him the doctor's report. 'But will it not be very difficult to get Mr Matthew into a chair without his feet touching the ground?'

'With Darrow's' help, I am sure it can be achieved, your Ladyship. But there may be another problem.'

'Something I can help with?'

'It concerns Mr Matthew's clothes—'

'His clothes! I don't think I've given them a thought. What's he been wearing, so far?'

'Nightshirts, My Lady, furnished by Mrs Soames.'

Rosalie could barely suppress a laugh. 'If they belong to Soames, Mr Matthew must be quite lost in them. But you are right. He will not want to sit in a chair dressed only in a nightshirt. I will give the matter some thought, Joseph. What about shirts and small clothes?'

'In anticipation of that, Mrs Soames has acquired some. Lord Hargreaves gave me a sum of money to spend on Mr Matthew's probable requirements, and I have taken the liberty of commissioning Mrs Soames to purchase the garments and toilet articles that Mr Matthew lacked.'

'Very good, Joseph. I will let you know what I have decided.'

After he had gone, Rosalie sat for some time, lost in thought. Then with a determined shake of her shoulders, she went out to the courtyard, where her daughter was play and summoned her in.

'Do you remember your Papa, Beth? I don't mean his portrait or the miniature Aunt Amanda did of him for you. I mean real experiences—the sound of his voice when he read to you, any special time he spent with you, that sort of thing.'

'Not a lot, I'm afraid, Mama. I remember him lifting me up on his horse and riding in front of him. He used to pretend he was a bear, and crawl round the room trying to catch me, and then we rolled on the floor. You see, Mama, you have told me so much about him, I don't know if it's that or if I really remember—except in my prayers. Why are you asking me?'

'Because I am going to do something, but I will only do it if it doesn't upset you.'

'Tell me.'

'Well, the doctor has said that Matthew can sit in a chair for a few hours each day, and he doesn't have any clothes to wear.'

'Yes, isn't it exciting? I don't mean about the clothes but about getting up.'

'You knew?'

'Yes. I heard Joseph telling Mrs Soames.'

Rosalie ignored this remark. 'Well, Beth, I have a mind to lend Matthew some of your father's clothes—for the time being, that is.'

'That's a splendid idea. Mama, I think Papa would be very pleased, don't you? You told me he always liked to help people.'

Rosalie had given no thought to this aspect, but Bethany was right; he would be pleased. Her mind was made up. She ascended the three flights of stairs to the attics—each one narrower than the last—and entered the furthest room. It was almost bare, only containing a large wooden box, a small table, and a simple wooden chair. Rosalie had not set foot in it for almost five years.

Without hesitation—because she knew that, if she did, she would probably turn tail—she went over to the box and opened it. The lid was heavy, as the whole box was tin-lined. She removed several layers of tissue paper and stared down at her darling Benedict's dress uniform of the Royal Horse Artillery. Removing these upper garments, she laid them carefully on the chair and then found the clothes she was looking for, returned the uniform and tissue to the box, and closed it firmly. On the table was a white cardboard box. She picked it up and quickly left the room.

She found Jenny in her bedchamber mending a lace flounce. 'I want you to go up to the far attic, Jenny. You will find a suit of clothes, some waistcoats, and cravats on a chair. Please take them to Joseph to undertake any refurbishment that may be required. I do not wish to be disturbed for the next half hour. I will ring when I am ready.'

'Yes, M'lady, are you feeling all right?'

'Thank you, Jenny. I have been thinking of Lord Benedict.'

Rosalie sat with the white box beside her on the couch. She noticed a thin film of dust on the lid and went to get a handkerchief from a silk sachet in her dressing table drawer, brushing the dust off before opening the box. She removed a pink leather-covered book, tooled in gold and bearing the word 'Journal'. The first page bore the inscription, 'To my best friend Rosalie, with all love, from her bridesmaid, Sophie Carstairs.'

She turned to the first entry, dated September 1817. She read:

> *This has been the happiest day of my life. I married my darling Benedict today. It took place in the private chapel in Coverdale Hall, with only a few friends and family, but to me it was just as wonderful as if it had taken place in Westminster Abbey. Benedict is far from being fully recovered. But I know that all he really needs is rest and peace in the place he loves, and with the care I can give him. We leave for Mairsford tomorrow.*

The next entry was for March 1819:

> *Amanda and Justin came to stay. She is expecting! I envy her. Justin is like a mother hen; I expect Benedict will be too— when the time comes. He is so much better. Justin says he is almost back to his old self. But I know he still has nightmares,*

though not so often. Amanda's daughter was born in May and called Julia. I am her godmother.

In July 1821, she had written:

King George the fourth was crowned in July, and Amanda gave birth to a son the very next day! Justin will be ecstatic. I can't help feeling a little jealous.

In April 1823:

I told Benedict today we can expect a happy event in November. The silly man wanted me to go upstairs to rest immediately!

November 1823:

The worst day of my life. I can barely write even now, although it happened three weeks ago. We lost our son. Benedict is devastated. The baby died in his arms, two hours after he was born. I was too ill to know. The doctor said I nearly died too. Benedict has been wonderful to me. We cried together, and when I was better, we took great consolation in our music. The doctor says no more babies.

April 1824:

We are in Paris! Benedict and I played Clementi's sonatina for harp and piano opus 36 no. 3 at a private musical soiree, and Frederic Chopin was there! He asked if we would play at one of his concerts. I can't believe it.

December 1824:

We are in Vienna for Christmas. What a place Europe is for music! So many wonderful composers and the opera. Mozart,

Rossini, Donizetti. But I still love Mairsford and long for the summers we spend there.

September 1829:

I can't believe it! I'm pregnant! The doctor says three months already. How am I going to tell Benedict? He will worry himself into a frazzle.

March 1830:

Bethany has arrived. A perfect little girl. Benedict is in ecstasies. I had no trouble giving birth. For now, our travels are at an end. There are more important things to keep us occupied. Bethany goes to sleep every time I play the harp!

Rosalie sat with the book open on her lap, unable to turn the next page. Tears sprang into her eyes. She closed it and got up and then changed her mind, sat down, and opened it again, turning to the last page. All down the cream-coloured paper was scrawled and scattered with blots: *No … No … No … I can't. I can't.*

Using the handkerchief she had dusted the box with, Rosalie dried her cheeks. And taking the book over to her bureau, she wrote:

21ˢᵗ august 1833:

Today my darling Benedict died in my arms.

She blotted the ink, closed the book, and returned it to the box. It held the past—not the present. She rang the bell for her maid.

When Jenny appeared, she asked. 'Did you give the clothes to Joseph?'

'Yes, M'lady.'

'What did he say? Did he think they would fit Mr Matthew?'

'Mr Joseph isn't one to say much, M'lady. But I saw 'im sort through them, and 'is expression seemed favourable.'

Rosalie was excited to see Matthew when he was dressed in proper clothes—not exactly new, of course, or in the latest fashion but, nevertheless, of the finest quality. 'Did he say when they would be ready?'

'He was a-brushing, an' a-sponging of them when you rang. An' I 'spect he will be done pressing them by now, M'lady.'

'Good. Please tell him to bring them to me in the drawing-room, when they are ready, Jenny.'

'Yes, M'lady.' Jenny, whose eagle eyes missed nothing, when it came to anything concerning her mistress's wardrobe, saw the soiled damp handkerchief lying on the couch and picked it up and left without making a comment.

Rosalie had not been in the drawing room long before Joseph appeared with several items of clothing over his arm. 'Your Ladyship wished to inspect these garments, I understand.'

'Yes, Joseph. Spread them over that chair.' She rose to inspect them. 'What is your opinion?'

'They are of the finest quality, M'lady, and have not suffered from damp or been got at by moths. It is a pleasure to work with such fine tailoring again, if I may be so bold.'

'What have you brought?'

'A pair of trousers; two waistcoats, the one Mr Matthew was wearing when he arrived and another, so he may have a choice; the velvet dressing robe; and two silk cravats. In my opinion, the gentleman will be more comfortable in a cravat, rather than a formal collar, M'lady.'

'Quite right, Joseph. Have you devised a method of getting Mr Matthew into a chair without further injury to his feet? The doctor was very firm on that point.'

'Yes, M'lady. Darrow and I have devised a method, and arranged a chair and footstool, which I have taken the liberty of acquiring from another room.'

The bracket clock struck twelve. 'Is there time to prepare Mr Matthew to have his first meal at a proper table? I am sure it will improve his appetite. Eating in bed is always tiresome.'

Picking up the clothes again, Joseph replied, 'I will see to it straight away, M'lady.'

Chapter 11

Washed, shaved, and dressed, Matthew was seated in a comfortable chair beside his bed. His left leg was supported on a long stool, his foot heavily bandaged. But at last he was able to wear clothes—black trousers, waistcoat, and the velvet robe. He had chosen a paisley pattern cravat. He was looking at himself in a handglass and put a hand up to adjust his hair. 'Ouch!' he exclaimed.

'Sir?' enquired Joseph.

'I seem to have a bump on this side of my head,' replied Matthew.

''That is not the side of your head that was injured. Would you allow me to have a look, sir?'

'Please.' Matthew pointed to the place. 'Just there.'

After careful examination, Joseph announced: 'You are right, sir. There is definitely the remains of a swelling and also a large but fading contusion. But I do not think the skin has been broken. It must have been hidden by the bandage covering your other wound.'

'Isn't that rather odd, Joseph?'

'It is certainly unusual to have had two head injuries. There is no doubt the bruising on this side occurred some time ago. I can only suppose it got overlooked in the concern for the more serious one.'

'Oh, well. There are so many things I don't know.' Matthew sighed. 'This is just one more.'

'I need to know what the time is, sir. Could you tell me?' Instinctively, Matthew's left hand went to his waistcoat pocket, and he drew out a silver watch. He looked at it in amazement. 'This is not my watch.'

'No, sir, it is mine. I was just making a little experiment, sir. Do you remember what your own watch is like?'

'Yes ... yes ... I believe I do. It's a gold one, a hunter. You can't see the dial till you open the case ... And when you do, my name is engraved inside.' Matthew leant back against the cushion that was supporting his back, looking a little pale. 'It's Matthew! My name really *is* Matthew. Isn't that extraordinary?'

'Yes, sir, indeed it is. It may help you remember more, but I shouldn't worry about it. Just let it come in its own time. Now, I'm going to ask for your luncheon to be brought.' As he spoke, Joseph carried a table from across the room and set it in front of Matthew, carefully avoiding the stool his leg was resting on. Before he left, he asked, 'Would you like me to tell Her Ladyship that you have recalled your name, sir, or would you rather tell her yourself?'

'You tell her, Joseph. After all, you made it happen.'

Joseph smiled. 'Very well, sir.'

When he went up later to fetch the tray, Matthew was fast asleep in the chair. Joseph took great care not to disturb him.

Rosalie and Amanda were in the drawing room discussing when they should send a note to Lord Hargreaves and his sister, apprising them of their intention to call. 'I don't think we need to make it too formal, Amanda. After all, it's not as if we haven't met already, is it?'

'No. And his sister, Mrs Clayborne, has had time to settle in, which is just the sort of thing a man wouldn't consider. What about tomorrow afternoon? We could go in the phaeton. Would you let me drive? Justin doesn't like me to drive in town; he says there are too many bad drivers in London already!'

Rosalie laughed. 'I hope you rapped him over the knuckles for that remark.'

Their discussion was interrupted by a discreet tap on the door. On command, Joseph entered. 'My apologies, My Lady, for disturbing you, but I have a message from Mr Matthew.'

'He's all right?'

'Yes, indeed, M'lady, very all right, if I may say so. He has remembered his name—or at least part of it.'

'Go on,' said Amanda. 'What is it?'

'It seems that it is, indeed, Matthew.'

'I knew it,' exclaimed Rosalie. 'Didn't I say all along that he looked like a Matthew?'

'Hindsight is a wonderful thing, Rosalie.' Amanda grinned. 'But tell us, Joseph, how did it come about?'

Joseph cleared his throat. 'A little ruse of my own devising, Your Ladyship. For some time I have been noticing things that indicated the fog in his mind has been clearing. Nothing definite, just small signs. And this morning when I was dressing him, I held out two waistcoats. Without hesitation, he chose his own—the one he was wearing when he was found, so Soames informed me.' He hesitated.

Rosalie spoke at once. 'Go on, Joseph. Don't keep us in suspense.'

'Well, M'lady, when I was cleaning and pressing the garment, I noticed that a pocket on the left—Mr Matthew is left-handed—was slightly stretched, as if it had once contained a watch.'

Amanda interrupted, 'Do you remember, Rosalie? Lord Hargreaves mentioned that too. Sorry, Joseph, carry on.'

'So I took the liberty of putting my own watch in the pocket before easing Mr Matthew into it and, a little while later, asking him if could tell me the time, M'lady.'

'That was so clever of you. What did he do?'

'Just as I had hoped. He went straight to the pocket and took out the watch. But my plan succeeded even further.' Joseph went on to explain how the timepiece had triggered the memory of his own name.

'Did he remember anything else—his surname, for instance?'

'No, M'lady, and I didn't press him on the matter. I believe he is feeling a little confused. When I went to collect his luncheon tray, he hadn't eaten his dessert and was fast asleep.'

'Let me know when he wakes. I am sure the sleep will do him good.'

When he had gone, Rosalie and Amanda returned to the subject of the visit to Staplewood. 'What about tomorrow afternoon, shall I say three o'clock?'

'I am sure that would be perfect,' replied Amanda.

'I shall send Darrow with a note at once.' As Rosalie rose to go to her desk, she asked Amanda, 'Do you think it would be all right if I allowed Beth to visit Matthew—now that he is out of bed?'

'I'm sure it would be perfectly all right.' She smiled. 'Then they can continue their chess game face to face.'

'What *do* you mean?'

'They have been conducting a covert game of chess, passing moves back and forth, via Joseph, or anyone who would do it—'

'And how long have you known about this, may I ask?' Rosalie raised her eyebrows.

'Now don't get on your high horse, my dear. Remember, I was once your guardian,' Amanda said in mock severity. 'There has been no harm done. And in fact, if I had thought, for one moment, that it was wrong, I would have told you at once. I actually believe it has done them both good.'

Rosalie's temper subsided. 'You are right—as usual, Amanda. And I don't think it is wrong; it was only that I hadn't been told.'

'And if you had been, would you have put a stop to it?'

Rosalie thought for a moment, before saying, 'No, probably not. But I suppose I might have spoiled Beth's enjoyment of the secret.'

A little while later, Rosalie went up to see Matthew and found him wide awake and smiling as she entered the room. 'You look very pleased with yourself, Matthew,' she observed.

'Oh, Lady B, I have remembered my full name and where I've come from!'

'That's wonderful. So what is it?'

'Matthew William Stuart, and I've come from America. I'm still a little confused about exactly where, but it's either Philadelphia or New York, or possibly both. I remember getting on a boat but nothing after that, until I came to in this bed.' He pointed to his waistcoat. 'I think this is mine.' He slid his left hand into the pocket. 'I had a watch.'

'Well, Mr Matthew Stuart, welcome to England, although not the start you had hoped for, I'm sure. And I'm afraid there was no watch in your pocket when we found you. Can you remember what happened at all?'

Matthew shook his head. 'No, but I remember what I do—or did—for a living. I'm an engineer and surveyor, and I worked in New York. I was coming to England to study railroad building. I wanted to meet someone,' Matthew made a face. 'I just can't think of his name.'

'I shouldn't worry,' said Rosalie. 'I'm sure a lot of other things will come back to you in time. Who is winning the chess game?' she smiled.

'Oh, you know about that? Beth said it was a deep dark secret. But in answer to your question, she is.'

Chapter 12

Emily Clayborne was all of a dither, which was most unlike her. 'Relax, my dear,' said her brother. 'They are very charming ladies. I can assure you.'

'I know, so you've said a dozen times. But I don't think you realise just what a great lady the Marchioness of Coverdale is, Charles. The fame of her parties and political dinners has even reached Bath, and this place still looks so shabby. I think having the windows cleaned was a mistake. It makes it even worse. And they're sure to want to be shown round.'

'Yes, I expect they will. But they know I've been here only a few months. They won't expect miracles. Just enjoy their company—and make sure your monster dog is shut away.'

The plan to drive in an open carriage was thwarted by the weather. So promptly at three o'clock, a chaise, drawn by two carriage horses and with a postillion, drew up to the portico of Staplewood House. Parsons was waiting to help them alight. Contrary to formal etiquette, Lord Hargreaves and his sister were in the hall to receive their guests. And Royston, in his role as footman, was there to relieve them of their outerwear.

After the introductions were over, Amanda couldn't help exclaiming at the grandeur of the hall—just at that moment the sun appeared. The newly cleaned Venetian window gave full rein to the gilded staircase and doors, making them look as if King Midas himself had recently been in residence.

'Oh!' said Rosalie. 'For once, the reports I've heard of this place were actually true. It *is* magnificent.'

'Perhaps just a little too much,' said Lord Hargreaves deprecatingly. 'We will sit in the long saloon. I hope the fire has stopped smoking.'

Comfortable seats had been arranged around the heavily carved marble fireplace, and Amanda managed to seat herself beside Mrs Clayborn. 'I understand you have been living in Bath, Mrs Clayborne,' she began.

'Yes, I have a house there. Of course, Bath is not what it was in its heyday. But I like it. The parks and gardens are still lovely, and there are good walks by the river for my ...' She was going to say dog but quickly altered it to, 'Health.'

'All this will be a great change for you.' Amanda waved her hand to indicate the extent of the room.

'Of course, Lady Coverdale. But it will give me something to do, and I like to keep busy.'

'Lady Benedict.' Said Amanda, 'is very pleased there will be someone living here at last. Big houses like this need to be occupied, and I expect you will soon be overwhelmed by callers.'

'Especially as my brother now has the seal of approval from you and Lady Benedict.' Emily smiled, raising an eyebrow.

'I expect Charles has explained to you the circumstances under which we first met.'

'Yes, a most unfortunate accident. How is the young man? He was quite seriously injured I understand.'

Amanda looked towards Rosalie. 'Tell Mrs Clayborne and Lord Hargreaves the good news about our invalid. I'm sure they are all dying to know.'

'Well,' Rosalie began, 'he is certainly a great deal better. And he has recovered some of his memory. The extraordinary thing is, his name really is Matthew.'

''No, really; that is amazing,' put in Hargreaves.

'Yes, Matthew Stuart. And he is an American, as we guessed he might be.'

'What else does he remember? Why was he in your drive?'' Hargreaves enquired eagerly, adding, 'Does he know what happened to him?'

'I can answer some of your questions,' said Rosalie, 'but not all. Matthew's last recollections seem to be just before the ship sailed from New York; he can't remember exactly. After that, he has no memory of anything.'

'How about why he was coming to England in the first place?'

'It seems he has come to study railway engineering—he calls them railroads. I think he would like to meet Mr Brunel.'

At this point Parsons, followed by a maid, arrived with a tray containing a silver tea kettle with a spirit lamp and several other silver containers. The maid carried another tray with a China tea set and plates of thin bread and butter, fruit cake, and almond biscuits.

'Thank you, Parsons. We will serve ourselves,' said Emily, turning to Rosalie. 'I haven't gotten used to servants hovering about, not,' she added, 'that we have many. The butler came with the house, and Charles brought the husband and wife who looked after him in Ludlow. The rest are mostly girls from the village. He was quite surprised to find that they were all virtually illiterate.'

'Yes, I know. Such education as there is in rural areas, is mainly directed at boys. Benedict and I started a small school in Mairsford, which has gone some way to address the problem.'

'Oh, Lady Benedict, Charles will be very interested to hear more. But now I must attend to the tea. I see the kettle is boiling.' As she went over to the table, Emily caught a tiny nod of approval from her brother.

Halfway through the repast, which was clearly being enjoyed by all, from the hallway, came a shout of, "No!" This was followed by a deep bark and a yelp as something hit the door with a thump.

'Emily!' The look from her brother was far from approving this time.

'Will you excuse me a minute, Lady Benedict?' Laying her teacup down, Emily rose and went to the door. When she opened it, she found what she was expecting—Bedford splayed out on the floor, looking puzzled.

Rosalie, who was sure an animal had made the yelp, followed Emily. Immediately upon seeing the dog, she exclaimed, 'Oh, the poor darling. Is he hurt?'

From back in the room, Hargreaves said, 'I give in. You'd better bring him in, Emily, but make sure he doesn't knock the tea table over.'

'I'm afraid, Lady Benedict, Bedford doesn't see very well. That's why he sometimes bumps into things.'

'That's terrible. Was it an accident?"

'No, when I was in Bath, I spoke to a retired kennelman, and he said he was probably born that way. So at least he doesn't know any different.'

Amanda, who had been watching the reactions of the other three people with interest, now joined in, asking what his parentage might be.

Hargreaves replied, 'There's certainly Great Dane there. His ears and colouring might be part bloodhound, perhaps.'

The unexpected arrival of the dog somehow managed to loosen the somewhat stilted conversational atmosphere that had prevailed earlier, and the visit ended cheerfully with a quick tour of the main rooms.

Before their departure, Rosalie issued an invitation to dinner the following week. 'The Marquis and his elder daughter, Julia, will have arrived by then, and I hope Matthew will be well enough to join us for dinner,' she said. But privately she wondered how difficult it might be to get him down the narrow winding stairs of Mairsford, which were in total contrast to the gilded magnificence of those at Staplewood.

'There now, you see, Emily. There was nothing to worry about. Both ladies are charming, just as I told you,' said Hargreaves as Parsons was closing the front door.

'I think it was Bedford who made all the difference. He really took to Lady Benedict. He's such a clever dog. Aren't you, darling?' Emily said, fondling his ears.

'Humph,' said her brother, frowningly. 'Bedford will take to anyone who surreptitiously feeds him almond biscuits.' But privately, he had to agree.

In the carriage, on the way back to Mairsford, Rosalie was excited. 'I'm sure the Hargreaves are going to be a great asset to the neighbourhood. The area has lacked a great house and active occupants for so long.'

'I shouldn't get your hopes up too high yet, Rosalie. They may decide not to stay.'

'Mrs Clayborne wouldn't have been asking me about local tradesmen if they weren't planning to make improvements.'

'Well, it could certainly do with some, although one can't deny that the rooms they showed us have their own elegance, despite the wear and tear. I dare say nothing has been changed since the day the place was built. And there's another consideration.'

'What?'

'Money, Rosalie, money. You mustn't forget that the new Lord Hargreaves was only a country solicitor—even if a very successful one, he may not have the finances to make big changes, never mind the upkeep of a place that size. I very much doubt he was left a fortune to go with the title and estate.'

Rosalie sighed. 'I hadn't thought of that, although Benedict said that the first Lord Hargreaves was rumoured to be a Nabob,' Then she added more cheerfully, 'Never mind. They are both really nice people.'

'How do you know that? You've only just met them,' Amanda said sternly.

'I just do, that's all.'

Amanda looked out of the carriage window and gave a little smile. From long experience, she knew Rosalie's instincts as far as people were concerned, and animals, too, were always right. She certainly had been about Benedict.

Chapter 13

In his Bristol office, the solicitor Mr Pettigrew and his chief clerk, Mr Fitton, were debating what to do next. 'Should we not inform the police, sir?' suggested Mr Fitton.

'Yes, we could. But that would be rather hard on the pawnbroker. He hasn't actually done anything wrong—yet. And the police would undoubtedly want to take the watch and probably turn the whole place over. The law on receiving stolen property is "knowing it to be stolen". He may have made an educated guess about the watch, but anyway he came to us.'

'He did, sir. But I have to say it was in the hope of monetary gain, rather than from any altruistic motives.'

'Nevertheless, Fitton, we have gotten one step further towards finding out about Mr Stuart. I'll have to think about how to proceed next. Meanwhile, it is time to resume our normal duties.'

Various courses of action occurred to Pettigrew in the next twenty-four hours. But none of them seemed to be quite the right or the most fruitful thing to do. He was aware that an apparently well-to-do American citizen had disappeared almost without trace. The only innocent explanation was that he had found himself without funds and sold his watch. But why should he? He had been in correspondence with Pettigrew, so the obvious thing would be to apply to the solicitor to help him out of his difficulty. He was looking at a conveyance document, but his mind kept wandering to the problem of the missing Mr Stuart, when Fitton came in holding a newspaper.

'A moment of your time, sir, if you please.'

'Yes, yes. Have you more news?'

'Not exactly, sir. But I see from the Lloyd's shipping list that the ship Mr Stuart arrived in, the SS *Marianna*, is due back tomorrow. We may learn more from the captain and crew. Perhaps he told someone of his plans.'

'An excellent suggestion, Fitton. Send a message to the shipping office immediately, stating our requirements. Tomorrow we will go to the docks and find the ship. As you say there must be more information to be had there.'

By mid-morning, Pettigrew and Fitton were in the hallway of the shipping company, awaiting the arrival of members of the crew of the SS *Marianna*. They did not have to wait long. Two men, accompanied by an office clerk, entered. The older of the two was wearing an officer's uniform, and the other, a seaman's dark jacket and trousers.

'This is the first officer, Mr Green, and the senior steward from the ship you are interested in, Mr Pettigrew. I am sure they will be happy to answer any questions you may have, sir. You may use this office,' he said, opening another door.

Once seated, Mr Pettigrew explained, 'We are from a firm of solicitors in Bristol. And some weeks ago, we were expecting the arrival of a Mr Stuart, who we know was a passenger in the SS *Marianna*. But he has not contacted us, and we have reason to believe that some ill may have befallen him. I am hoping you can throw some light on the matter.' Pettigrew addressed the first officer.

'Indeed, I can, a little,' the grey-haired Mr Green said. 'But Mr Craigie here knows a lot more than I do.'

'Aye, I do that, sir,' said the younger man, betraying his Scottish origins. 'I was that sorry for the poor gentleman. I'd ne'er seen the like of it before, that sick he was.'

'Taken ill was he?' Pettigrew asked anxiously.

'Aye, but not wi' a disease, mind, with the seasickness.'

'Don't people get over that after a few days at sea?' Fitton put in.

'That is usually true,' answered the first officer, 'but not in this case. Describe what happened, Craigie, if you please.'

'From the moment he set foot on the ship to the moment I helped him off, he was sick. And we had a terrible bad crossing, sir. Two days late, due to the storm.'

'Craigie came to me, Mr Pettigrew. He was very worried. We have no doctor on board, and Mr Stuart had been unable to keep anything down, if you will excuse the expression, for more than a week.'

'I had tried everything—weak tea, dry biscuit. Mr Stuart was'nae a fat man, an' now he was jist skin an' bone. I was sair worrit, sir.'

'I can imagine you were.' Pettigrew turned to Mr Green. 'So what did you do?'

'There wasn't much I could do, but I am in charge of a small quantity of medical supplies—mostly for injuries, you understand. And I had some laudanum, so I suggested administering a few drops in brandy.'

'And did that work?'

'Well. It knocked the poor gentleman out while the worst of the storm was raging. And after that, he seemed a bit better and was able to drink some tea and nibble a rusk. He was very weak when we docked and had to be helped up the gangway.'

'Aye, but he was that glad to be on dry land.'

'What about his belongings? What did he have with him?' asked Fitton.

'There were a big trunk unloaded onto the quayside, and he had a wee valise and some sort of document case. I helped him pack the valise. He seemed to be a well-to-do gentleman. Judging by his pairsonal items, ivory and silver mounted brushes an' that—'

'And then what did you do?' asked Fitton.

'I had duties to attend to on the ship, sir, and I left him there. He was very grateful for my attention to him and generous with a tip.'

'He didn't mention any plans?' Pettigrew enquired.

'Not exactly.' The first officer intervened. 'I wanted to make sure he was all right—not that he looked it. But he asked me to send the trunk to the shipping office and asked me if I knew of a reputable hotel he could put up at. I recommended the George on Queen Charlotte Street, and I'm afraid that was the last I saw of him.'

'Can you describe Mr Stuart to us?'

'He was tall, about six foot or a wee bitty more. Dark hair, blue eyes, an' no looking himself, I doot—with the sickness, you understand,' Craigie explained.

'Yes, perfectly.'

The two seamen were about to leave when Fitton asked, 'Mr Craigie, could you describe the valise—for identification if it is found.' He turned to Pettigrew for confirmation.

'Sound thinking, Fitton. Well, Mr Craigie?'

The steward gestured with his hands the size of the case, saying, 'It were light, tan-coloured leather. One o' they cases with two compartments. It had a lock, an' two straps wi' buckles.'

'Any markings, labels, that sort of thing?'

'Aye, there were initials on the top, in black—M.W.S.'

'That could be very helpful, Mr Craigie.'

Pettigrew looked at Fitton. 'I think we now know all these gentlemen can apprise us of. Thank you, Mr Green, Mr Craigie. I can see you both did your best to help Mr Stuart. We will make enquiries at the George. That may take us further.'

But it didn't. Their questions drew a blank. No one of that name or of that description had ever enquired about or booked a room there.

Leaving the hotel, Pettigrew and Fitton looked at each other. 'Now what should we do?' Fitton asked his employer.

'I think I'll have to inform the police, now, about everything we've learnt, previously and today, suggests foul play has occurred.'

The following day, Mr Pettigrew did just that. Being slightly acquainted with the superintendent of police in Bristol, he was able to speak to him in person. Having laid everything he and Fitton had learned in the last few weeks, before that individual, he added. 'My concern, Superintendent, is that a well-to-do gentleman from America seems to have gone missing, and the American embassy in London could get involved. I wouldn't want to think my firm had not done enough to remedy the situation.'

'I think you have done all you can, Mr Pettigrew. And you were quite right not to make any attempt to recover the watch. The pawnbroker must keep it for the required time before the pledge is void.'

Mr Pettigrew left the station, consoled the matter was in other hands but still worried about the welfare of Matthew Stuart.

Chapter 14

Two days before the dinner party Rosalie was giving to welcome Lord Hargreaves and his sister formally to the neighbourhood, Amanda's husband and daughter arrived at Mairsford. As the carriage pulled up beside the bridge, as usual, Bethany managed to be the first to greet the new arrivals. Julia disembarked first and immediately hugged her little cousin but then went to the rear of the carriage, where a superb black gelding, led by a groom on another horse, had been following the carriage. 'Oh, Julia,' cried Bethany, 'you've brought Gladiator. Can I ride him?'

'Perhaps. We'll see.' Julia turned to the groom. 'Is he all right, Eckersly? No problems on the road?'

'He behaved perfect, M'lady.' He handed Julia a carrot from his pocket, which she gave to the eager horse.

'Can I give him one, please?' asked Bethany.

'If Eckerslys got another.'

The groom smiled and produced another carrot, which Bethany offered to Gladiator.

'Bethany,' her mother called, 'I think your uncle deserves a greeting too.'

Bethany looked a little shamefaced. 'Sorry, Uncle Justin.' She dropped a curtsy.

The big figure of Marquis of Coverdale smiled and held out his arms. 'I can do better than that.' He scooped the child up and kissed her cheek. 'You've grown since I last saw you—well, you got heavier, anyway,' he said, laughing, as the party went through the gatehouse door.

While Soames and Darrow organised the unloading of the trunks and suitcases and directed the coachman and groom where to take the horses, Rosalie led the way to the drawing room.

'Bethany, show Julia to her room. I will see if Mrs Soames has tea ready.'

This was entirely against normal procedure. Rosalie knew that tea was certainly awaiting her order to bring it in, but she wanted to give Justin and Amanda a few minutes privacy. She knew they hated being apart and would appreciate the opportunity to embrace in private.

During tea, the marquis was apprised of all that had been going on since his wife had been staying at Mairsford. Admittedly, he had trouble getting everything straight, listening to Rosalie, Amanda, and Bethany all trying to talk at once. Eventually, he said, 'This young American you have secreted upstairs, my sweet sister-in-law, will I be allowed to see him?'

'Yes, and he's not secreted,' she admonished but knew she was being teased. 'I will take you up for a visit after dinner. I know he will enjoy some male company—other than Joseph's, that is. What I would have done without him, I just don't know.'

'Joseph?' queried the Marquis.

'Rosalie is right,' put in Amanda. 'He has been a tower of strength, and a great help to Matthew, who is struggling with loss of memory. Only last week, he remembered his surname was Stuart, and Joseph said it was then recalled a lot of other things, too.'

'But who is he?'

Amanda continued. 'He was sent over by Lord Hargreaves. Ros and I were in a bit of a difficulty, not having a suitable manservant to look after Matthew, especially when he was so ill.'

'You will have plenty of time to check Joseph over, as I have arranged for him to look after you, since you haven't brought your own valet,' added Rosalie. 'Ah, I think I heard my niece arriving.'

With a sigh that was entirely humorous, Amanda said, 'One can always hear Julia arrive. The idea of a silent approach is unknown to her.'

True to her words, the door was flung open, and Julia bounced in. 'I have him settled. You know he's very sensitive to new surroundings.'

'Now that you have the love of your life fed and watered, perhaps you might sit down. And your aunt Rosalie might, just might, offer you a cup of tea.'

'Sorry, Aunt Rosalie.' Julia sat demurely on the sofa and accepted a cup of tea and a slice of fruitcake. 'Now you can tell me about this handsome young man you've hidden in the attic.'

'Julia! That is no way to talk to your aunt,' Justin exclaimed and then realised he had said almost the same thing himself.

Rosalie just laughed. 'How did you find out about him? You've hardly been here five minutes.'

'I went through the kitchen to go to the stables, and I saw a tray, loaded with fine bread and butter, scones, cake, and the best tea service. Jenny was about to carry it, when a servant I'd never seen before took it from her and told her to go and see to my unpacking. She didn't look too pleased, so I asked her who it was for. "'Im wif the bad feet, though 'e's ever so nice, an' 'andsome too." Julia imitated Jenny's cockney accent.

Amanda sighed. 'If you want to know anything about anybody, ask the servants. I don't know why we bother with politicians. Servants would run the country much more efficiently. Wouldn't they?' She smiled at her husband.

'Sometimes I think they probably wouldn't do any worse!' he replied.

'Talking of politics, Justin,' said Rosalie, 'my new neighbour, Lord Hargreaves, is looking forward to meeting you. He holds the same opinions. And I think is hoping to take his seat in the Lords next session, but he is in an awkward situation.'

'How so?'

'Well, you see, in his former life—as a solicitor—he had no social contact with the peerage and, of course, never expected to be raised to it, being the descendant of a fourth son. He will need sponsors, won't he?'

'Yes, I suppose he will. What do you want me to do?'

'He and his sister, a Mrs Clayborne, are coming to dinner the day after tomorrow. Perhaps you could tactfully introduce the subject—after dinner perhaps? He's very nice and has been a great help to me, allowing Joseph to come here and insisting on paying his wages. As I have already said, I honestly don't know what I would have done without him.'

Justin quirked an eyebrow. 'Joseph. Or Hargreaves?'

'Really, Justin, Joseph of course!'

After dinner, Rosalie took Justin upstairs to meet Matthew. Julia was quite vociferous about the fact that she was not to be included.

'He's been very ill, Julia,' her mother explained, 'and even although he is getting better, one visitor at a time is enough for now. Anyway, you will have plenty of time to get to know him later.'

Matthew was fully dressed, and his right foot was now encased in a soft slipper, the left still bandaged. Joseph opened the door and announced, 'The Marquis of Coverdale to see you, Mr Stuart.' Then he withdrew discreetly.

'I'm sorry I can't get up,' said Matthew, holding out his hand.

Justin shook it warmly, saying, 'That's the last thing I would expect you to do, having had a full account of your injuries from my wife and sister-in-law.' He smiled, taking the chair placed by Matthew's table.

'I expect, My Lord, what you really want to know is what sort of cuckoo has landed in Lady Benedict's nest. Is that not so? My memory of recent events is, as yet, almost non-existent. But lately, more of my early life has returned.'

Justin's golden eyes twinkled. 'You read me like a book, Mr Stuart. A Scottish name, I presume.'

'Yes, but I believe my father left Scotland as a young man – he was an officer in the British Army, posted to Canada. He died when I was ten years old.'

'So, you are a British citizen then?'

'I suppose so, My Lord. But after the war, my parents went to live in Philadelphia, and I consider myself more American than British, sir.'

'Which war?' Justin enquired.

'The war with the United States in 1812, sir.'

'That's interesting. My brother fought in that campaign. He was in the Royal Artillery.' Justin smiled. 'But we were talking about you. What has brought you to England?'

'To study railroad engineering. My Lord, my father was a military engineer. And although he died when I was young, I followed in his footsteps and qualified as a surveyor. I remember working as one in New York. But what has happened since is a complete blank, I'm afraid—until, that is, I woke up in Lady B's guest bedchamber.'

'Ah, railways, the future of the world. You have the right idea, Mr Stuart. The St Maure family, too, takes an interest in progress.' Justin saw a puzzled expression pass over Matthew's face. 'Are you feeling all right?' he said anxiously.

'Oh, yes, My Lord. Something vaguely familiar flitted through my head but went before I could catch it.'

'Did something I said remind you of your past?'

'I don't know—perhaps. The doctor said I was not to try to remember but, rather, to let it come in its own time. So I try not to worry. But it is a very strange experience to wake up and not even recognise your own face!'

'It must have been,' Justin said, rising from his chair. 'I think it is time I rejoined the ladies, and I can hear someone outside the door.'

'That'll be my keeper—the inimitable Joseph. I expect he wants to bring me hot milk or something.' Matthew knew the something included his foot being redressed, an ordeal he had to endure twice daily. He held out his hand. 'Thank you for coming, My Lord. I hope I have allayed some of your doubts about my presence here. They saved my life, you know.'

Justin returned to the drawing room and immediately accepted a cup of tea, seating himself beside his wife—who said, 'Well, Justin, we're all waiting for your opinion.'

He addressed Rosalie. 'I have no anxiety about your foundling. He seems to be an intelligent young man. And although he has lived all his life in the Americas, he is, nevertheless, a British citizen.'

'Is he as good-looking as Jenny says, Papa?' Julia asked.

Justin shook his head. 'Gossiping again, Julia. I'm no judge of male beauty. But yes, his features seem to be arranged in a satisfactory manner, and one can't help noticing his very blue eyes, and ...' Some fleeting memory shot through Justin's mind, and he paused.

'And what?' said Julia.

The moment passed, and Justin finished, 'And off course one can see the marks of illness and injury are still apparent.'

'But there's good news,' said Rosalie. 'The doctor called this morning and said Matthew will soon be able to leave his bed during the day and join us downstairs.'

Chapter 15

It didn't take twenty-four hours for Matthew and Julia to become friends. He spent most of the day out of bed, largely being entertained by Julia and Bethany, who had a poor opinion of his chess-playing skills' but had to give him best at backgammon. Amanda worried and expressed her anxiety to Justin.

'I am sure your concern is unfounded, my dear, Nothing untoward can happen. And anyway, it is a relief to see Julia happily entertained, instead of moping about in Berkeley Square, and refusing to go to balls or help you with social events.'

'I suppose you're right, Justin. You usually are.' she smiled.

'She wants some independence and something to do. If young Matthew can give her that, then we should be grateful.'

Amanda wasn't wholly satisfied. But she dropped the subject as Rosalie entered the room, a frown on her face.

'Something the matter?' asked Justin.

'That depends. The doctor has just left, and he has said that Matthew can come downstairs for the first time. But I can't think how we are going to manage it. He looked so pleased. I don't want to disappoint him. But our stairs are so narrow and twist round corners, and he is not allowed to put a foot to the ground.'

'Don't worry, Rosalie. There are at least three strong men in the house. Between us, we will manage something.'

'If you're sure. I'd better go and tell Soames there will be seven for dinner. As she approached the dining room, Rosalie could hear an altercation taking place. The voices stilled the moment she opened the door, observing Soames and Joseph both looking somewhat peeved.

'Ah, Soames,' she began, 'Mr Matthew will be joining us for dinner this evening.'

'Yes, M'lady. I have already been apprised of that fact,' he said, his voice dripping with disapproval.

'It is my fault,' said Joseph immediately. 'I was unaware Mr Soames had not already been informed, and I came to ascertain how best to arrange for Mr Matthew to be seated.'

Rosalie could see that hurt feelings had occurred in both parties, and diplomacy was called for. 'Perhaps, Soames, you could explain to me what the problem is?'

'Mr Joseph, My Lady, wants Mr Matthew's place to have no one opposite him, and that will leave a gap.' The gap, in Soames's mind, was roughly equivalent to the Cheddar Gorge and should play no part at a lady's dinner table.

'What is your reasoning for this … er …gap, Joseph?'

'I wish to place a footstool for Mr Matthew's foot under the table. And any person sitting opposite might accidently hit it or, indeed, touch Mr Matthew's foot.'

'That seems very sensible to me, Joseph.' She turned immediately to the butler, whose lips were compressed in a rigid line. 'You see, Soames, none of us is able to follow our own ideas in this matter. We must all bow to the doctor's decree, and he has been most specific about the care we must take of Mr Matthew's injuries. It is barely a month since he arrived in that terrible condition, and he is still far from fully recovered, so doctor's orders must prevail over common etiquette. I suggest you set the table accordingly, while Joseph goes to find a suitable piece of furniture for Mr Matthew to rest his foot on.'

Joseph leapt to open the door for her.

'You may find something in the great hall, that suits the purpose,' she told him.

The family was assembled in the drawing room, ready to receive their guests. All were arrayed in attire suitable for an intimate country house dinner. As the only man present, the marquis, in sober black, as was now the fashion, made a contrast to his ladies' colourful gowns. Even Rosalie had donned a dove-grey dress, the silk shot through with pink and a front panel of cream satin edged with lace. A double string of perfectly matched pearls set off to perfection her still delicate complexion.

'My dear!' exclaimed Amanda. 'You look delightful. Is that a new dress?'

'No, indeed not. But I have never worn it before. I thought it was time I gave it an outing. I see you still favour green, Amanda.'

Amanda sat on the sofa, spreading out a silk dress the colour of summer leaves, trimmed with a row of tiny bows down the front. Each one was set with a tiny diamond, which sparkled as she moved.

'And my darling daughter in primrose yellow completes my bevy of garden flowers.' Justin laughed.

But it was Amanda who was secretly the most pleased. At last, Rosalie was taking the first steps away from her grief. She had even discarded the ugly widow's cap with its ribbons tied under her chin. True, she still wore a cap, but it was no more than a wisp of ecru lace, secured with a pearl comb.

The rumble of wheels on gravel proclaimed the arrival of Lord Hargreaves and his sister, and shortly afterwards Soames announced them. After the introductions, Hargreaves and the marquis gravitated to one end of the room—as men do.

But this arrangement did not suit Amanda. 'Lord Hargreaves,' she began, 'I remember your expressing an interest in this house, and it is certainly worth exploring. I am sure Lady Benedict would be delighted to show you some of it. Is that not true, Rosalie?'

'If that is what you would like, it would be my pleasure,' replied Rosalie, keeping surprise at this turn of events out of her voice. 'We had better take the advantage of the light before it fades.'

Emily Clayborne, who was quick on the uptake, immediately said, 'There is something I particularly want to ask Lady Coverdale, and this is an ideal opportunity. You are the one interested in architecture, Charles. You can tell me all about it later.'

The marquis also found something else that demanded his attention and enjoined Julia to join him. Thus, Lord Hargreaves and Lady Benedict found themselves alone in the courtyard. 'The house is entirely timber-framed, apart from the gatehouse and chimney stacks.'

'Do you have to draw all your water from the well?' asked Hargreaves, who still hankered for the running tap water installed in his Ludlow home.

'We did when we first came here. But Benedict had a pump installed, and the water comes up—something to do with underground pressure. He was an artillery officer, and they learn all about engineering. You'd better ask Lady Julia. She takes an interest in all that sort of thing.'

'How old is the building?'

'We don't exactly know,' answered Rosalie. 'The name exists in the Domesday Book, but we don't think it refers to this house.' Rosalie gave a little stumble, and Hargreaves put a hand on her arm to steady her. She smiled. 'We are about to enter the great hall. It is not particularly great when compared with others—like the one at Coverdale Hall, but I love it.'

'I can see why, Lady Benedict, it is truly beautiful.' The ceiling timbers had been painted in the Italian style. At one end was a massive fireplace, and at the other, a minstrels' gallery.

'It is a shame it's hardly used these days, but I still host the Harvest Supper here, and a traditional Twelfth Night Ball. If we take those stairs, you can look into where the musicians play as we go up to the long gallery.' Rosalie led the way.

'Do you have a lot of documentation regarding the house?'

'Alas, no. It only came into the St Maure estate about a hundred years ago. Before that, it had numerous different owners, and much of the archive has been lost.' It was getting dark as they reached the gallery, so they did not linger, but Rosalie said, 'It is believed the hall once extended to the height of the roof, which you can see is vaulted. But when it became fashionable to have a long gallery, one was inserted. It is used now as Bethany's schoolroom and play area.'

Hargreaves insisted on holding Rosalie's arm as they descended the steep flights of stairs. Once back in the drawing room, she was surprised how much she had enjoyed talking to Lord Hargreaves—even if it was only on architecture. There was something else she had liked, but she banished that thought to the back of her mind.

'Did you enjoy your tour, Hargreaves?' enquired Justin.

'Very much, My Lord. Who could not, with such an excellent guide,' he replied, bowing in Rosalie's direction.

Amanda thought she detected slight colour rising into Rosalie's cheek. But then again it might be a flicker of candlelight. Soames came in and announced in sepulchral tones that dinner was served.

The party entered a room ablaze with light. Three magnificent six-branch candelabra marched down the centre of the table. In each corner of the room, a torchère bore more lights, and a fire blazed at one end of the room. Matthew was already seated, as this had been considered the safest thing for him. Mrs Clayborne was the only one he had not previously met, and he apologised for being unable to get up on being introduced.

Mrs Clayborne immediately said. 'No need for apologies, Mr Stuart. I have been told about all you have endured, and it is delightful to see you able to join Lady Benedict's dinner party.'

At Rosalie's request, Justin took the head of the table, with Mrs Clayborne on his right. Rosalie sat at the other end with Lord Hargreaves on her right. The meal was a simple but carefully chosen one, starting with fresh green pea soup and followed by buttered lobster, Romney Marsh lamb, creamed chicken breasts, a raspberry sorbet, and several other cold desserts—each course served with the appropriate wine.

Talk was general and rather slow to start. But both Julia and Emily Clayborne were enthusiastic conversationalists and soon managed to break down barriers, and the social sin of 'talking across' was forgotten. Only Matthew, who answered politely any questions put to him, forbore to offer his own opinions. It was not long after the ladies had risen to allow the men to enjoy their port and nuts that Justin noticed Matthew had gone very pale, and beads of sweat had appeared on his brow.

'You know, Hargreaves, I think our young friend here is ready for his bed. He has been up long enough for his first time in company.'

Matthew gave a wan smile and said a little weakly, 'I believe, My Lord, you are right. If you would be so good as to summon Soames.'

'How did you get down here?'

'I was supported by joseph and Darrow, and sort of hopped, too.'

'You are in no fit state to hop anywhere. Is he, Hargreaves? I will carry you.'

'Oh! But, My Lord—'

'No buts,' said Justin, gently pulling Matthew's chair back from the table. 'Hargreaves, if you would be so kind, grab one of those candlesticks, and go in front of us. You can direct the way.' He bent down beside Matthew. 'Put your arm round my shoulders, lad.' And with that, he scooped the young man into his arms, taking great care not to bump the injured foot against any protruding table legs. 'Let us proceed.'

Halfway along the passage, they encountered Darrow. 'Tell Joseph he is required by Mr Stuart. And tell Soames we are coming back to the dining room.'

'Very good, M'lord. Mr Joseph is already in Mr Stuart's room, M'lord.'

Laying Matthew gently on his bed and leaving him to Joseph's tender care, the Marquis and the Baron returned to the dining room. Justin kicked the fire into life with the toe of his shoe, a habit deplored by his valet, and angled his chair towards that of Hargreaves, saying, 'Bring that decanter down this end—there's a good fellow—and we can at last have a chat.'

Hargreaves steady grey eyes twinkled. He was well aware that the marquis wanted to quiz him in a covert sort of way as to his suitability as a neighbour for his sister-in-law to consort with. But the conversation opened with a different subject.

'Have you considered taking your seat in the House when Parliament sits again in October, Hargreaves?'

There was a slight pause, as he sipped his port before replying. 'Considered, yes, but not, as yet, made any decision.'

A little puzzled, the Marquis asked, 'Why not? I understand from my wife you are of the Liberal persuasion—as I am. And I am sure you would be an asset to the party.'

'It's like this, Your Lordship. I was not born to this position. Neither had I any expectations of ennoblement. It has come entirely due to the failure of others in my family to live long enough.' He gave a deprecating smile. 'I have never aspired to high society. I am just a country solicitor.'

'But a very successful one and highly thought of in your community, in many different ways,' interpolated Justin, giving a reassuring grin. Stretching his hand out for the decanter, he topped up Hargreaves's glass.

The grin and the gesture disarmed Hargreaves, and he just raised his eyebrows. 'You've been making enquiries?'

'Yes, and I find Lady Benedict has acquired the perfect neighbour. Now, about the matter of your seat in the Lords. I would be delighted to act as one of your sponsors, and I can easily find another, if you don't have anyone in mind.'

'I should be very pleased to accept your kind offices, Lord Coverdale. May I ask why you do not have a position in the government? You seem to me to be ideally suited to high office.'

'A brief spell as an MP before my father died somewhat put me off what I might call organised politics. Since almost the beginning of the late wars with France, I have been a gatherer of information. I can be of more use to the country—no matter who is in power—that way. My wife, likewise, has no desire to enter court politics by taking a position as one of our new queen's ladies.'

'I see.' Hargreaves nodded. 'But on another subject entirely, I am concerned about Mr Stuart. I know he has received care and attention second to none while he has been here. But now he is going to be more mobile, and this house—beautiful as it is, has real problems with stairs and so forth. Do you think it would upset Lady Benedict if I suggested he continued his convalescence at Staplewood?'

Justin cracked a walnut and picked out the flesh with a silver nut pick. 'I'm sure she would be very sorry not to have him here, but her first concern will always be for his welfare. Do you have downstairs accommodation he could use?'

'Yes, there's a billiard room.' He laughed. 'It has everything for the game except a table! I believe it would be ideal, as it is big enough to use as a sitting room as well. He might not always want to be with the family, and of course Joseph already has a room at the house.'

'It sounds ideal. Would you like me to introduce the idea to the ladies?' Justin rose. 'I think it's about time we joined them. But before we do, I want to say how very pleased I am that you and your sister have come to live in the neighbourhood. It will be an undoubted boost to the area to have Staplewood Park occupied once more.' He held out his hand, and Hargreaves shook it warmly.

'Thank you, sir. It will take a bit of getting used to. But I'm sure we'll soon settle down. My son, Nicholas, too. He will be coming home soon. He's been staying with school friends.'

Tea was under way when the gentlemen entered the drawing room, and both men accepted a cup, seating themselves comfortably.

Rosalie immediately asked after Matthew.

'Lord Hargreaves and I have taken him up to bed. I think the experience of a dinner party tired him somewhat, so we thought it best. Joseph is with him now.'

'Thank you both,' said Rosalie. 'I will go and see him shortly. Julia has been regaling us with her visit to the Royal Observatory at Greenwich, with the astronomer royal,' remarked Rosalie and caught a brief frown crossing Julia's father's brow. 'You disapprove, Justin?'

Justin shook his head. 'Not exactly, but I cannot see any future for a woman in trying to pursue an interest in that sort of thing. It certainly hasn't done the longcase clock in the hall any good, since she dismantled it.'

'At least it goes now, Papa,' Julia said, a disgruntled expression on her face.

'A clock that doesn't keep time is worse than one that doesn't go at all,' he replied shortly. 'But I'll say no more. Just leave your Aunt Rosalie's timepieces alone while you're here, Julia. Now I believe Lord Hargreaves has something he would like to discuss with you, Rosalie.'

Lord Hargreaves placed his cup on the table by his chair but didn't start to speak.

'Please, My Lord, do not hesitate. You are among friends,' urged Rosalie.

'It is this, Lady Benedict. I have realised the stairs in this house could present a great problem to Mr Stuart once he becomes more mobile. And my suggestion is that he should relocate to Staplewood, where I can offer ground floor accommodation.'

Emily Clayborne immediately clapped her hands together in agreement.

Rosalie and Amanda looked at each other and smiled.

'You know, Lord Hargreaves,' said Rosalie, 'I shall be very sorry to lose him, but your offer is just what he will need. Subject to the doctor's approval, of course.'

'Of course, Lady Benedict, that goes without saying.'

'And also, Lady Benedict, you must feel free to visit Mr Stuart any time you like. We will all be pleased to see you and your family at Staplewood. Shall we not, Charles?' Emily addressed her brother.

'It will be our pleasure, Lady Benedict,' said Hargreaves.

'It will make Justin and me happy to know that you have good neighbours again. We used to worry sometimes. Mairsford is a lovely house, but it is somewhat isolated for an all-female residence. Didn't we, my dear?' said Amanda pointedly.

Justin, to whom this idea was a complete surprise but quickly realising his wife had a hidden agenda, replied, 'Indeed it will, Amanda. And I am certainly desirous of making further acquaintance with Lord Hargreaves. We have been talking about this after dinner.'

Hargreaves smiled. 'Lord Coverdale has kindly offered to be one of my sponsors and to find another, when I decide to take my seat in the House of Lords.'

Amanda gave a self-satisfied smile and inwardly thanked God for a husband who was quick on the uptake. 'Perhaps,' she said, 'it is time to ask our hostess if she would play something for us.' She turned to Emily. 'Lady Benedict is very accomplished, you know.'

'That would be delightful. Charles and I are both very fond of music, although neither of us are adept on an instrument. Charles,' she added, 'has a fine baritone voice.'

'Emily!' exclaimed Hargreaves, mortified by her disclosure.

'What would you like me to play?' Rosalie quickly intervened.

But Amanda filed the information away, believing it might do much to forward her plans.

Rosalie rose from her chair. 'Before I play, would you excuse me? I would like to go and see how Matthew is, after his first visit downstairs.'

The company murmured their assent, and she rustled out of the room. Encountering Joseph just as he was quietly closing Matthew's chamber door, she asked. 'How is he?'

'Mr Matthew is comfortable now. He has had a cup of tea, and I hope he will sleep well, My Lady.'

'I understand Lord Coverdale carried him all the way upstairs.'

'Indeed, he did, a noble endeavour, My Lady.' Joseph did not add that, as the Marquis had left, there had hardly been time to grab the washbasin before Matthew lost most of his drink and all of his dinner.

The doctor's approval of Matthew's move to Staplewood was given wholeheartedly, along with the recommendation that exercise and stimulation was now required for his recovery—in moderation, of course.

Rosalie realised Matthew would need more clothes now that he would soon be leading a more active life. She summoned Joseph. 'I believe Mr Stuart and my late husband are of a similar size and build. If you go to the furthest attic, you will find a trunk full of his clothes. Apart from the regimentals you will find there, please take anything that may be of use to Mr Matthew.'

'Yes, My Lady.'

'Oh, and if you can find a suitable piece of luggage to put the clothes in, take that as well.'

'Very good, Your Ladyship. Will there be anything else?'

'No, Joseph, just ... just treat the uniform with respect.'

'Of course I will, My Lady,' he said gently and left the room before the tears he could see forming in Lady Benedict's eyes fell.

Rosalie dashed them away with the back of her hand and, after a few seconds felt, unexpectedly, as though some sort of burden had been lifted from her spirits.

Chapter 16

The move took place three days later, when Justin and Amanda were due to return to Coverdale Hall—the marquis's comfortable travelling coach having been deemed the best way to transport Matthew. Goodbyes had been fondly said, and the equipage was ready to move off when Julia appeared, riding Gladiator and dressed in a dashing royal blue riding habit trimmed with scarlet braid. Her groom was waiting a little further back.

'There is no need for this,' said her father, leaning out of the coach window and speaking sharply.

'But, Papa, it may be some time before I see you and Mama again. I want to spend every last minute with you,' Julia replied plaintively.

Since she was riding and her parents were in the coach, they didn't believe a word of it, but this was no time to argue. She rode up beside the carriage so Matthew could see her and her magnificent horse, before trotting off down the drive.

The sound of a horn had alerted the Staplewood household to the imminent arrival of the Marquis's coach, and Parsons and Royston were already stationed at the portico as the vehicle drew up. The Coverdales were not to disembark, as they had a long drive ahead of them. But Joseph got down immediately, from his outside set, and signalled to Parsons to help him get Matthew out of the coach.

It was a difficult process, as the door was narrow, and care had to be taken to prevent damage to Matthew's foot. As soon as he was on the ground, standing on one leg, with an arm around the shoulders of his supporters, Lord Hargreaves emerged from the portico, bearing a pair of crutches. 'I hope these will make your progress more comfortable. They are adjustable, if the fit is not quite right. And welcome to Staplewood Park.'

Matthew released his hold on the two men and fitted the crutches under each arm. 'My Lord, this is splendid. Thank you so much.'

'I am merely the go-between.' Hargreaves smiled. 'It is Lady Benedict and Joseph you have to thank. But we all hope you will benefit from being able to get about more. Now, if you would like to try, shall we go in?'

'May I have a word with Lady Julia?' Matthew had noticed her groom coming forward, as if to help her dismount.

'If you think you can manage, I will.'

Tentatively, Matthew started to advance on the crutches and take his first one-legged step forward. Joseph hovered, and Mrs Clayborne, who had come out to speak to Amanda, watched with equal concern—but without cause. Although slow, Matthew showed no sign of falling.

Gladiator sidestepped as he saw the unusual sight of a man on crutches approach. But Julia held him steady. 'I was just going to dismount, and—'

'I could see that you were.' Matthew looked up at her as he patted the horse's glossy neck. 'But I am very anxious about Lady Benedict. I am sure I caught a glimpse of tears as she said goodbye. She must be feeling very lonely, bereft of all her relations.'

Julia looked down with narrowed eyes into Matthew's appealing, dark blue ones and then smiled. 'I believe you are right, Matthew. I think I have been selfish. I just wanted to see Staplewood for myself. I will return to Mairsford immediately.'

Mrs Clayborne caught the end of this conversation as she approached Matthew. 'My dear Lady Julia, perhaps you would be so good as to convey an invitation to Lady Benedict. We should be delighted if she would grace us with her presence tonight for dinner—and you too, of course, Lady Julia. Only send a reply if it is inconvenient. We shall look forward to seeing you this evening.'

'Thank you. I am sure my aunt will be delighted. Now I must say farewell to my parents.' She moved off towards the carriage.

Bedford had remained in his new bed by the hall fireplace and was sitting, nose in the air, ears forward, alert for the new arrivals. His saviour and the fount and source of all his comforts was his goddess, Emily Clayborne. And by now, he and Lord Hargreaves had assumed a polite respect for one another. The recent arrival of Nicky from school had given him a playfellow and exerciser. He ignored all the other occupants—except

Mrs Royston, for whom a pleading expression, intended to convey near starvation, inevitably produced a snack or a good-sized bone.

He heard the front door close and smelt the presence of two new males. He got out of his bed to investigate. He moved his head from side to side and saw that one of the men appeared to have three legs and then, from the smell of them, realised that two of them were made of wood.

'This must be Bedford,' said Matthew. 'I've heard a lot about you, old fellow, from Lady B.'

'Don't let him get too close, Emily,' Hargreaves said anxiously. 'You know how boisterous he can be. We don't want him to knock Mr Stuart over when he has just acquired his crutches.'

'He won't do anything of the sort, Charles. He's just trying to sort things out in his head. He can't see you properly, Matthew. He just wants to acquaint himself with your smell.'

But Bedford had already learnt a great deal about Matthew. He knew he was young, he knew he had something wrong with the foot that was being held off the ground, and he knew he needed taking care of. This last discovery filled him with pleasure. At last, there was someone who needed him. He circled Matthew and sat down beside him but not close enough to impede the wooden sticks.

'There now, you see!' said Emily triumphantly. 'That dog understands perfectly. Now I will show Mr Stuart his room.'

Joseph had already gone with Parsons to make final arrangements for Matthew's arrival. The room had been transformed. All evidence of billiards had been removed—except the scoreboard, which remained screwed to the wall. Emily had scoured the house for better—if not new—curtains, a four-poster bed, a washstand, and a side table, which occupied one end of the long room and was screened off. The end with the fireplace, had been furnished as a sitting room, in which a chaise longue was the main feature. Joseph was waiting to receive its new occupant.

Matthew, preceded by Emily and accompanied by Bedford, was amazed at how weak he was. He had only travelled about thirty yards in all on his new crutches, and already his right leg felt like jelly. The daily exercises Joseph had insisted upon, but of necessity confined to a chair, had not prepared him for the effort required to propel himself upright.

'Do you like it, Mr Stuart?' said Emily, a hopeful note in her voice.

Matthew rested on his crutches just inside the doorway and looked round. 'It looks absolutely splendid, Mrs Clayborne. If this was ever a billiard room, no one would know it now. It is a perfect room for me. I am so grateful.'

'I know the floor looks rather bare, but Joseph said there should be no rugs, to avoid the danger of slipping. Still, I thought just a hearthrug would be all right.' She turned to Joseph, who was arranging cushions on the chaise.

'Yes, ma'am. That is not a problem, and I think your dog appreciates it already.' He gave a slight smile.

'I will leave you now to get settled, Mr Stuart. Refreshments will be brought presently. Which would you prefer, coffee or ale?'

'Coffee would be just dandy, Mrs Clayborne, thank you.'

Joseph helped Matthew onto the couch and saw that his foot was fully supported. Matthew didn't admit it, but it was starting to throb painfully. 'Oh, Joseph, I did not realise how damnably weak I had become. Will I ever …?' He left the question hanging in the air.

'I have every reason to believe that you will make a complete recovery, sir. But I cannot emphasise enough that it will take time. Rash actions on your part could put healing in danger. That's why I recommend you remain in this room for the rest of the day. But I am sure you will welcome visitors. I will go and request your coffee, now, sir.'

The moment he had gone, Bedford rose from his place before the fire and cautiously approached the couch. He sat down in front of it and laid his head on Matthew's thigh. 'Well, old fellow,' Matthew said, starting to fondle Bedford's ears. 'We both seem to be people who need a helping hand from time to time, don't we?'

Bedford closed his eyes in utter bliss. He had found his god.

After lunch, various people dropped in to visit Matthew. Lord Hargreaves arrived with a pile of books, a recent copy *of Tatler* magazine, and one *of The Morning Post.* 'I must say you are looking rather better than when I last saw you.' He smiled.

Matthew gave a rueful grin. 'I'm afraid, My Lord, I had quite literally bitten off more than I could chew. I have to thank you for your assistance on that occasion.'

'It was mostly Lord Coverdale. He carried you all the way upstairs. I merely lighted the way. But now you're here, I am sure you will come on by leaps and bounds.'

'Not if Joseph has anything to do with it. He has specifically warned me against any form of leaping and bounding.'

Hargreaves laughed. 'Quite right, too.'

'I was very surprised to be given these crutches; they look new.'

'Yes. They were made by my carpenter. I *say my*, but he lives in the village and works on the estate as required. I think he made a good job.'

'Excellent, but how did you get the right measurements?'

'The whole thing was Lady Benedict's idea, and Joseph sent the measurements over a few days ago.'

'Lady B is the most amazing and generous woman I have ever met. Without her, I should probably be dead. I shall never be able to repay her.'

'She wouldn't want repayment. And I agree with you. She is amazing, and beautiful with it. It is just so sad that she lost the husband she adored, so young.'

Matthew gave his host a shrewd look. 'Yes, that is true, but it was five years ago. I believe she is really beginning to appreciate some male company again. She quite sparkled at the dinner party.'

'Keep your mind on getting better, young man,' said Hargreaves, sternly, but he smiled as he spoke.

Other members of the household dropped in on Matthew throughout the day. Nicky came not only to apologise in person for being the cause of Matthew's condition, which that individual hotly denied; he also expressed the desire to show Matthew round the grounds as soon as he felt able. And finally Emily came to make sure he had everything he required.

'I worry, Mrs Clayborne, that I am causing unnecessary expense and nuisance to this household that I have no means to repay.'

'Now listen to me, young man,' Emily replied sternly, 'you will only delay your recovery if you lie awake worrying. It will be payment enough to see you fit and well again. And besides, I am firmly of the belief that there is a higher purpose in life that we cannot understand. I am sure your chance to repay is waiting, somewhere in the future.' She patted his hand. 'Now, sleep well. I will see you in the morning.'

Chapter 17

'Wozzat?' PC Jones pointed to a triangular lump showing above the water in Bristol's Floating Harbour.

'You'd better find out, lad,' said the sergeant. 'We don't want it clogging up the lock gates, do we, now?'

A bow wave from further up the harbour caused the object to bob up and down, and a leather strap with a buckle briefly showed above the water. 'Go and borrow a boathook from one of the bargees.' The sergeant pointed to the row of narrow boats moored by the quayside.

The day was hot, his uniform thick and scratchy, and PC Jones didn't fancy fishing about in the water with a long pole, but he had no option. When he returned with the pole, the sergeant instructed him to catch the hook onto the leather strap. Jones's first attempt merely served to push the object farther away, and he nearly toppled in after it.

'Here, I'll hold your belt,' the sergeant growled. 'Now, try again.'

A second attempt brought the object closer to the side, and Jones managed to hook it out. It was sodden, and water trickled out of it as he held it clear of the canal. 'Bring it in carefully. It might sink if you drop it in again.' Jones swung the pole, so that what was now clearly a suitcase, was on the towpath, but he had forgotten the other end of the long pole and it fetched his colleague a hefty blow on his side. The sergeant's comment would have shamed even a bargee.

'Sorry, Sarge. What shall I do with it?' He pointed to the bedraggled suitcase.

The sergeant kicked it with his foot, and it tipped over. 'Better throw it on the tip. It's no good to anyone no more.'

Jones examined it more closely. The water had darkened the leather to slimy black. "'Ere, Sarge, look. It's got them initials on it. You know, them ones on the notice board at the station wot we was to look out for.'

The sergeant took a closer look. 'I believe it has. You'd better carry it back then. The super'll want to see it. We can ask if anyone knows anything about it as we go.'

The broken handle meant that the heavy wet luggage bumped against Jones's legs with every step he took.

The barge community treated the police with deep suspicion, and no information was forthcoming from most of the people they asked, until a young lad said, 'Did they mean the dummy? Bloke who was touched in the 'ead, Mister.'

'Who was touched in the head?'

'Bloke they found on the *Jennie Lee*.'

'When?'

'Dunno. Maybe middle o' June.'

'Where is the *Jennie Lee* now?'

'Dunno, Mister.'

The sergeant was exasperated and turned to Jones. 'These people are no use at all. Even if they know something, they're not going to tell.'

'Lock-keepers would be a better bet, Sarge. They know all the comings and goings of the narrow boats.'

'D'you know where the nearest one is, Constable?' The sergeant was not a local man.

"'Bout 'arf a mile from 'ere. Lock-keepers look after several locks, Sarge.'

'I see.' He pulled a large watch from his breast pocket. 'It's too late to do anything more today. Besides, we need to take that back to the station.' He pointed to the sodden leather case.

Jones knew precisely what the sergeant meant by 'we' and hoicked the case, trying unsuccessfully to tuck it under his arm.

Later that evening, the superintendent contemplated the case, sitting on damp newspaper in the corner of the office. 'Is there anything inside it, Sergeant?'

'I don't know, sir. I was waiting for your permission to open it.'

'Well, you'd better do it now.'

The sergeant hefted it onto a table, and the initials 'M.W.S.' were clearly visible, despite the staining of the leather. Two straps and two catches had once secured the case, but now the only thing holding it shut was one of the straps. 'Go on, then, undo it, man,' the superintendent said impatiently. The strap was stiff, and the leather was swollen with the damp. But eventually the sergeant managed to undo it and lifted the lid.

Disappointingly, all that was revealed was one wet sock and a broken ivory comb. 'Well, well, well,' the senior officer exclaimed, 'that's not going to get us very far, but I don't think there's any doubt that the case belonged to the missing man. You'd better visit the lock-keeper first thing tomorrow, Sergeant.'

'May I make a suggestion, sir?'

'Go ahead, man.'

'I believe Constable Jones would be a better man for the job. He is a local man, and people might open up to him more.'

'Very well.' The superintendent looked at the clock. 'Time for my supper. Make any arrangements you like.'

The next day, after a long towpath walk, Constable Jones knocked on the door of the lock-keeper's cottage. A woman, wiping floury hands on her apron, opened it and enquired his business. 'He's gone to the next lock. Dunno when he'll be back. I can give you a cup o' tea, if'n you want to wait.'

Jones was about to say no, very regretfully, when he realised he could mix business with pleasure. 'Very kind, I'm sure, and mebbe you can help me.'

'Not in trouble with the law, is he?' She picked up a teapot from a trivet by the fire and poured a tar-like brew into an earthenware mug. 'Take a seat.'

'Not at all. I am here to enquire after a missing person. Do you remember a tall young gent—a stranger—on any of the boats?'

'There's a mighty lot o' boats, Mister. Have you got a name?'

'*The Jennie Lee* has been mentioned.'

'Ah, that stranger. Proper queer he were. Looked sick as a dog an' thin as a rake, but I seen him work a lock.'

'Do you know what happened to him?'

'Went off on the *Jennie Lee*, I s'pose.'

'Do you know where that boat is now?'

'No, but she were goin' to Reading. Must be on her way back by now.'

At that moment the door opened, and the lock-keeper came in rubbing his hands. 'Me dinner ready, woman?' He stopped abruptly on catching sight of the policeman. 'What's up?'

'Constable's asking about the strange cove on the *Jennie Lee*.'

'Is there any chance I could talk to the bargee soon?' queried Jones.

'You're in luck, Constable. She's just gone through the lock before this'n. Should be here any minute.'

Jones put down his mug. 'I'll just wait outside, then, sir. Thanks for the tea, missus.'

Ten minutes later, a narrowboat drawn by a stout-looking piebald horse came into sight. 'You Mr Lee?' he asked the helmsman.

'What of it, if I am,' was the surly reply.

Mindful of the suspicion that accompanied the presence of all policemen, Jones became conciliatory. 'There's nothing to worry about, Mr Lee, but I understand you had a passenger a little while ago—tall young man.'

'Oh, 'im; strange thing that—'

'How did he come to be on your boat?'

'Don't rightly know. The wife found 'im one morning lying on the deck when we was moored back at the harbour. Best you talk to 'er, Elsie!' he shouted into the cabin.

A youngish woman with a child on her hip emerged. 'What d'you want?'

'Constable wants to know 'bout Bill.'

'He was just lying there.' She pointed to the small area in front of the doorway. 'I thought 'e were asleep or drunk. But then I seen the great big lump 'o the side of is 'ead. 'E were spark out. Came to quite quick like, but we never got 'ardly a word out of 'im—'cept please an' thank you when I give him a bowl of stew. Not even 'is name—we just called 'im Bill. 'E seemed to be livin' in a sort of fog, if you take my meaning.'

'Funny thing, tho',' her husband added. "E knew 'ow to work locks, so we let 'im stay.' He shrugged. 'Then one morning, 'e were gone.'

'Did he say where he was going or wanted to go?'

'No.' Mr Lee paused. 'But 'e had this bit o' paper. I don't know letters, but the wife does. What was on that paper, Else?'

She hitched the child higher up on her hip. 'Nothin' much. Some letters I couldn't make a word of, there was an M an' an S, and then "Kent"; that were quite clear.'

'How long was he on your boat?'

''Bout five or six days. 'Is clothes were terrible. My 'usband tried to fix 'is boots wi' a bit o' leather and some newspaper. 'Is shirt, now that were quality. I washed it for 'im.'

'One last question. Did he have any money or anything of value on him?'

Lee shook his head. 'Nothin' but what he stood up in. I give 'im a few bob for doin' the locks, that's all.'

'Thank you very much. You've both been very 'elpful.' As they'd been speaking, the lock had done its work, and the *Jennie Lee* was ready to proceed.

When he returned to the station, Jones repeated all he had learned to the superintendent, who decided to relay the information to Mr Pettigrew at once.

Mr Pettigrew received the superintendent's note that afternoon and called in his chief clerk. 'I've just got this from the police station.' He held out the paper.

Fitton read it carefully. 'Well, sir, it seems that our Mr Stuart may be alive, although it seems almost certain that he has been robbed.'

'That is the good news, but we still have no idea where he might be. It says in the note that he left the barge just before Reading and had a piece of paper with the word "Kent" on it.'

'That's some distance away, sir.'

'Yes, indeed.' Mr Pettigrew laid one pair of spectacles on the desk, drew the second pair from the top of his head, and placed them on his nose. 'I think it is time, Fitton, that we opened that trunk that is inconveniently blocking up our front passage. Put aside what you were doing and get it open. Call me when you have done so.'

It was quite some time before Pettigrew got the call and found a red-faced chief clerk kneeling in front of the cabin trunk, a heap of strong cord by his side and a screwdriver in his hand. 'You haven't damaged it I hope,' said Pettigrew eyeing the tool.

'No, sir. But not having the key, it was necessary to take the locks off. They can be reaffixed quite easily.'

'Very well, let's see what we have.' Fitton raised the lid to reveal an upper tray containing items for the use of a surveyor, a flat wooden box fitted with drawing instruments, and several cloth-bound notebooks. 'Hand me one of those books, Fitton. They might contain the information we require.' Pettigrew flipped through the first one, but it only contained architectural drawings and various neatly written notes and measurements. The other books were the same. 'It seems as if we will have to delve deeper.'

Fitton, whose knees were killing him, lifted out the tray and handed it to Pettigrew, who was obliged to place it on the floor. Nothing but a quantity of clothing appeared. Fitton removed layer after layer, until, at the bottom, were several pairs of boots and shoes, and beneath them, some books.

'What are they?' Pettigrew enquired.

'I don't think they will advance our search, sir.'

'Well, man, what are they?' asked Pettigrew impatiently.

'A novel by Sir Walter Scott, a Bible, a treatise on mathematics by Isaac Newton, and this.' He handed up a large vellum-covered tome to his employer.

Pettigrew looked at the title—*Castles and Great Houses of England*. He was about to open it.

'Be careful, sir. There's a marker at one of the pages. It might tell us something. If it falls out, we won't know where it came from.'

'I'd better take it upstairs then. You can put all this stuff back, Fitton.' He tucked the volume under his arm and left his disappointed employee to it.

Back in his office Pettigrew exchanged his glasses once again. Opening the book at the front page, he saw it had been published in 1800. Then he turned to the place with the paper bookmark. The volume had engravings on one page and a description of the property, its owners, and its history on the page opposite. The page showed a fine etching of Coverdale Hall in the County of Essex, which the accompanying text described as the country seat of the Fifth Marquis of Coverdale, titular head of the St Maure family.

Chapter 18

August was drawing to a close, and those members of the county set who had not gone North for the shooting were entertaining each other to dinners and carriage drives, frequently including al fresco lunches, plagued by wasps. To accommodate the extra work that entertaining required, changes had taken place at Staplewood Park. It soon became clear to Emily that the house was severely understaffed, and the existing servants were finding it hard to cope. 'We need at least one more manservant and two—if not three—more women, Charles,' Emily announced.

Her brother demurred. 'How can we possibly need so many, Emily? There only us two and Matthew, and he has Joseph.'

Emily heaved a sigh. 'My dear, you simply do not understand. You are not living in a modern house anymore. This place is a barrack. It is so cold we need to keep fires burning on all but the hottest days, and that takes a huge amount of time and effort. And that's just the beginning. I won't trouble you with all the other inconveniences. Just authorise me to hire more staff, or the ones we have will leave—including me. And then where will you be?'

Years of experience had taught Lord Hargreaves the futility of arguing with his sister. 'Oh, very well then. But just remember my pocket—it's not all that deep.'

Emily went off to consult Parsons. In less than a fortnight, a footman, George; another kitchen maid; and two more house parlourmaids arrived. And a more contented household was the result—especially as it turned out that Joseph, many years ago, had served under George in the Duke of Alloa's London mansion, and they had gotten on well.

Nicky, Julia, Matthew, and Bethany—or the young people, as Lord Hargreaves and Rosalie referred to them—often joined forces at Staplewood to enjoy rides and be company for Matthew, who was getting along famously on his crutches. The doctor was pleased with the progress of his foot.

One morning, Emily and Rosalie, who had been invited for luncheon, were in the conservatory, trying to sort out what could and could not be saved from the neglected plants. 'The only thing that has flourished in this place is the vine,' said Emily, looking up at the canopy of green that rambled above her and was already showing numerous bunches of grapes, just tinged with pink. 'I hope they are Black Hamburgs,' she said. 'But they need pruning.'

'Whatever they are, you'll be able to set up a winery.' Rosalie laughed. 'What do you want me to do with this?' She held up a plant apparently welded into its pot.

'I think the poor thing is past praying for, Lady B. See if you can get it out and then put it on that pile of stuff to be thrown away. But the pot looks quite nice.'

'Oh look!' exclaimed Rosalie, momentarily diverted from gardening. She pointed through the newly cleaned conservatory glass. Nicky and Matthew were on the lawn beyond the formal garden, teaching Bedford to fetch. Emily joined her to watch. 'How does a nearly blind dog manage that?'

'That is all due to Nicky. He realised that, if Bedford could hear the stick flying through the air and landing on the ground, he could probably find it.'

'That's a clever idea. What did he do?'

'He fixed some bells to a piece of wood, and they began by just throwing it a few yards, until the dog got the idea. It didn't take him long. He is a very intelligent dog, you know.'

'Does he retrieve it—the stick, I mean?'

'He didn't at first. He just sat beside it until someone else fetched it. Then Matthew had the idea that, if he wrapped one of his unlaundered handkerchiefs round the stick, Bedford might think Matthew had dropped it and bring it back to him.'

Rosalie watched as the big dog set off to find the stick Nicky had just thrown. 'I can see that the scheme has worked, and Bedford looks really pleased with himself. But,' she added, 'this will never get this place tidied up. What are you planning to do with the pond?' She peered into the murky green depths.

Whatever Emily was going to reply was forestalled by Parsons announcing that luncheon was being served in the alcove. This was an area at the far end of the long dining room, where less formal meals were served.

'Thank you, Parsons. Would you mind going out and telling those two out there that it's time for lunch while Lady Benedict and I clean up?'

After luncheon, the two ladies retired to the drawing room. Nicky, determined to find a way for Matthew to ride without damaging his foot, went off to the stables to discuss the possibility with the head groom. Matthew was thankful to retire for a rest. He was very pleased to be more mobile and explore more of Staplewood, but it came at a price. Keeping one foot off the ground at all times made that knee ache abominably, and his good leg still tired quite quickly. Keeping up with the others was sometimes a real effort, and only Bedford seemed to be aware of his god's distress and would simply sit down and refuse to move when he considered it was time to go home.

Seated comfortably in the drawing room, Rosalie asked. 'Are you enjoying life here, Mrs Clayborne? This place has none of the diversions present in Bath.'

'I've hardly had time to miss Bath at all. I've had such a lot to do here, and there still is. But I am used to being busy, as, indeed, I know you are Lady B.'

Rosalie said: 'You know, Mrs Clayborne, I am very glad you asked me over today.' She paused.

Emily noticed her guest's clenched fingers. 'There is something special about today, my dear? Can you tell me?'

'It is the fifth anniversary of the day my husband died. And I ...'

'Oh, Lady B. I am so sorry. If I had known, I would never have intruded on your grief.'

'Please, Mrs Clayborne, do not apologise. I have found lately that my feelings are changing—oh, not towards my beloved Benedict, but to the world I live in now. I wouldn't describe myself as a recluse, but I have tended to eschew occasions devoted entirely to enjoyment. But now, and I don't really understand it, but I am finding much more pleasure in being with people than being alone, or only with Beth, as I have been in the past.'

'I do understand, Lady B. I have been a widow for many years, and the memories become more bearable—good, rather than grief-stricken. Are you able to tell me what happened to your husband?'

'He ... he,' Rosalie began. 'He came in from riding, and just as Soames was opening the door, Benedict collapsed. Soames and Darrow—no, no, it wasn't Darrow, then ...I can't remember—'

'Don't distress yourself, Lady B. I'm sorry. I should never have asked.'

Rosalie heaved a long sigh. 'No, I must go on. It is time. They got him upstairs, and the doctor was sent for. Benedict became very restless and shouted out about the time he was in the army. He had been in the Royal Artillery and had fought in the American War of 1812, and at Waterloo. I held him in my arms, and he suddenly went quiet, and then opened his eyes and looked into mine. "Play your harp for me, my darling," he said. And then he was gone ... I have never been able to play it since.' Rosalie gave a sad little smile. There was a silence between the two ladies, before Rosalie said: 'May I ask how long you have been a widow, Mrs Clayborne?'

Emily stared into the empty fireplace for a moment before replying. 'Forty-one years, Lady B.'

'Good gracious!' The exclamation escaped Rosalie's lips before she could stop it. 'Now it's my turn to apologise. Could you tell me about it? Or is it still too painful?'

'Do you know, Lady B, I really think I would like to. There has never been anyone in the family I could confide in. My parents disapproved of the marriage, and Charles was too young—'

'Please, take your time,' Rosalie said sympathetically.

'Daniel Clayborne was a first lieutenant in the Royal Navy. He was visiting Bath, waiting for a new commission. I've always lived in Bath, you know, and we met in the Pump Room. He was rather shy but nice-looking, with a lovely smile.'

'So it was love at first sight, a whirlwind romance—how exciting!' exclaimed Rosalie.

'Yes, I suppose you could say that. Anyway, we were both of age, so no one could legally object to an engagement. But my parents wouldn't let him visit the house.'

'That must have been very upsetting for you.'

'Well, it certainly made things difficult. But then he got orders to join a ship—a frigate that was due to leave in four weeks—so we got married and had our honeymoon in a boarding house in Plymouth. I saw him off on the quayside.' Emily paused. 'I never saw him again.'

Rosalie threw down her embroidery and rushed over to sit beside Emily on the sofa. 'Oh, my dear, how dreadful for you,' she cried, putting her arms round the older woman's shoulder. 'How could you bear it? Do you have something to remember him by, a miniature, perhaps?'

Emily put her hand to her neck and drew out a small gold locket attached to a fine chain. She unclipped it and passed it to Rosalie. 'I have always been so grateful I was persuaded to have this done while we were in Bath. It was executed by a pupil of the well-known miniaturist, Mrs Kendal. It is a very good likeness.'

Rosalie examined the tiny portrait of a young man in naval uniform. He was not stunningly good-looking but had the blue eyes often associated with seafaring men and a firm chin. She handed it back. 'He looks very nice, and it is interesting because Mrs Kendal was Amanda's, that is Lady Coverdale's, paternal grandmother.'

Emily placed the locket round her neck again. 'It was a long time before I was notified that he had been killed at the Battle of the Nile. And by then I was four months—' Tears appeared in the older woman's eyes.

'Oh, no!' exclaimed Rosalie, 'You didn't lose his child?'

Emily nodded dumbly. 'The only part of Daniel that was left in this world, and I failed him. But you wouldn't understand—"

'Oh, but I do, Mrs Clayborne. I really do. We lost our first child. He only lived for two hours. And I was told I'd never have another, but then we were blessed with Bethany.'

'I'm sorry. I can see that you really do understand.' Emily wiped her eyes and patted Rosalie's hand. 'You and I, and Charles, have all lost loved ones before their time. Life is very cruel sometimes. I think it was especially so with Charles.'

'I believe his wife died three years ago.'

'Yes, that is true. But he began to lose her many years before that. She had a derangement of the brain, which meant she gradually lost her memory, until she could no longer recognise him—or Nicky, which was particularly hard on so young a boy. My brother had to look after him, as well as seeing that Frances was well cared for, and running his legal practice. I just hope this big change in his life will be a happier one for him—a new beginning.'

'I'm sure it will be, Mrs Clayborne. It is such a pleasure having you and your brother as near neighbours. When does Lord Hargreaves return from London?'

'The day after tomorrow,' Emily replied.

'Then you must both come to dinner the next day. That is a firm invitation, Mrs Clayborne. It's just a pity Matthew cannot join us at present.'

'We shall be delighted. I'm sure Matthew will understand, Lady B. But Lady Julia will be disappointed. Was there a reason she did not accompany you today?'

'Yes, indeed. After we visited my husband's grave earlier this morning to lay flowers, she and Bethany went with the rector's wife to visit the hop pickers' huts' to collect hop bines, to decorate the church for Harvest Festival. She gives sweets and cakes to the hop pickers and their children, who come down from the poorer parts of London each year.'

Emily smiled. There was a lot she was going to enjoy in learning the ways of her new home.

That evening after dinner, Rosalie took the cover off her harp and began to tune it.

Chapter 19

Some days later, Matthew was crossing the hall from his room to the library, and passing the stairs, he thought to try a few steps on his crutches. Leaving one crutch at the bottom—and Bedford, for whom stairs were an anathema—he grasped the wide brass rail and, with the remaining crutch under his right arm, hopped onto the first step. The steps were broad and shallow, and he soon found himself about eight steps higher up. Looking down, he could see Bedford getting increasingly anxious and decided he had proved a point, and would come down. It didn't take long to discover that descent was quite a different matter. His bad foot, which had previously been clear of the steps, would be, when he turned round, perilously close to the wood; and, furthermore, the crutch was now on the wrong side. An attempt to change the crutch to the other side had a disastrous result. Somehow the end of it went through the ironwork of the banister, and pulling it back caused one of the gilded grapes that adorned the balustrade to fall off and bounce down the stairs. The sound immediately alerted Bedford, who, following the noise of the grape's progress across the marble floor, set off in pursuit.

Matthew sat down on a step to reconsider his strategy, just as Joseph was crossing the hall. Taking in the situation, he said suavely, 'Perhaps you would care for some assistance, sir?'

'That would seem to be the case, Joseph. I think this has been a step too far, and I fear I have done some damage. I must find Lord Hargreaves at once and confess.' Together they managed to reach the foot of the stairs without further mishap, and Matthew continued his progress towards the library, where he hoped to find his host.

His search was successful, and he began at once. 'My Lord, I fear I have been very foolish, and my stupidity has resulted in some damage to your property.' Matthew hitched himself uncomfortably on his crutches.

Hargreaves looked at the embarrassed young man. 'The building is still standing, so I do not suppose the damage is terminal. What precisely has occurred?'

'Well, sir, I was attempting a few steps of the staircase—'

'That accounts for the stupidity. Would you care to sit down?'

'Thank you, sir, but I need to show you what happened. I was trying to come down, and in doing so I managed to dislodge one of the gilded grapes on the balustrade. If you follow me I will point out the damage.'

The pair stood beside the staircase, and Matthew was able to reach up and show Hargreaves where the gilded grape had broken off. 'I am afraid I do not know where it went exactly. I was having a bit of trouble balancing at the time, but I heard it bounce across the floor.'

'My dear Matthew, please do not refine upon it. I am sure it will turn up and can be reaffixed.' He laughed and looked around. 'There are, after all, plenty more where that came from. Now let us repair to the library and have a drink. I will remind Parsons to keep an eye out for the errant grape, but I suggest you abandon mountaineering until you are in a better condition to do so.'

Meanwhile, Bedford put his recent training to good use. Having heard something bounce down the stairs and rumble across the floor, he had followed his ears until he came up against the hall curtains. He snuffled under them, and his nose bumped against a small round object, which he picked up in his mouth. It was heavy and he didn't care much for the taste. But it had been thrown by god, and, therefore, had to be returned to him—but Matthew was no longer there. Bedford took the object back to Matthew's room and buried it under the blanket in his own bed, where it joined the rest of his precious belongings—a large marrow bone, which was maturing nicely; a fir cone, bearing the scent of an animal he had never seen; and half a slipper, which he had won in a tug-of-war with Nicky. With these treasures comfortably disposed, Bedford curled up and went to sleep, happy in the knowledge of a job well done.

Mr Pettigrew sat at his desk, *Castles and Great Houses of England* open at the page displaying Coverdale Hall. In his hand, he held the gold watch the police superintendent had returned to him. But there had been no further information regarding its sojourn in the pawnbroker's shop. No one had come to claim it.

He flipped open the outer case of the gold Hunter pocket watch and examined the inscription again, but it afforded no new information, only Matthew, and the date. Pettigrew collated in his mind every item of information he had so far gleaned. He knew when Matthew Stuart had arrived in England and that he was not in good health, having been ill during most of the voyage. He was the holder of some, if not all of his possessions. If he was the man who had travelled on the narrow boat, then he was also headed towards Kent. He turned the pages of the book to examine the contents. The buildings were arranged in counties, so he found the pages related to Kent. There were not many entries. Dover Castle, Knole House, Hever Castle, and Staplewood Park, seat of the second Lord Hargreaves. It could be any or none of these, probably the latter. He turned back to Coverdale Hall. It would be a long, not to say impertinent, shot, to write to the marquis, in case there was a connection. After several minutes thought, he took out a sheet of headed writing paper, and began:

> *To the Most Noble, the Marquis of Coverdale*
>
> *My Lord, I beg your indulgence in a matter in which you may be able, with your greatest condescension, to be of help to me concerning a young American gentleman, about whom I am greatly troubled.*

Having outlined the case, and the tenuous reason for involving the Marquis, he signed the letter:

> *Your most humble and obedient servant,*
> *Stephen Pettigrew,*
> *Attorney at Law.*

And after some thought, he addressed it to "Coverdale House, Berkeley Square, London."

Ten days later, the office boy brought the day's post to the lawyer's office. A letter sealed with a crest and franked, so Pettigrew did not have to pay for it, stood out among the other more mundane correspondences, but the content was disappointing.

Dear Mr Pettigrew,

I am instructed by My Lord Coverdale to thank you for your letter. His Lordship is currently not in residence at Coverdale House. Your correspondence will receive his Lordship's attention on his return.

The letter was signed:

Your obedient servant,
Jeremy Stinton,
Secretary to the Marquis of Coverdale.

Pettigrew smoothed out the expensive writing paper while he contemplated his next move. His almanac showed that Parliament would sit again on 3 October. Coverdale would surely be back in London by then. He decided to wait before pursuing the tenuous Kent connection.

Chapter 20

Rosalie's dinner party, in contrast to the one she'd held when the Coverdales were staying, was a much more informal affair. All the extension leaves had been removed, and a single four-branched silver candelabrum illuminated the table. Hargreaves sat with Julia on his right, and opposite, Rosalie had Mrs Clayborne on her right. With servants in the room, the conversation was general.

'I hope your recent sojourn in London was not too fatiguing, My Lord,' said Rosalie.

Emily laughed. 'Lady B, I can assure you my brother is quite recovered from the ordeal—especially as I finally persuaded him to take advantage of Lord Coverdale's kind offer to put his Mount Street house at Charles's disposal.'

'Yes, indeed, Lady B. My every comfort was catered for.'

Soames, who was at the sideboard carving the goose, which was the central course of the meal, silently took note of this piece of information. Servants rated their masters in a similar way to that which their masters rated each other. Heredity and hierarchy were as important to a servant as to a master. Soames had been in service with Lord and Lady Benedict since they first came to Mairsford. He had been recommended by Clarkson, the marquis's own butler. Consequently he was very protective of the family, especially since Lord Benedict's death. It was reassuring to hear that Lord Hargreaves was approved of by the marquis.

Further talk during dinner concerned the forthcoming Harvest Festival celebrations. 'I don't understand why the Upper Mairsford church should be the centre of activities. Staplewood church is the larger,' said Hargreaves.

'Yes,' replied Rosalie. 'I can see why you are surprised. It is all to do with tradition. At one time, Upper Mairsford was the more important village. Staplewood didn't even have a church. And although it has one now—two if you count the Methodist chapel—and has many more shops and businesses, Upper Mairsford still keeps its local prominence. And of course, it still has the mill.'

'Yes, I can see that now. What form do the celebrations take?'

'There is a procession from the mill, which is surrounded by corn sheaves, to the church. It always looks lovely.'

'Bethany and I have been to collect the hop bines, and local farmers will bring apples, pears, and all manner of vegetables.'

'We are going to help the vicar's wife to decorate the church,' interjected Julia.

'Can we come too?' inquired Mrs Clayborne.

'Of course you can. You will be expected to—although Lord Hargreaves's predecessor never did. It will be a good opportunity for the local populace to have a good look at you.' Rosalie smiled.

'What can we contribute? I'm afraid the gardens at the Park have been sadly neglected for years; the yield is very poor.'

Rosalie thought for a minute and then exclaimed. 'I know! Remember, Mrs Clayborne, you said the vine in your conservatory needed pruning. Some vines, especially those with grapes, would look wonderful.' She turned to Hargreaves. 'You would have no objection, My Lord?'

'Of course not. I should be delighted. Emily, take as much as you want. When is the event?'

'The Sunday after next,' Julia and Rosalie chorused together.

'What happens to the produce after the ceremony?' asked Emily.

'It is distributed to the poor and pensioners of the two parishes. But the wheat from the sheaves round the mill is milled, and the baker in Staplewood makes bread from it. On the following Sunday, the congregation from each parish is given some as they leave the church...' she hesitated, 'traditionally by the owner of Staplewood Park – that's you, Lord Hargreaves.'

'What a lovely tradition. Where did it originate?'

Rosalie smiled. 'Ah, I fear the origin is lost in the mists of time.' She rose from the table. 'Now, ladies, I think we should leave Lord Hargreaves to his port and walnuts.' She turned to him. 'We shall look forward to you joining us in due course, My Lord.'

In a very short space of time, the drawing room door opened, and Soames ushered in Lord Hargreaves, who gave a deprecating smile. 'I got lonely,' he said.

Rosalie, who was still at the tea tray, smiled back. 'We missed your company, too. Tea or coffee? Mrs Clayborne and I are still old-fashioned enough to prefer tea, but modern girls like Julia now choose to drink coffee after dinner.'

'I am old-fashioned, too, Lady B. Tea will suit me admirably. Let me carry it.'

'If you haven't had a cigar, I hope Soames showed you where they were.'

'Yes, indeed he did. But I have never acquired a taste for them, Lady B.'

Rosalie resumed her seat on the sofa, and Lord Hargreaves took the armchair next to it. 'Perhaps you prefer snuff, although I know some people think any form of tobacco is bad for the health.'

'No, it was because of my late wife, Lady B. She became addicted to striking matches—not that she was an arsonist. But like a child, she thought the flames were pretty, and she would just strike a match and throw it away. It was so dangerous that we only kept one box locked away in the kitchen, so I gave up smoking my pipe.'

'Oh, Lord Hargreaves, I am so sorry!' Rosalie was near enough to put her hand out and touch his sleeve and nearly did so. But just at that moment, Emily gave a little cry, and they all looked towards her.

She was dabbing at her lace fichu. 'Oh dear!' she exclaimed. 'I've been so stupid. I've spilt some tea on my lace. Lady Julia, would you be so kind as to show me where I can rinse it off before it stains.'

Julia was about to say she would call a maid, when she caught the expression on Emily Clayborne's face and was quick enough to realise it was a ploy to leave Hargreaves and Rosalie together. 'Of course, Mrs Clayborne. We will go to my room, where we can soon remedy the matter.' Her words sounded a little stilted, but they left the room together.

'You must have had a very difficult time, Lord Hargreaves,' said Rosalie sympathetically. 'Mrs Clayborne told me a little about your wife the other day. I would very much like to hear more about your life today, and how you and Nicky are settling in. But there is another matter I wish to discuss with you. And now that Lady Julia is out of the room, it is a good opportunity.'

'I think I know what you're going to say. You're concerned about her friendship with Matthew Stuart.'

'That is very clever of you, Lord Hargreaves. Are you a mind reader?'

He laughed. 'No, Lady B, but I am aware that your niece is in your care, and her moral and physical welfare is of concern to you. Firstly, I can assure you that Lady Julia is in no moral danger from Matthew. He is a very nice, respectful young man, who has been well brought up. I know he would consider it not only a breach of good manners to compromise any lady but also utterly dishonourable to abuse my hospitality. Besides,' he added, 'there is very little opportunity for him to do so.'

Rosalie gave him a shrewd look. 'I feel sure you are right. But my niece is a very headstrong young woman, with unorthodox ideas. She is also the daughter of a marquis, and we know nothing of Matthew's background and antecedents.'

'I hope you do not wish to deny them each other's company. Lady Julia is doing Matthew a great deal of good. He is very frustrated by his lack of mobility, and he is still recovering from his head injuries. The innocent pleasures Lady Julia and Nicky can provide are both a stimulation and a distraction from the very real problems he is facing.'

'No. I see that would be unkind. but I felt I had to voice my concerns. I am sure you and Mrs Clayborne will monitor the situation carefully.'

'Please rest assured that no harm will come to Lady Julia when she visits Staplewood.'

'I knew I could rely on you. Now, I want to know about the things that interest you, Lord Hargreaves.'

'I am very interested in the past—especially the people who have lived in this country long ago. I am a member of the Antiquarian Society.'

'Digging up bones and things?'

'That is only part of it. We are all heirs of the past, Lady B. Every man, woman, and child alive today is only here because their ancestors all lived long enough to procreate. Your chain of inheritance and mine is unbroken since man first walked the earth.'

'My goodness! That is a thought indeed!' interposed Rosalie.

'So everything, however small—a bone hair-comb or a flint axe-head—can give us insight into who we were. I find it a very fascinating subject, but I expect you might find it dull.'

'No,' Rosalie replied thoughtfully. 'I don't think I would. It's just that it's never occurred to me. Nor have I ever before met anyone who is interested. Is there any particular period that appeals to you?'

'There is a growing interest in Roman Britain. But there were people living here before that—and after. They all have contributed to the country we live in today. My interest is very general and, I have to say, in no way expert. Unlike your talent for music. I hope you will honour us with something later. I see your harp is no longer covered—'

'Yes, I have tuned it. But my fingers are not ready yet. It is a very unforgiving instrument. I seem to remember Emily saying that you sing.' Rosalie got up and carried a branch of candles over to the piano and pointed to a pile of music nearby. 'Is there anything there that you would like?'

Hargreaves smiled. 'Am I being coerced?'

'Not really, but why don't we try. Nobody's listening.'

But they were. Julia and Emily had just come downstairs and heard the piano and a rich baritone joined in song. Emily put her finger to her lips. They retreated partway up the stairs till the music stopped and then made a noisy entrance.

Rosalie turned on the stool. 'I hope the stain came out, Mrs Clayborn. Lord Hargreaves and are just deciding what to play. He has kindly offered to turn the pages for me.'

Julia and Emily exchanged speaking glances.

Four people went to their respective beds that night, each content with an evening well spent. Julia was surprised that two people as old as her Aunt Rosalie and Lord Hargreaves seemed to be making sheep's eyes at each other. Emily was pleased her beloved brother's loneliness could be coming to an end. Charles lay thinking about the way the candlelight glinted on Lady B's still-blonde hair and the way her eyes sparkled, as well as the delightful curves of her more intimate charms. Rosalie was amazed at how much she had enjoyed the company of a nice-looking man. The warm feeling she had, had nothing to do with the bedclothes.

Chapter 21

September was proving to be a glorious month. The sun shone from a sapphire sky, day after day, and the temperature soared into the seventies. The only hints of autumn were the shorter evenings and heavy morning dew, which sparkled on the grass, decorated with a myriad of tiny cobwebs. With his summer holidays drawing to a close, Nicky was determined to spend his last few days exploring as much as possible of the woods and countryside that surrounded Staplewood Park. And an exciting discovery saw him rushing headlong into his father's study. 'Papa, I've found something really interesting. It's down in the woods—' His speech stuttered to a halt when he saw Lord Hargreaves expression.

'You seem to have brought a considerable amount of them back with you, son.'

Nicky looked down at his boots and the mud and leaves adhering to them. 'I'm sorry, I didn't think—'

'I suppose the evidence of your expedition is all across the hall too.'

'I'll call George or one of the maids to clear it up—'

'You will do no such thing, Nicholas. The staff are not employed to run after you with a dustpan and brush. You will go out again, clean your boots, and then ask Mrs Royston for the necessary utensils and clean the mess up yourself. Then'—Hargreaves smiled—'you can come back and tell me all about your momentous discovery.'

Nicky never remained chastened for long, and soon he was recounting his adventure. 'Down the sloping lawn on the right of the house, there's a large area of woodland. It's got a good path through it, but I found another path—or rather what had once been one, but it's now all overgrown. So I thought I'd see where it went. Perhaps there might be an old building or a ruined chapel, or something. You know, Papa, something that would interest you.'

'It is certainly comforting to know my concerns are at forefront of your mind at all times, son,' Hargreaves interjected.

Nicky looked at his father and realised he was being teased. 'Yes, well, I did find something. It's really strange. I know you'll think so when you see it. You can't imagine what it is—'

I certainly can't, until you tell me. Perhaps now would be a good time to do so.'

'It's a chimney!' announced Nicky triumphantly.

'Is it attached to anything, this chimney?'

'No, that's the funny thing. It just seems to be growing out of the ground, but it's a real chimney with a pot, although that looks badly damaged.'

'It certainly seems unusual. How tall is it?'

'I dunno, taller than me—about seven or eight feet, I suppose.'

'Perhaps the building it belonged to has fallen down—or rotted away. Chimneys always had to be built of brick or stone, so the fires didn't set the house ablaze. The estate was here long before this house was built, so it would not be a surprise to find the remains of buildings scattered about the place.' Lord Hargreaves was being pragmatic, and Nicky's face fell with disappointment.

'I still think it's a strange place to find a chimney, right in the middle of a wood.'

One of the joys of Hargreaves's life was watching his son grow into manhood, but he realised that boyish enthusiasm should not be curbed. 'All right, son. There's an old map of the estate hanging in Matthew's room. If he's there, why don't you and he have a look and see if you can identify any kind of building in the wood? I shall be keen to see if you find anything.'

Spirits restored, Nicky flung out of the room, banging the door behind him. Lord Hargreaves winced.

The next day, Nicky rode over to Mairsford. He was excited on two counts. He wanted to tell Lady Julia about his discovery, certain she would show more enthusiasm than had his fathe,r and, he hoped, a desire to see his mysterious chimney. Secondly, she had promised to let him ride

Gladiator. This was to be a special treat before he went back to school. He was delighted to know Julia considered him a good enough rider.

'Only in the home paddock,' Julia explained when he arrived. 'But I have got them to set up a jump—not a "facer".' She laughed. 'But it will give you an idea of his ability.'

Nicky was a sensible boy and well aware that Gladiator was a blood horse, who usually carried his rider side-saddle. So he took his time accommodating his seat to the horse's action and, when he was satisfied, turned to the jump. The horse cleared the obstacle, but Nicky knew he had given the wrong signal for take-off. The second time, they sailed over the jump with feet to spare, and he was amazed by the sheer power generated by Gladiator's quarters. Reluctantly, he dismounted and handed the horse over to the groom to change the saddle so he and Julia could go for a hack.

'He really is a splendid horse, Lady Julia. Surely he would have made a wonderful stud?' Nicky queried.

'That,' replied Julia, 'is a very sad tale. My uncle, Piers, owns and runs the Abbots Court stud farm in Somerset, and the horse doctor was supposed to geld a different black horse. Piers was devastated. Gladiator is the same get as Dominator, Colonel Fortescue's famous grey that carried him all day at Waterloo. He is, by descent from the Godolphin Arabian.'

'Good God!' exclaimed Nicky. 'What a terrible tragedy. I can understand why your nncle was devastated; a terrible loss.'

'He was—so much so he never wanted to see the horse again, so he gave him to me.' Julia let the groom catch up and open the gate to a stubble field. 'Come on, race you to the other side.'

It wasn't really much of a contest. Julia arrived a good ten seconds before Nicky, despite giving him a head start.

Over luncheon, Nicky explained to Rosalie and Julia his exciting, in his opinion, discovery of the chimney. Lady B wasn't really interested and said, 'It's probably just the remains of a woodcutter's hut or something.' But Lady Julia was much keener.

'I'd really like to see it. We could poke about a bit and see if there's anything more to find.'

'I knew you'd be the one to take an interest. When can you come over?'

'Not tomorrow, Julia dear. Remember we're going to help decorate the church for Harvest Festival,' said Lady B.

'Yes, of course, Aunt Rosalie. I wouldn't want to miss that. Would the next day suit you, Nicky?'

'Yes, that would be great. But make it the afternoon. I have to go to the village to collect something from the saddler. I've had a saddle altered so Matthew can ride without having to put his foot in a stirrup. And he said it would be ready then. Then you'll be able to see it too.'

'Is he going to be allowed to ride?' asked Rosalie. 'That certainly shows he's improved, doesn't it?'

Nicky looked abashed. 'Well, I haven't actually asked anyone. I just thought, if I could show how my invention worked, he might be allowed to.'

'I see. I'm sure it's very thoughtful of you, Nicky. But you mustn't be too disappointed if the doctor or Joseph say no,' said Rosalie gently.

Two days later, Julia and Matthew were standing outside the portico of Staplewood Park awaiting the arrival of Nicky. Bedford's tongue was hanging out in eager anticipation of a walk. 'You know, Matthew—I'm going to call you that, at least in private. And please will you drop the "Lady". When we're together, I'd much prefer Julia. But that wasn't what I was going to say. I think it would be a good idea to start towards the wood. I'll just leave a message with George to tell Nicky we've gone on ahead.'

He was a little stunned by what Julia had just said, but Matthew replied. 'Do you not think it might spoil Nicky's surprise if we went before he got here, Lady ... er ... Julia?'

'Oh, I don't mean all the way—just a little way along the path. After all, you will have to take it slowly. Joseph would hang me out to dry if anything happened to you.'

Matthew laughed. 'I'm sure he wouldn't, but I promise to take care.'

'So we'll start off then?'

Julia was right. Their progress was slow, and they took the long way round to the edge of the wood, where the lawn sloped less steeply. The path through the copse was firm but rough. They had travelled about thirty yards when Julia exclaimed, 'Oh. Look! That must be the way to the mysterious chimney.' She pointed to a much narrower entrance that could barely be described as a path, so overgrown with briars it was. You can't possibly go down there, Matthew.'

'We'll just wait here until Nicky turns up. I'm sure he won't be long now.'

But Julia was impatient. 'I'll just go a little way along it and see if I can see the chimney. I won't go near it. This may be the wrong path anyway, and then I'll come back.'

Matthew sighed. He knew it was no good arguing with Julia, and even if he tried, the outcome would be the same. 'All right, but don't go too far,' he warned.

Picking up her skirts and holding them close, Julia set off along the narrow path. Matthew watched anxiously as she turned at right angles. She waved, pointing forward. 'I can see the chimney,' she called.

'Then you'd better come back, now you know it's there,' Matthew called back.

But Julia disappeared from view. He leaned on his crutches, resting his bad leg on the other foot, and rather wished there was somewhere he could sit down. His thoughts wandered, as they so often did, to his situation. What was he going to do? What exactly had happened to him? And what had brought him here in the first place? He still had no memory at all, of recent events. And although a lot of his earlier life had come back, the closer to the present, the hazier it became, until it disappeared altogether.

These thoughts were violently interrupted by an ear-piercing scream, followed a few seconds later by a fainter shout. 'Matthew! Help!'

Chapter 22

The Marquis of Coverdale descended from the hackney carriage and rang the front doorbell of his Berkeley Square house. The Hackney driver deposited the small amount of luggage on the step, receiving a gold sovereign, which was as much of a surprise to the driver as his lordship's arrival was to the hall porter.

'My Lord, we were not expecting—'

'I know, Baxter. But I was just in time to catch the Night Mail from Dover, and the lure of my own bed was too tempting. 'Don't rouse all the staff. If you can just rustle up a sandwich, I'll have a brandy in the library while my room is got ready.'

As he was speaking, a footman, hastily shrugging himself into his coat, came forwards to collect the luggage, and another started to light the gas lamps.

'I'm sorry to put you to so much trouble at this late hour.' he he apologised to his staff, divesting himself of his travelling cape.

'My Lord, it shall be as you wish. Do you desire a fire to be lit in the library?'

'No, Baxter, just the sandwich. I'm for my bed as soon as possible. I have been travelling for nearly two days non-stop.'

'Is there anyone else you wish me to inform of your arrival, My Lord?'

'No … yes, send round to Mr Stinton—but not until the morning—that I wish to see him at nine o' clock.'

In the morning, still tired after only a few hours' sleep, the marquis, having breakfasted, was scanning the *Morning Post*, when his secretary arrived.

'Good morning, My Lord. I trust the results of your visit to France were satisfactory.'

'Yes, Stinton. And I shall shortly be reporting my findings to the Foreign Office, which is why I wish to deal with any correspondence you have received in my absence. I have every intention of travelling to Coverdale Hall today, if that is at all possible.'

'Indeed, My Lord. I have everything here.' He placed a document case on the desk and began to extract several sheaves of paper.

The Marquis groaned. 'That looks like the devil of amount of work, Stinton.'

''No, My Lord. I have appended a copy of all my replies to each item of correspondence, so it may look more than it is.'

'That's a relief. Let me see the worst.'

They spent the next hour going over the official and business documents. And apart from one or two minor alterations, the marquis was satisfied with his secretary's work. But there was no time to consider the private correspondence. 'Put it all together, Stinton. I will take it down with me to the hall. Lady Coverdale may have an interest if there are invitations. I have an appointment with the foreign Secretary in half an hour. Send my carriage to wait for me there. I will leave for Essex directly from Horse Guards.'

'Very well, My Lord. Shall I put the private correspondence file in the coach? Or do you wish to take it with you now, sir?'

'Put it in the coach, Stinton. I'll read it on the way down.'

But the marquis didn't. He fell asleep almost immediately and only woke up when the lodge keeper opened the gates to Coverdale Hall. He was just in time to hug his younger children before they went to bed. Jamie had gone to stay with a friend, so he and Amanda had an informal dinner in the small dining room.

He covered Amanda's hand with his. 'It's so nice to be home, my darling. I miss you all so much when I'm away. What has been happening here in my absence?'

'Not a lot,' his wife replied. 'Mainly the preparations for the Harvest Feast. Remember it's the day after tomorrow.'

'I could hardly forget. You've told me often enough—including dire threats of unmentionably appalling torture, if I didn't get back in time! But as you see, I have saved my skin.'

Amanda's warm brown eyes smiled into her husband's unusual golden ones. He was just as handsome as he'd been when they married twenty years ago—if a bit greyer and, perhaps, a little thicker round the waistline. 'I've been thinking about the robes, Justin.'

'You've given up the idea.' There was a note of relief in his voice.

'Certainly not. The guests will love it.'

'I suppose so.' He sighed.

'After all, our young queen could reign for sixty years; her great-uncle George did. Even Jamie might not ever get a chance to wear them.'

'Probably not. They'd all be too moth-eaten to wear by then.'

Amanda frowned at him. 'No, Justin. I was thinking it would not be a good idea for you to do the carving wearing them. So, I've told Larkin you will carve the barons of beef first, and then we will both make an entrance in our full coronation regalia.'

'As usual, my dear, you have a practical solution to everything, and you are quite right. Ermine and gravy don't mix well. Now, I shall forego a lonely glass of port and join you in the drawing room. Stinton has given me some correspondence that might involve us both. I shall fetch it from the library.'

Seated together on the sofa, Justin opened the file and removed a sheaf of papers. The first two letters he discarded as being correctly replied to by Stinton. The third he passed over to Amanda. 'It's from Sir James Appleby, inviting me to a shooting party in November. Lady Appleby will be writing shortly to you.' He passed the letter to his wife. 'Your department, darling.'

'What do you want me to say when she writes?'

Justin didn't reply. He was deeply engrossed in the next letter. 'Listen to this, Amanda. This is extraordinary.'

'What is?'

'This letter. It's from a solicitor in Bristol—a Mr Pettigrew. He starts by apologising for the intrusion and then goes on to say he is very concerned about the welfare and whereabouts of a young American man called Matthew Stuart.'

'That *is* amazing. Read on.'

Justin rapidly scanned the small but very legible writing, giving Amanda the gist of the letter. 'He says that Mr Stuart arranged to come to England, Bristol in particular, on the SS *Marianna* but never arrived, although his cabin trunk apparently did. Pettigrew put a notice in the local paper asking if anyone knew of Mr Stuart's whereabouts.'

'And did they?' interjected Amanda.

'No, but he was eventually able to retrieve what he believed to be Mr Stuart's gold watch from a pawnbroker!' Justin exclaimed. 'When the *Marianna* returned to Bristol, he was able to question the steward, who had looked after Mr Stuart on the voyage. And he said Mr Stuart had been very ill with seasickness. He had last seen him on the quayside, with his trunk and personal luggage.'

'This is indeed an extraordinary tale,' remarked Amanda. 'He must surely be referring to Rosalie's accidental guest. Does this Mr Pettigrew say when all this occurred?'

Justin looked back at the first sheet. 'Yes, sometime between the fifteenth of June—when the ship docked—and more or less now.' He read on. 'It seems the police got involved because of the watch, and a man they think was Matthew, was traced nearly to Reading. He had been on a narrowboat on the Kennet and Avon canal. But after that, nothing.' Justin read on. 'According to the bargee, this man just turned up on the boat overnight, apparently penniless and in a very confused state of mind. The police superintendent seems fairly certain this man had been the victim of a violent robbery.'

'Why has Mr Pettigrew written to you? What can possibly be the connection?'

'There isn't one—not really. He says that, with some reluctance, he opened the missing man's trunk, in the hope of finding a clue as to Mr Stuart's destination. But there was only a book called *Castles and Great Houses of England*. Apparently, there was a marker at the page on which Coverdale Hall was illustrated. His only other clue was a piece of paper that Matthew showed to the bargee's wife, but she could only read the word "Kent" on it.'

Amanda clapped her hands together. 'I know that scrap of paper. I've seen it. Lord Hargreaves rescued it when he went looking for Matthew. Rosalie must still have it.'

'Pettigrew says there was nothing in the section on Kent that might indicate which house—if any—Mr Stuart might have an interest in. So he decided, with many apologies, to write to me, as *"My Lord, your humble and obedient servant, Stephen Pettigrew, attorney at law"*. Well. Well, well,' said Justin, handing the letter to his wife. 'This throws a new light on events of the past few months. What do you suggest we do?'

'I will write to Rosalie. You know, this letter confirms a lot she and I—and Lord Hargreaves, as well—speculated on what had happened to Matthew before he turned up at Mairsford. It addresses his near starvation, his loss of memory, and his shabby clothes. She will be delighted to have a bit more information. I think you should write to Lord Hargreaves, perhaps enclosing Pettigrew's letter. After all, Matthew is staying with him now.'

'And what about Mr Pettigrew. I should let him know at once that Matthew is alive and more or less well. He has clearly been very worried about him.'

'Yes, of course you should, but in the morning. You must be tired, my dear.'

'Do you know, Amanda?' said Justin, as they were leaving the room. 'I believe we have a copy of that book about castles and houses in the library. I'll just—'

'Tomorrow,' replied his wife firmly.

The next day, despite it being the day of the Harvest Feast, Justin made time to look for the book, and thanks to meticulous cataloguing, he found it quite easily. 'Look, my dear,' he said to his wife, 'it is just as Pettigrew described.' He plonked the large volume on Amanda's desk, putting the inkpot at risk.

Annoyed at first and then intrigued, she read the entry for Coverdale Hall, which gave a fulsome account of the Jacobean house. She turned the pages to find Staplewood Park. 'The author's not so complimentary about Lord Hargreaves's house, is he?'

'Except for the entrance hall, which he describes as "magnificent in its gilded glory." Is it, indeed, magnificent?'

Amanda smiled. 'It's rather overpowering, actually, not to my taste, and I rather think not to Lord Hargreaves's either.'

'That's all rather by the way, though. The real question is, Why was Matthew Stuart in Kent, at all? When this feast is over, I think I will try to find out more about him. I believe you said Matthew remembered that his father was an army officer. Perhaps the Army List might help to track him down. What do you think?'

'I think it is time you went to the great hall to confirm the arrangements for tonight and let me get on with this letter to Rosalie.'

Chapter 23

'I'm coming, Julia!' shouted Matthew. 'Where are you? Are you hurt?'

Bedford, alerted by the shouts, stood at Matthew's side, ready for action.

'Stay there. Good dog,' Matthew urged. 'Stay there. I'm coming back.'

He hoped the dog would obey as he set off down the path as fast as he could, catching his crutches in the briars and stumbling over exposed tree roots. 'I'm coming, Julia!' he shouted, 'Where *are* you?' He could see no sign of her anywhere.

Then, at last, a reply. 'I'm down here. I've fallen into a hole!'

'Good God, Julia! Are you hurt?' He moved towards where her voice was coming from, his heart hammering from exertion and fear.

'No, no. I'm all right, only a few scratches and bruises—nothing serious.'

As she spoke, Matthew could see a huge gap in the path where the earth had given way. 'I can see the hole—'

'Don't come too near the edge.' Her voice was closer now. 'It's still crumbling away.'

Matthew, as a surveyor, was well aware of the dangers of soil collapse and subsidence. He lay down flat on his stomach and elbowed his way to the edge of a deep hole, at the bottom of which—some ten or twelve feet below—he could see Julia, standing and looking up at him, smiling in relief. 'You're sure you're not hurt?' he asked again, anxiety in his voice.

'Quite sure. But it's too deep to climb out.'

'What happened?'

'I don't really know. It all happened so fast. One minute I was walking along the path looking at the chimney, and the next I was sliding down into this hole. I didn't really fall, and it's quite soft and muddy down here. Can you get me out?'

'I'll try.' He slid one of his crutches towards her. 'Can you grab onto this? Then I might be able to pull you out.'

But the crutch didn't reach far enough, and more soil began to trickle into the hole. Fearful of a landslide, which could bury Julia, he said. 'It's no good. I'll have to go and get help. Now listen very carefully, Julia; your life may depend on it. Stay as still as you can. Do not try to climb out. Do not touch the sides. I will leave my crutches with you. If the hole collapses, you may be able to push the earth away with them or use them to stand on. Have you got that?'

'Yes, but I'm sure there's no danger—'

'You don't know that. And neither do I. But I know soil, and it's a possibility. Please do as I say. I'll be as quick as I can; help won't be long in coming.'

'I hope not, it's not very nice down here.' The second crutch slid down the muddy slope. 'But, Matthew, you need them. How will you manage without them?' Julia wailed.

'I'll manage. Don't worry.' In his mind he silently added, *my darling Julia*. But that would remain forever unsaid.

Matthew started back down the path. The first few steps gave him no pain, and then his foot stepped on a sharp stone, and it felt as if a red-hot poker had gone up his leg, but he kept going as fast as he could. He was relieved when he saw that Bedford had obeyed him and was still sitting on the path. 'Good dog,' Matthew said, grabbing his collar.

Together, half hopping, half stumbling, they made their way out of the wood. The pain became excruciating, and his good leg started to weaken. A few yards onto the lawn, it gave way altogether, and he crumpled to the ground. With the last of his strength, he ordered. 'Go and get help, Bedford! Go on find someone—' Tears of pain and frustration were running down his face. Bedford licked them.

'No, stupid. We need help.'

But the dog didn't know where he was. He couldn't see the house, and all his peripheral vision showed him was green grass. He knew his limitations. Then ancestral voices told him what to do. Bedford stood up, pointed his nose skyward—and howled. His howl was a thing of awe and wonder and would put Cerberus to flight. It started deep in his chest and rose to a munificent note a coloratura soprano could be proud of.

The household were alerted by the second howl. But only Joseph, who was in Lord Hargreaves dressing room on the first floor, could see the cause—Mr Matthew lying on the sloping lawn with the dog by his side. He flew down the main stairs, taking the last three in one and nearly crashing into Parsons, who was carrying the afternoon post to Lord Hargreaves's study. 'I'm sorry, Mr Parsons, but Mr Matthew has had an accident. He is lying on the lawn, and Lady Julia is not with him, although I saw them together earlier. I fear the worst. Please inform His Lordship, at once. I must go!' Joseph sped out of the front door, across the gravel drive, and down the sloping grass. 'Mr Matthew, what has happened? What have you done—?'

Matthew didn't let him finish. 'Never mind about me,' he gasped. 'It is Lady Julia. She has fallen down a hole. She is not hurt, but I fear for her life. You must get help immediately. I couldn't ... I tried, but I couldn't—'

Joseph could see Matthew was on the point of collapse. 'Tell me where, Mr Matthew, and I will go for help at once.'

With relief in his voice, Matthew managed to explain where the accident had happened before passing out in a dead faint.

By now, Lord Hargreaves was halfway down the lawn, and Joseph left Matthew and rushed towards him. 'My Lord, there has been a subsidence in the wood, and Lady Julia has fallen into a deep hole. Mr Matthew fears for a further collapse of earth. You must organise a rescue at once, sir.' This was an impertinence on Joseph's part, but he didn't care, and Lord Hargreaves didn't seem to notice.

'Yes, Joseph. I have instructed Parsons to find Royston and George and bring them here immediately.' He looked up towards the house. 'They're coming now. Give me the directions for finding Lady Julia. I will see to her rescue. You must go back to Mr Matthew and take George.' The elderly portly footman was lagging behind Parsons and Royston, and Hargreaves realised he would be more of a hindrance than a help to the rescue mission.

Just as all this was occurring, Nicky appeared, driving a trap at a spanking pace up the drive. He pulled up sharply and was about to jump down, when his father shouted. 'Drive round to the stable and get Hampton to ride to Tunbridge Wells for the doctor at once, Nicky. See if you can find some rope, and then come to your chimney path. Hurry, son. I'll explain when you get there.'

Nicky whipped up the horse again and disappeared round the side of the house towards the stable yard.

Lord Hargreaves and his rescue party soon disappeared into the wood. He was desperately worried. He was not convinced Lady Julia was unhurt, and worse could yet have befallen her. He recalled, with chagrin, his words to Lady B, only two days ago, that Lady Julia would come to no harm in his house. The narrow path to the chimney was now more visible, since it had been trampled down by both Julia and Matthew, and the men had no difficulty finding the hole.

Julia heard people approaching and looked up. 'Don't come too near the edge!' she shouted. 'It may give way, and you will fall in too.'

'Are you all right, Lady Julia? Are you hurt? I've brought help.' Looking into the hole, Hargreaves could see a pale face, surrounded by a mass of muddy dark-red hair.

'I'm not hurt, just a few scratches and bruises, perhaps, and I may have turned an ankle a little, but nothing serious. However, it is really not very nice down here, and the sooner you can get me out, the better.' She laughed.

The laugh was music to Hargreaves's ears. Nevertheless, the situation was serious. And he could see at once that it was not just a matter of manpower, to get Lady Julia out of her predicament.

'How is Matthew, Lord Hargreaves? He insisted I keep his crutches in case there was a further fall of earth. I know he could do himself damage without them.'

He obviously had, thought his lordship, but this was not the time to tell her. 'Joseph and George are looking after him. He will be all right, I'm sure. Royston and Parsons are here to help me. I told them to stand back till I had assessed the situation. Now, Lady Julia, can you give me an idea of what it's like down there?'

'If I face the muddy slope, which is what I slid down—the ground just seemed to give way; I didn't fall at all hard—the two sides are quite solid. I gave them a prod with a crutch. I think, beneath all the tree-roots, they may be brick built. Behind me there may be some sort of passage, again with a solid roof. Nicky will be thrilled.'

'Nicky will not be at all thrilled when I have finished with him,' said his father sternly.

'Please don't be too hard on him. He wasn't to know.'

'I don't think trying to pull you out is the best idea. We need a ladder, although Nicky has gone to get some rope. I'll have a word with Parsons; he will know the quickest way to get a ladder here.'

Lord Hargreaves disappeared from Julia's view, and she could hear him talking to the butler.

Moments later he reappeared. 'That is in hand. I will stay with you. I would join you if I could. But two people in a hole would probably be more than twice as difficult, don't you think?'

'I beg you not to consider it, and before you lay the blame for my being here, I must tell you it is all my fault. I insisted we should not wait for Nicky, who was going to show us his mysterious chimney. Matthew begged me not to go along the path alone, but I am an impatient creature, Lord Hargreaves. Curiosity got the better of me, and you know what that did to the cat, so here I am.'

'Well, it certainly could have been a lot worse, I suppose. Anyway, we will just have to wait until the ladder arrives. Royston is here in case of a further emergency.'

While they waited, Hargreaves speculated as to what the structure—as it certainly seemed to be one—could be. The antiquarian in him dared to hope it might be Roman, but his common sense told him otherwise. Either way, once the immediate problem had been solved, further investigation was paramount.

Chapter 24

Joseph took one look at Matthew's blood-soaked foot and groaned inwardly, praying the damage was not as bad as it looked.

Matthew came round from his swoon. 'Julia … Lady Julia,' he said faintly.

'Do not worry, sir. Everything is in hand. It is you we have to see to now. George is here to give me a hand. If we lift you up and support you on either side, you would be able to reach the house?'

Once they had managed to raise Matthew up, Joseph could see that he was barely able to stand on his good leg. 'This won't be comfortable, sir,' he said, heaving Matthew onto his shoulder. In a fireman's lift. 'George, see that Mr Matthew doesn't fall off. Walk beside me,' he instructed briefly.

Bedford, satisfied he had done his duty, plodded along behind.

As Joseph arrived with his burden at Matthew's room, Mrs Clayborne emerged from the drawing room. 'Oh! What has happened? Has Mr Matthew been badly hurt? Oh dear me! What can I do to help? I've been in the conservatory.'

'Is Shephard still there, Mrs Clayborn?' asked Joseph as George opened the billiard room door.'

'Yes, we've been tying up the vine.'

As Joseph was laying the semi-conscious Matthew on his bed, he spoke to the footman over his shoulder, 'George, tell Shephard that Lord Hargreaves wants his presence immediately on the woodland path. Tell him to take the ladder.'

'The ladder!' exclaimed Mrs Clayborne. 'Whatever has happened?'

'I must attend to Mr Matthew immediately, Mrs Clayborne. Then I will explain what has happened, and I would be very grateful for your help.'

At that moment, Matthew opened his eyes. 'Have they got her out? Lady Julia, is she safe?' His voice was laden with anxiety.

'Yes, Mr Matthew, all that is being attended to.'

'Lady Julia! Oh no! No!' wailed Emily, bringing her hand up to her mouth.

'Please, Mrs Clayborne, do not distress yourself. She is not hurt. But now, as you can see, Mr Matthew needs our help.' He pointed to the blood seeping through the sock he wore on his left foot.

Despite her initial shock, Emily quickly pulled herself together, snatched two towels from beside the washbasin, and handed them to Joseph. 'Now just tell me what you need.'

'More towels, clean linen, plenty of hot water—for Lady Julia as well as for here—and an infusion of tea, made with boiling water. I have everything else I need here. Lady Julia will doubtless require the attention of a maid and possibly somewhere to rest too.'

'I will see to it immediately, Joseph.' As she bustled out of the room, she could see Joseph's attention was focussed on Matthew.

'Is it very bad?' asked Matthew as Joseph began to cut the sock and started to peel off the dressing. The sight was not encouraging, but Joseph maintained a calm expression. 'We will know the extent of the damage once it has been cleaned up, sir. While we wait for the water, I will get you a small brandy. That will revive your spirits.' He returned with a glass, to which he had added a drop of laudanum. 'Now, Mr Matthew, perhaps you will tell me exactly why you felt it necessary to abandon your crutches.'

After Matthew had explained what had happened, Joseph said, 'That is certainly the act of a gallant gentleman, sir. It is a pity it has had such an unfortunate result.'

With the opening of the screen, Emily was revealed bearing an armful of linen and, behind her, a maid with a large jug and a teapot. At the sight of Matthew's bloody foot, Emily ordered, 'Stay there, Elsie.' And dumping the towels on a chair, she relieved the maid of her tray.

The next half hour was very painful for Matthew and equally disappointing for Joseph. The newly healed skin on the sole of Matthew's foot had been torn open again. And, although by the time Joseph had bathed it in the tea, it had stopped bleeding, it would certainly start again if his patient attempted to move.

With his foot freshly dressed and elevated on pillows, Matthew dared to ask about the damage. 'I am afraid you have set the healing process back by about three weeks. However, there are several circumstances that could make it quicker. Firstly, your general health is much better than the last time, and I do not expect infection to set in. I could detect no foreign matter in the wound and have cleaned it thoroughly. But you must stay in bed until I, or the doctor, say you may get up.'

Matthew made a face of disapproval, but he was too exhausted to argue.

Having made all the arrangements for Julia to be well taken care of, Emily was waiting anxiously at the front door for the arrival of the rescue party. And it was not long before they appeared. She was relieved to see that Julia was walking quite freely, albeit with Charles holding her arm. On her other side, she could clearly see Nicky was being quite exuberant. Bringing up the rear were Parsons, carrying Matthew's crutches; Royston; and Shephard, without his ladder.

Nicky rushed forward and reached her first. 'Isn't it exciting, Aunt Emily—,an underground passage!'

'Never mind that,' Emily reproved. 'How is Lady Julia?'

'Oh, she's fine,' declared the irrepressible Nicky. 'Well, a bit grubby, perhaps, but nothing serious.'

'I wish I could say the same for Matthew.'

'Oh.' Nicky looked shamefaced. 'I'd forgotten about that. Is he very bad?'

But there was no time to answer his question, as Lady Julia and Lord Hargreaves reached the front door, and Emily could see the full extent of Julia's disarray. 'My dear,' she exclaimed, 'you are in a bit of a mess. But I have everything ready for you. Are you sure you are not hurt at all?'

'Just a few scratches and bruises. I'm afraid my clothes have taken the brunt of the damage. But never mind me, Mrs Clayborne, it is Mr Matthew I'm worried about. He should never have gone without his crutches, but I couldn't stop him.'

Emily turned to her brother. 'Charles, you must send a note to Lady Benedict at once, informing her what has happened and asking for a change of clothes for Lady Julia; nothing of mine will fit her. Send the trap, so she may bring them herself if she so wishes.'

Charles recognised the authority of an elder sister. 'Yes, of course. I will go myself and invite her back for supper. But like Lady Julia, I want to know how Matthew is.'

'Not too good, according to Joseph. His wound has opened up again and caused a major setback, and not inconsiderable pain.'

'It's all my fault,' wailed Julia. 'He *said* we should wait—'

'Come now, we must get you cleaned up.'

At that moment, Parsons, who, with Royston, had entered the house by another door, appeared, looking as if he had never spent the last hour hauling someone out of a muddy hole. 'May I be of assistance, Mrs Clayborne?'

'Yes, Parsons. Please arrange for tea and something to eat for Lady Julia to be sent to the blue bedchamber.' said Emily.

'And send round the trap. I need to go to Mairsford immediately. I'll drive myself,' added Hargreaves.

'At once, Mrs Clayborne.' He bowed. 'M'lord.'

'But Matthew,' said Julia agitatedly. 'How is he?'

'I'll tell you all I know while you tidy up. My maid will help you. The doctor has been sent for, so do not worry. I'm sure you'll be able to see him soon—after the doctor has been. Charles will want him to take a look at you too, Lady Julia.'

'I'm all right, really I am, Mrs Clayborne.'

'Yes, dear. But you've had a shock, and that can make you feel badly later on. Besides, my brother feels responsible for you.'

'For a complete idiot, you mean,' Julia replied ruefully.

130

Chapter 25

The closer Lord Hargreaves got to Mairsford Manor, the heavier his heart got. How on earth was he going to explain to Lady B, that her niece had fallen into a hole, and the young man she had taken such care of, while he stayed in her house, had now suffered further damage? It was just after four in the afternoon when he drew up beside the moat.

He waited in the gatehouse while Soames announced him.

'Show him in at once, Soames.'

'Lord Hargreaves, M'lady.'

Rosalie came forward, both hands extended, a smile of greeting on her face. Then saw his lordship's grave expression. 'Something has happened!' she exclaimed, the smile turning to distress.

'Yes, Lady Benedict. I am afraid I am the bringer of bad news.'

'Oh, please, tell me quickly.'

Hargreaves drew in a deep breath. 'Lady Julia was in the woods, and she fell into a hole—'

'Is she badly—'

'No, Lady B. I am glad to say she suffered only minor injuries.. But she was rescued in a very dishevelled and muddy condition.'

Rosalie laughed, partly in relief and partly with humour. 'If I know my niece, I am sure she engineered her own downfall. Julia has forever been getting herself into scrapes. But I see from your expression that there is more, My Lord. Please sit and tell me everything. But first I will ring for some refreshment.

'I hope Julia is suitably contrite about the damage she has caused by her impetuosity.'

'I am sure she will be, Lady B. But my first mission is to secure some clean garments for her. Those she has now are in a sorry state, and the disparity in size between my sister and Lady Julia does not permit borrowed plumage.'

Rosalie laughed at the thought of her tall slender niece trying to struggle into the raiment of the short, plump Mrs Clayborne. 'Will you excuse me while I get my maid to pack the necessary items? Then you can tell me everything. Please, Lord Hargreaves, ring for Soames and tell him what you would like to drink.'

Hargreaves, gratefully sipping on a tall glass of ale, regaled Rosalie with as accurate an account of the last few hours as he was able to piece together, ending with the consequences of Matthew's courage.

'It sounds as though it might be an underground passage. How exciting,' said Rosalie, 'especially with your interest in Roman remains.'

Hargreaves smiled, pleased that Lady B had remembered but replied, 'Any exploration of it will have to wait until I'm satisfied it is safe. Or the hole will have to be filled in, I'm afraid.'

Rosalie, who had accepted the invitation to supper at Staplewood, tried to convince Lord Hargreaves on the drive back that in no way was he responsible for Julia's mishap, and that she did not blame him in any way for it. But she could see that he still believed he *was*.

On arrival Emily greeted them with the news that the doctor had been, and apart from slight superficial damage, Lady Julia had suffered no lasting harm.

'But what about poor Matthew? What did the doctor say about him?' Rosalie asked anxiously.

Emily's lips tightened. 'Well, he certainly considered it a serious setback in the healing process. But again, he is not fearful of lasting damage and has left him in the capable hands of Joseph, for whom he has great respect.'

'I would like to see him as soon as possible, Mrs Clayborne.'

'Of course. But first, I must take you up to Lady Julia. My maid has been attending to her, and they are waiting for the clothes you have brought.'

As the two ladies disappeared upstairs, followed by George, carrying the valise, Lord Hargreaves retreated to his study, rather less worried than he had been earlier. Lady Julia, at least, was going to be all right. The first thing that caught his eye was the letter, still on the salver, that Parsons had been about to deliver when all the furore had started. The thick letter, with numerous seals on its outer covering, was intriguing, even more so when he recognised the seals as being those of the Marquis of Coverdale. He took it over to his comfortable chair by the fire, placed a pair of gold-rimmed spectacles on his nose, and broke the seals. Folded inside a covering letter, headed with the Coverdale coat of arms, were several other sheets of writing paper. Hargreaves laid these aside as he read the Marquis's letter first:

My dear Hargreaves,

I am glad you were made comfortable during your stay in Mount Street. I am enclosing a letter, and when you read it, you will be as astonished by its contents as I was. As you see from the date, it was received when I was abroad, hence the delay. After you have read it, I suggest you are in the best position to make any arrangements you think necessary.

I think you will find that several of the questions raised by you and Lady Benedict concerning Matthew will be answered, but several intriguing new ones raised. My wife has written to her separately to apprise her of the new developments. But I am sure you will want to discuss the matter with her, too. I am not, in general, a believer in random circumstance, so I am sure there is a logical explanation for Matthew Stuart's presence at Staplewood Park.

On another matter, I have secured another sponsor for your induction into the House of Lords. Viscount Uttoxeter is only too pleased to perform the office, and I look forward to you joining us when Parliament resumes in two weeks' time.

Yours sincerely and in anticipation,
Coverdale

With every page of Pettigrew's letter he read, Hargreaves's amazement grew. It was not a law office he was familiar with, although as a solicitor himself, he'd had dealings with Bristol lawyers. As he perused the closely written pages, his admiration for Pettigrew's persistence in endeavouring to find his missing client increased. Now, at least, it would be possible not only to put the lawyer's mind at rest, but also to return to Matthew some of his missing belongings.

How best to proceed was his next problem. Should he gather all the interested parties round Matthew's sickbed and tell everyone the good news? Or would it be best to have a private word with Lady B, and they could decide together what was the best course of action?

After some cogitation, he decided on the latter option, at the same time wondering if he had chosen it just so he could be alone with Lady B. There was no doubt she was taking up a lot of time in his thoughts these days. Intending to leave a message with George, he encountered the three ladies descending the stairs, all impeccably dressed for dinner.

'We are going to see Matthew and find out how he's doing,' said Emily. 'Lady Julia is beside herself with worry. Are you not, my dear? Although I was able to reassure her with the doctor's opinion.'

This was Lord Hargreaves's opportunity. 'Emily, do you not think that he might be somewhat overwhelmed by the sudden appearance of three beautiful ladies all at once? Lady B, perhaps you would care to join me in the library. I have something to tell you that I am sure you will find of interest.' He smiled.

Rosalie detached herself from the group and came towards him. 'That sounds like a mystery. I love mysteries. Let us go at once.'

The library was furnished exactly as if it had been copied from a manual called *"The Nobleman's House.. (1) The Library."* It had a pair of globes, a writing desk, library steps, and two button-back armchairs with reading stands. Busts of the great and good of classical and English literature were arranged at intervals along the top shelf. It was dull, cheerless, and the fire had nearly gone out. 'Please, Lady B, won't you take a seat.'

'Not in here, Lord Hargreaves, unless you want me to die of cold and, therefore, lose all interest in what you have to say.'

His Lordship was both slightly taken aback and secretly pleased, but he felt obliged to explain himself. 'My study is much warmer, Lady B, but I thought you might consider it too intimate—'

'Fiddlesticks!' exclaimed Rosalie, 'I'm sure you have a nice cosy study. Lead me to it, My Lord.'

Hargreaves did so.

'Now what is this exciting news?' said Rosalie, seating herself on the well-upholstered settee.

'You will no doubt be surprised to hear I have received a communication from Lord Coverdale concerning Matthew.'

When he had finished giving Rosalie a brief outline of Mr Pettigrew's letter, stating all the salient points, she was as astonished as Justin and Amanda had been.

'But what does it all mean? Why did he land up outside Mairsford? Or was he intending to come to *this* house?' Her questions rapped out one after another.'

'Lady B, I have no more an idea than you do. And since Matthew has no recollection of anything that happened to him—even before he set foot in England—he can be of no help either. However, it is quite pleasing to know how accurate our early detective work has turned out to be.'

'And,' added Rosalie with a mischievous smile, 'how pleased I am that we have become friends as a result. Are you going to tell him?'

'Of course, but not tonight. I'm sure Joseph would disapprove of anything that might overexcite Matthew. For the time being, we must just be glad it won't be too long before his trunk and gold watch is returned to him. They, at least, may make him feel he is less of a lost soul.'

'I think that's wise. He will undoubtedly be excited by such good news. So, for just now, we will keep it to ourselves.'

Emily took Lady Julia to Matthew's room. At the door she said, 'Remember, my dear, do not do or say anything that may cause him further pain.

But as soon as she entered, Julia pushed past the screens that separated Matthew's living area, rushed to his bedside, and knelt down. Taking hold of the hand that had been stroking the dog, she cried, 'Oh Matthew! I'm so sorry … I'm so sorry! You told me not to go, but I'm so stupid and thoughtless. Will you ever forgive me?' Tears flowed down her face and splashed onto Matthew's hand.

Emily stood at the end of the bed, observing Julia's outburst, which ignored all the proprieties, and realised that perhaps there was a deeper current of feelings between the two of them than she had hitherto imagined.

Matthew turned towards Julia, ignoring the stab of pain the slightest movement caused him. 'Please, Lady Julia,' he said, using her title, 'you really must not distress yourself so.'

'But I have caused you such pain—'

He shook his head.

'But I have!' she exclaimed. 'I can see it in your eyes.'

'I will recover, and you should consider this. If you had waited for Nicky, you would both have fallen into that hole and probably have done a great deal more damage to yourself and him. And I would still have had to go for help.'

Ignoring Matthew's reasonable explanation, Julia said. 'You were so brave, and help came so quickly—'

'That was entirely due to Bedford. When I collapsed on the lawn, he gave two massive howls, and everyone came running out of the house— like rabbits out of a hole when a ferret is put into a warren. So it is he you should be thanking.'

'Maybe so. But you left me your crutches. You must have known what damage that would cause. That was very brave, and I won't have it otherwise.'

Emily realised Matthew had, probably by design, managed to lower the emotional tension, and the meeting was ended by the arrival of Joseph with Matthew's supper.

'Mrs Clayborne,' he said, 'Mr Parsons has asked me to say that dinner is served.'

'Thank you, Joseph. Come along, Lady Julia. We must not keep your aunt and my brother waiting.'

As they left, Julia turned back and gave Matthew a little smile and a wave.

Chapter 26

Two days later was the day of the Mairsford Harvest Festival at St Saviours Church in Upper Mairsford. It began with a procession to the church from the mill, led by a farmer carrying a symbolic sheaf of barley, followed by all the members of the congregation, each with a single offering, normally an apple or a pear, to lay in front of the altar.

This time, the congregation was exceptionally large, the cause of which was curiosity to see the new Lord Hargreaves. With Staplewood Park empty for all but a few weeks of the year, the three villages lacked a centre, and a figurehead. Lord Patrick had been greatly missed, and his successor unknown: the inhabitants were now optimistic about the future.

Following the service, Lady B was curtsied and bowed to by those leaving the church. But there was no doubt that eyes were upon Lord Hargreaves and Mrs Clayborne, who were standing behind her. The harvest supper took place at five o'clock in the hall of Mairsford Manor. Two long tables stretched along either side of the hall—one to serve the food from, the other with benches for the guests. It was tradition for the Lady of the manor to serve the food. And this time with Lord Hargreaves, Mrs Clayborne, and Lady Julia by her side, Rosalie managed to spill some soup on her gown. Quickly, Hargreaves snatched up a napkin. and began to dab at the stain. Then realising what an intimate thing he was doing, he looked up, and his eyes met hers. They both laughed.

The next day, Hargreaves took Nicky to Tunbridge Wells to catch the stage coach to London, where he would spend the night with a cousin of his late mother, before travelling to Shrewsbury in the company of other boys returning to school. On the way back, he called in at the estate office in Staplewood to see if his agent knew anything about the chimney. He didn't mention the hole, as he didn't want news of it getting about.

But the agent could tell him nothing, and there seemed to be no papers or documents relating to the house, only numerous account books, dating back to the time of the first Lord Hargreaves. He took a couple of the oldest ones with him. As he drove back through the village, he was greeted with touched forelocks, raised hats, and curtsies by those who noticed his progress, and he returned the courtesies. He was beginning to feel more at home and comfortable in his new position. And although he knew the big house would seem empty without Nicky, now was the time to give Matthew the good news about his belongings. And there was the mystery of the underground tunnel to solve.

Matthew was now allowed to resume his position on the couch in his living area, as Joseph had satisfied himself that neither fever nor infection had set in as a result of his adventure. So, mid-morning, Hargreaves entered the erstwhile billiard room with a letter in his hand and a smile on his face. 'I have some news, my boy, that will, I am sure, cheer you greatly,' he said, seating himself in the armchair.

'I sure could use some, sir. Disregarding this little setback,' he pointed to the bandaged foot resting on a pillow, 'I am beginning to feel that my life has got stuck in some sort of limbo. There is still so much of the past I can't remember, and nothing to look forward to.'

Hargreaves put on his spectacles. 'This letter may be a great help. It is from a solicitor, a Mr Stephen Pettigrew, in Bristol, and it concerns you. Would you like to read it, or shall I?'

'Please, Lord Hargreaves, I should like to hear it.'

When Hargreaves had finished reading the letter word for word, Matthew exclaimed, 'But that is extraordinary! Absolutely extraordinary! Are you sure it refers to me?'

'I think there can be no doubt about that, despite the obvious gaps. Mr Pettigrew, his staff, and the Bristol constabulary have made a very good case. Besides, the trunk, currently residing in Pettigrew's office, is certainly yours. So, when I arrange for its transport, you will at last have something of your own. And it will make you feel less like the orphan of the storm than you do now, won't it?'

Matthew's face lit up, and he moved on the couch, wincing a little as Hargreaves offered him the letter, then his expression changed.

Observing this, Hargreaves remarked, 'Are you not pleased? I will put matters in hand for the return of your trunk immediately, if that is what you wish.'

'Of course it is. But the cost—'

'My dear boy, do not give it another thought.'

'But I do, My Lord, all the time,' Matthew interrupted. 'I am living entirely at your expense, and I have nothing to repay you—or Lady Benedict, for that matter. You pay Joseph's wages and my food—'

'Listen, Matthew. Joseph does a lot of other things in this house besides looking after you. And as for food, that hound whose ears you are fondling costs me more to feed than you do. So, on that head, let us hear no more. Besides, I do not believe you are penniless. You cannot have arrived in this country, travelling first class, without any means of support. It will just be a case of finding out where your money lies, and the arrival of your trunk may well solve that puzzle.'

Matthew smiled. 'I suppose you are right. I should just consider myself very lucky to have had two such wonderful people as yourself and Lady B to rescue me.'

Bedford gave a grunt.

'Yes, you too, old fellow.'

Letters were sent to Mr Pettigrew—of gratitude from Matthew and with directions for the transport of the trunk from Lord Hargreaves. The distance was quite considerable, so its arrival was not expected in much less than a week.

Meanwhile, His Lordship decided to explore the cavity that Lady Julia's fall had exposed. He took only Royston with him, as at this point, he considered that the fewer people who knew about it, the better. Armed with shovels, shears, rope, and a lantern and suitably clad, they set off on a voyage of discovery. When they reached the spot, Hargreaves insisted he should go down the ladder first. The bottom had received some more soil. But otherwise, it seemed merely damp.

'Send me down the shovel, Royston,' he shouted to the anxious man at the top. The tool was tied to the rope and lowered to Hargreaves, who used it to test the strength of the walls. To his surprise, he found that, by pushing the shovel through the area of soil Lady Julia had slid down, he encountered a solid wall on that side too. 'Lower the lantern on the rope and then come down yourself, Royston. I believe it to be safe to do so.'

When the manservant arrived, Hargreaves said, 'Well, what do you think?'

Royston clipped some of the roots from the side wall and gave it a good scrape with the shovel. A patch of well-built brickwork was revealed. He gave the mortar a poke. 'Seems sound enough, sir, M'lord, he corrected himself.'

Hargreaves heaved a sigh. The Roystons had been with him for over twenty years and could not get used to his new title. 'Sir is quite sufficient, Royston, or My Lord, but please, not both. Shall we proceed?' He produced a silver vesta case and struck a match to light the lantern.

'Let me go first, M'lord.' He tapped the brickwork arch that formed the roof of the passage and began clearing roots and rubble from the entrance. 'Seems like there were a door here at some time, Sir, M—' He grinned. 'Must've all rotted away.'

When a large enough opening was made, Hargreaves lifted the lantern high, and they both scrambled through. The passage was quite high enough for a man to walk upright and was remarkably free from growths and intrusions, although the air was musty and stale, the lantern throwing their shadows on the walls. 'This is a very strange place, Royston. I suppose it leads to somewhere below that chimney stack.'

A few yards farther along, Royston's shovel, which he had been using to test for safety underfoot, struck an obstruction.

Hargreaves brought the lantern closer. 'What is it?'

But he didn't need to ask. They had clearly reached a door—this time, one that had not rotted away. The light revealed a rusty latch and a handle. Royston lifted the latch and pushed. Nothing happened.

'Try pulling it,' Hargreaves suggested.

This time, there was a slight movement.

'I think the dirt and stuff on the floor is stopping it, sir.'

Hargreaves stepped back to allow Royston to get to work with his shovel. A couple of further strong pulls on the door handle, and with a screech of rusty hinges, the door opened. Cautiously, the pair entered and found themselves in a chamber about twenty feet square, with a vaulted roof and stone-flagged floor. 'What do you make of this, Royston?'

'Dunno, sir.' He kicked at a pile of bricks and rubble, above which a construction of some sort had once been present. 'Must have been a hearth here. Looks as if someone's destroyed it, deliberate like.'

Hargreaves flashed the lantern in a circular motion, revealing a stone bench running the whole length of the side opposite the chimney and, much to his surprise, the glint of glass. 'That's odd, Royston. Surely it can't be a window?'

But it was. It was a porthole of heavy glass that looked as though it had, indeed, once been on a ship, completely dust covered on the inside, and earthed up on the other. 'Whoever heard of an underground window?'

'Don't rightly know, sir,' replied his henchman, uncertain what to reply. And then he had an idea. 'The wood is on a steep slope, M'lord. Perhaps the window overlooks it—if it were dug out on the other side.'

'You could be right about that. But I think, for today, we've seen enough. Time to go home. Back in the wood once more,' Hargreaves said. 'I don't want to leave the ladder here. Can we pull it up, and return it to Shephard?'

'I can do that, sir, no bother.'

'Good. And I would appreciate it if you didn't talk about what we have found. They're bound to ask. So, say it was just a hole that led nowhere.'

'My lips are sealed, sir ... M'lord.'

After dinner that evening, Hargreaves entered Matthew's room, bearing the two leather-bound volumes he'd taken from the estate office and placed them on the table by Matthew's couch. 'Now, I know you're eager to hear what Royston and I discovered this afternoon.'

'Sure am, sir.'

'We took a lantern and some tools and eventually found a tunnel or passage, about twenty or so feet long, which ended in a door. After some excavation, Royston managed to get it open, and we found a square chamber with the remains of a hearth. Royston thought it had been deliberately destroyed, rather than decayed by time.'

'I wonder why,' interjected Matthew.

'So do I, but that's not the only strange thing. The room has—or seems to have had—a window. Circular in shape and about eighteen inches in diameter.'

'An underground window?' queried Matthew. 'How odd.'

'Exactly my thoughts, too. That's why I've brought you these books. They are a record of all the estate transactions at the time of the first Lord Hargreaves. You might care to occupy your time by looking through them and seeing if there have been any payments or invoices referring to materials or labour. It may take some time, as you won't know exactly what you're looking for.' He placed an oil lamp on the table. 'Meanwhile I will take that hound out for a run before bedtime.'

Chapter 27

It wasn't until two days later, and with a guilty feeling of neglect, that Hargreaves finally managed to find the time to discuss Matthew's findings—if any—from the account books. 'I'm sorry, Matthew. My consultancy for my Ludlow practice has been taking up my time. But now you can tell me what you've found. Good news, I hope.'

Matthew drew down his lips and shook his head. 'I've been through every page. And it seems that, although the accounts appear to be well kept, I can find nothing that does not relate to estate matters.'

'That is very disappointing. Nothing concerning the building of the house, at all?'

'No, sir. But there is just one thing I thought rather odd.' Matthew picked up one of the volumes and opened it where he'd put a marker. 'It seems the building of an apple store has been ordered.'

'Yes?' Hargreaves leaned forward and took the book. 'What about it?'

'It may be nothing, but it looks to me that a much greater quantity of building materials, mostly bricks, were ordered, unless the store was to be very large indeed.'

Apple storage was an important part of the estate's production. Well-preserved apples that could be sold in the winter months brought in a good income. Hargreaves had made it his first duty to visit every farm, orchard, and building on the estate as soon as he took up residence. 'There are a number of such sheds on the property, Matthew. But as far as I could judge, they are mainly of wooden construction, with a few courses of brickwork as a base. it doesn't seem very likely. I'm afraid. That is all I have been able to come up with. But I must say it has been a great pleasure to have something to do. I only wish there was more.'

'There must be more records connected with this house and family, if only I knew where to look. I've already scoured the library and looked in every drawer and cupboard in my study. But I found nothing older than household receipts for the years before I arrived.'

Matthew thought for a moment, really wanting to make a useful suggestion. Eventually he said, 'Perhaps you could ask Parsons. He has been coming here for a number of years with your predecessor. You never know. He might be able to help.'

'A good idea. It's certainly worth a try. I'll ask him at once.'

'Good luck, My Lord.'

Parsons was quickly summoned to the study. 'Something you require, M'lord?'

'Yes, Parsons. I am in need of information, and I hope you will be able to supply it.'

'When we were in the process of extracting Lady Julia from the cavity into which she had so unfortunately fallen, and she said it seemed to have solid sides, did anything, then or later, indicate what the purpose of the structure might be?'

'Yes, M'lord.'

Hargreaves raised his eyebrows. 'Indeed, Parsons. Perhaps you could give me the benefit of your opinion.'

'It is an opinion, M'lord, based on service in country houses as well as working in town. The structure seemed similar to the icehouses that may be found in large estates such as this.'

'An icehouse?' Hargreaves scratched his head. 'An icehouse,' he repeated. It was, of course, possible but did not account for the chimney or hearth. But then, that could have been added later. 'That is certainly a possibility, Parsons. I will look into it.'

'Will that be all, M'lord?'

'No, there is another matter you may be able to help me with. Now I know you only worked here for a few weeks each year. And because of that, you may not have the information I require.'

'I will do my best, M'lord.'

'I have been trying to find out more—or, indeed, anything—about this house. But so far, apart from books referring to the estate, I have not come across any records, papers, or documents pertaining to any aspect of Staplewood Park itself. I have searched the library and the study to no avail. Have you any suggestions as to where else I could look?'

The butler cleared his throat. 'You might try the muniment room, M'lord.'

Hargreaves looked up at Parson's impassive face. Surely he could be being sarcastic or joking. 'The ... er ... muniment room?' he queried.

'Yes, M'lord.'

'I was unaware that there was one. Where is it situated—in the loft?'

'No, M'lord. It is at the end of the long saloon. It occupies a similar space to that of the area you refer to in the dining room as the alcove. Perhaps you would permit me to show you.'

'I should be delighted, Parsons. Its existence, hitherto unknown to me, may hold the answer to all my questions.' Hargreaves rose to his feet. 'You had better lead the way.'

The two progressed through the library to the long saloon and reached the far end. A large somewhat faded and worn tapestry depicting a biblical scene covered almost the entire wall, to a height of about two feet from the ceiling.

'Permit me, M'lord,' said Parsons, stretching his arm behind the hanging and retrieving a long pole, fitted with a brass hook.

Hargreaves was intrigued. 'Carry on, man.'

The tapestry was suspended from rings arranged along a brass rail. The butler, using the long pole, unhooked one end of the rail and began walking towards Hargreaves, swinging the tapestry away from the wall. Then he stopped.

'Something the matter?'

'Yes. M'lord, I have omitted to uncover the floor socket.' He pointed to a small circle of brass set into the floor to the right of where Hargreaves was standing.

'I'll do it.' Hargreaves bent down, lifted a small ring, and with it, swivelled the cover to one side, exposing a metal-lined hole.

'Thank you, M'lord.' Parsons proceeded to fit the end of the pole into the socket. Now that the tapestry was at ninety degrees to the wall, a door was revealed. It was the same size and design as all the other doors on the ground floor, but devoid of a pediment and any form of gilding, bearing only a doorknob and keyhole. No key. The excitement Hargreaves felt as the door was revealed, dissipated when he tried to open it. It was, of course, locked.

'Have you any suggestions, Parsons?'

'Not really, M'lord. I only ever saw this place once. I was looking for the late Lord Hargreaves, and as I entered the long saloon, he was just emerging through this door. He locked it behind him.'

'Where did he put the key? Can you remember?'

'In his pocket as I recall. It was some time ago.'

'Where are keys generally kept? I'm afraid I am rather ignorant of such matters,' said Hargreaves ruefully.

'Your Lordship is not expected to be cognisant with such matters. But since Mrs Clayborne has taken over most of the housekeeping duties, she is in charge of the appropriate keys. There is also a board in the housekeeper's room, with spares and those too big to carry around. I keep the keys to the wine cellar and the silver vault. Shall I put the tapestry back, M'lord?'

'Might as well, Parsons. What did you say just now? A silver vault?'

'Yes, M'lord.'

'Where is this silver vault? I've never heard of such a place.'

'It is beneath the butler's pantry. It is accessed by a trapdoor in the floor.'

'I see. Do I have a vast hoard of silver?'

'I wouldn't put it quite like that.'

'How would you put it?'

'Adequate, M'lord.'

'Adequate for what?'

'A gentleman's establishment of moderate size, although judging by the size of the cupboards and the number of drawers in the vault, I would suggest it once held a great deal more.'

'All sold off, I suppose,' said Hargreaves.

'I'm sure I couldn't say, M'lord.'

By this time, they had reached the door of the long saloon. 'Thank you for your help, Parsons. I have learnt a great deal more about this house. I will give some thought to where the missing key may be found. And if you have any ideas, please do not hesitate to convey them to me. I should also like to visit my ...er ... adequate supply of silver in the near future.'

146

'Very good, M'lord, any time you wish.' They had just gone their separate ways when Parsons halted, midway across the hall. 'Your Lordship.'

'Yes, Parsons?'

'It has just occurred to me that the person to ask about his Late Lordship's keys would be Mr Joseph, being, as it were, closer to him than I was.'

'An excellent suggestion. Send him to me as soon as possible. I shall be in my study.'

A few minutes later, Joseph entered the room. 'You wished to see me, M'lord?'

'Yes, Joseph. Parsons has shown me the room where I might find the documents and records I have been searching for. Unfortunately, it is locked, and there is no key present. He suggested you might know where your late master kept his keys.'

'He did not have many, M'lord, living in an hotel as he did. There was one for the door to his apartment, but that was returned to the management. Likewise, he had a key to a bureau. But that, too, belonged to the hotel so remained in the lock. The only other one I was aware of was the one to his strongbox, and that, he kept on his watch chain.'

'I didn't know there was a strongbox. Where is it now?' asked Hargreaves, giving Joseph a frowning look.

'I imagine, M'lord, that Mr Parsons has put it in a safe place. When my master died, it was, as you know, just before Christmas last year. A solicitor's clerk came to the hotel and made an inventory of all his late Lordship's possessions, and asked me to pack them all up and bring them here, sir, which I did. It was fortuitous that Mr Parsons was already at Staplewood, making ready for the Christmas visit that, in the end, never took place.'

'So they must all be somewhere in this house then? You didn't unpack them?'

'No, M'lord. Since my master was deceased, they were no longer my concern.'

'What happened to the watch and key?'

Joseph looked a little embarrassed. He cleared his throat. 'Er ...' He stopped.

'Well, man, spit it out,' Hargreaves said impatiently.

'It's like this, M'lord. It may have slipped your mind. But under the terms of his late lordship's will, the watch was left to me. The clerk took it away with him, pending the grant of probate, and eventually it was sent to me. Do you wish to see it?'

'Yes, you are right. I had forgotten. Is it the one you are wearing now, Joseph?'

'No, M'lord. I'm afraid it doesn't keep very good time. I prefer to use my own.'

'I see. But what happened to the strongbox key?' Hargreaves felt he was finally going to acquire the information he needed.

'I made sure the box was locked and then attached the key to the underside with a court plaster, M'lord.'

Hargreaves felt he was wading through treacle. Why couldn't Parsons have told him about this? He wondered. But he already knew the answer. Because he hadn't been asked, that was why! He drew out his watch. 'It is too late today to start a search, and it's better done in daylight anyway. Tomorrow will do.'

'Yes, M'lord. Is there anything else you require?'

'I would like your opinion on Mr Matthew's progress—not only his injury but also his state of mind.'

'His foot is progressing slowly, despite the recent setback. As to his state of mind, I think he is becoming rather depressed. With the departure of Master Nicholas, he has no one close to his own age to talk to. And with his improving health, he is feeling the insecurity of his position and increased anxiety for the future.'

'Thank you, Joseph, I rather feared as much. But if I can get the door to the muniment room open, there may be something there to keep him occupied.'

'Indeed, it is to be hoped so, M'lord. I might add that Bedford is a great comfort to him when he is downhearted.'

But next morning, all thoughts of an early search for the missing key were put aside, as Matthew's trunk arrived.

Chapter 28

Royston and George entered Matthew's room, bearing between them a large, heavily corded, brass-bound trunk. Joseph brought up the rear. The trunk was carefully placed in the window embrasure. But Joseph immediately said, 'I think Mr Stuart would prefer it to be closer, so he can examine its contents himself.'

Matthew smiled as the trunk was relocated beside his couch.

'Will that be all, sir?' enquired Royston.

'Thank you, yes. If we need any more help, I will call. Joseph, you will stay, of course.' Matthew looked at the trunk, observing the labels, in particular the one assigning it to Pettigrew's office. He recognised his own handwriting but still had no recollection as to why he had done so.

'Would you like me to assist in opening the trunk, sir?' Joseph enquired.

Matthew grinned. 'In my position, I think the assistance will be yours alone.'

'Shall I commence?'

'Cut the cords, my good man!'

Joseph produced a small folding knife from his pocket and proceeded to cut through the restraints, which fell away, leaving only two leather straps and a flap concealing the lock. Joseph undid all three. But the trunk remained locked. Disappointment flooded through Matthew's being. Of course, he knew a locksmith could be summoned, and the trunk would soon yield up its secrets, but he had so wanted it to happen now.

Lord Hargreaves entered the room. 'I thought you might be in need of this.' He held out a key. 'It came yesterday, in a separate cover. Mr Pettigrew explained that he'd had to remove the lock when he was trying to find out more about you and needed to open the trunk. He had employed a locksmith to replace the lock and make a new key.' Hargreaves handed the key to Matthew.

'There is no end to the trouble that man took on my behalf.' Matthew leaned over but could not reach the lock. 'Will you do the honours, please, Joseph?'

The manservant knelt down, fitted the key, and lifted the lid. Matthew's eyes unexpectedly blurred. He wasn't prepared for the emotion he felt on seeing something that really and truly belonged to him. His purpose in the world lay in front of him. There lay all the tools and instruments of his profession, and some personal items too. Noting Matthew's emotion 'I can see you are pleased to find your own things again.' Hargreaves remarked.

'Of course I am.' Matthew smiled. But 'without your good offices, the trunk would not be here at all. Shall we see what else will be revealed?'

Among the surveying instruments, Hargreaves saw two round leather boxes, the larger stamped, 'collars', the smaller 'studs'. But it was a third box that caught the eye of both Matthew and his lordship. Matthew leaned over, but his trembling hand couldn't quite reach it. Joseph handed it to him. With a slightly croaky voice, Matthew said, 'This was my mother's. She always kept it on her writing bureau. I remember it so well now.'

'Well,' remarked Hargreaves, 'it's certainly travelled a great many miles to finally reach home again.'

Matthew, still smoothing the lid with his fingers, looked puzzled. 'What do you mean, sir?'

'That inlaid design of tiny wooden tiles is called Tunbridge Ware. Your mother's box was made not ten miles from here, in Tunbridge Wells. That's really quite extraordinary.'

As he was speaking, Joseph lifted out the tray from the top of the trunk to reveal tightly packed clothes.

Hargreaves pulled out his watch. 'I must go. I'll leave you to discover whatever else you can truly call yours.'

Matthew placed the box on his table. 'I must thank you, My Lord, for all the trouble you have gone to—'

'Nonsense, my boy. I'm just pleased that you now have some things of your own. I will see you later.'

With his Lordship's departure, Joseph, who had been looking out of the window, asked, 'Would you like me to continue with the unpacking?'

'Of course. Let's get on with it.'

Joseph lifted garment after garment from the trunk, including a frock coat, several pairs of trousers, waistcoats, and a velvet smoking jacket. Nestled underneath this was a small package, the paper sealed with wax. He gave it to Matthew, who broke the seal.

'My watch, Joseph! It's my watch.'

'Indeed, it is, sir.'

Matthew searched through the paper. 'There's no key.'

''I expect it got lost when you were robbed, sir. Perhaps there's a spare key in that box.' He pointed to the one on the table.

The lid was hinged, but one of them was loose. The inside was stained with ink, and it was clear the box's main purpose had been to hold the instruments associated with writing. There was also a small tin box, and a military button—but no watch key. Matthew shook his head.

'May I suggest the stud box, sir? In my experience they often contain more than shirt studs.' When opened, it was clear that Joseph was right. The box contained a generous assortment of buttons; studs; tie-on labels, used and unused; and a quantity of pins. A few pokes around by Joseph's fingers produced what he was looking for—a small double-ended watch key. 'I hope it fits your watch, sir.'

Matthew held this treasured possession in his hand, minutely observing the fine engine turning on the case and his initials engraved on the escutcheon before flipping the cover. He was relieved to find there was no damage to the face or hands. But of course, it wasn't going. He took the key and, opening the back of the watch, inserted the key and gingerly began to turn it. After a few turns, he shook it gently and put the watch to his ear. The smile on Matthew's face told Joseph all he needed to know.

The remainder of the unpacking consisted mainly of small clothes, nightwear, and accessories. The room was beginning to look like a gentlemen's outfitters. Brown paper covered the final layer, revealing, when removed, boots, shoes, and books, including the one that had ultimately led to the knowledge of Matthew's whereabouts. He peered over the side of the trunk but couldn't reach it.

'Is this the one you want, sir?' Joseph picked up the large volume,

Matthew nodded and was immediately immersed in *Castles and Great Houses of England*. He turned to the flyleaf, which bore two inscriptions.

One was in a hand he didn't recognise. It read, *"To my dear wife of twenty-five years. 20 July 1805."* The other was in his mother's writing, with just her name and the date 1824. Matthew was puzzled. His mother was born in the United States and had never mentioned any close connections with England, and yet she had, presumably, bought this book second-hand. He riffled through the pages, and exactly as it had done with Mr Pettigrew, it fell open at Coverdale Hall.

At that moment, Emily Clayborne came into the room. 'Oh my!' she exclaimed, seeing the clothes piled up on the chairs and threatening to spill onto the floor.

Joseph appeared from behind the screen that concealed Matthew's sleeping area. 'I believe, Mrs Clayborne,' he said in his soft voice, 'that you may be able to make a suitable suggestion for the disposition of Mr Matthew's newly discovered wardrobe.'

'I think it is you who should make the suggestion, Joseph.'

'Very well, madam. If it is at all possible for a chest of drawers to be brought here for the small clothes, nightwear, and accessories'—he pointed to a pile of cravats, scarves, and gloves perched precariously on the back of a chair—'I will undertake to see to Mr Matthew's outerwear, which will all require refreshing.'

'I'm sure that can be arranged.' She turned to the person whose belongings were under discussion. 'Will that be all right, Matthew?'

'What?' Matthew had been so engrossed in the book he hadn't taken in a word.

'Joseph and I were discussing where to put your clothes.' She smiled, adding, 'Now that you are a man of property once more.' Matthew was looking a little overwhelmed by the events of the last hour. Emily and Joseph exchanged glances. 'You know, Joseph, perhaps we could discuss this a little later. I think Mr Matthew would like to enjoy his newfound possessions in peace.'

'Indeed so, Mrs Clayborne.' He gathered up an armload of coats, jackets, and trousers and followed Emily from the room.

Matthew was left with a multitude of feelings to sort out. He hadn't imagined that seeing his things again would have had such an emotional effect. Certainly there was pleasure. He picked up the watch, and held it to his ear, still ticking. He flipped it open and stared at the inscription—'Matthew' and a date. That's my birthday. His memory loss had made keeping track of dates—both past and present—confusing. But now he remembered getting the watch.

He had come down to breakfast, and his mother was there, an unusual occurrence, as she normally took her first meal in her bedchamber. 'Happy Birthday, son,' she had said, giving him a kiss and pointing to a small package on the table. 'I promised your father you would get a gold watch for your twenty-first birthday.'

To get it back now was a wonderful feeling. Matthew slipped it into his waistcoat pocket. It felt just right. He gave a sigh of contentment.

He was keenly interested in the contents of his Tunbridge ware box, as he now knew it was called. He dismissed the pens and pencils and concentrated on the military button. It was made of brass, he thought, but needed a good polish to bring it up to military standards. The centre had the cypher 'GR' and, on a stylised ribbon round the rim, the words, 'Royal Regiment of Artillery'. He supposed it could have belonged to his father. The other item of interest was the small tin box. He opened it carefully. Inside was a small scrap of paper and a lock of black hair. Written in faded ink on the paper was the date 181—— The last figure was partly concealed by an inkblot. Matthew held it up to the light. It could be a 12 or a 13. And below it, in pencil, was his name, 'Matthew'.

He smiled at his mother's two souvenirs and then frowned. A vague memory fluttered through his mind like a butterfly but disappeared before he could catch it, leaving the feeling that something was not quite right. He closed the box and picked up the book to examine the entries for Coverdale Hall and Staplewood. But somehow sleep overcame him. And when Lord Hargreaves entered, he was just in time to catch the volume before it hit the floor.

Chapter 29

The movement woke Matthew with a start, and he looked sheepish. 'I'm sorry, My Lord, I don't know what came over me.'

'Too much excitement all in one day, I expect.'

'But I'm not a child. I should be able to stay awake during the day.' He grimaced.

Still holding the book, Hargreaves sat down in one of the armchairs. 'No, but you are not properly fit yet, and the body has a way of saying enough is enough. Anyway,' he changed the subject, 'have you found everything in good order?'

'Yes. It's wonderful.' He pulled the watch from his pocket and held it out. 'Look, it still goes, even after all its adventures.'

'I have more good news, Matthew. I have found the muniment room. Or rather, Parsons has shown me where it is. But there is a problem. It's locked. And so far, the key hasn't turned up. Parsons thinks it might be in a box in the silver vault, yet another room I was unaware of.'

'It's like my mind, My lord, areas of it are still locked away, but the keys are gradually coming to light. But if I may say so, it seems to me the key you want is more likely to be found in your study—or the library.'

'Why do you say that, Matthew?'

'Well, the keys to the doors are quite large. Why carry one to a place you can't use it, when it could be hidden in the house. I suggest a secret drawer in your desk, sir.'

'That's a good idea, I'll look into it later.' Hargreaves turned the pages of the book until he reached 'Kent' and found 'Staplewood Park' and laughed.

The writer didn't think much of this place. He read, *"A typical mid-century edifice, distinguished only by an impressive, rather overbearingly heavily-gilded grand staircase.*" He goes on to say, *"The house is pleasantly situated, and the park well-laid out"!'* He laid the book down. 'I hope I can find that key before I leave for London on Monday. Lord Coverdale has invited me to stay at Berkeley Square to introduce me to Viscount Uttoxeter and other like-minded peers, but,' he said ruefully, 'I have to preside over "Bread Sunday" at the church.'

'Yes, Mrs Clayborne told me about that. Well, if you run out of bread, you'll just have to give them cake.' Matthew grinned.

'Impertinent boy!' Hargreaves said as he left the room, almost colliding with Royston and George, carrying a chest of drawers.

Following Matthew's advice, concerning the missing key, Hargreaves decided to explore the desk in his study. It was of the knee-hole variety, with a cupboard on one side and a set of drawers on the other. The writing surface was accessed by a roll-top, which, when up, revealed a leather-covered surface in front of a multitude of small drawers and pigeonholes. When he had first arrived at Staplewood, the desk had been all but empty, containing only a few bills and invoices; even the inkpots had dried out. Hargreaves was continually being amazed by the lifestyle of his predecessor. He seemed to have little interest in any of the normal pursuits of a nobleman and certainly none in his estate.

He began his search for the missing muniment room key. He commenced by removing all the small drawers from the top of the desk and feeling around all sides of the empty spaces left by them. There were eight in all, and he had completed his search of six when he felt a small unevenness on the underside of the seventh. His hand trembled a little as he pressed a finger into the slight recess. Success! There was a dull click, and what appeared to be a decorated frieze below the pigeonholes, fell away, revealing a hidden recess. It was barely deep enough for Hargreaves to get his hand in, so he poked about in it with a ruler. Apart from a quantity of dust, it was empty. His disappointment was almost tangible, but there were still other areas to explore.

He tried the drawers down the side first, but they were all solid mahogany and unproductive. His last resort, in which he had little faith, was the cupboard. The door swung open, revealing a set of pull-out shelves, all empty and a single deep drawer. *With my luck*, he thought, *this has to be locked, too.* But it was not; nor was it empty. It contained a number of bound account books.

Hargreaves removed them one by one, giving a cursory glance at each. They were full columns of numbers and letters in different coloured inks, which meant nothing to him. Resigned to believing his search in the desk had been fruitless, he picked up the last volume and was about to return them all when something pale against the dark wood caught his eye. He bent over and fumbled at the back of the drawer. His fingers touched metal. He straightened up, clutching a key, attached to which was an ivory label bearing the words, 'Muniment Room.' He leant back in his chair and let out a yell. 'Yes!'

Parsons, who was about to enter the dining room with a lamp, heard the unusual sound and hurried to the study. Fearing an accident, he did not knock and was confronted by his noble master swinging round and round in his swivel chair, with a stupid grin on his face.

Without a flicker of surprise or amusement, Parsons said, 'You called out, My Lord?'

Hargreaves gave his chair one more turn, and holding the key towards his impassive butler, exclaimed, 'I found it! Mr Matthew was right! Come with me.'

Parsons followed his master through the library and along the full length of the saloon, stopping in front of the tapestry. 'Open Sesame, at last! Come on, man, let's see what's what.'

The butler did what he had done previously with the tapestry, and stood, waiting for further instructions.

'You have the key, Parsons. Open the door.'

'Just as you please, M'lord.' He inserted the key, and although it was a little stiff, it turned with a satisfactory click. But turning the handle did not have such a satisfactory result. The door was stuck. Parsons leaned against it and pushed hard, but it did not budge.

'We'll both push.'

Together they thrust their combined weight against the heavy door, which suddenly gave, propelling them, head first, into the room. Both men managed to keep their balance. But the swirl of dust-laden air, disturbed by the draught, made them both cough. ParThe butler cleared his throat as if to speak but said nothing.

Lord Hargreaves said excitedly, 'Look at this, Parsons!' He pointed to the shelves and cupboards, piles of dusty papers, pigeonholes stuffed with scrolls. 'History, at last!'

'Yes, M'lord.'

'This'll give Mr Matthew something to get his teeth into, eh, Parsons?' The last of the evening light was making poor progress through the grimy, cobwebbed windows. 'I'll need a lamp,' said Hargreaves, oblivious to his butler's agitation.

Summoning up courage, Parsons said nervously, 'My Lord, Mrs Clayborne has ordered dinner to be served in half an hour's time. Do you wish me to say you want it postponed?'

Hargreaves banished the euphoria of the discovery. 'Good heavens! No! She'd kill me,' he exclaimed and then realised this was not an appropriate thing to say to his butler. He then said, 'Of course, Parsons, all this will have to wait. Go about your duties as usual. I'll lock up. He glanced at the dust that had settled on both of them. 'We must clean up before dinner, or we'll both be in the soup!'

As soon as the meal was over, Hargreaves took his sister to see the newly discovered room. Her main concern was the appalling state of it. 'With this amount of dust and cobwebs, I doubt anyone has been in here for decades.'

'Well, the previous Lord Hargreaves went in it for some reason, or Parsons would never have known it was there.'

'No matter. What do you want to do about it?'

'I was thinking, Emily, my dear, that sorting this lot out would give Matthew some real work to do. But as you know, tomorrow is "Bread Sunday", and we are bidden to luncheon with the vicar and his wife. And I leave for London early next morning. I'm sorry, but I'll have to leave it to you and Joseph to find a way for him to manage it.'

The journey to London gave Hargreaves time to take stock of his position. It was barely eleven months since he had been catapulted into the aristocracy, having been a small-town solicitor, albeit a very successful one. Ideally, he would like to become an active member of the House of Lords, fully believing his legal background would be welcomed among lawmakers. But there was an obstacle—a big one. Staplewood Park was proving to be far more expensive than he had at first envisaged. As well as extra indoor staff, the estate and park required much remedial work. He was not inclined to leave his tenant farmers struggling to make ends meet and pay their rent for buildings unfit for use. The perimeter walls of the park were falling into disrepair, and the main lodge was on the point of collapse. His predecessor, who had held the title for eleven years, had done the barest minimum, and that mostly on the house itself. How could he justify renting a London apartment, absolutely necessary if he wished to attend Parliament regularly, when his present income barely covered his current expenses.

There hadn't been time to explore the possibilities of the mysterious strongbox, which Joseph had said was in the vault where his 'adequate' amount of silver was kept. There had been less than four hundred pounds in the late Lord's bank account—most of which had already been spent on urgent repairs.

There were other concerns, too. What was going to happen to Matthew? This was certainly not an immediate matter, as he was unlikely to be fit enough to leave Staplewood for some time yet. And Emily? Would she want to stay at Staplewood permanently? Throughout these dire imaginings, there ran a golden thread—his growing friendship with Lady B, who combined beauty with a charming personality and, at the same time, displayed practical common sense. She was, undoubtedly, a woman in a million, and the belief that she liked him, too, warmed his heart.

Despite Amanda and Justin's warm welcome, it was not long before his spirits suffered another blow. He soon realised just how different London living was from both that of a small town or, indeed, that of a country estate. It only took one or two dinner parties for him to realise that it was far beyond his meagre financial resources.

It was all settled that his induction into the House of Lords should take place when Nicky was on his half-term from Shrewsbury, so he could come and watch. And it would be an opportunity for him to meet James, the Coverdale's eldest son, as they were both going to be up at Oxford at the same time.

It wasn't until nearly the end of his stay in Berkeley Square that there was an opportunity for a quiet dinner, with only Amanda and Justin present. 'Don't be too long over your port, Justin. There are so many things I want to ask Lord Hargreaves and have not yet had the chance,' said Amanda firmly.

'My darling, we will insult my finest port by gulping it down intemperately and be with you in quite a short time, I assure you.' When the servants had left the room, he turned to Hargreaves. 'Now you can tell me what you really think of what you have seen of life in town.'

'I have barely scratched the surface, Coverdale. But I strongly suspect that, if I dig deeper, much that is regrettable will come pouring out.'

'I know that is true. But one can hope the recent Reform Acts will give government—any government—the power to improve matters. What did you think of Melbourne?'

'He is very charismatic, and I understand he has the ear of our young queen.'

Justin smiled. 'Or she has his. I'm not sure she understands the relationship a monarch should have with a prime minister, and I'm afraid she may yet learn a hard lesson, when a different party is in power. But enough of politics. You said you had something you particularly wanted to ask me, Hargreaves.'

'Yes, when I was talking to several men that you kindly introduced me to in your club, I got the impression, although nobody said anything outright, that the late Lord Hargreaves was something of a gambler. Is that right?'

'I never met him, although I occasionally saw him at the club. I do know he made a maiden speech in the Lords and never darkened its doors again. But yes, I had heard he played heavily on the tables and the horses.'

Hargreaves drew in a deep breath. 'I think that explains quite a lot. Thank you.' He didn't enlarge on the subject, and Justin didn't enquire.

'If you've finished your drink, shall we join the lady?'

Chapter 30

'**I**'m so glad you are here,' said Amanda, holding out a cup of tea. 'There's so much I want to ask you, Lord Hargreaves. Do sit down.'

Accepting the cup and the invitation to sit, he replied, 'Quite a lot has happened at Staplewood. Where would you like me to begin?'

'Tell us about Matthew. Justin has told me he has his trunk back from Bristol but not what Matthew's reaction was.'

'Of course he was delighted to get his watch back, and it was still in working order. He recognised all his surveying instruments. But most of all I think it was a box that triggered memories.'

'What sort of box?' Amanda asked eagerly.

'Well, Lady Coverdale, that's the funny thing. As soon as I saw it, I said to him how well travelled it was. It must have crossed the Atlantic Ocean at least twice, only to arrive not ten miles from where it was made.'

Justin raised his eyebrows. 'Where *was* it made?'

'In Tunbridge Wells. It is a perfect example of what is called Tunbridge ware. It is unmistakeable, decorated with all that wooden mosaic.'

'Did he say how he acquired it?'

'Yes. He said it was one of his mother's most precious possessions, which, he supposed, was why he brought it with him, although he has no recollection of packing it—or, indeed, packing the trunk at all.'

'And the book. I have our copy here. Justin, darling, it's over on the Boulle table.'

Hargreaves took the volume from his host. 'Yes, this is the one, although yours is in rather better condition than Matthew's copy.'

'Was there any inscription in it?'

'Why is that important, Justin?' inquired his wife.

'You know what Rosalie has been writing to you about. We need to know as much as possible about him.'

'Before Julia runs off with him to Gretna Green.' Amanda laughed.

Hargreaves looked a little embarrassed. 'I can assure you, Lady Coverdale—'

'I'm sorry,' Amanda said quickly. 'I know our daughter is well chaperoned. And anyway, Matthew is not in any state to run anywhere.'

'If I may get a word in edgewise,' said the marquis, 'perhaps Hargreaves might like to answer my question. Was there an inscription in the book?' he repeated.

'Nothing significant, although it had clearly belonged to someone else before Matthew's mother wrote her name, Isabella Stuart, in it and the date 1823.'

'Not much more than you've found out, Justin. You'd better tell Lord Hargreaves.'

'I discovered a William Stuart had joined the Royal Engineers. It is unfortunate that not only is Stuart a common name in Scotland, but also, back in the eighteenth century, the spelling of it seems to be exchangeable with Stewart. However, knowing his wife was called Isabella may help. I will look into it further.'

Amanda excused herself, saying she had a busy day on the morrow, leaving the two men to their brandy, and it was not long before Hargreaves followed suit. Justin sat by the dying fire, swirling his glass. The memory of an event in his childhood had been triggered by the mention of Matthew's Tunbridge ware box.

He, aged fourteen, and his eight-year-old brother, Benedict, had been taken to visit the great-aunt who lived at Mairsford. He remembered being rather bored, but cheered up when the aunt offered each of the boys a present. Justin and Benedict were invited to choose either a gold guinea or one of the aunt's Tunbridge Ware boxes, of which she had numerous examples. Immediately he had accepted the money, but Benedict had taken much longer to decide, finally choosing a box.

'Very wise,' his aunt had said. "You will have something to enjoy long after your brother has spent the guinea, and has nothing to show for it.'

How true, thought Justin, drinking up the last of his brandy, remembering the pleasure Benedict took in his great aunt's gift, and thinking how foolish he had been. I wonder what happened to that box. A startling thought shot into Justin's mind. He shook his head to rid himself of it. You're getting fanciful in your old age. He put the glass down and went to join his wife.

As Staplewood Park hove into view, Hargreaves couldn't help a momentary regret for his small convenient house in Ludlow. But this large barrack of a house was his now, for better or worse. However, the welcome from his staff and the blazing fire in the hall raised his spirits somewhat. As he was relieved of his cloak and hat, by George, and he went over to warm himself by the fire, other members of the household emerged to greet him. Emily came from the drawing room, and Matthew came accompanied by Bedford. Hargreaves bent to kiss his sister's cheek, looking over at Matthew on his crutches. 'Back on your feet again, then that must feel good.'

'Yes, sir, it does. But I'm not allowed outside yet. I think Joseph would like to put me on a lead, too!

Hargreaves laughed. 'Have you managed to make any discoveries in the muniment room?'

Emily interrupted. 'Charles, you must go and change before dinner. All our news—and yours—must wait. Now away upstairs with you. Royston has everything ready.'

During a simple but enjoyable meal, he concentrated on what Emily had to tell him. Lady B, Lady Julia, and Bethany had paid an all-day visit during the week, and the two younger ones had been fascinated by Matthew's surveying instruments. He had shown them how they were used, and from the conservatory, had instructed them how to 'survey' the formal garden.

'Young Bethany is a real smart girl,' Matthew said. 'She understood the principle right away.'

Emily smiled. 'But Lady B has issued us with an invitation, Charles, and it sounds exciting. There is to be a special concert in the Assembly Rooms in Tunbridge Wells, and she has invited us both to accompany her. She and her late husband were both patrons of the Music Society there. I do hope you will agree.'

'It should be interesting,' he said calmly, trying to ignore—and failing—the emotion he felt at the thought of being in close proximity to Lady B.

Taking that as an acceptance, Emily went on, 'It takes place in ten days' time, and we are to travel in her chaise. The concert starts at five o'clock, and we will have a light collation here before we leave.'

Hargreaves gave a wry smile. 'Since it is all arranged, I don't have much choice, do I, sister dear?'

'None at all. But it will make a nice change. 'Now,' she changed the subject, 'would you and Matthew like to take your port in the library, so he can show you what progress he has made with the documents from the muniment room?' She rose from the table, and Parsons opened the door for them all to leave.

'I will bring the decanter and glasses to the library directly, M'lord.'

Matthew carefully seated himself at the table and footstool that had been arranged for him. 'If you draw that chair up here, My Lord,' he indicated to his right, 'you will be able to see what progress I have made so far.' With Hargreaves beside him, he went on to describe the system he had devised for examining the scrolls and documents. 'The pile of papers in front of you summarise the contents of each file, one page per pigeonhole, and are numbered accordingly, so you should be able to lay your hands on any particular item of interest in the future.'

'That sounds excellent, Matthew. But have you found anything that might relate to the underground chamber?'

'Not as such, but I believe there was definitely a house here before Staplewood Park was built. The original deed of sale to the first Lord Hargreaves included property described as a dwelling. But as yet, I have found no evidence as to its whereabouts.'

'That's a pity. But I must say the middle of a wood were Nicky found the chimney doesn't seem promising.'

'I believe the drawers beneath the pigeonholes may hold the answer, but I did not want to explore them without your permission, sir.'

'You have my permission to do anything you want.' Hargreaves smiled, pushing back his chair. 'But not tonight. Parsons has brought the decanter and glasses. Let's take them to my study, and drink to future discoveries.'

The following day, Hargreaves certainly made a discovery, but not the one he was hoping for. He had called for Parsons after breakfast. 'It is time I made my acquaintance with my wine cellar and the so-called silver vault. Would you conduct me there?'

'Certainly, M'lord, if you will just follow me.' They entered the butler's pantry, Parson's private domain. 'You will see'—he waved a hand at shelves loaded with china, and at further shelves containing glassware—'that we are plentifully supplied with dinner services, all, if I may say so, of the finest quality. Here is the cutlery, M'lord.' He pulled out several baize-lined drawers.

To Hargreaves eye, there seemed to be an inordinate quantity of it. 'Is this what you call adequate, Parsons?'

'It is, sir, for anything but a banquet, and it is almost all that is left. Would you care to see the silver vault now, M'lord?'

'Of course. It is what I came for, and the strongbox that was put there after my predecessor died.'

Parsons went to the centre of the room and lifted a ring set into the floor, revealing an irregular-shaped brass-rimmed hole. He took from his pocket a similarly shaped key and lifted a trapdoor. 'We shall need a lamp, M'lord. Will you excuse me while I fetch one?'

While he was away, Hargreaves peered into the hole. A little light from the pantry window showed him a set of narrow steps, but not much else. Parsons returned with a lighted oil-lamp.

'If you permit, sir, I will descend first. Please be careful, the steps are steep.'

The first thing Hargreaves noticed was a table, on which stood a brass-bound box. It measured about eighteen inches by twelve and was about twelve inches deep. He hoped it was full of gold. The rest of the vault was fitted with slotted shelves lined with baize. Every one of them was empty. As before, Parsons pulled open cupboards and drawers, all of which proved to be similarly bereft. Only the bottom deepest drawers, held anything, some candlesticks and entrée dish covers.

Even in this dim light, Hargreaves could make out Parson's expression, as he said, 'Plated, M'lord. There is one more thing.' Parsons pointed to a mahogany cabinet on the floor. 'If I take the strongbox up to the pantry, I can put that on the table.'

'Very good, Parsons. I hope it contains something valuable.' The butler said nothing, picking up the strongbox and ascending the steps. When he returned, he placed the cabinet on the table. And by the light of the lamp, Hargreaves could see it had a fall front and that the key was in the lock.

'With your permission, M'lord?'

'Go ahead.'

Parsons opened the cabinet halfway and peered in. 'It is as I had feared, Your Lordship.' He opened the container the whole way to reveal a velvet-lined triangular space, each side measuring about three feet.

'What did it contain?' said Hargreaves in hollow tones.

'A ship, M'lord, a magnificent silver galleon in full sail. I believe it dated from the late seventeenth century—'

'This all too depressing, Parsons. Let's get out of here.' He turned and mounted the stairs.

'Do you wish to examine the wine cellar, sir?'

'Another time. For now, just bring the strongbox to my study.'

'Very good, M'lord.'

As they left the pantry, Hargreaves said, 'What is your opinion concerning the absence of the silver?'

'It is my belief that the Late Lord Hargreaves extracted some silver every time he visited the residence. Every shelf and drawer was full when I was first employed here.'

Hargreaves heaved a sigh, as Parsons placed the strongbox on the desk. 'Well, it was his silver to do what he liked with, but I wish I had seen that ship.'

'Yes, indeed, it was very fine. Will that be all, M'lord?'

'Yes, thank you, Parsons. You have been very helpful.'

Hargreaves was left alone in his study, contemplating the brass-bound box. From the ease with which his butler had carried it, he was certain it did not contain gold. But perhaps the fourth lord had kept his winnings in it, and it was bursting with ten- or even hundred-pound notes. He felt underneath, where Joseph said he had taped the key, and found it easily and stood with it in his hand, staring at the box.

Well, he thought, *here goes.*

The key was a little stiff to turn, and the box resisted his attempts to lift the lid. But it gave eventually.

165

At that moment, the sun went behind a cloud, and the room darkened. When his eyes adjusted, Hargreaves could see there was something in the box, glinting in the black interior. He put his hand in and drew out a piece of paper, a five-pound note. His second dip produced three gold sovereigns. Hargreaves mentally added this to the 368 pounds, 7 shillings and 11 pence, which was all that was left in the third Lord Hargreaves's bank account, after all expenses had been paid. *A rich inheritance indeed*, he thought sourly, as he went through to the library to see if Matthew had better news.

Chapter 31

'**A**nything about the chimney?', asked Hargreaves hopefully.
'Not today,' replied Matthew. 'More deeds, sir. It seems the
first Lord Hargreaves was keen on enlarging the estate. I have
made a note of them. They are in that bucket. George is bringing the last
of row "A", and will collect those ones to replace them.'

'Is it very boring for you, Matthew?'

'Not at all. And I have something I'm sure *will* interest you. I have
kept them back, as you may want to keep them in your study.' Matthew
pointed to a long, narrow box at the far side of the table. 'Be careful how
you open it, sir. There is a seal that might fall out.'

Hargreaves opened the box and carefully took out several scrolls,
unrolling the first, which had, as Matthew said, a seal, precariously
attached. He spread it out and read, *'"I, George the Second, by the Grace
of God, King ..."* These are the letters patent creating Henry Charles
Hargreaves, Baron Staplewood. It's very fancy and signed, I see, by the
king himself.' He raised his eyebrows and unrolled the second scroll. It
was even more highly decorated and depicted the Hargreaves coat of arms.
There was also some correspondence from the College of Arms, concerning
the addition of a baron's coronet to the helm.

'Yes, thank you. Matthew, I will put these in my study.'

Over the next few days, Matthew made more discoveries, including
maps of the estate and surrounding countryside, one of which showed that
the original house had been built on the same site as the present one, but
much smaller. The only part remaining was the basement area.

George was kept busy, to-ing and fro-ing with the paperwork and
ledgers and one day ventured a comment. 'This book, sir'—he held out a
small cloth-bound volume—'was concealed. I pulled out another book,

and I'm afraid I stumbled coming down the ladder, and this book fell out. All the pages of the bigger book had been cut out, like. I thought I'd better tell you, in case there was any damage, sir.'

'I'm sure there is nothing to worry about, George. Which book did it fall out of?' Matthew said, taking hold of the volume.

'That on the bottom of the pile, sir.'

'Thank you, George. I have enough to be going on with for the rest of the day. I'm sure Parsons will be glad I have released you.'

'Very good, sir, but ring if you want anything else.' George bowed himself out.

Matthew opened the small volume immediately he had gone. It was certainly a ledger of sorts. The writing was small and neat, and the front page had a single word on it, 'Benares', and the date 1750. There was a column of figures down the right-hand side of every page, some in red. On the left, there were letters, sometimes a single one, sometimes as many as three. Matthew reckoned there were about twenty pages filled in this way; the rest of the book was unused. Hargreaves was out all day, so he wasn't able to show it to him until after dinner.

Both men were excited by the find, and Hargreaves brought out the book he had found in his desk drawer. But there were no similarities between the two. On examination, it was clear from the dates on the one he had found and Matthew's one that they were written nearly eighty years apart. 'I am fairly sure now, Matthew, that my predecessor was a heavy gambler, and my recent descent into the so-called silver vault, seems to confirm it. I believe he was systematically raiding this house of everything of value.'

'But surely that's stealing, sir?'

'No. He had a perfect right to do so. Only the house and estate is entailed upon the male heir, not the contents—which is just my bad luck. But there is still one question to be answered.'

'And that is?'

'Where did the supposed fortune go? According to my sister, who always kept an eye on the inheritance, it was immense.'

'I may be able to help with that,' said Matthew, laying his hand on the pile of ledgers he had yet to examine. 'I have had a quick look in these, and they are all meticulous records of everything that was spent on the building and equipping of this house. I should soon be able to give an idea of what the first Lord Hargreaves spent, but it will take a little time, I'm afraid.'

'Take as much time as you need, I have plenty of other matters to attend to, not least this concert in Tunbridge Wells, that Lady B is taking me and Emily to. The very thought makes me nervous. I am such a newcomer to society.'

Matthew laughed. 'I'm sure you will do very well, sir.'

On the afternoon of the concert, an event took place that increased Hargreaves's apprehension a hundredfold. Emily took to her bed, declaring that weak tea, advised by Joseph; Bath Oliver biscuits, by which she swore; and twenty-four hours in bed was the only possible cure for her unspecified condition. Hargreaves was on the horns of a dilemma. To go meant leaving Emily. And what if she took a turn for the worse? Not to go meant letting Lady B down, leaving her to go on her own. The second option troubled him the most. The decision was made when a note from his sister, delivered by Emily's maid and written in what he considered to be a suspiciously steady hand for one so stricken, apologising to Lady B foer absence.

Rosalie's light chaise, with two horses, arrived at Staplewood at two thirty, giving, as she explained, plenty of time to enjoy drinks and light refreshments in the patron's room and the opportunity to introduce the new Lord Hargreaves to local society. Lady B didn't seem the least put out when Hargreaves explained that his sister would be unable to join them. After sending her best wishes for a speedy recovery, via Parsons, Rosalie turned to Hargreaves with an impish smile. 'Now we'll be able to have a nice cosy chat together on our journey.'

Hargreaves was still concerned. 'You don't think it is improper for us to travel without a chaperone?'

'Fiddlesticks! My Lord. We are an elderly widowed couple. Why would we possibly need a chaperone?' Rosalie said with a chuckle.

The chaise was comfortably upholstered in dark red velvet and superbly sprung. The distance was not long, and there was no need to travel at speed. There ensued a discussion on the best way for Hargreaves to instigate a plan close to his heart, a way of enabling those adults. Living in the village, who wished to, to have the opportunity to learn to read and write. Rosalie had some very good ideas, which he considered putting into practice as soon as possible. Then the conversation turned to family.

'You must be very proud of your son, Lord Hargreaves. He is such a nice boy.'

Hargreaves smiled. 'I'm so glad you think so, Lady B. I know he can be rather headstrong at times, and he has been responsible—at least in part—for several commotions in your family.'

'But that is just it; he faces up to his responsibilities. I always admired the way he told you at once about what happened to Matthew. I know a lot of boys that age would have just kept quiet. But instead, you both did your best to find the injured man.'

'And if he hadn't found that chimney, Lady Julia wouldn't have had a very muddy fall—'

'That,' said Lady B firmly, 'was entirely her own fault. But she was really upset that it ended in more damage to Matthew's foot. How is he now?'

'Much better and well occupied with sorting out the Hargreaves's archives, which I finally managed to locate.' He went on to tell her about the discovery of the muniment room.

'Has he found out anything about the hole Julia fell into?'

'Not yet, but he may well do so in time.'

'I think Matthew is a fine young man, too, although a little lost at the moment. It must be very distressing to lose your memory.'

'The arrival of his belongings from Bristol has given his recollections a boost but not, unfortunately any recent ones.'

Rosalie looked out of the carriage window and didn't face Hargreaves, as she said, 'Benedict would have liked a son like him. We had one, you know, but he only lived a few hours.'

'That's tragic, Lady B.' Hargreaves wanted to comfort her with a touch but felt he could not. 'I'm so sorry. You must both have been devastated.'

'We were. But we still had each other and the music we loved, and then Bethany came along.' She turned back to look at Hargreaves. 'She was such an unexpected joy.'

The chaise pulled up outside the Assembly Rooms, and a lackey helped them out. It gave Hargreaves an opportunity to admire Rosalie's apple-green, silk gown and silver-buckled, satin slippers, beneath a fur-trimmed travelling cloak. Divested of their outer garments, they mounted the stairs and entered a well-lit room, filled with the chatter and colour of animated guests wearing evening dress. The moment Rosalie was spotted, she was surrounded by people of both sexes, eager to welcome her back and to look with barely disguised curiosity at the man standing beside her.

She smiled and murmured politely but turned to Hargreaves, who was looking a little overwhelmed. 'Don't worry, My Lord,' she said in a low voice. 'They won't eat you.' Loudly she announced, 'I want to introduce you to my new neighbour. I know he will be a great asset to our Music Society. Please welcome Lord Hargreaves of Staplewood.'

A woman in purple satin and an elaborate old-fashioned turban, pushed forward, offering her hand and dropping a curtsey. 'Oh, Lord Hargreaves, I am so pleased you've come. I know Staplewood so well. We used to dine there often, not recently, of course. But when Lord Patrick was alive— Such a shame he didn't have a son, just the two daughters. But then of course you wouldn't be here, would you?'

'No, madam, I would not,' replied Hargreaves, rather wishing he wasn't.

'My name is Mrs Thompson. That's my husband over there, talking to the high sheriff. He's a high court judge, my husband, that is, a law lord, but I'm not allowed to call myself a lady. I do think that it's all wrong, don't you, Lord Hargreaves?'

'Indeed so, Madam.' Hargreaves looked over her shoulder for help, but Lady B was fully occupied.

'Well. As I was saying, Patrick Hargreaves gave wonderful dinners. And the table—all that silver and, of course, the ship sailing down the table on a glittering sea. The candlelight almost made the little figures on deck and on the rigging come alive.'

There seemed to be no stopping Mrs Thompson, but she had said something that interested him, and when he could get a word in edgeways, he said, 'Mrs Thompson, you mentioned the third Lord Hargreaves's daughters. They would be distant cousins of mine. Do you happen to know where they are?'

'Oh, yes. The youngest is married now, of course. Lady Jeffries, wife of Sir Gerald. He's a baronet, you know, lives in Sussex. And poor dear Harriet lives in a village—'

Hargreaves was never destined to know why Harriet was described as a 'poor dear', as Rosalie finally came to his rescue to introduce him to the chairman of the Musical Society. The concert was better than he had expected, a fine well-disciplined chamber orchestra, which played within their capabilities. The opening and closing performances were by the famous Amonetti Quartet, with whom Lady B had played in the past. Refreshments were served during the interval, and Hargreaves and Lady B were back in the chaise by half past nine. It was a bright moonlit night but bitterly cold. They sat opposite each other, but the fur rug was not large enough to provide warmth for them both.

'You must sit beside me, Lord Hargreaves,' said Rosalie, so we can share the rug. I'll never forgive myself if you were to catch your death because my staff didn't provide for you.'

'But it wouldn't be proper—'

'Oh, fiddlesticks! My Lord.' exclaimed Rosalie, using her favourite expression, 'keeping warm takes precedence over propriety every time.' She pulled back one side of the rug. 'Come on.'

Hargreaves took her at her word and changed his seat. The mutual warmth and the diversion of the evening lulled Rosalie into a doze, and Hargreaves found himself supporting her head on his shoulder—a situation he was happy to endure.

This idyll was torn apart by a loud cracking sound. The carriage tipped sideways at a precarious angle, throwing its occupants onto the side of the coach, accompanied by the sound of terrified, squealing horses.

Chapter 32

Hargreaves put his arms round Rosalie, whose frightened blue eyes looked up into his, but she didn't scream. 'Oh! What's happened?'

'Lady B, are you hurt?' He felt her wriggle.

'No, I don't think so. Are you all right? What has happened?' She repeated anxiously, 'The horses—?'

'Yes, Lady B, I'm fine.' Hargreaves reassured her. 'I think we've lost a wheel.' They could both hear the groom trying to calm and control the frightened animals. Rosalie tried to sit upright again. 'I think it would be best if we stayed quite still for the moment. Any movement might make things worse, until your groom has assessed the damage.'

Rosalie had no argument with this. Surprisingly, she was quite enjoying being in the arms of a man, despite the discomfort of the carriage door handle pressing on her thigh. Hargreaves, with one arm braced against the side of the chaise, so Lady B would not be crushed by his weight, nevertheless managed to pull down the window and peer out into the darkness. Almost immediately, the coachman appeared at the aperture. 'What has happened? Are we in a ditch?'

'No, M'lord, M'lady, the wheel has broke. We can go no further.'

'Are the horses all right?'

'Yes, M'lord. No hurt taken. The young 'un took fright an' tried to run off, but I got 'un under control now.'

'Good man. Now we will have to get out of here. Lady Benedict, I will go first, and then we can help you down.' He turned to the groom. 'Is the carriage secure from falling further?'

'Yes, M'lord. I think so. It ain't right down on the axle. If you will, please, to open the door.'

Hargreaves turned the inner handle and pushed gently, but it didn't move. A second harder push had the desired effect, and the door creaked open. Very cautiously, he eased himself forward on the tip-tilted seat and away from Lady B. Due to the angle of the coach, it was impossible to lower the steps, so he felt around with his foot till he found solid ground and got out of the vehicle.

'Have a care, your Lordship. We'em precious close to the ditch.'

By the light of the moon high in the sky, Hargreaves could see that only a thin strip of grass verge separated the coach from a ditch, and a high hedge. Once he had both feet on the ground, he turned to Rosalie. 'It's going to be difficult. There's not much room down here.'

'My Lord, if I may be so bold,' the groom suggested shyly, 'if you can lift My Lady out of the carriage, together we can see that she doesn't fall into the ditch.'

'An excellent suggestion. What is your name?'

'Beddoes, M'lord.'

'Well, Beddoes, stand by.' Hargreaves reached into the chaise. 'Lady B, if you could edge forward carefully, I will lift you down.'

'I do not require lifting, Lord Hargreaves. I can see that the distance to the ground is not far, but if you will give me the benefit of your arm, I will manage quite well.'

And so it proved, and soon all three were standing in the road in front of the horses, to which Rosalie immediately went. 'They seem unscathed, Beddoes, but I think the young one is still a bit scared. They should be rugged up while we consider what to do next.'

Hargreaves felt himself also at a loss. As the man, he felt he ought to take charge. But he was Lady B's guest, the carriage and horses were hers, and Beddoes was *her* servant.

Almost as if she understood his dilemma, Rosalie turned to him. 'What do you suggest we do now?'

'One thing I think is certain. There is no chance of getting the wheel fixed tonight—'

'But our people. They will be so worried,' said Rosalie anxiously, pulling her cloak tighter.

'There are several possibilities. The first one is we walk; you can ride the horse with the saddle. But Beddoes told me when you were looking at the horses there are still nearly nine miles to go. The second option is for us to stay here, while Beddoes goes to Staplewood to report what has occurred. But I'm not at all sure the coach is safe to sit in, apart from being very cold and uncomfortable.'

'I do not care much for either of those suggestions.'

'No, neither do I, Lady B. So I have a third one.' He turned to his left and pointed. 'Do you see a light, about two or three hundred yards away? You can just make out the outline of a cottage or farm.'

Rosalie followed the direction his arm was pointing. 'Yes, yes, I see it. They might let us stay there.'

'Let us hope they have a good fire we can sit beside.'

'But what about Beddoes?'

'He can take one of the horses and ride to Staplewood and give them the news and then on to Mairsford, so no one will be worried.'

'That is an excellent plan, Lord Hargreaves. But what about the other horse?'

'You will ride it, and I will lead it. I couldn't help noticing your charming satin slippers as you dismounted from the chaise at the Assembly Rooms. But they are hardly suitable for even a short walk on grass, let alone several hundred yards on a stony farm track.'

Beddoes quickly set to unharnessing the horses and checking them over by the light of one of the carriage lamps, held by his lordship. Not long after, the two parties set off for their different destinations.

With Rosalie perched sideways on the saddle and Hargreaves leading the horse and still carrying the lantern, they soon arrived at a garden gate. He tied the horse to the gatepost and lifted Rosalie down. As they walked the short distance to the front door, and even by the light of the moon, they could see that the flower beds on either side were well tended and the house larger than they had first thought. Hargreaves gave the knocker a sharp rap.

It was not long before the door opened less than halfway, and a bewhiskered man, holding aloft a lighted chamberstick, grunted, 'Yes?'

Before Hargreaves could utter a word, Rosalie pushed forward. 'Oh, sir!' she said in a pathetic but appealing voice. 'We have had a carriage accident, and wondered if you could be so terribly kind and let us sit in your cottage until a repair can be effected?'

The man looked them both up and down but said nothing, merely opening the door a little further. Another face appeared, topped by a mob cap and grey ringlets—and wearing a frown. 'Nate,' she abjured, 'what are you thinking? Let these poor people in at once before they catch their death of cold.'

The door was opened wide, and the two were led into a cosy and well-appointed kitchen. 'Sit ye down by the range and warm yourselves.'

'Oh, thank you, thank you so much. We were on our way home from the Wells, and a wheel came off our carriage. No one was hurt, I'm glad to say. But it was very frightening. I nearly swooned.'

Hargreaves was shocked into silence. The competent fearless Lady B was transforming before his very eyes into a delicate hothouse flower, but her revelations had not yet ended.

She was seated by the range and looked up at the farmer's wife.

'Our name is Clayborne.' Rosalie turned to Hargreaves. 'He was so brave when the carriage nearly tipped over, and now he's managed to bring me to your lovely cottage on one of the horses.'

'Gotta 'orse, 'av ee?' growled the man.

Hargreaves found his voice. 'Yes, I tied him up to your gatepost.'

'Nate will see to it,' the woman said firmly. 'We've a spare stable.'

Hargreaves rose to help the farmer. 'Nay, nay, sir. Sit ye down, and warm you 'sen.' The improvement in the man's tone followed his wife's acceptance of the couple's story.

Meanwhile, the farmer's wife, who said their name was Worthy and explained that it was not a farm they owned, but a market garden, one of many in that area that supplied London with fruit, flowers and vegetables, on a daily basis. As she was speaking, she put some cider in a muller, and thrust the "toe" of the boot-shaped vessel between the bars of the kitchen range, and in no time. Hargreaves and Lady B were being warmed by the deliciously flavoured brew.

As soon as Mr Worthy returned, announcing that the horse was well-founded, his wife unhooked a copper warming pan from beside the range and put a shovelful of hot coals into it. 'The bed will not be damp,' she said. 'But there's nothing like warm sheets on a cold night.'

'But—' exclaimed Hargreaves in a startled tone.

But before he could get another word out, Rosalie silenced him with a look.

'Oh, Mrs Worthy, that is so kind, and I do so agree with you. There's nothing like a warm bed on a cold night. And you think so too, Charles, don't you?'

'Er … yes,' he mumbled, staggered at the unimaginable prospect opening up before him.

'Perhaps I could come with you, Mrs Worthy. I do feel a little tired— the accident, and all that, you know.'

'Of course, madam.' If you would be so kind as to take that chamber stick and go up first, and I will bring the warming pan.' Of the three doors on the landing at the top of the stairs, Mrs Worthy indicated the one on the left. 'That one in the middle is the girl's room. She's already abed.'

Rosalie immediately opened the door indicated.

'Thankee, Mrs Clayborne.'

She went over to the large brass bedstead and thrust the copper pan between the sheets. 'I hope you and your husband will be comfortable here. 'Tis the room my daughter and her husband use when they come home. He works at the Royal Docks at Chatham.'

'I'm sure it will be perfect, Mrs Worthy.' She glanced at the washstand with a bowl and jug. 'But I do feel a little grubby. Would it be possible for me to have a wash?'

'I'll fetch a jug of hot water at once, mistress.'

When she returned with a large brass can, she placed it on the washstand and lit two more candles. Immediately, the pleasant scent of beeswax assailed Rosalie's nose.

'Do you keep bees, Mrs Worthy?'

'Aye, we do. The honey is very useful, and I insist on wax candles. Although Worthy says it's a 'stravagance,' she smiled.

'Before you go, Mrs Worthy, would you mind undoing the buttons on the back of my gown? I'm afraid my maid has to do it at home. Such a nuisance not to be able to take one's own clothes off.'

The older woman did as she was bid, and then asked if help was required with Rosalie's stays.

'If you would just loosen them a bit, that is all that is necessary, thank you.'

Rosalie had no intention of undressing one garment further. It was embarrassing enough having to share a room with Lord Hargreaves, let alone a bed. But there was no help for it now. She was regretting having announced that they were man and wife, but a tiny corner of her mind seemed to disagree. She removed her dress, stockings, and two of her three petticoats, and washed her face and hands, leaving the stays and the chemise over which they were laced.

The bed had a magnificent patchwork quilt, several blankets, and fine linen sheets smelling of lavender, which surprised Rosalie as she struggled to put the bolster down the centre on the bed. The Worthy's standard of living was quite a surprise. She blew the wax candles out, leaving only the chamber stick, which she placed on the farther nightstand and got into the warmed bed, immediately getting out again. There was no way she would get a wink of sleep wearing stays—loosened or not. After wriggling out of them, she fell asleep almost immediately.

When she woke up, it was still dark, but dawn was approaching. For a brief moment, she wondered where she was, and then was shocked into remembrance. The bolster, so carefully placed the night before, had somehow slipped down the bed, and she realised she was nestling into Hargreaves shirt-covered back, one arm halfway across his gently rising and falling chest. With the greatest care, so as not to disturb him, she slid out of the bed, and, leaning over, gently pulled the bolster back to its original position. She gathered up her clothes and left the room, hoping to find somewhere to dress in private.

The door to the small room at the top of the stairs was open, and the room was empty. In no time, she was dressed, with all but the buttons on her gown to do up. Mrs Worthy obliged.

Chapter 33

By ten o'clock, Lord Hargreaves and Lady B were on their way home, a new wheel fitted and no further damage to the chaise. They sat in opposite corners of the vehicle, both deep in thought, and neither inclined to talk. Rosalie was not in the least bothered by the fact that she had spent the night in the same bed with a man she was not all that well acquainted with, and then realised that she liked Lord Hargreaves very much. He was pleasing to the eye, intelligent, conscientious, and had a wry sense of humour. She knew Benedict would always be the great love of her life. But life had moved on, and she had not moved with it—until now. She looked across at him and observed the worried frown that creased his forehead. It was obvious his thoughts were not so pleasurable.

Charles Hargreaves's thoughts were, indeed, far less pleasurable. In fact, they were thoroughly confused. He and Mr Worthy had sat in the kitchen long into the night. At first, the conversation had centred on the methods employed to be a successful market gardener. But it seemed to him now that the cider was considerably stronger than he'd thought. He remembered going up to the bedroom and seeing, by the light of the flickering candle, a mass of golden curls splayed out on the pillow, but little else, until he had woken up in the same bed, dressed only in his shirt and under drawers, with a throbbing head, and a mouth like the bottom of his sister's parrot's cage. He was alone. But somewhere in his confused mind, he thought he had sensed the feel of a warm body close to his, and the weight of an arm across his chest. Or had it just been a dream? And anyway, what right had he to dream about warm bodies, especially that of the lovely Rosalie. The frown deepened. But when he looked up, Rosalie was smiling broadly.

When the delayed coach finally reached its first destination, Lord Hargreaves took punctilious leave of his hostess—not to say bedfellow— and vowed to put the whole episode behind him, although this proved rather difficult under the penetrating interrogation by his sister. She was clearly dissatisfied by the way he brushed off her questions about sleeping arrangements. He took the earliest opportunity to visit Matthew in the library, where he found that gentleman busy at work.

'Any new discoveries, Matthew?'

'I'm not sure, sir. But I think it would be interesting to discover exactly what kind of bricks were used to construct the underground chamber.'

'How so?'

'Well, sir, the original house was built sometime in the 1580s. There are documents that suggest this. And this house was finished in 1756, again according to the documents. Therefore, it would be reasonable to suppose bricks from the old house were reused to construct the chamber.'

'But could it not have been built at the same time as the older house?' Hargreaves interrupted.

'Possibly, My Lord, but it can be tested.'

'How?'

'By measuring the bricks and analysing the mortar.'

Hargreaves sighed. 'That's something for the future then. Anything else?'

'So far I've only been looking at the specifications for this house. They are very detailed and meticulously priced for every aspect of the build. And then there's the strange thing.' Matthew selected a rolled-up chart and spread it out on the table. 'This is the plan for the foundations, sir.'

'I can see it's a plan, but I'm no architect. What's so strange about it?'

'In itself, nothing, sir. But *this* house was never built. Matthew placed a finger on the centre of the plan.

'But I'm living in it. And so are you,' Hargreaves added. 'And what's more'—he moved his finger to the elaborately decorated name written on the chart—'it says Staplewood Park.'

Matthew smiled. 'But if you look again, sir, you will see that you are the owner of half—well, just over half the house this plan depicts. It was clearly intended to be almost twice the size.'

'I wonder why? I suppose he must have run out of money, and that is strange. My sister, who always kept an eye on the Hargreaves family, said the first lord was reputed to be as rich as Croesus.'

Matthew shrugged. 'These things can sometimes be exaggerated and grow bigger and bigger every time they're told. But I'll go on looking to see if I can find the reason.'

'Don't wear yourself out. I never intended you to become a slave to it'—Lord Hargreaves grinned—'especially as Mrs Clayborne and I will soon be going to London for my induction into the House of Lords and the State Opening of Parliament by the new Queen.'

With Hargreaves and his sister gone, together with her maid and Royston, the house felt very strange. But all that was about to change. Before she left Staplewood for London, Emily had begged Lady B to visit while they were gone. She did not like leaving Matthew without any entertainment, as he was still confined to the house. Two days later, a party of four ladies, Rosalie had brought her companion, Mrs Sylvia, as well as Julia and Bethany, arrived at Staplewood in time for luncheon. Matthew was surprised and pleased.

During the meal, Rosalie noticed that Matthew remained largely silent, and this was not in character. He usually had relevant and humorous comments to make. After the meal, Julia and Bethany wanted to show Mrs Sylvia the delights of Staplewood while the weather was fine. So Rosalie went in search of Matthew.

'I believe you will find Mr Matthew in the library, My Lady,' Joseph informed her.

She found him poring over several large and meticulously drawn images of the grand staircase. He looked up and smiled.

'You look very busy, Matthew. Lord Hargreaves keeping your nose to the grindstone?' she joked.

But Matthew frowned. 'No, indeed not, Lady B. But doing this work is, in some way, a small repayment for all his kindness. You see—'

Rosalie did at once see. She realised Matthew was downhearted and understood the reason. She drew up a chair beside him and put a hand on his arm. 'You really mustn't worry,' she said reassuringly. Her tone of voice must have alerted Bedford, who left his place in front of the fire and padded over to the table but, unaware of the new position of the chair, bumped into it. Unhurt but puzzled, he sat down to think things over.

'Matthew put a hand down to reassure him. 'I'm afraid, Lady B, that his eyesight is deteriorating. Mrs Clayborne was told by the kennelman she consulted, that it might be so.'

'That's a shame, but I'm sure he is happy, with you to look after him. And you are a great help to Lord Hargreaves, too, and I don't just mean all this.' She gestured to the piles of paper on the table.

'I don't know what you mean, Lady B.'

'No, I don't suppose you do, Matthew. But have you ever considered what a difficult transition it must be from small-town solicitor to a peer of the realm and the ownership of a large estate? I know he often feels like a fish out of water, and having another fish, so to speak, to keep him company is a great help.'

'I never thought of that. But now you say it, I can understand it might be true. But Lord Hargreaves is now swimming in a bigger pool, and I can't stay in this one forever.' Matthew continued the analogy.

Rosalie stared out of the window, marshalling her thoughts, and then said. 'I owe you a great debt of gratitude, too, you know.'

Matthew raised his eyebrows at this unexpected statement.

But before he could query it, Rosalie continued. 'Yes. Before your dramatic arrival on my drive, I was merely existing. I think I had forgotten how to live, and if I had wanted to do something about it, I had no idea how to—until you came. I would never have made such good friends as I have with Lord Hargreaves and his sister. I would never have played the harp again, although I can't explain to you how significant that is. I know none of this has been a conscious effort on your part. Nevertheless, it is all due to your presence. Sometimes just being is more important than doing.'

'That is a very philosophical approach to life, Lady B, and one which I am in an ideal position to appreciate. But I still can't help worrying about the future.'

'Well, my dear, you are young and will soon be returned to full health. I am sure, with your ambitions and ingenuity, anything is possible. Now, can you show me what you are working on? Or is it all a deep secret?' she queried with an amused expression.

'There can be nothing secret about these drawings, Lady B. You have seen the grand staircase, and,'he pushed the folio towards her—'as you can see, these drawings show not only every detail, but also every measurement.

The firm commissioned to do them has also submitted a complete costing. And in somewhat flowery language, begs to inform hislLordship—we are talking here of the first Lord Hargreaves.' Matthew explained—'of their best attention to every aspect of the work.'

'The staircase certainly bears out the quality of their craftsmanship, doesn't it?' Rosalie commented.

'But that's what is so puzzling.'

'What is?'

'There is no evidence they ever carried out the work! Everything else the firm did in the way of furnishing and decoration is fully accounted for—invoices, receipts, everything, but nothing for the staircase.'

'But it's there, nevertheless.'

Further speculation was interrupted by the return of the walking party and Bethany bouncing in. 'Oh, Matthew, can you show Mrs Sylvia the surveying instruments? I've been telling her all about what you told me and Cousin Julia. So I want to show her what I've learnt'. The words all came out in a rush, until she caught her mother's eye.

Barely suppressing a smile, Rosalie said, 'Manners, Bethany!'

'Sorry, Mama.' Bethany dropped a curtsy and began again. 'Please, Matthew, may I show Mrs Sylvia the surveying instruments?'

Matthew reached for his crutches. 'Of course you may, Beth. Lead the way.'

'You shouldn't let her disturb your work, you know, Matthew,' Rosalie remonstrated.

He smiled. 'It'll still be there when I get back. And anyway, Joseph gets cross with me if I sit for too long.'

Back in Matthew's living quarters, Lady Julia and Mrs Sylvia were waiting. 'Go ahead, Ju- Lady Julia,' he corrected himself, colouring slightly. 'You know where the surveying material is.'

Julia went straight over to the window beneath which Matthew's trunk was situated and lifted the lid, taking out the theodolite and handing it to its owner. 'If you can lift the tray out, there are some books on architecture and surveying at the bottom.'

Bethany immediately went over to help and leant into the trunk to retrieve the books. But she was not tall enough to reach, so Julia joined her. She was able at once, to reach the books and handed them to Bethany but remained bent over the trunk. 'That's funny,' she said, her voice muffled. 'Come and look, Matthew. There's a hole in the bottom. I wonder …'

Matthew hopped towards the trunk and bent over beside Julia, their two heads close.

'There,' said Julia, 'just where my finger is.'

'It must just be a tear in the fabric, isn't it?'

'I don't think so. Can you see it's perfectly round?'

But whatever it was was instantly superseded by Bethany announcing, 'Mama, did that man on the horse call on you?'

'What man, darling?'

'The one we met on the road.'

Rosalie turned to her companion. 'Sylvia, is this true?'

'Oh, yes, Lady B. Oh, yes, indeed. He asked the way to Staplewood Park. No, more accurately, he asked if he was on the right road to Staplewood Park.'

'What was he like?'

'He had a nice horse, a blood-chestnut with a Roman nose—the sort of mount who'd carry you for miles but wouldn't win any races,' said Julia.

'I didn't ask about his horse, Julia, my dear,' Rosalie said a little sharply.

'Sorry, Aunt. You'd better ask Mrs Sylvia.'

Well, Sylvia?'

'I couldn't tell much,' the governess replied. 'He was polite, wished us good day, doffed his hat, that sort of thing. He seemed well dressed, polished boots, tan gloves. I believe his riding coat was green.' She thought for a moment. 'Oh, yes, he asked if we were on Staplewood land. And before I could reply, Bethany said, "Yes, it's huge." I remonstrated with her for speaking before she was spoken to.'

'Then what happened?' Rosalie asked, frowning.

'He wished us good day and cantered off.'

During this time, Matthew had closed the lid of the trunk and was leaning against it, his bad foot resting on the other one. Fortuitously, at that moment, Parsons arrived to say that tea was ready in the blue drawing room, and Rosalie was able to ask him if any gentleman had arrived at the park that afternoon.

'No, M'lady. No one has called today. Had any one done so I would have informed your ladyship immediately.'

'Of course, you would, Parsons.' She sensed ruffled feelings. 'It is just that someone asked the way here when the party were out walking. Come on, people. Tea awaits.'

Julia fetched Matthew's crutches for him—a gesture not lost on Rosalie—before they all left the room, not forgetting to allow Bedford to follow them.

The Mairsford party left after an early dinner. But before that, much amusement was had with cards and lottery games. And no more was said about the hole Julia had thought she'd found on the floor of Matthew's trunk. But he had not forgotten, and when Joseph was massaging his feet with oil, as he did twice a day to keep the healing skin supple, he brought the subject up again, explaining what Lady Julia had said.

'Would you like me to have a look, sir? The lamp there is still lit.'

'The trunk is so solid. I can't imagine it has a hole in the bottom. Surely if that is the case, dampness must have damaged the contents, and there was no sign of that, was there, Joseph?'

'Indeed not, sir.' He folded back the leaves of one of the screens, so Matthew could see the trunk without getting up.

'Go on, then,' Matthew urged.

Joseph lifted the lid and set the inner tray aside, bringing the lamp closer, but the interior of the trunk was still in too much shadow for a really good look, so he resorted to kneeling down and feeling around with his hand. After a few moments, his head emerged. 'I think Lady Julia was correct, sir. There is, undoubtedly, a small hole in the floor of the trunk.'

'Can you feel anything if you poke your finger into it?' Matthew inquired, hitching himself further down the bed.

'It feels a bit like some sort of paper, sir.' He got up and went back to Matthew's bed. 'What would you like me to do now?'

'I think we'll have to leave it till tomorrow for further exploration; it's too dark now. But I'd like to look into it before the party from London returns.'

'Very well, sir, tomorrow it is.' Joseph put back the screen and wished his master goodnight.

Chapter 34

The following morning, Matthew returned to his room after breakfast to find Joseph putting the finishing touches to his room. He was always very particular about doing this himself, as he had no faith in the machinations of housemaids. 'Ah, Joseph, just the man,' exclaimed Matthew. 'Perhaps we could continue the exploration of my trunk and the reason for the hole, you and Lady Julia discovered.'

'Very good, sir. May I remove the tray?'

'Go ahead.' With the floor of the trunk exposed and now in full daylight, the hole, although small, was quite visible. Kneeling on a chair, Matthew peered in. 'Do you think it really is a false bottom?'

Joseph felt round the edges. 'Yes, sir. I believe it might be. If I press down firmly, there seem to be some give there, but it is cleverly concealed. I think it will be necessary to remove some of the lining before we can know for certain. It may result in some damage.'

'Never mind that, Joseph, Rip it all to pieces,' said Matthew, throwing caution to the winds.

'I have no intention of doing any such thing, Mr Matthew, sir. A small incision is all that should be necessary in the first instance.'

'Go ahead and do it then. The suspense is killing me.'

Joseph took a small folding knife from his pocket and inserted it carefully through the lining at the edge of the trunk. The blade entered for about the depth of two inches. Joseph looked up at Matthew and gave one of his rare smiles. 'I believe there is, indeed, a cavity here, sir. Do you wish me to explore further?'

'Of course I do,' Matthew said impatiently. 'Carry on.'

Joseph slid his knife round the entire perimeter of the floor of the trunk, releasing it from the lining. I believe the purpose of the hole is to enable the false bottom to be lifted. Do you wish me to do that, sir?'

'Yes, Joseph, I do. I very much want you to. And if the entire world disappears in a puff of smoke, you can put the full blame on me.'

'Yes, sir,' Joseph replied with a straight face, at the same time hooking his forefinger into the hole and giving a tug. At first, nothing happened. But a second one started the false bottom moving. Matthew stretched his arm into the trunk and grabbed the loosened end. It took only a few more pulls for the wooden cover to give up its grip entirely. Joseph laid the false panel on the floor, and both men stared into the trunk.

Matthew had no expectations. But at least the space wasn't empty. Covering the entire area was a series of paper-wrapped packages, each— judged by eye—about six inches by four and neatly tied with fine string. Matthew and Joseph looked at each other with raised eyebrows. Joseph spoke first. 'Do you remember, sir, placing these in here?'

'I haven't the slightest recollection, Joseph. They might not even be mine. Suppose my father purchased the trunk second-hand?'

'Would you permit me to extract one of the packets for your perusal?'

'Go ahead. I can't reach anyway.'

Joseph eased one of the little parcels from the trunk and handed it to Matthew, who examined it closely. But it bore no writing. He turned it over and saw the other side was sealed with red wax, impressed with a signet. 'What do you make of that?' he said, showing it to Joseph.

'I believe it confirms that it belongs to you, sir. The impression in the wax is "WS", in a similar style to the ring you wear on your right hand, sir.'

Matthew looked more closely. 'You are right, Joseph. My father was called William, so it must be mine after all. May I borrow your knife?'

'Sir,' Joseph said a little hesitantly, 'of course you may have the knife, but I feel I should withdraw. Whatever is in those packages is a private matter for you, Mr Matthew. It is none of my business.'

Matthew sighed. 'You are the soul of discretion, Joseph. But if that is what you wish, so be it. I will keep this one out. And before you leave, perhaps you would be good enough to replace the false bottom. As you say, until I find out more, it is best kept hidden.'

The moment Joseph closed the door, Matthew hopped back to his couch. He cut the string and ripped open the package, breaking the seal. Before he could stop them, a quantity, of what appeared to be banknotes fluttered out, covering his knees, Bedford's head, and the floor.

Just before lunch the following day, Hargreaves, his sister, and Nicky returned from London, all eager to tell Matthew about their experiences at the House of Lords. Since the Palace of Westminster had mostly been burnt to the ground four years previously, the ceremony of introducing Lord Hargreaves to the chamber and the taking of his oath of allegiance took place in a very crowded space that had once been the monarch's robing room.

'He looked splendid in his scarlet robe and fur collar,' said Nicky. 'And we could all hear Papa take the oath, and then he made his maiden speech.'

'And did it go down well?' Matthew addressed Mrs Clayborne.

'I believe so, but the tradition is never to criticise a maiden speech. It concerned education, a subject dear to my brother's heart. Lord Melbourne himself came up afterwards and congratulated him.'

'I'm not sure if he was praising me because it was short or because he approves of the content.' Hargreaves smiled. 'But either way, it was very gratifying. Of course, I had the very best of sponsors in Lords Coverdale and Uttoxeter. Lady Coverdale gave a wonderful dinner party that night.

'She is a great hostess and so kind, too,' put in Emily. 'And the next day was the State Opening of Parliament. Nicky and I sat in the gallery. It was a splendid affair.'

'Papa wore his coronet, and the queen wore a splendid crown; she's so tiny but really, really regal.' Nicky joined in.

The descriptions and emotions went on throughout lunch. But afterwards Lord Hargreaves said to Matthew, 'If you could spare a few moments, I have some news I wish to convey to you.'

'And I to you, sir.'

Both sat on either side of the fire in Hargreaves's comfortable study, waiting for the other to start. Matthew smiled. 'Would you like to tell me your news first, My Lord?'

'I suppose it is really Lord Coverdale's news. Last time I was there, we discussed your circumstances.'

Matthew raised his eyebrows.

'We were both concerned about you, and his lordship was sure there might be someone in this country who knew you, or a family member somewhere. He was also convinced you could not have arrived penniless, and perhaps there were funds lying in a London Bank waiting to be claimed. Please don't think I wanted to get rid of you—far from it,' he added quickly. 'Your presence has done much to improve the mausoleum-like atmosphere of this house. But I know you worried about your future.'

'I'm not at all resentful of *any* attempts on my behalf. Quite the opposite. In fact, I'm merely surprised that one so eminent as Lord Coverdale should involve himself.'

'Well, as to that, he put his secretary to work.'

'With any success?'

'Not, I'm afraid, as far as the money is concerned. But he found out quite a lot about your antecedents. I don't know how much you have remembered. But when you turned up at Mairsford, you didn't even know your own name!'

'That is true, but I have recovered some memories. My father was in the Royal Artillery, but he was retired by the time I was born. I think he died when I was ten years old.'

Hargreaves frowned and shook his head, 'No, Matthew he was in the Royal Engineers. The marquis has discovered most of his military history and also who his father, your grandfather was.'

'Really!?' Matthew exclaimed. 'I don't recall him ever mentioning his father. But perhaps that's not strange, as I was quite young when he died.'

'According to Coverdale, he was a well-respected Edinburgh lawyer, a senior partner in the firm. Your father was articled to him at the age of sixteen, but presumably had no taste for the law. And his father, Alistair William Stuart, paid for him to become a cadet at Woolwich, the establishment for training military engineers, after which he was commissioned as a lieutenant in the Royal Engineers and was sent out to Canada.'

Matthew straightened in his chair. 'How did he find all this out? And why Canada?'

'Fortunately, the army keeps very good records. And for a man of Coverdale's rank and standing, access to them is no problem. As to Canada—Quebec, to be precise—apparently there was always a fear the Napoleon would send a force to recapture it, and there was no doubt the populace would rise up to help them. Stuart was sent to advise on reinforcing the garrisons in the city.'

'That's interesting.' Matthew leaned forward in his chair. 'I know he was in York—the town that has recently been renamed Toronto.' He paused, knitting his brows. 'Now how do I know that, I wonder?' He continued with his original train of thought. 'He was there during the War of 1812, although he retired immediately after, and I was brought up in Philadelphia. Do you know anything else?'

'No,' said Hargreaves. 'I'm afraid not. But he certainly retired in 1814. The War Office paid his pension into a bank in Canada.'

Matthew slumped back in his chair in disbelief. 'That is incredible, My Lord.'

'What is?'

'This.' Matthew extracted one of the banknotes he had found, from his waistcoat pocket. He held it out.

Hargreaves examined the elaborate printing, scrolled writing, and depiction of the seated figure of Britannia, turning it over and over, rubbing the paper between his fingers. 'Where did you get this?' he asked, holding it up to the light.

'In my trunk, sir. It's the news I was going to tell you about. Do you think it's real—I mean, real money?'

'I think it could be, but I'm no expert in these matters. I see it is for twenty pounds. Are there any more?'

'Yes, sir. Lady Julia found a small hole in the bottom of the trunk, and Joseph and I found that it did, indeed, have a false bottom. And the money was packed in underneath.'

'How much?'

'I don't really know, but the packet this one came from had a thousand pounds worth of notes in it.'

Hargreaves attempted to keep the surprise out of his voice and failed. 'How many packets?'

'Thirty-six, My Lord.'

'By God! Man, you're as rich as Croesus!'

Matthew gave a wry smile at his host's enthusiasm. 'Possibly, sir. But there are a lot of factors to take into consideration before that happens.'

Hargreaves returned to being a solicitor. 'Of course. You are right. We must find out if this'—he waved the banknote he was still holding—'is legal tender.'

'I don't even know if all the other packets contain the same amount. And although I have no memory of having put them in the trunk—or where they came from in the first place—they do appear to belong to me. I wondered at first if they were even mine at all, until Joseph pointed out they bore my father's seal.'

'Joseph knows about them?' Hargreaves sounded worried.

'No, sir. He helped me with the trunk but insisted that he left the room before I opened one of the packets. He is the very soul of discretion, you know.'

'Yes, I suppose he is. But nevertheless, the fewer people who know about this, the better, until we—that is, you—know more about it. Now, I must go and sooth the ruffled feathers of my impulsive son, who also has something he wishes to tell me.'

Chapter 35

'But I wanted to show Matthew now, Papa. I've waited ages. And think how great it will be when he can ride again.'

'Yes, Nicky, I'm sure it will be. But have you given any thought to how it is to be done?

Nicky looked crestfallen. 'No, not really, sir.'

'Well, I suggest you do. You will have to consult with Hampton about choosing the right horse—fitting the saddle with suitable girths and devising a method for a man with only one useful leg to mount a horse from the wrong side. You don't want to drag Matthew round to the stables when nothing is prepared, do you?'

'No, Papa. I'll see to it right away.'

He was halfway to the door when his father shouted, 'Tell Hampton, I said it's all right to do whatever you and he think is best.'

Hargreaves sighed as he turned back to rejoin Matthew. There was no doubt his son's heart was in the right place. He just wished that sometimes his head was, too. But then there was plenty of time for that to happen.

On entering his study once more, Hargreaves addressed Matthew. 'What do you want to do now?' he asked, seeing the young man twiddling the banknote between finger and thumb.

'I don't really know, My Lord. I am not really in any position to do anything, am I?' He gestured to the crutches propped up against his chair.

'Would you like me to take the matter in hand, although, as I have already said, I am no expert in financial matters? But, on the other hand, I know someone who really can help and I'm sure would be willing to do so.'

'I suppose you mean Lord Coverdale, sir?'

'Yes. I know he has your best interests at heart—'

Matthew made a face and interrupted. 'I think he is more concerned with Lady Julia's interest.'

'And how do you feel about that? Anyone can see she has a *tendresse* for you.'

An expression of annoyance passed across Matthew's face. 'I am in no position to have any feelings in the matter. She is the daughter of a great nobleman and will enjoy a life among her own kind,' he said stiffly.

Hargreaves narrowed his eyes and looked shrewdly at his young friend.. 'That remark makes me feel that you do care.' Matthew started to speak, but Hargreaves continued. 'Let us get back to the best way to verify that banknote you have nearly shredded.'

Matthew acquiesced with a wry smile. 'Yes, sir.'

After further discussion, it was decided the banknote should be despatched at once to Lord Coverdale, with a request to discover its validity. George was sent to the post office in Staplewood to express the letter.

The following day, he had more immediate matters to attend to, although much as Hargreaves would have liked to observe Matthew's first attempt at riding, he deemed it kinder to stay away—in case it proved an embarrassing failure. So only Nicky and Matthew went to the stables, although unbeknownst to either of them, Joseph had checked out the arrangements beforehand and reluctantly approved of them.

'You see, Matthew,' said Nicky excitedly as they entered the yard, 'everything is ready for you.'

A black cob, saddled and bridled, was standing quietly beside a stepladder, Hampton at the horse's head and a stable boy to steady the ladder. 'That is how you will mount. The ladder has handles near the top so you can hop up the steps. I know old Ben is not what you were used to riding, but—'

Matthew eyed the scene with some trepidation. He knew he was not the greatest rider at the best of times, but this was altogether different. He approached the ladder cautiously, with Nicky beside him. 'Good morning,' he said to Hampton. 'I hope I can manage this.'

Hampton touched his cap. 'I'm sure you will, sir. We shall see you right.'

Matthew approached the stepladder and handed his crutches to Nicky, who leaned them against the wall.

'Grasp the handles I have had put there, you know—and see if you can hop onto the first step.'

Matthew did so without any difficulty.

'Now if you go up about four more, you should be level with Ben's back.'

The horse made a slight shudder, unaccustomed to someone apparently mounting him from the wrong side.

'Don't 'ee worry, sir. 'E won't move,' said Hampton as he patted the horse's neck.

'Now,' said Nicky as Matthew reached the fourth step, 'can you manage to get your left leg over Ben's back?' The horse was broad, but Matthew had long legs and achieved the manoeuvre without difficulty. Still, he found himself half on and half off his would-be mount. 'Hold the pommel with your right hand and ease your right leg away from the ladder. I'll make sure you don't fall off on the other side.'

'You'd better,' said Matthew grimly, clinging onto the saddle. But after he put his good foot into the stirrup and adjusted it for length, he felt quite secure.

'This is the part I've been waiting to see!' Nicky exclaimed, fastening the leather strap that would keep Matthew's left leg in place without the use of a stirrup. 'There, is that quite comfortable? I'm sure it will work,' he stated, with all the confidence of youth.

But just at that moment, there was a clatter of hooves, and Lady Julia swept into the yard aboard Gladiator. Ben gave a start, and Julia immediately reined in her horse. 'Oh, Matthew!' she said. 'This is wonderful. I had no idea.'

'It's his first time,' Nicky replied a little grumpily, feeling somewhat put out by the look of delight at seeing each other that passed between his two mounted friends.

'It is all due to Nicky, Lady Julia,' said Matthew. 'But as yet, I am like a bronze statue. I haven't actually moved.'

'We'll have to remedy that.' Julia laughed. 'What have you in mind?'

'A walk round the paddock,' put in Nicky.

'Splendid. I can go on one side, and you on the other. I see your horse is already saddled and waiting.'

One circuit of the home paddock adjacent to the stables proved quite enough for Matthew, who discovered that his months of inactivity had made him weak as a kitten. Dismounting in the same way as he had climbed aboard proved impossible, so he slid off from the nearside. Nicky was standing by to hand him his crutches, but even they, were hardly enough to prevent his good leg from buckling. Nevertheless, his first outing on horseback was considered a great success, and it only required more to improve his strength and regain his ability. Another ride was proposed for the following day.

Meanwhile, Rosalie, who had driven over to Staplewood with Bethany, had been having a cosy chat with Emily in the blue drawing room, leaving her daughter feeling bored. 'May I go to the library, Mrs Clayborne, and look at the globes?'

'Of course you may, my dear. I know how much you like playing with them.'

'But be sure you don't disturb Lord Hargreaves. He is working on his speech in the Lords for next week,' said her mother.

'I won't.' Bethany skipped off. The celestial globe was her favourite, with all the constellations and the signs of the zodiac beautifully illustrated on its varnished surface.

It was not long before Hargreaves emerged from his study, and Bethany jumped back. 'I'm, sorry, My Lord. Have I disturbed you? Mama said—'

'No, my dear, not at all. I have finished my work. Do you like looking at the globes? They are a fine pair, I believe.'

Once free from reproof, Bethany was not a child who suffered from shyness, and she had no hesitation in asking Hargreaves the question that was troubling her. 'My Lord, I understand that globe.' She pointed to the terrestrial one. 'But I cannot make sense of this one. The stars are not really all on the outside of a globe, are they?'

'No, Bethany. But if you imagine yourself very, very small and standing in the very centre of the globe, and all the stars and pictures were painted on the inside, then it would make sense.'

'Oh, how clever. Of course it would. But then no one could see it, could they?' She laughed.

Hargreaves picked up the small cloth-covered book containing all the columns of numbers that both Matthew and himself had puzzled over to no effect. 'You are a clever child, I'm told. What do you make of this?'

'May I stay here and study it? I promise not to touch anything else.'

'Of course you may, my dear child.' Hargreaves gave a mischievous smile. 'I shall go and spoil the ladies' tête-à-tête.'

Just before luncheon, Nicky, Julia, and an exhausted but elated Matthew returned from the stables, all talking at once about the success of the experiment. Bethany emerged from the library, barely able to conceal her excitement. 'Good news, Beth,' said Julia. 'Matthew has had his first ride!'

Bethany ignored this remark, instead asking, 'Cousin Julia, could you say I'd very much like to speak to Lord Hargreaves?'

Julia looked her cousin up and down. 'What about?'

Bethany looked embarrassed. 'It's sort of private.'

'I have to go and change, but all right then.' She popped her head around the door of the drawing room and managed to catch Lord Hargreaves's eye. 'Bethany wants to talk to you, My Lord.'

Rosalie immediately spoke up. 'What's my daughter been up to now?'

'Nothing sinister at all, Lady B, I assure you,' he replied, moving towards the door. 'Now then, young lady. What's this all about?'

Bethany was just about to tell him when Parsons appeared to announce that luncheon was served. 'I'm afraid whatever it is will have to wait. We don't want to let the food get cold, do we?'

Matthew and Bethany were both noticeably silent during the meal, Matthew because every bone and muscle in his body was aching and he could only think of the comfort of his couch, and Bethany because she could only think of what she believed she had discovered in the cloth-covered book.

Chapter 36

With luncheon over, people went their various ways—Matthew to his longed-for couch; the ladies to the drawing room; and Julia and Nicky to the stables, where he was going to have his promised ride on Gladiator.

'Bethany, my dear,' said Hargreaves, 'will you ask your Mama to give you permission to join me in the library?'

Back from her quest, Bethany announced, 'Mama says yes, but I'm not to be a trial.'

'I'm sure you won't be, and I'm really interested in what you have discovered.'

They went over to Matthew's table.

Bethany picked up the book. 'You see, My Lord, these three columns?'

Hargreaves nodded.

'I think the first column are dates. I haven't worked them all out.'

Hargreaves put a hand on her shoulder. 'That sounds very interesting, but do you know, I think you should explain it all to Matthew, too. All this'—he pointed to the scrolls and piles of paper on the table—'is his work. He should be the first to hear of your theory.'

'Can we ask him to come here?' said Bethany eagerly.

'I rather think he would prefer to learn of it in his own room. I think his morning ride has been rather tiring. Bring the book, and we will go and see.'

Hargreaves knocked on Matthew's door.

Matthew made a vestigial effort to get up as they entered.

'Don't even try, dear boy.'

'I very much doubt if I can.' Matthew grinned. 'To what do I owe this honour?'

Bedford, realising his period of ear-fondling was over, retired to the hearthrug as Bethany pulled up a stool to sit beside Matthew.

'Bethany thinks she has discovered what one of the columns in the "Benares" book means, and I thought you should hear it too. Bethany, the floor is yours.'

Bethany opened the book at the first page and gave it to Matthew. 'When you play chess, My Lord, you have to look for patterns. There are eight numbers in every line, and I couldn't see anything at first. So I concentrated on the very first group of numbers. There.' She pointed them out to Matthew. 'You have a 1 and a 7 and then four more numbers and then a 5 and a 6. And I knew I'd seen those numbers somewhere else, but I couldn't remember where. So I closed my eyes, and it suddenly came to me. On that triangle bit above the portico, it says, "This house was built in 1756." It's in Latin, of course, but that is what it says.'

This piece of information, delivered so casually by an eight-year-old girl, stunned her listeners to silence, broken eventually by Lord Hargreaves. 'Er … then what did you do?'

'I think I know,' said Matthew. 'You took those numbers out of every line.'

'Yes,' agreed Bethany. 'And you can make day and a month with the other four, although this might not be straightforward if they are all jumbled up, too.'

'Let me have a look,' said Hargreaves. 'We need paper and pencil.'

'I have pencils here,' Matthew opened his Tunbridge Ware box.

'I'll get some paper from my study.'

By the time he returned, Matthew and Bethany had worked out possibilities for the other four numbers if her theory was right; 0236 could either mean the 23 June 1756, or 26 March. On the first page, there were thirteen entries, one with the word "Benares" in the centre column. By taking four groups each, it didn't take long for all the possible dates for each set of numbers to be worked out. It was no surprise to Hargreaves and Matthew that Bethany finished first.

'By the way, Bethany, does Mrs Sylvia teach you Latin?' It was a question that was in both men's minds.

Bethany shook her head and seemed reluctant to answer.

'If it's a secret, we won't tell.' Matthew grinned.

'It's not exactly a secret, but Mama says everyone will think I'm some kind of stocking. It was when we were staying at Uncle Justin's last Christmas—we go there every year. I found some schoolbooks that belonged to my papa, and Uncle Justin said I could have them. I've been teaching myself Latin from them.'

No further comment was possible, as her mother came in and said the pony and trap was ready. 'Go and say goodbye to Mrs Clayborne, and then George is ready with our coats.'

'What about Lady Julia?' enquired Hargreaves.

'Oh. She'll ride home with Nicky, with your permission, my Lord.'

'Of course. And I hope we will see you all here again soon.'

When he returned from seeing them off, they continued to work on the numbers until there was no doubt at all that Bethany had been right about them being dates.

Hargreaves said, 'You know, Matthew, I think that child is definitely going to become a something-stocking!'

The following day, breakfast was just finishing, when the sound of gravel being scattered drew Hargreaves to the window. An Express Post rider was already ringing the doorbell, and it was not long before Parsons entered with a package, which he presented on a silver salver to Matthew.

'It's from Lord Coverdale,' Matthew said, turning it over in his hand, and examining the several wax seals that kept the contents safe.

'Do you wish to open it in private?' asked Mrs Clayborne.

'Not at all. I have until now,' he replied, 'only spoken to Lord Hargreaves about the discovery in my trunk of some banknotes. And he has kindly begged the good offices of Lord Coverdale to establish if they are valid.'

'They were drawn on the Bank of Nova Scotia, you see,' put in His Lordship by way of explanation.

'Now,' said Matthew, breaking the seals on the letter, 'we shall see what the marquis has to say.' He unfolded the outer cover and took out a letter, inside which were four Bank of England five-pound notes.

'I say!' exclaimed Nicky, flushing red when he caught his father's expression of disapproval.

Unfazed, Matthew began to read:

Dear Mr Stuart,

*I have been able, on your behalf, to ascertain from my man
of business, that the banknote Lord Hargreaves sent to me is,
indeed, valid currency in this country.*

'That's great news,' Hargreaves murmured as Matthew continued:

*The notes are equal in value to English currency, but there
would be a small commission payable to effect the exchange.
Hoare's Bank is willing to act in this matter. I am aware
your circumstances do not permit you to come to London at
this time, but Lord Hargreaves will be in town next week. If
you could send with him a small deposit and a signed letter,
empowering the bank to open an account on your behalf.
Because you are known to me, this can soon be accomplished.
I hope this arrangement finds favour with you.*

Yours, very sincerely,
Coverdale.

*Post Scriptum. My dear wife, Amanda, who is wiser than me
in these matters, thought you might like to have something to
put in your pocketbook. I am, therefore, enclosing £20, the
value of the note Hargreaves sent me for validation.*

'Good news, indeed,' said Mrs Clayborne. 'I'm sure it will be a great
relief to you. To be stranded in a strange country without means of support
must surely have preyed on your mind.'

'Emily, my dear, Matthew has become like one of the family, and he
we would never turn him penniless, into the world.'

'No, Charles, of course not, but—'

Matthew came to her rescue. 'You are quite right, Mrs Clayborne. I
do, indeed feel that one of my problems seems likely to be resolved now.'

After some discussion between Matthew and Lord Hargreaves, it was
decided he should take with him to London two of the packets of notes,

amounting to £2,000. These, Hargreaves said, could easily be concealed in an inner pocket, and he had no fears for his safety.

Their other discussion was rather more argumentative, as Matthew wanted to reimburse his host for all the expenses he had incurred, and Hargreaves stubbornly refused. A compromise was finally agreed. Matthew would pay Joseph's wages from the day he first went to Mairsford but nothing else.

When Matthew asked him, Joseph expressed his pleasure at becoming Matthew's official valet. At the same time, he imparted the good news that his foot was now sufficiently healed to allow him to walk on it, using a stick, adding, 'But only for a limited time each day, and certainly not outside,' where he would still require his crutches.

On the day of his visit to town, Hargreaves rode to Tonbridge to catch the London Stage, and having left his horse at the livery stable, was walking through the market toward the coach stop. Suddenly, a voice he didn't recognise said, 'Good morning, Mr Clayborne, sir. I trust I find you well?'

Hargreaves froze in his tracks, and then he remembered—Mrs Worthy! There was nothing he could do but turn back and acknowledge the greeting.

The lady was standing behind a table laden with cheeses. He lifted his hat. 'Mrs Worthy, what a pleasant surprise. I hope I find you well, too.'

'Oh, indeed, sir. And Mrs Clayborne?'

'Yes, I thank you.' Hargreaves was desperate to get away. 'I am for the stagecoach to London and must not miss it. He lifted his hat again. 'My best wishes to your husband, Mrs Worthy.'

He bowed and strode off hoping against hope that no one had seen the little exchange.

But in this, he was wrong. A gentleman in corded breeches and a green riding coat had been standing in a nearby shop doorway.

Chapter 37

The end of a wet November turned into a frosty December. And it would be time for the Mairsford occupants to leave for Coverdale Hall, where it was traditional for the family to spend Christmas. The Hargreaves and the marquis had agreed this would be the best time to transfer Matthew's remaining fortune to London. Packed in a nondescript cloak bag and accompanied by coachmen, as well as the family, it would be unlikely to attract attention. As Lord Hargreaves pointed out, since the establishment of a regular police force, highway robbery was largely a thing of the past.

Matthew's progress, both on horseback and on foot, was a source of pleasure to all at Staplewood and to one in particular at Mairsford. Lady Julia rode over frequently to join him on his rides, always accompanied by a groom. However, Hargreaves had his suspicions that the groom was not always as closely in attendance as he, or indeed Lady B, would have liked. Nevertheless, he couldn't help but think the two young people were well suited in most ways, except rank.

With some time yet before Lord Coverdale was due, Hargreaves decided to explore further the origins of the mysterious underground room. He discussed the topic with Matthew, and they wondered if there was still anyone in the village who might remember the house being built. Enquiries brought the knowledge that the village blacksmith had been there for many generations, and the present owner's grandfather was still alive and might be able to help.

Hargreaves entered the smithy's yard and dismounted. Immediately, a young man with dark curly hair and wearing a leather apron abandoned the horse he was shoeing and came forward, tugging his forelock. 'M'lord, how can I be of service?'

'I think Monty here has a loose shoe on his off hind. Perhaps you could take a look?'

'At once, M'lord.'

'No … no. Mr Berrow, you must finish that other horse first. I have business in the village, I will come back.'

'Very good, Your Lordship. Beggin' your pardon, folk all call me Nathan.' He led Monty across the yard to tether him.

Hargreaves followed, 'I understand, Nathan, that your family has been working this forge for a long time.'

'Aye, M'lord, dunnamany years, great-great-granfer were first here.'

'Then perhaps you, or someone in your family can help me,' Hargreaves said. 'I am trying to find out more about Staplewood, particularly the house. It was built about eighty years ago.'

'Granfer might remember summat. 'E be ninety now.'

'Could I ask him?'

'Mebbe difficult, he being stone deaf.'

At that moment, a middle-aged man emerged from the forge, clad in the same way, his sinewy arms pocked with scars made by sparks landing on them. 'Da,' said Nathan, 'His Lordship wants to know if Granfer can tell him anything about the big house.'

'M'lord,' said the older man, scratching his head, 'me father were nobbut a lad when house were being built. But like the nipper in there'—he indicated the forge—''e worked the bellows.'

Hargreaves looked through the door of the heat-filled forge. The red heart of the fire was contained in a waist-high hearth. A young boy was giving the fire an occasional puff with outsized bellows, causing sparks to fly up to the flared-out chimney breast. 'Your son says his grandfather is deaf. Would he understand my questions?'

'He took ill when 'e were about Nate's age and weren't expected to recover, but 'e did. But 'is hearing were quite gone, but 'e can speak; 'e's not dumb.'

Although the back door of the blacksmith's cottage was the nearest, Hargreaves was led down a side road and was ushered through the front door of a surprisingly spacious dwelling. The old man was seated in a rocking chair by a glowing fire. He was certainly feeble of body, but his eyes were still sharp, set beneath bushy brows, and he seemed pleased to be consulted.

The next half hour consisted of a mixture of signing, lip-reading, and a few written words. But Hargreaves came away, with many thanks and the refused offer of a gold sovereign, with the information that the forge had made a large number of identical wrought-iron bars for the newly built Staplewood. These had apparently been ordered by what the old man described as a 'furriner', with a strange hat'. After several attempts at drawing various types of headgear, Berrow senior nodded vigorously when he saw the picture of a turban.

Hargreaves rode away with not a great deal of useful information, except that it seemed the wrought-iron banisters had been made at Berrow's forge. From the size and number of the rods ordered, they could have been for no other use. But the presence of a man in a turban, probably an Indian gentleman, was all rather mysterious. Furthermore, there was something in the forge that rang a bell in his mind, but he couldn't recall what it was.

Some ten days before Christmas, Lord Coverdale arrived in his magnificent travelling coach, drawn by four Cleveland Bays. This was followed by a smaller vehicle, which would carry the ladies' maids and the not inconsiderable luggage. Lady Julia's groom would lead Gladiator.

'My Lord, it is such a pleasure to welcome you to Staplewood.' Emily greeted him with a curtsey.

'It is a pleasure to be here, I am only sorry it is to be such a fleeting visit. .We are all for London tomorrow and then on to Coverdale Hall for Christmas.'

'A cold collation is being got ready. But perhaps you would prefer to have your talk with Matthew first, My Lord.'

As he was being divested of his outer garments, Coverdale remarked, 'You know, Hargreaves, this is the most remarkable, or perhaps I should say magnificent, hallway.' He looked round at the gold leaf ornamentation that glittered even though the day was a dull one.

'It is a pity, My Lord, that the original builder didn't spend more of his money on convenience rather than glorification,' interjected Emily with a rueful smile.

Matthew was already in the study when Hargreaves and Coverdale entered. He came forward immediately, extending his hand. 'My Lord, how can I thank you for all you have done on my behalf?'

'Do not give it a thought,' replied the peer. 'It has been an enjoyable exercise and quite out of the common way. I see that you have indeed improved since I last saw you!'

'Please, sir, don't remind me. I'm afraid I wasn't quite myself at the time.'

His lordship laughed. 'No, but you had every excuse. However, I have been kept well informed about your progress. My sister-in-law writes frequently to my wife, who insists on reading out the letters at the breakfast table!'

Ale was brought in. And once Parsons had departed, the three men got down to business. Hargreaves produced the bag with Matthew's money from beneath his desk.

'I can't believe it is really mine,' said Matthew, poking the bag with the end of his stick.

'Well now that it is,' replied Justin, 'what are your plans for it?'

'I suppose I should invest it in something that will bring me an income. I plan, when my foot is good enough, to go somewhere I can learn all I can about building railroads. And no one may want to employ me, so I will have to have enough to live on, without squandering my capital.'

'Very sensible,' said the marquis. 'Don't you agree, Hargreaves?'

'Yes. I suggest you put some of it in government funds, Matthew. They may not pay as much as more speculative investments. But at least, your money will be safe.'

'I thought,' Matthew said tentatively, 'perhaps railroad stocks would be good—'

To his surprise, Coverdale immediately said, 'No. They may be attractive in the short term, but there are so many unknowns about rail travel. Although it will soon be universal, money put into them can soon be eaten up in unforeseen costs.'

'I think that is very true, My Lord,' said Hargreaves, 'although I wouldn't have thought of that myself.' He took a long drink from his tankard. 'What do you suggest?'

'I was talking to the Marquis of Bute the other day. You know he's mining coal in Wales, and expanding Cardiff docks. I'd put my money in coal and steel. Whatever happens to individual railway companies, those two commodities will always be in demand. That's where I'd put my money; in fact, I already have.'

'That seems to be excellent advice, Matthew. I'd take it if I were you,' said Hargreaves.

'Well, it's still a little way in the future,' said Coverdale. 'Let's get the money safely stowed away, firstly in my coach and then in the bank. I will get my man of business to look into suitable investments for you.'

'I am indebted to you once again, Lord Coverdale.' Matthew sighed.

'I do very little. I have a host of people who do it for me, and to whom I am very grateful. I never take them for granted, but I expect them to earn their keep. Putting them to work on your behalf is my pleasure, Matthew. However, there is something you could do for me.'

'Anything at all, My Lord, although I cannot imagine what it could be.'

'A simple matter, I assure you. When he was in London, Hargreaves said you had found a Tunbridge Ware box among your possessions. Is that not so?' He turned to his host, who nodded agreement. 'I would very much like to see it—if you do not mind.'

'I should be delighted to show it to you, sir.' Matthew made to rise from his chair, but Hargreaves forestalled him by ringing the bell.

Parsons arrived almost immediately.

'That was quick.' Hargreaves smiled at his butler.

'I was on my way to inform you that the cold collation is ready, My Lord.'

'Tell Mrs Clayborne we will be along shortly. Meanwhile, Mr Matthew would like to ask Joseph to bring his Tunbridge Ware box to the study.'

Very shortly, Joseph appeared carrying the box, which Matthew handed over to Lord Coverdale, who examined it closely before asking, 'May I open it?'

'Of course, My Lord, please do so,' replied Matthew. 'But one of the hinges is a little loose.'

Walking towards the window for better light, His Lordship smiled. 'I will take great care. It was your mother's, Hargreaves told me?'

'Yes, she always kept it on her writing bureau. I think it was precious to her, which is presumably why I brought it with me. But I have no memory of packing it, nor, for that matter, any recollection of the money in that bag,' Matthew said, pointing to the cloak bag sitting at his feet.

Coverdale caressed the lid before carefully lifting it. He stared into the box, giving the contents a gentle stir with his finger. Matthew watched the older man start as if he had received a shock of static electricity and the colour drain out of his face. Matthew was about to ask him if he was feeling all right, but His Lordship drew in a deep breath, and seemed to pull himself together, laying the box down on the desk with a trembling hand. 'Thank you, Matthew. It is certainly a very interesting box,' he said in a tightly controlled voice.

Hargreaves, who had been poking the fire during this brief exchange, stood up, saying, 'I think we might proceed to the dining room, where luncheon awaits us.'

Chapter 38

Christmas Day at Staplewood was a quiet celebration. The family attended church in the morning and returned to the house for a later than usual lunch, as the vicar and his wife had been invited to join them to share the meal.

Letters of seasonal goodwill were received by Charles and Emily from friends in Ludlow and Bath respectively—one of which caused Emily to exclaim, 'Oh, my!'

'What's the matter, Em?' her brother enquired.

'This is from the people renting my house. It seems that Precious—you remember, that's my parrot, Charles?'

'Who could forget?'

'Don't interrupt. Well, it seems she has laid an egg! What a clever bird, don't you think, Charles?'

Her brother, who always disliked the noisy parrot, replied a little acerbically, 'Isn't that what birds are supposed to do?'

Boxing Day was a much jollier affair. Hargreaves had decided to revive the tradition Lord Patrick Hargreaves had maintained throughout his time at Staplewood, and treat the outside staff—not that there were many of them now—to cakes and ale in the servants' hal,l before lining up to receive their annual gift of money. In addition Emily and Mrs Royston had made boxes of biscuits and sweetmeats to take home to their wives and children. Hargreaves was particularly keen to show his son that good staff should be valued. This was continued in the evening when the indoor staff were waited upon at supper by the family, before receiving their Christmas boxes.

In private, and as he retired to bed, Matthew gave Joseph a silver chain for his pocket watch.

'That is most kind of you, sir,' Joseph said in a formal tone. But Matthew detected the glimmer of a smile and knew his gift was appreciated.

The Mairsford household, including Lady Julia, whose parents had reluctantly agreed, returned on the day after New Year's Day and immediately invited the Staplewood party to dinner. Christmas at Coverdale Hall had clearly been a much more entertaining and, according to Lady B, exhausting time than that at Staplewood. But everyone seemed to have enjoyed it. The talk soon turned to the forthcoming Twelfth Night Feast at Mairsford. 'It is a very old tradition, explained Rosalie. 'The Lord of Misrule is voted for each year by the people of Mairsford and Staplewood, and he rules the feast, ordering the dances, musicians, and general merriment.'

'Doesn't it ever get out of hand if the drink is flowing freely?' asked Emily.

Rosalie laughed. 'Not really. It is well watered down, and the festivities end promptly at midnight. There used to be a tradition the Lord of Misrule was thrown into the moat. But Benedict put a stop to that. He considered it too dangerous.'

'What part do you play?' enquired Hargreaves.

'Not a great deal. I sit on a dais opposite "the Lord" and open the proceedings with a short speech and make a toast to the coming year. I have the first dance with the Lord and then slip away. I hope you will all join me this time.'

Hargreaves cast a dubious glance across the table at his sister, who disappointingly gave Lady B an enthusiastic, 'Yes.'

After the men had rejoined the ladies in the drawing room and tea had been served, Rosalie suggested some music, and Hargreaves was enchanted by hearing her play the harp for the first time. 'That was so lovely, Lady B. No wonder you were the toast of Europe.'

'I'm afraid I'm still rather rusty, but I have been practising more recently.'

'There is something I really want to ask you, Lady B,' said Hargreaves. He looked across at the young people getting out a card table and at Emily, who was rapidly being overcome by sleep.

Rosalie grinned. 'Let us go over and sit on the sofa. We can talk quietly there. What is your question?'

'When we had that little accident on the way back from the concert, why did you say we were man and wife?'

'Well,' Rosalie put her head on one side, in the way Hargreaves found delightful, 'if you think about it, there was no way we were going to get home that night.'

'No, I suppose not.'

'Then just imagine how embarrassing it would have been for the Worthys if we'd said who we really were. As husband and wife, they could easily put us up for the night. And anyway,' she added, 'I never *said* we were married; the Worthys just assumed it.'

'I see. It was very quick thinking of you.'

'Not really. I decided to do it on the way there. I always believe in planning ahead, don't you, My Lord?'

'Indeed, Lady B. But I lack your ingenuity in such unusual circumstances.'

Rosalie gave a little laugh and patted his hand. 'But nevertheless, I think you can be relied on in many other ways. I am expecting you to sit beside me on the dais and bow to the Lord of Misrule.'

Hargreaves looked a little shocked. 'Won't that give the guests the wrong impression? I mean—'

This time her laugh was full-blooded. 'Oh, My Lord! You think they'll believe we are a couple, but they won't. You see, Lord Patrick used to always be on the dais—until he got too old. It was quite the custom.'

Hargreaves looked relieved, until Rosalie added. 'Of course, if they knew we had shared a bed, they might well think differently.' She looked at the man sitting next to her with a mischievous twinkle in her eye.

'You are a terrible woman, Lady B,' Hargreaves said severely and then smiled.

It had been dry since Christmas, and Hargreaves decided it would be a good time to have another look at the underground passage and strange room at the end of it. So, he chose a morning that Nicky was visiting Mairsford, and accompanied by Shephard carrying a ladder, and himself, a lamp, they proceeded through the wood and uncovered the hole. A slight argument ensued about who should go down first, both wanting to protect the other. But Hargreaves prevailed and cautiously descended without mishap.

They reached the chamber, which was remarkably dry, a testament to the original builders. Setting the lamp on the stone shelf, Hargreaves turned to Shephard. 'What do you make of it?' he asked the gardener.

'I can't rightly say, M'lord. But I don't think that's no ordinary chimbly, there being no hearth, so to speak.'

'You're right there, Shephard.' Hargreaves looked at the bricks and pieces of masonry scattered across the floor. 'Let's see if we can piece some of this together. It might give us some idea of its purpose.'

After several minutes work, they were able to reconstruct something that resembled a raised hearth of some sort. But it had been badly damaged, deliberately, Hargreaves thought. He picked up the lamp and swung it round to reveal all corners of the room, catching sight of the crumpled metal object he had noticed on his first visit. Pointing to it, he asked, 'What do you suppose that is?'

, Shephard picked it up and placed it in the centre of the room. And instantly a memory entered Hargreaves's mind. The object was battered, but if straightened out, it was undoubtedly a smaller version of the flared hood over the hearth, that he had seen in Berrow's forge. He was now sure that the underground room had been used for metalwork, and then destroyed. But why? It was all very puzzling. And did it have any relevance to the present day? Hargreaves turned to Shephard. 'I've seen enough now, thank you. We'd better be getting back.' He raised the lamp to show the way through the passage, only a little wiser than he had been before.

At exactly eight o'clock on Twelfth Night, Lady B and Hargreaves—followed by Julia, Bethany, Nicholas and the rest of the Staplewood party—took their seats on the dais. A significant item of the decorated hall was a very large bunch of mistletoe suspended from the centre of the painted ceiling.

At the other end of the hall, on a raised throne decorated with ivy, sat the Lord of Misrule, dressed in scarlet and crowned with a gilded circlet. 'Behold!' he declared. 'My courtiers have arrived.'

Lady B rose and curtsied deeply. 'My Lord,' she said, 'we come to do your bidding.'

'Let us eat, drink, and make merry,' said the lord.

'Your wish is my command,' replied Lady B, and she clapped her hands. 'Food! Drink! Music!' she announced, and the assembled company clapped and cheered.

Half an hour later, Lady B had led out a dance with the Lord of Misrule, and the merriment was well under way. Lady B rose and bowed once more to the Lord of Misrule, and the dais party took their leave of the festivities. Emily and Nicky went upstairs to keep a promise of a bedtime story for Bethany, who had been allowed to stay up late. Tea had been ordered for the drawing room, but when Hargreaves and Rosalie entered, the room was deserted. 'I wonder where Julia and Matthew are,' Rosalie exclaimed.

Hargreaves, who had seen them slip away down another corridor, quickly offered to go and find them. It didn't take long. In a small anteroom, lit only by a single candle and through a slightly ajar door, he saw them in a deep embrace and wondered what he should do. He was not one to tell tales. He sneezed loudly, hoping it would have the desired effect. When he returned to the drawing room, it was once again empty. Hoping to prevent Lady B from finding the young lovebirds, he went in search once again and came upon her at the foot of the stairs.

'Any luck?' she asked.

'I expect they'll be in the drawing room by now,' he replied, hoping this was true. 'Shall we join them?'

''Before we do, my Lord, I want to thank you.'

Hargreaves raised his eyebrows. 'What for, Lady B?'

'For being so kind and helpful and giving Matthew somewhere to stay while he gets better, and for bringing Staplewood Park back to life, and ...' She stretched up and gave him a kiss on the cheek.

'Lady B!' he exclaimed, taken by surprise, and then smiled. 'There isn't any mistletoe here.'

Rosalie brought a hand from behind her back, and held the sprig she was holding above Hargreaves's head. 'There is now.' She laughed and kissed him again.

Two days later, Hargreaves was in his study after a lonely dinner, the rest of the household having gone up to London—Emily to visit a friend in Wimbledon and Matthew, together with Joseph, to buy all the new clothes he would need for the future, and Nicky to return to school. His lordship was trying to work, but his mind kept returning to that kiss. Should he have swept Lady B into his arms—as he would love to have done—or backed off? In the event he had done neither. He had just stood there with a look of surprise on his face, managing to say, 'Perhaps it is time to join the others.'

There came a knock on the door, and Parsons entered. 'There is a gentleman asking to see you, M'lord.'

'At this hour?'

'Yes, M'lord.' expression said everything he thought about persons who eschewed etiquette.

'Did he give his name or a card?'

'No, M'lord.'

'Oh well, better show him in. I will receive him in the library, but stay close, Parsons.'

The butler went to the door and signalled to the visitor. 'His Lordship will receive you now, sir.'

A gentleman of medium height, wearing a green riding coat, beige buckskin breeches, and a mustard-yellow waistcoat entered the room, and came towards Hargreaves with his hand extended.

'Who have I the honour of addressing?' Hargreaves enquired.

'I am the fifth Lord Hargreaves,' the man announced.

Chapter 39

Hargreaves's heart rate leapt up the scale. But years of experience dealing with unexpected revelations from clients enabled him to maintain a neutral expression, and move forward to shake the proffered hand. 'I think you had better explain yourself, sir. Please be seated.' He indicated a chair to the right of the fireplace.

There was a heavy thump on the adjoining door to the study, followed by a basso profundo bark.

'Excuse me a moment.' Hargreaves opened the door to find Bedford standing there hopefully. He grabbed the collar of the huge dog and led him to the hearthrug, 'There now, you be a good dog and lie down.' He gave a quick glance out of the corner of his eye and found a certain satisfaction in seeing his visitor draw his feet back nervously. He did not reassure him that the dog was completely harmless.

The interruption had given Hargreaves time to gather his turmoiled thoughts together. He took the other chair. 'Now then, sir, what are your reasons for believing you are the fifth Lord Hargreaves?'

The man gave a satisfied smile. 'I am Sebastian Hargreaves, the grandson of the first Lord Hargreaves's third son. I have every reason to believe you are the great-grandson of Charles, the fourth son. Therefore, my claim supersedes yours.'

'If that is true, you are perfectly correct. Your claim would certainly supersede mine. By the way,' he added casually, 'how did you get here?'

'Somewhat nonplussed by this apparent capitulation, the man muttered, 'I ... I ... rode here.'

'Where is your horse?'

'Tethered outside.'

'It is a very cold night. I hope he is well rugged up.'

The man shuffled in his chair. 'Er ... well, no.'

Hargreaves rang the bell.

Parsons appeared immediately. 'My Lord?'

'Tell George to go out and rug up this gentleman's horse immediately. Then bring some refreshments.' He turned to his visitor. 'What is your pleasure? Tea? Coffee? Ale?'

'C-coffee,' was the stammered reply.

'And some sandwiches, Parsons,' ordered Hargreaves. When the butler had departed, he said, 'I always believe in looking after my animals first.' Bedford stretched and turned over to warm his other side. 'I must ask by what means you can prove who you are, Mr Hargreaves. Claims such as yours have to be very thoroughly examined before they can be verified.'

'I have papers and this ring.' He thrust his hand forward to show a signet on the third finger of his right hand.

'Would you be kind enough to take it off so I can examine it by the light of this lamp?'

'Yes, but no funny business, mind.'

Hargreaves raised an eyebrow.

The man, regretting his comment, quickly covered his mistake, removed the ring and handed it to Hargreaves. 'Of course, you may look at it all you wish.'

His lordship could see at once that the ring, gold with a carnelian stone, bore the same coat of arms as his own ring, but with the addition of a bar across the top of the shield. He handed it back. 'It certainly bears the Hargreaves blazon. But unlike mine'—he held up his hand—'it shows the arms of a younger son.'

'That doesn't prove I'm not the heir.'

'No. But you'll have to do a lot better than that, to verify your claim, sir.'

'As I say, I have papers.' He reached into an inside pocket. 'This is a letter to me from my father.'

Hargreaves made no move to take it. 'It is not me you have to prove your identity to. It is a thing called "the Court of Privileges", and "the College of Arms". And it can go through the law courts if I decide to challenge your claim. My advice to you is to employ a good lawyer. I can give you the name of mine, and you can communicate through him. However, there are some questions I would like to ask you.'

At that moment, Parsons entered with a tray containing cups, a silver coffee pot, and a plate of sandwiches.

'That will be all, thank you, Parsons. I will pour.'

'Yes, M'lord. If I may,,' the butler added, 'I can inform the gentleman that his horse has been rugged up and given some water.'

Hargreaves placed the plate on a table beside his visitor, followed by a cup of coffee. 'Now, I am curious,' he said, carrying his own cup and sitting down, 'why you have taken so long to come forward. The fourth baron has been dead for over a year.'

'I've been abroad,' Hargreaves's visitor replied through a mouthful of ham sandwich. 'Didn't know the Lord Patrick was dead, let alone his successor.'

'Did you know Lord Patrick?'

'No. My father did though. He's been here.'

While he was eating, Hargreaves was able to observe the man seated opposite him more closely. His clothes seemed to be of good—if not the top—quality. His boots were well-polished, if a little dusty from his ride. But it was his visitor's hands that intrigued him. They looked strong and were tanned and more indicative of manual work than of a life of leisure. His speech was of an educated man but had an inflection, Hargreaves couldn't quite place. 'Were you abroad for long?'

The man hesitated a moment before answering, 'Twelve years.'

'I see. Have you come from London today? It's a long ride.'

'No, I've been staying in Tonbridge. I didn't mean to be so late. I got lost.'

Suddenly, Hargreaves remembered something Lady B had told him. 'But you've been here before, have you not? Were you not the gentleman who asked the way to Staplewood Park in the autumn of last year? Spying out the land, eh?'

With an air of bravado, the man said, 'I wanted to see what my inheritance looked like. Didn't you when you thought it was yours?'

'Actually, no. I wasn't even aware of its existence.'

'So it must have been a real honeyfall for you. I mean this grand house and estate'—he glanced at the silver coffee pot—'all the valuable contents and the money.'

216

Hargreaves got up to pour another cup and accidently touched Bedford's leg. The big dog gave a start and a deep woof. Sebastian Hargreaves pressed himself further into his chair. 'More coffee, Sir?'

'Thank you. I, of course, have always known about this place, from my father, you understand, although this is the first time I have been inside the house. My father came here in Lord Patrick's time.'

'He died eleven years ago,' Hargreaves retorted

'I was unaware of that or of his successor, until I returned to this country, only to find that you had inherited in my place.'

Hargreaves returned to his chair and steepled his fingers beneath his chin. 'What exactly do you expect from your inheritance, in the event your claim should succeed?'

Mr Hargreaves gave him a rather surprised look. 'This house and lands; the town house; the money; and, of course, the contents.' He waved a hand to signify the furnishings in the room.'

'I am afraid I am going to have to disillusion you about a few things. In the first place, there is no town house.'

'But I saw you, in London, leaving a very nice house in Mount Street—smallish but a very good address,' interrupted the visitor.

Hargreaves frowned. 'You may well have done, but that house belongs to the Marquis of Coverdale. He very generously allows me to stay there when the House of Lords is sitting.'

'But I was told my predecessor lived in London.'

'So he did, but in an hotel. The only thing he actually possessed was a desk. Everything else belonged to the hotel. Now, I suspect what you really want to find out about is how much money you might come into. Is that not so?'

'Yes. Isn't that what anyone in my position would want to know?' he replied a little defensively.

'I'm afraid you are in for another disappointment. The last Baron Hargreaves was a gambling man. By the time his debts and expenses were paid, there was very little left in his bank account, and I regret to say I have spent most of that—'

'Spent it!' exclaimed Mr Hargreaves. 'But that's outrageous. How much?' He jerked forward in his seat, and the dog let out another bark.

217

Hargreaves smiled. 'There is no need to get upset, sir. It all went on essential repairs to this house. All the accounts are freely available—as are grants of probate, deeds, and any other papers you wish to consult. You only have to get your lawyer to get in touch with mine. They are situated in Lincoln's Inn Fields.'

'Of course,' mumbled the man opposite. 'But the estate must be worth a pretty penny. I'm sure there would be plenty of people who would be interested in buying—'

'Perhaps. However, it is out of the question. The entire property is entailed on the eldest male heir. Are you married? Have sons?'

'No.'

'In that case, my son Nicholas will inherit when either of us dies.'

Mr Hargreaves looked round the room again. 'I believe entails can be broken. Is that not so?'

Hargreaves rubbed his chin thoughtfully. 'Only with the consent of the entailee—who must be of age. My son is only seventeen.' He smiled. 'Your prospects seem to be deteriorating by the minute.' Then he added, 'But there is one moderately bright spot.'

'Oh, I'd be glad to hear it.'

'The contents would be all yours, to do with as you wish.'

Hargreaves's visitor's eyes gleamed. 'The silver!' he exclaimed. 'My father told me about it. The wonderful silver galleon in full sail—'

'A magnificent sight, I am sure,' said Hargreaves regretfully, 'but alas, not one I have been privy to.'

'What do you mean?'

'Our predecessor sold everything he could lay his hands on—silver, paintings, oriental carpets, tapestries, anything—to fund his gambling habit. My butler will tell you. He was the fourth lord's servant, too. You certainly won't be able to live the life of leisure and luxury you probably imagined—that is, if your claim succeeds, Mr Hargreaves.' His Lordship stood up. 'I think I have given you a fair account of how things stand.' He drew his watch out. 'It is barely half past nine, plenty of time to reach Staplewood and put up for the night in the village. The "Rose and Crown" is a good hostelry. Mention my name,' he added with an ironic smile, 'if you encounter any difficulty.' He rang the bell.

The butler entered almost immediately. 'Ah, Parsons, this gentleman is leaving. Tell George to ready his horse for him.'

The visitor had no option but to stand up, causing Bedford to growl. He was clearly at a loss as to what to say, as Hargreaves ushered him towards the door. 'I expect to hear from my solicitors as soon as you have decided on your next course of action.'

'Yes, sir, yes indeed. It will be put in hand at once.'

Parsons was in the hall, holding the visitor's riding cloak. which he expertly eased the man into, and then handed him his hat, gloves, and whip. 'Your horse is at the door, sir.'

Hargreaves watched as the man trotted briskly down the drive in the bright moonlight. *I don't suppose for one minute that that is the end of this matter*, he thought and turned to go back into the house. But Bedford was standing at the door, anxious to go out, and Hargreaves was obliged to take him.

On their return five minutes later, the dog put his nose to the floor and crossed the hall, bumping into the bottom of the stairs. Putting his huge front paws on the third step, he raised his head and sniffed the air.

Parsons was locking the front door. 'I think he's trying to find Mr Matthew, My Lord. He doesn't understand that he is not in the house.'

'You are quite right, Parsons. Take him to Mr Matthew's room and bed him down for the night. He'll be happier if you can find something of Mr Matthew's for him to look after. Then bring me a brandy to my study.'

Chapter 40

Hargreaves came down to breakfast the next day after a surprisingly good night, perhaps helped a little by the brandy. He had lain awake for a short while, wondering how much he would really mind giving up Staplewood Park and all that went with it. He'd decided the only thing he would really regret was his seat in the House of Lords. And with that thought, he'd turned over and gone to sleep. He made two firm decisions. The first was that he would keep last night's encounter to himself for the time being. And the second that he would have to make an effort and find out more about Sebastian Hargreaves, starting immediately.

The family tree Matthew had found was still rolled up in the corner of his study. But realising it was too long and cumbersome for that room he took it to the dining room. The butler was polishing the table. 'Ah, Parsons, you can give me a hand with this.'

'Certainly, M'lord.'

'Take one end and put one of those candlesticks on it, so it doesn't roll up again. My end is weighted, so it will be all right. Have you seen it before?'

'No, M'lord. I don't think that sort of thing interested your predecessor.'

'Do you remember any of the names on it?'

Parsons gave a good look at the long parchment scroll, which covered about a third of the table. 'Other than his lordship who employed me, I don't recollect seeing any of them here, although some were mentioned by name.' He pointed to one. 'That is His Lordship's father, I believe, the honourable Arthur Hargreaves; and Lord Patrick, of course, he was His Lordship's uncle.'

'No one else?'

'I'm sorry, M'lord.' Parsons shook his head. 'I don't recall anyone else.'

'Never mind. I won't be long. Then you can have your table back,' Hargreaves smiled

'Very good, M'lord.' the butler withdrew.

Hargreaves studied the first lord's four sons—Clifford, the eldest; Henry, who had died in infancy; and then Sebastian; and, finally, Charles, his own great-grandfather.

Sebastian's son was another Clifford, and his son was another Sebastian. This was the man Hargreaves's visitor had purported to be. The later entries had been written in a different hand, much less neatly. And he noted wryly that he himself was not even named, merely called 'a son'. Most names were given the dates when they died but not that of the second Sebastian. Hargreaves removed the candlesticks and rolled up the chart. The only positive to come out of this research was that a Sebastian Hargreaves had existed. And if he still did, he was undoubtedly the rightful heir to the title and the estate.

Hargreaves returned to his study and propped the family tree back in the corner. Then took out all the papers relevant to his own succession and scrutinised them carefully for any reference to Sebastian. They seemed to be definite that he was dead, but the circumstances were rather vague. And there was no mention of a burial, either in this country or abroad. A visit to the graveyard surrounding the parish church might be fruitful.

Taking Bedford with him, he set off for the village.

The sexton was tidying up after a recent burial and stood, head bowed as Hargreaves approached. 'Have you been doing this job long?' he asked.

'Aye, M'lord, and me father before me; dunnamany years.'

'So, you were here when Lord Henry, my predecessor, was buried?'

The sexton sniffed and rubbed a finger across his nose. 'Aye, M'lord,' he said in a disapproving tone.

'And Lord Patrick?' continued Hargreaves.

'Aye, M'lord. A proper funeral that was, everything done just as it should be. Black horses with plumes brought 'is late lordship from the park. All the gentry come. An' next day the two ladies laid wreaths, all in black—the ladies, not the wreathes, you understand.'

'Which two ladies?'

'Why, M'lord, his late lordships two daughters, Miss Alice and Miss Harriet. Proper cut up, they was.' The sexton rubbed his nose again. 'Well. They was going to lose their 'ome as well as their father, weren't they?'

After looking at that part of the cemetery given over to his family, Hargreaves set off for home, pondering the sexton's words. Then the memory of the garrulous Mrs Thompson at the Tunbridge Wells concert came back to him. And what she had said about one of Lord Patrick's daughters being married to a deputy lieutenant of Sussex. It shouldn't, he thought, be too difficult to find her. Then another thought struck. Of course, the vicar would surely know their address. 'Come on, dog. Back we go.'

The reverend was only too pleased for any diversion from a sermon that was not going right, and was able to furnish Hargreaves with all the information he wanted regarding Lord Patrick's two daughters. And on his return home, he lost no time in writing to Lady Ascourt.

The reply was not long in coming, and included an invitation to stay at their Sussex home, the Hustings, for a couple of nights.

Still on his own at Staplewood, since Matthew had been invited to stay with the Coverdales in Berkley Square, Hargreaves set off for the Sussex home of Sir Geoffrey and Lady Ascourt, a distance of some forty miles. He arrived just before the winter sun was setting—to the warmest possible welcome. Lady Ascourt was a tall slender woman in her late fifties, fashionably attired and coiffed. She greeted Hargreaves with enthusiasm, saying, 'We were so delighted to get your letter, weren't we, Geoffrey?' She turned to her more reserved husband.

'Indeed, we were,' Sir Geoffrey replied, shaking Hargreaves warmly by the hand. 'My wife has longed for news of Staplewood. I'm afraid your predecessor had no interest in the family at all.'

'You must tell us everything. How did you feel when you came into your inheritance? Do you like Staplewood? Do you live alone?'

'My dear,' interrupted Sir Geoffrey, 'let the poor man get settled. I am sure he will tell us everything in due course.'

'Oh, I'm sorry, Lord Hargreaves. Pringle is here to take you up to your room, so you can refresh after your journey. We will be in the drawing room'—she indicated a door on her left—'when you are ready,' adding, 'I can hardly wait.'

Hargreaves inclined his head. 'Thank you, Lady Ascourt. I do feel a little dusty.'

'Oh, don't let's be so formal. Call me Cousin Alice. May I call you cousin, too?'

Sir Geoffrey raised his eyebrows. 'You don't object, My Lord?'

'No, of course not. I should be honoured to be called Cousin Charles. After all, that is what I am—if a bit removed,' replied Hargreaves.

'You're not removed at all now, so that's settled then.' The vivacious Alice smiled. 'Now I expect you would like to see your room. Geoffrey's man will be seeing to your clothes, and I shall get some refreshment up. We keep country hours here, so dinner is at 6.30,

As he mounted the stairs, Hargreaves was able to appreciate the classical proportions of the hall, the delicate plasterwork in the neoclassical taste, and pale apricot-coloured walls. He was sure the rest of the house would be equally delightful. And all his hopes were realised when he found a basin with taps, as well as a roaring fire in a large bedroom.

When he came downstairs, a footman opened the door to a charming drawing room, decorated in pale blues and greens, with classical motifs picked out in gold. Another lady, older than Alice, was seated by the fire. Lady Ascourt came forward. 'I do hope you found everything to your satisfaction, Cousin Charles. My sister is joining us for dinner. Harriet, my dear, this is Charles Hargreaves, our cousin.'

Hargreaves bowed over the proffered hand. 'I am delighted to meet you, Miss Hargreaves. It is so kind of your sister to invite me.'

His lordship was scrutinised by the older sister, through long-handled lorgnettes. 'You have a look of Papa about the eyes, but he was much taller—and thinner,' she added.

'Really, Harriet!' exclaimed Alice, 'I'm sure Cousin Charles is well aware of how much he resembles other family portraits. There are enough of them at Staplewood for him to scrutinise. Now, Cousin, please be seated. May I offer you a glass of sherry wine before dinner?'

Hargreaves was of two minds whether to tell the two ladies that the home they had grown up in and loved was but a shell of its former self, stripped as it was from so much of what they had known. But he was obliged to tell the truth at dinner when the subject of the silver ship came up once more.

Alice pointed to a quite attractive silver centrepiece, saying, 'Of course, it is nothing like the Hargreaves galleon. I don't suppose there is anything as beautiful as that ship. Don't you agree, Cousin Charles?'

Hargreaves heaved a sigh and laid down his knife and fork. 'I am very much afraid, ladies, that I have some bad news regarding the ship and indeed other things as well. The estate, as you know is entailed, but whoever created the entail did not include the contents. My predecessor sold almost everything he could lay his hands on, to feed his gambling habit. The ship and most of the other silver, pictures, and ornaments—in fact, almost everything of any value—had long gone before I got there.'

'Good heavens,' exclaimed Sir Geoffrey. 'Surely not the family portraits?'

Hargreaves nodded. 'I'm so sorry to have to tell you this.'

The two sisters looked at each other in horror. 'Oh dear, how awful. Our poor house. And I don't suppose he looked after what was left either. But it does explain one thing.' Alice looked at her sister. 'Doesn't it, Harriet?'

'Yes, indeed.' Harriet explained, 'You see, Cousin Charles, I offered to stay on and look after the place after Papa died. We knew our cousin lived in London. But I got very short shrift—virtually an eviction order. So of course, I packed my bags immediately, and dear Geoffrey found me a lovely little cottage in the village.'

'If I may say so,' Hargreaves remarked, 'my predecessor doesn't seem to have been a very pleasant fellow.'

'We hardly knew him. Our father fell out with his younger brother, and the two families never met—except at funerals. Poor Papa was devastated that Staplewood would go to his son, and you have just proved how right he was.'

After dinner, when the men rejoined the ladies in the drawing room, where tea was being served, Alice said, 'Now I know you said in your letter that, as well as being anxious to get to know us and learn more about Staplewood, you also had something else you said we might be able to help you with.'

Hargreaves laid down his cup of tea and told them, in as much detail as he could remember, about the late-night visit of the man who claimed to be the true heir to the title and the estate. When he had finished, there was a moment's silence.

Then Cousin Harriet announced firmly, 'That's all nonsense, of course. Sebastian Hargreaves is dead.'

'You can't know that for certain, Harriet dear,' her sister said gently.

'Yes I can. Captain Whatshisname came and told me.'

'Captain who?'

Harriet hit her head with the heel of her hand. 'Howard—that's it, Captain Howard ... of the *Daffodil*.'

'You're not making any sense, Harriet,' her sister said impatiently.

Sir Geoffrey intervened. 'Perhaps you'd better explain, Harriet, before Alice explodes.' He gave Hargreaves a conspiratorial smile.

'At the time,' Harriet said, 'it hardly seemed to matter. It was a week or so after dear Papa's funeral. You and Geoffrey had gone back home, and I had just received the letter from the solicitor telling me to leave. I suppose I was in a bit of a state ... Well, anyway, I was trying to choose which mirror to take—they were both mine, you know—when Pringle ... He came here with us. He didn't want to stay at Staplewood without His Lordship, our father, that is.'

'Harriet, my dear. I think you've wandered off the point a bit,' suggested Sir Geoffrey.

'Oh, yes, of course. Where was I?'

'Captain Howard of the *Daffodil*?'

'Pringle announced him. A tall, spare man, weather-beaten face, blue eyes, just as a sea captain ought to look. He said he was sorry to disturb me, but he had hoped to see my father. And I had to explain that, unfortunately, he was too late, but that I was his elder daughter. Would I do?'

Chapter 41

'So what *did* he tell you, Harriet?' asked Alice eagerly.

'He said it had been nearly two years ago. He was sailing to Australia with a shipload of convicts who were being deported to the colonies. But he had some paying passengers too—one of which was a Mr Hargreaves.'

Her listeners gave a gasp of surprise. Sir Geoffrey cleared his throat and was about to say something but changed his mind.

'Well, it seems that, about a month out to sea, a virulent fever broke out. It raged through passengers, prisoners, and crew alike. The weather was very bad too, and Mr Hargreaves became very ill. The captain could not spare a crew member to look after him, so he asked for a volunteer from the deportees to take on the job. However, after a week, Mr Hargreaves unfortunately died. He wasn't the only casualty. Captain Howard told me he buried six of the convicts on one day and three others a few days later, along with a Royal Marine, his second officer, and Mr Sebastian Hargreaves.

'I remember that particularly,' said Harriet, 'because I asked him what the Marines were for. And he said to keep order and relieve a unit on Van Diemen's Land.'

'Are you absolutely sure about this?' asked Hargreaves, his eyes alight.

'Oh, yes, Cousin Charles, quite sure.'

'Is there any proof—I mean other than his word?' enquired Sir Geoffrey.

'There was,' replied Harriet. 'He said he took a ring from Sebastian's finger and a bundle of documents and put them in his own cabin. It was a very stressful time for the captain, especially as the ship was quite badly damaged by the storm. When things eventually improved, he looked for the papers and the ring, but they had disappeared. He was very apologetic.'

'So, there's no written proof then?' Hargreaves was disappointed.

'Not, I suppose, of anything directly connected to Sebastian, but captains have to keep records of everything that happens on board— especially things like deaths at sea. And he assured me he'd kept his log meticulously, even giving the co-something-or-others of where the burials took place.'

'Coordinates?' suggested her brother-in-law.

'You should have told me all this before, Harriet,' Alice said a little resentfully.

'Probably,' replied her sister, 'but it didn't seem all that important at the time. And then I'm afraid I forgot all about it. After all, Sebastian wasn't the heir, at least not then.'

'I don't think that matters now,' put in Sir Geoffrey, forestalling a sisterly argument. 'It's what happens now, isn't that so, Hargreaves?'

Hargreaves felt like giving a whoop of triumph, but his better judgement as a lawyer prevailed, and he said, smiling broadly, 'Well, ladies, you have certainly exceeded my expectations, and is something I can work to give this imposter the short shrift he deserves.'

'Will you prosecute?' Alice said tentatively.

'Not if I can possibly help it. In my experience, court cases are invariably messy and not always successful.'

His newly found relatives looked relieved, and then Harriet looked at the enamel and diamond-studded fob watch pinned to her ample purple-covered bosom and exclaimed, 'Nine thirty already! My carriage will be here. You must excuse me, Cousin Charles.'

With Harriet gone and Alice deciding it was time for bed, Sir Geoffrey said, 'Now then, Hargreaves, I think it's time for something rather stronger than tea. Come into my study.'

The room was very similar to Hargreaves's own study and, unlike the rest of the house, oak-panelled and low-ceilinged. Ascourt noticed Hargreaves's surprise. 'It is the only part of the house that escaped a rigorous remodelling at the end of last century, and I'm really rather glad. But we're not here to talk about architecture. Brandy? I want to tell you some more, which might help you. Alice and Harriet are unaware of it, and it might upset them.'

In well-worn but comfortable armchair and a brandy at his elbow, Hargreaves concurred. 'I'm all ears.'

'It must have been about fourteen years ago or thereabouts. Alice and I were staying at Staplewood, and Clifford Hargreaves came to dinner. I'd never met him before, but he seemed to be very agitated during the meal, and we didn't stay long with the port afterwards. His Lordship and Mr Hargreaves disappeared into the study. And by next morning, Clifford was gone. With a gave face, this is what his lordship told me: Clifford's son, Sebastian, had got himself into very deep water. He had apparently been selling worthless shares in a non-existent emerald mine in South America, on the promise of huge returns, and had been found out.'

'My goodness!' exclaimed Hargreaves.

'Yes, well ... Naturally, the parties concerned wanted recompense, and/or punishment. Clifford had come to Patrick for help.'

'Did he give it?'

'Of course. Otherwise, there would have been a dreadful scandal. Patrick agreed to pay back all the defrauded parties all their money, plus interest—provided they did not bring criminal charges or sue for their money. However, some aggrieved victims felt Sebastian should not go scot-free, so his father ordered him to Australia and not to return for twelve years at least. Thus, a scandal was avoided, and the family name was safe. My wife and sister-in-law are unaware of all this, and I would like it to remain so, My Lord.'

'Naturally, sir Geoffrey, they will never hear it from me. But it is quite a story,' agreed Hargreaves, 'and it certainly explains a lot. The so-called claimant could easily have discovered much about Sebastian and his father—including knowledge of that ship.'

'And with the bad weather and the fever, I don't suppose it would have been too difficult to slip into the captain's cabin and steal the ring and the papers.'

Hargreaves left the Ascourts a much happier man. He had discovered some delightful new relatives, and it would not be long before they came to visit Staplewood. He had enough ammunition, with a bit of digging, to blow the imposter out of the water. God was in His heaven, and almost all was all right with the world. But his heart still yearned for the lovely

228

Rosalie. The fact of the matter was, though, his finances were becoming so tight he only managed to scrape through each month. How could he ask any woman, let alone the widow of a son of a marquis, to share a life, of what to her, would undoubtedly seem like poverty? And there was no way his conscience would allow her money to supplement his income, although the law, as it stood, allowed him to do so.

By the end of the week, both Emily and Matthew had returned from their respective visits. Matthew, wearing the latest fashion and carrying a silver-topped cane was greeted by an ecstatic Bedford. He was full of his experiences, not least because his visit to London Bridge Railway Station had reignited his enthusiasm for railway engineering, but also because he had enjoyed the social life the Coverdales had introduced him to. Hargreaves told Emily the entire saga of the visit of the man claiming to be the true heir, and all he had learned from his visit to the Ascourts.

'Well,' she said sternly, 'here was me thinking of you all alone at Staplewood. And all the time, you've been gallivanting all around the countryside in search of new relations.' Then she smiled. 'I'm glad you found them and were able to put an end to that man's ridiculous pretentions.'

'I don't think it's quite finished with yet, my dear. I'm sure Cousin Harriet's recollections are correct. She's that sort of person. But I need to confirm them with witnesses and documentation too, if possible.'

Emily was supremely confident. 'Of course you will, Charles. People like him never get away with it.'

Hargreaves lost no time in putting everything in motion to establish the truth of Captain Howard's story. His Lincoln's Inn lawyers were in a better position to find records and track down crew members of the *Daffodil* who were on that voyage. And it was not long before advertisements in national and local newspapers bore fruit in the form of the third mate, a Mr Jepson, who had been on that passage. Mr Jepson was in Bristol, where he had seen the advertisement in the local paper, but was about to sail for America. He was persuaded to swear an affidavit to the effect that he had been present at the burial at sea of a passenger known as Sebastian Hargreaves.

From the claimant himself, nothing more was heard—until a letter arrived from a firm of solicitors, announcing they were looking into their client's rightful claim to the barony of Staplewood and the estate of Staplewood Park.

Chapter 42

By the middle of the third week in January, the occupants of Staplewood and Mairsford woke up to a countryside blanketed in six inches of snow. Big fat, feathery flakes were falling so thickly visibility was reduced to a few yards. But worse was to come. The wind got up, and the flakes turned to icy needles that quickly piled up against hedges and fences, blocking roads and cutting off all communications. It was nearly three days before a path could be cleared to the village, and Hargreaves was able to send Royston with a message to the vicar, to ensure that Staplewood pensioners and, indeed, any other old people were not left without food or fuel. This was something, he later discovered, that had not occurred since the death of Lord Patrick Hargreaves. As far as Staplewood House was concerned, they were well stocked for a long siege, but the only exercise available was shovelling snow.

One evening after dinner, Hargreaves brought the strange cloth-bound book into the drawing room, so they could all have another attempt at deciphering its purpose.

After flicking through the pages, Emily announced, 'I'm sure it must be an account book, and the figures in column three must represent money.'

'I think that's fairly obvious,' her brother said a little scathingly.

She gave him a withering look. 'What does "Benares" mean?'

'It's a place in India,' replied Hargreaves. 'Well, we know that the first Lord Hargreaves made his fortune there.'

'Perhaps it's not about the place. But could it be a code word—for something or someone?' Matthew queried. 'How many times does it appear?' Emily handed him the book.

'You know, Emily,' said Hargreaves, 'Bethany worked out that all the figures in the left-hand column are dates.'

'She's done better than you, then, Charles, hasn't she?' His earlier remark obviously still rankled.

'There are thirty-five entries for the word, or name, "Benares"—at least one in every month, sometimes two.' Matthew looked up from his counting.

'Let me have a look.' Emily put down the lace collar she was crocheting. Matthew passed her the book.

'It looks very like the account books I keep for the household expenses, only you can't see what they are for. In my books, the entries for staff wages are the same for each person, each month. If Benares is a person, perhaps the figures refer to payments of his wages. What do you think, Charles?'

Hargreaves thought for a moment. 'Yes,' he said, slowly, 'yes, I think that's quite possible. I believe tje first Lord Hargreaves may well have had an Indian servant.'

Two voices spoke as one, and two pairs of eyes stared at him in surprise. 'How do you know?'

'Well, old Berrow at the forge told me. He remembered seeing a man in a turban come to the forge. He was only about ten at the time, but—'

'Charles! What have you been hiding from us? It's disgraceful behaviour—keeping secrets from your only sister and dear Matthew, who has been helping you.'

'Now, don't get on your high horse, Emily. I just didn't want idle speculation—or gossip.'

'So we're gossips now. Who, pray, are we supposed to be gossiping to?'

To hide his embarrassment at this family quarrel, he got up and rang the bell and, when Parsons arrived, asked him to bring in some sherry wine and brandy. 'I think a little refreshment will do us all good,' he announced when the butler had gone.

Sipping sherry wine and nibbling the ratafia biscuits Parsons had thoughtfully supplied, Emily said, in a more conciliatory tone, 'I think you had better explain yourself, Charles.'

So he told them both about his visit to the underground chamber with Shephard, and the subsequent trip to the forge. 'I really wanted to find out more about the building of this house, and old Berrow is the only person left who can tell me anything.'

'So, what did he tell you, sir?' asked Matthew.

'Not a great deal; he is stone deaf, so communication was difficult. But he remembers this Indian man coming to the forge and ordering lots of iron rods and being very particular about the exact size. I imagine they were for the bannisters and balustrade in the hall.'

Matthew looked thoughtful. 'Nothing else?'

'No, I'm afraid not.'

'I hardly think that piece of information would be worthy of gossip,' Emily said pointedly, not having forgotten her brother's secretiveness in the matter.

'Well, I've told you everything, now. Matthew, will you look at the book again, tomorrow, and see if anything we've discussed is relevant? I suggest we have a game of three-handed whist before we go to bed.'

After three days of severe frost, on the first of February, the weather changed dramatically—the temperature rose, accompanied by rain. The snow slithered into ditches and disappeared from the fields, leaving only heaps by the roadside where drifts had accumulated. The roads themselves, which had become impassable, were now almost as difficult, as they turned to slushy swamps. However, the postal service was able to resume, and Parsons brought a large pile of letters to the breakfast table. Most of the letters were for Lord Hargreaves, but two were for Emily, and one for Matthew.

Emily was the first to divulge the contents of one of hers. 'Listen to this, Charles,' she said excitedly. 'You'll never believe this.'

'Not until you tell us. Good news I hope, Emily.'

'Amazing! Precious's egg has hatched! What do you say to that? I'm a grandmother!'

'What I say, my dear sister, is that it is the nature of birds' eggs to hatch.'

'Oh, really Charles, you have no imagination. What do *you* think, Matthew?'

'You and Precious are to be congratulated. I believe it is quite rare for parrots to breed in captivity,' said Matthew, who had broken the seal on his letter and seemed prepared to share its content. 'This is from Mr Pettigrew. You remember the lawyer in Bristol who was so helpful in finding my watch. I wrote to him while I was in London, asking him where I should stay if I came to Bristol, and did he know anyone who could help me to acquire the knowledge of railroad engineering that I am keen to pursue?'

'You're leaving us, Matthew? I can't believe you're ready for it yet,' said Hargreaves.

'Not immediately, of course. But I can't stay here forever. And I thought it wise to make inquiries.'

'Quite right, too, but you must be absolutely sure that you are fit enough. But what does Mr Pettigrew have to say?'

Matthew looked closely at the letter. 'He says rooms can easily be gotten at the George Hotel, and he is well acquainted with Mr Brunel's lawyers. Imagine that!' He broke off excitedly. 'Mr Brunel himself!' He rose from the table. 'I must write back at once!'

When Matthew had left, brother and sister looked at each other. They knew Matthew was right. A young man of Matthew's ability and ambition must make his own way in the world. Emily heaved a deep sigh. 'We shall miss him very much. He's been such a lovely person to have about the place. Bedford will be very upset, too. He's devoted to Matthew.'

'I know someone else who will be devastated, too.'

For a moment Emily looked puzzled. Then she realised what her brother meant. 'Oh!' she said, 'You mean Lady Julia. But I don't think there is anything serious between them; they just enjoy each other's company.'

Hargreaves knew better but said nothing.

Chapter 43

Matthew and Joseph were to travel to Bristol in fourteen days' time, but there was plenty to do before then. Lady B gave a farewell dinner party for Matthew, and Bethany was allowed to attend for the first two courses. Seated next to Matthew, she engaged him in lively conversation concerning any further discoveries in the book that she had already helped to decipher. Before answering any specific queries, Matthew looked across at Lord Hargreaves, who nodded his assent.

'Well, Bethany, Lord Hargreaves has discovered that the first Baron had an Indian servant. And we think that the word "Benares" probably refers to him, because the figures next to his name each month are the same—maybe his wages. But the amounts seem very large.'

Bethany thought for a moment and then said, 'Perhaps he paid him in rupees. That's what they use for money in India.' She said it rather loudly, and conversation round the table stopped. Bethany blushed scarlet. 'Sorry, Mama.'

Hargreaves intervened immediately, before her mother could utter the words that were clearly on her lips. 'Please, Lady B, I believe the child could well be right. Sometimes young people can get a little over-excited—'

Rosalie smiled. 'Of course, you are right, Lord Hargreaves.' She turned towards her daughter. 'In future, Bethany, remember to keep your voice down at the dinner table.'

'Yes, Mama,' whispered the girl, apparently glad to be let off with a mild rebuke.

After dinner when the men had rejoined the ladies, there was music. Several of the guests, as well as the hostess, contributed with varying displays of talent. The exception was Lady Julia and Matthew, who sat at either end of the room, studiously—in Hargreaves's opinion—avoiding each other's eyes.

The Staplewood coach was drawn up outside. Hargreaves and his sister were waiting under the shelter of the gatehouse, when Lady B suddenly said, 'Oh, I nearly forgot. Will you excuse me for a moment?' She rustled off in her pink-flounced silk dress and returned a minute or two later with a small scrap of paper. 'You may remember, Lord Hargreaves, that this is the scrap of paper you found when you were looking for Matthew. It seems such a long time ago now. We will all miss him very much—'

'Yes, I know,' he said, tucking the note into an inside pocket. 'But I also know he will always keep in touch, won't you Matthew?' He addressed the young man, who had just appeared from the courtyard.

Lady Julia also arrived but from the drawing room. The lock of hair that had descended to her neck from her elaborate chignon was enough to tell Hargreaves that, despite the subterfuge, he was not deceived. He guessed that Matthew and Julia had been saying a very private farewell.

With just three days to go before Matthew left, most of his preparations were in place. Mr Pettigrew had confirmed that rooms at the George Hotel in Bristol had been engaged for himself and Joseph. The journey would be taken in easy stages, starting with a night in London at Coverdale House in Berkely Square.

Matthew and Joseph were in his room discussing which clothes should be packed in the newly restored valise. The local saddler had repaired and polished it, so it was now good enough to use again. A piercing yellp was followed by the sound of something heavy falling. Doors to Matthew's room, drawing room, and study opened simultaneously, Emily and Hargreaves emerged. But Matthew was first on the scene. Bedford was lying at the foot of the stairs. ' Oh, Bedford!' he exclaimed. 'What *have* you done? Are you hurt?' He knelt down, and the dog raised his head a few inches. The others all stood around horrified but not knowing what to do.

Hargreaves noticed with dismay that the dog had not responded by wagging his tail. If he was unable to, he feared the worst. He went forward and put a hand on Matthew's shoulder. 'I'm afraid he's badly hurt. I think his back may be broken.'

Matthew's anguished face turned up to Hargreaves. 'We *must do* something.'

Hargreaves shook his head, as he saw a trickle of urine appear from beneath Bedford's body.

'I'm afraid there's only one thing *we can* do.' He made a significant gesture to his butler, who had just entered the hall.

Matthew sat on the floor with Bedford's broad head on his lap; the dog's great golden eyes seemed to be pleading. Matthew fondled his ears. The dog heaved an enormous sigh, and then the breath shuddered out of his mighty chest, and his eyes closed.

'I'm sorry. He's gone.' Hargreaves squeezed Matthew's shoulder.

Matthew gently eased Bedford's head off his lap, got to his feet, rushed into his room, and slammed the door. He was not seen again that day.

Emily, who had been standing stock-still with her mouth in a silent 'O', burst into tears and rushed into her brother's arms.

Parsons returned, holding a pistol, pointing downwards. Over his sister's white lace cap, Hargreaves shook his head, and Parsons retreated.

George came into the hall and paused for a moment while he took in the tragic scene. 'I am taking Mrs Clayborne to the drawing room. Please bring brandy and tea there as quickly as possible. Then ask Parsons and Joseph to meet me here. I wish to make suitable arrangements. I want to emphasise that, at all times, Bedford is to be treated with respect.'

By noon next day, the grave, lined with evergreens, had been dug at the edge of the shrubbery, where it joined the formal garden. Bedford's body was lying on a blanket, with only his head exposed; he looked as if he was peacefully asleep. The entire household was gathered round the grave, and when Hargreaves gave a sign, Shephard bent down and pulled the blanket over the dog's head.

Emily, with tear-bright eyes, placed Bedford's collar and lead on the blanket. Next, Matthew, pale but seemingly composed, carefully put his dog's favourite toy—the cloth-wrapped stick with the bells attached—beside the lead and then walked quickly away.

Just at that moment, Lady Julia came bursting through the conservatory door. 'There you all are!' she exclaimed. Then stopped dead in her tracks as she saw the mound of earth. Hargreaves came quickly towards her and explained in a few words what had happened.

'Oh, poor Bedford, por Matthew!' She glanced round the assembly. 'Where is he?'

Hargreaves pointed to one of the seats that surrounded the fountain. Matthew was sitting there, facing away, head bowed.

Lady Julia swiftly crossed the grass towards the seat. Hargreaves watched as she sat down beside Matthew, not speaking, not touching, just waiting. Everyone had dispersed, Shephard was filling in the grave. Hargreaves returned slowly to the house. And before he went in, he just caught sight of Matthew, held close in Lady Julia's embrace.

Matthew was going through Bedford's sleeping box before it was removed. He found several items the dog had treasured. He discarded most of them—especially the two smelly marrow bones but put the half-chewed slipper into his valise. To his great surprise, he discovered a heavy bright metal object. For a moment he couldn't think what it was. Then he remembered the gilded grape he had carelessly dislodged from the grand staircase. Bedford must have found it and kept it as a prized possession. Matthew put it on the mantelpiece to return to Lord Hargreaves.

The day before his departure, Matthew distributed to each member of the staff his heartfelt thanks and a handsome gratuity. 'I would like to speak to you, Parsons, in my room, in, say, five minutes.'

'Certainly, sir.'

Parsons entered to find Matthew sitting at his table with a pile of gold sovereigns in front of him.'

'I have a commission for you, Parsons. I am particularly desirous of doing something for Lord Hargreaves, and I have come up with a plan. But I need you to execute part of it for me.'

'I am at your service, sir, in any way I can help.' The butler glanced at the amount on the table. 'What precisely do you wish me to undertake, Mr Matthew?'

'I want you to find the whereabouts of this.' He gave the butler a folded note. 'I'm sure your knowledge and experience will stand you in good stead.'

Parsons unfolded the note, raised his eyebrows, and smiled.

Matthew pushed the pile of ten gold coins towards him 'These should cover any expense you may incur. Keep any that are left over. But do not hesitate to let me know if more is required. Write to me at the George Hotel, Bristol, as soon as you have news. If all goes well, I will do the rest.'

'With the greatest of pleasure, sir. A wonderful gesture if I may say so.'

Matthew smiled. 'But remember, absolute secrecy. Tell no one.'

'Naturally, sir,' he said, placing the note in an inside pocket. 'Will that be all, sir?'

After dinner, on Matthew's last day, he and Hargreaves were sitting in the study. Matthew put down his brandy. 'If you will excuse me, sir, I have something for you.' He left the room and quickly returned with a large book. 'I would like you to have this, sir.' He handed Hargreaves his copy of *Castles and Great Houses of England*. 'It has Staplewood Park in it.'

'That is very kind of you, Matthew. If I remember'—he smiled—'not a very flattering description.'

'Perhaps not, but it does praise the staircase.' Matthew dug into his pocket, 'Which can now be restored to its full glory with this.' He opened his hand to reveal the gilded grape.

'Now, where on earth did that come from after all this time?'

'It was hidden under Bedford's blanket. He must have found it and decided it was worth keeping.'

Hargreaves hefted it in his hand. 'It is really quite heavy; each bunch of them must weigh a pound or more.' He examined it closely. 'There is a hole at one end. It shouldn't be difficult to reattach it.' Both men were silent, thinking of Bedford, and how much he would be missed. At length, Hargreaves said, 'He would have been miserable without you, Matthew. You were his reason for being, his life's work, as it were.'

'Yes, I know. He will always have a huge place in my heart.'

'I was thinking of a headstone. What would you like?'

Matthew thought for a while, then said, "Bedford, a faithful friend", and the date he died.'

'It will be there when you come and visit us again.'

The gloomy hiatus caused by the departure of Matthew and the death of Bedford was somewhat relieved by the arrival of the irrepressible Nicky for his half-term holiday. Also, there were definite signs that spring was in the air. Daffodil spears were showing buds, single primroses appeared under sheltered hedgerows, and birdsong increased in intensity. Nicky returned from his first visit to Mairsford in rather a pensive mood.

'What's the matter, son?' enquired his father. 'Didn't you get to ride Gladiator?'

'Oh, yes,' he replied enthusiastically, 'and Julia allowed—'

'Lady Julia to you, Nicky,' put in Emily firmly.

'Oh, all right, *Lady* Julia allowed me to put him to a proper jump for the first time. But it's not that. She seemed different—sort of distracted. And when we went for a hack, she hardly spoke at all.'

Hargreaves knew exactly what the matter was, but it wasn't a topic for general discussion. 'Lady B told me her niece was due to return to London soon.'

'For the season, you know,' interrupted Emily.

'Yes,' went on Hargreaves, 'and I don't think she really likes so-called polite society. That's probably what's concerning her.'

Nicky shrugged. 'It's just not like her, that's all.'

Chapter 44

Ten days later Hargreaves was having a late breakfast alone, brows furrowed, at the latest bills that had come by post. Sighing, he looked out of the window to see Lady B's travelling coach, driving at a smart clip up the drive. Parsons had barely time to announce her when she cried: 'Oh, Lord Hargreaves, I'm so glad you're here!' Parsons discreetly retreated and closed the door.

'You'll never guess what's happened! I don't know what to do!' she exclaimed dramatically and then contradicted herself, 'At least I do, but I need to know what you think.'

'My dear Lady B, please calm yourself. Sit down and tell me what has gone wrong.' He tried not to look anxious.

'It's terrible! I don't know what Amanda and Justin will think. She was in my charge.' The words spilled out of Rosalie in a torrent.

Hargreaves took a spare cup from the silver tray and poured the distressed woman a coffee. 'Now, Lady B,' he said, adding sugar and pushing the cup towards her. 'I cannot help you if you do not tell me what has happened.'

Rosalie appeared to pull herself together. 'No, you are quite right. I am behaving like a hysterical maidservant, and that's not like me. But I was just so relieved to find you at home. I feared you might have gone to London.'

Hargreaves smiled. 'As you see, I am here. Now, what's amiss?'

'Julia has run away!'

'On her own?'

'She has her maid, Ferguson, with her. But that's not the point, My Lord,' Rosalie said impatiently.

Somehow the news didn't altogether take Hargreaves by surprise. 'To be with Matthew, I presume?'

'You knew? How did you know? Was it arranged? Why didn't you tell me?' Rosalie said accusingly, anger flaring in her eyes.

'Please, Lady B, I am absolutely certain that any *arrangements* that were made were done entirely by Lady Julia herself. However, the signs that they were in love have been fairly evident for some time. And it is that, which makes me sure Matthew had no hand in this. The very last thing he would want is for Lady Julia to ruin her reputation.'

The anger died out of Rosalie's face. 'You are quite right. Matthew is a very honourable young man.' The glimmer of a smile touched her lips. 'He's going to be mightily surprised. But I must go after her.'

Hargreaves looked worried. 'Not on your own, surely?'

'How else would I go? Except I thought that Emily might—?'

'I'm sure she would. But unfortunately, she is laid low with a heavy cold. When did Lady Julia leave?'

'Very early this morning, by one of the wagons that take vegetables up to the market. She had a chaise waiting for her in Tonbridge. She wrote it all in this letter.' Rosalie pulled a crumpled sheet from her reticule and handed it to Hargreaves.

'Travel by private coach is very expensive. How could she pay for it?'

Rosalie took a gulp of her coffee. 'You'll never believe this, My Lord. She has *sold* Gladiator! Look in the letter.'

Hargreaves turned over the page and read parts of it out loud. '"Master of the hunt ... 500 guineas ... must take on my groom to look after him." Well,' he said at last, 'I must say Lady Julia is a very well-organised young lady.'

'Hmph,' grunted Rosalie. 'Yes. And she managed it all behind my back, the devious child.'

'I think it shows one thing, though. Apart from her family, the only person she loves more than that horse is Matthew. She has sacrificed a lot to be with him.'

'But she can't be, of course. I must fetch her back before any damage is done to her reputation.'

'I will come with you, Lady B. You cannot travel all that way alone.'

'Rosalie's eyes twinkled mischievously. 'What about *your* reputation, My Lord?'

Hargreaves quirked an eyebrow but otherwise ignored the r+emark. 'I imagine you have your maid with you. We can set off in about an hour.'

'An hour!' exclaimed Rosalie, 'but she already has had a six-hour start.'

'Exactly so, Lady B. We could never catch them—even if we were in a racing curricle. The best we can hope for is to arrive before nightfall tomorrow. She will have to put up for the night, as will we.' Hargreaves crossed over to the door to the hall. 'George, ask Lady Benedict's maid to come in and give her some refreshment. Ask Mrs Royston to pack a luncheon—and some wine. Then tell Royston to put up sufficient gear for me for a three-night stay.'

Just before they we ready to depart, Parsons requested permission to have two days leave. Hargreaves acquiesced readily, as his own attention was taken up by the fact that Lady B's maid did not appear to be in the carriage and enquired why.

'Jenny is a bad traveller, despite being with me all round Europe. But she is fine sitting beside the groom. She is well wrapped up, I assure you.'

The journey was uneventful. And after the subject of Matthew and Julia had been exhausted, they enjoyed lively conversation. As the day progressed, the temperature dropped, and Hargreaves unfolded the fur-lined rug from the seat beside him and placed it over Rosalie's knees.

'Oh no, Lord Hargreaves,' she said at once, 'we must share it.' Before he could argue, she had moved to sit beside him, covering them both with the rug. 'Remember, we've already shared one before—and a bed! Our reputations are already ruined.' She grinned mischievously.

After a night spent at an inn on the Bath Road, the coach pulled up outside the George Hotel in Bristol at four o'clock. Rosalie went directly to the reception desk. 'I am Lady Benedict St Maure. I want to know where my niece, Lady Julia St Maure, may be found. Is she staying here?'

'No, My Lady, I believe not.'

'Have you seen her?'

'Yes, My Lady. She arrived this morning with her maid—enquiring after a young gentleman currently resident here. A Mr Matthew Stuart.'

Rosalie turned round to face Hargreaves, who was standing patiently listening to this exchange. 'There, you see. I told you so. They've run off together.'

Rosalie addressed the clerk again. 'Do you know where they went?'

'Yes, My Lady.' He turned and took down a note from the rack on the wall behind the counter. 'Mr Stuart left this.' He handed her the piece of paper.

Her gloved hand trembled, 'Here,' she said to Hargreaves, 'you read it. Do not tell me they have gotten married.'

Hargreaves took his spectacles from his waistcoat pocket, and read:

> *To whom it may concern (Lady Benedict and/or Lord Hargreaves, I suspect),*
>
> *The arrival of Lady Julia at this hotel this morning came as a complete surprise, not to say shock, to me. I do not hesitate to tell you Lady Julia's welfare and reputation were my first concern. There is no question of her staying in this hotel, and my limited knowledge of the town renders me unable to recommend suitable alternative accommodation.*
>
> *We have, therefore, gone to see Mr Pettigrew, who has been such a help to me in the past, to resolve this dilemma. His address is appended.*
>
> *Should Lady Benedict require an escort, Joseph is available.*

'It is *signed Matthew Stuart*,' Hargreaves concluded.

Mr Pettigrew himself opened the door and smiled. 'I believe I have the honour of addressing Lady Benedict St Maure and Lord Hargreaves or, perhaps, Lord and Lady Coverdale?'

'Right the first time, Mr Pettigrew,' said Rosalie briskly. 'Now where is my niece?'

Hargreaves interposed. 'I am sure Mr Pettigrew would be much happier discussing everything in his office, rather than on his doorstep, don't you think'?

'Of course. I'm sorry. But you see. I am so worried.'

Once all were seated in the lawyer's office, Mr Pettigrew said, 'I will come straight to the point. Mr Stuart came here this morning, accompanied by a young woman, who he introduced as Lady Julia St Maure. He explained that she had arrived in Bristol with her maid, intending to stay at the George Hotel. This, he said, was impossible, as her reputation might be at stake if she did so.'

'Of course it would,' agreed Rosalie. 'So what did you do?'

Mr Pettigrew steepled his fingers and leant forward, smiling slightly. 'I am happy to say that, in the past few weeks, I have had quite a lot to do with Mr Matthew Stuart. He has dined several times with my wife and me, so I was certain my wife would be only too happy for Lady Julia and her maid to stay with us. There is plenty of room, as our children have all left home.'

Rosalie clapped her hands. 'Oh, Mr Pettigrew, you are an angel. Thank you so very, very much. You see, Lady Julia has been staying with me. So I feel responsible for her, so you will understand my anxiety.'

'So where is Stuart now?' enquired Hargreaves.

'He escorted Lady Julia to our house in Cliftonville. Then he said he had to return to work.' Mr Pettigrew glanced at the office clock. 'But I expect he has now returned to my house. We can all repair there now, if that is your wish, My Lady? My Lord?'

Lady Julia received a severe telling off from Rosalie, condemning her impetuous action that had put so many people to great inconvenience and worry. 'I'm sorry, Aunt Rosalie. But I was so afraid I would never see him again, and I love him—'

Rosalie, who understood Julia's feelings entirely, was inwardly sympathetic. But the consequences of her thoughtless escapade could have been disastrous, not only for her, but also for the man she loved. After dinner, Hargreaves and Matthew went back to the George Hotel. Two days later, Hargreaves returned to Staplewood Park. And the rest of the party left for London and Berkeley Square, where Julia was told, in no uncertain terms, by her mother that she must now stay there for the Season.

At Lord Coverdale's request, Matthew travelled up to London as soon as his work permitted, and was immediately called into Lord Coverdale's study. He stood in front of the large desk, pale but composed. 'Now then, young man,' the marquis began, 'I am very glad to see you have recovered from all your injuries. Is your foot quite well now?'

'Thank you, My Lord, almost completely, only rough ground is still somewhat of a problem. But I am assured that will pass in time.'

'Good. Now I understand that my daughter wishes to marry you. Are you of the same mind?'

Matthew was a little taken aback by such a direct approach. 'I love Lady Julia very much, sir. But that is not to say I would make a suitable husband for her or, indeed, that you would think so, My Lord.'

'Sit down, Matthew, and tell me why you think that is the case, and why she believes you will never ask her.'

'Well, sir, I am not an aristocrat. I am not of noble birth. And I want to work. These are not attributes for the husband of a noble lady.'

'Nevertheless, despite all these shortcomings, you have shown yourself in the best possible light. My only reservation—and I have discussed this with my wife—is Julia's commitment. She is always headstrong in the face of opposition, and she is quite convinced that we would oppose the marriage.' He smiled. 'On the other hand, the fact that she sold her beloved horse in order to have enough money to pay her way and be with you ...' He paused. 'She is not aware of your recent acquisition of a fortune, is she?'

Matthew shook his head in amazement. *Julia sold Gladiator!* For me!'

'Yes, which makes me believe she has serious intentions towards you. So this is what we propose. Julia will be twenty this August, and if you are both of the same mind, then we will give you both our blessing. Meanwhile, we will allow you to write to each other but no more than once a week. Do I have your word on this, Matthew?'

'Yes, indeed, sir. I ... I am quite overwhelmed by your—'

The marquis cut him short and smiled. 'Now, how about a drink, before you go and tell her the good news she has been longing to hear.'

Chapter 45

Hargreaves was in his study. Emily was still confined to her bed, and although he had work to do, his mind kept skipping back to the journey he had undertaken with Lady B.

Parsons entered. 'There is a gentleman to see you, M'lord.'

'Did he give his name?'

'No, M'lord, but he has been here before. Do you wish to see him?'

'Show him into the library but stay close,' Hargreaves said and added, 'George too.'

Parsons opened the door wide and stood aside to allow the quasi-Lord Hargreaves entry. But he stayed by the open door until His Lordship gave the signal to depart.

Hargreaves felt fully confident that he had the situation in hand. 'Well, well, well, Mr Quails, I presume.' This was a shot in the dark, but Hargreaves felt if it hit the mark; he had the upper hand.

The man standing in front of Hargreaves was wearing the same clothes as last time, but the green coat and cord breeches were considerably shabbier, and the boots more worn. 'You've discovered my name then,' he said sullenly.

'I have good sources. And even if I hadn't, your ridiculous claim would never have succeeded. What I do not understand is why you have come back. I could have you arrested for false pretences, you know.'

Joshua Quails's head went up, and a sly expression crossed his face. 'I don't think you will, My Lord, when you've heard what I have to say.'

'I suggest you say it and get out of my house as quickly as possible.'

'Not so fast, not so fast. You wouldn't want a lady's name dragged through the mud, now would you?'

'Don't talk rubbish, man!' Hargreaves exclaimed, racking his brains to work out what the man meant.

'I'm sure you'll recall it soon enough. A little roll in the hay with a lady who was not your wife. *Mr Clayborne*, eh?' Quails gave a knowing leer.

Hargreaves frowned, and then he recalled the accident to the carriage on the way home from Tunbridge Wells. But how had Quails got hold of the name, Clayborne? Of course. His brow lifted. Quails must have heard Mrs Worthy addressing him by that name in Tonbridge market. 'So now you're trying a little blackmail to add your list of misdemeanours. Is that it? Don't be ridiculous, man.'

'Hundred quid, and I'll keep my mouth shut. Or I go to the papers.'

'*You'll* be going to prison—for a very long time.'

'You won't pay?'

'Certainly not. And I'll tell you why. Mrs Clayborne is my sister. She is currently upstairs, suffering from a severe cold. However, I will call her maid. No, better still, *you* call her maid, so there can be no collusion.' Hargreaves went over to the fireplace and pulled the bell rope. The butler entered immediately. 'Parsons, this … er … gentleman requires you to do something. I wish you to perform the task.'

Parsons looked a little surprised, 'Yes, M'lord.'

'Go ahead, Mr quailes.'

'Please ask Mrs Clayborne's maid to come here at once.'

'Very good, sir. M'lord.?' Hargreaves nodded.

Two minutes later, a tall rather severe-looking woman arrived. 'Thank you for coming, Withers. I would like you to answer any questions this *gentleman* has to ask you.' He indicated Quails.

Withers dropped a curtsy. 'If that is your wish, M'lord.'

'Go ahead, Mr Quails. Ask your questions.'

Looking rather less sure of his ground, Quails asked, 'You are Mrs Clayborne's lady's maid?'

'Yes, sir.'

'What relation is Lord Hargreaves to this Mrs Clayborne?'

Withers could barely conceal her surprise. 'Mrs Clayborne is his Lordship's sister, sir.'

'Does she have a green evening gown?'

'No, sir. But she has a green velvet evening cloak.'

'Can you describe her to me?'

Withers looked questioningly at Hargreaves, who nodded assent. 'Mrs Clayborne is a lady in her sixties. She is not very tall, white-haired. Is that enough, M'lord?'

'Satisfied, Quails?'

'Yes, I suppose so,' he replied sullenly.

'Thank you, Withers, you may go.'

'I don't know where you got your misinformation from. I can only suspect it was from the Worthy's servant girl, trying to make a bit of extra money. But she never saw either Mrs Clayborne or myself, except possibly from a distance. Explanations are not due to you, Quails. But my sister and I decided to call ourselves man and wife, in order to share a room, and not to inconvenience the Worthys so late at night. Let that be the end of the matter. Now leave.' Hargreaves went to the door.

'Wait,' Quails said and then added, 'please.'

'Now what?

'I need money. I want to go back to Australia. And I don't have enough for the fare.'

Hargreaves heaved a sigh. 'You really are a tiresome fellow, but it is probably worth it to get rid of you forever. How much?'

'Fifty pounds, sir.'

Hargreaves knew he hardly had that much in the bank at the moment. But he had this month's wages in his desk drawer. He noticed that Quails was still wearing the Hargreaves ring. 'I will buy that ring for twenty pounds, or you will leave with nothing.'

Quails hesitated for a moment. Then he took the ring from his finger. 'Twenty pounds?'

'Go into the hall and collect your things. I will bring the money out to you.'

The exchange was quickly effected, and the unwelcome visitor was shown the door. Hargreaves watched him walk down the drive, before returning to his study and sinking into his chair with a sigh of relief. It could have been a lot worse.

Chapter 46

Several days later, Rosalie and Bethany arrived at Staplewood to enquire after Emily's health and eager to give Hargreaves the latest news about Julia and Matthew. She found Emily in the drawing room, red-nosed, surrounded by shawls, and a distinct aura of balsam.

'My dear Rosalie, pray do not come close. I would not wish this foul cold on anyone, although I believe the worst is now over. You and Bethany go and entertain poor Charles, who has had no one to talk to since he returned. Just tell me, was everything resolved?'

'Yes, I believe so. Julia was very much out of favour for her escapade, but Matthew was absolved from blame.' Rosalie gave Emily the magazines she had brought, copies of *La Belle Assemblée* and *Tatler,* and went in search of Bethany.

She found her daughter and Lord Hargreaves poring over a book in the library. 'Don't be a trial to Lord Hargreaves, Beth, darling.'

'Lady B, Bethany is never any trouble to me. We get on very well.' He smiled. 'Don't we, Beth?'

Hargreaves ushered Rosalie into his study, leaving the adjoining door open. 'Did you have a difficult time with the Coverdales?'

'I'm glad to say they didn't blame me for Julia's ill-considered flight. However, I do believe that you, My Lord, were not really surprised. I think you knew more of what was in the wind than I did. Is that not so?' She raised her eyebrows.

'Perhaps, but to separate them—as you would have felt it your duty to do, would, in my opinion, have done more harm than good. Lay the blame on me, Lady B.'

Rosalie laughed. 'For all you're a hard-bitten lawyer, I think you are just a romantic at heart!'

Hargreaves didn't deny it. 'Please, be seated.' He indicated a coffee pot and two cups on a small table. 'May I pour you some?'

Before she sat down, something glinting on Hargreaves's desk caught Rosalie's eye. She pointed to it. 'What is that?' she asked.

'Pick it up. It is quite heavy. I have been using it as a paperweight.'

'But what is it? I have an insatiable curiosity. Benedict used to tease me about it.'

Hargreaves was amazed. It was the first time Lady B had mentioned her late husband in such a casual way; somehow, it gave his heart a little lift.

'Well,' said Rosalie again, 'what is it?' She sat down to examine the object more closely.

'It's one of the gilded grapes from the staircase. Matthew dislodged it during an ill-advised attempt to go upstairs on his crutches, and then we couldn't find it.'

'So where was it?'

'Under Bedford's blanket. He must have found it and hidden it.'

'Poor Bedford. I think it was partly Matthew's distress that decided Julia to go to him.' Rosalie looked closely at the small hole at one end of the grape. 'That's strange,' she said.

'What is?'

'If you look into this hole, it's all gold. I mean inside. I've never heard of gilding where no one can see it. It should be black—like iron.'

Hargreaves picked up a silver-mounted magnifying glass, and Rosalie handed him the grape. After careful inspection, he said, 'You're right, Lady B. It *is* gold inside. Too.'

'Have you ever paid attention to all the drawings for the staircase, My Lord? I was in the library when Matthew was looking at them, and of course, I had to have a good look, too.' Rosalie chuckled.

'I gave them a cursory glance. They're back in the muniment room now.'

'Matthew said it was strange that the plans had all been paid for but there was no record of the work ever having been undertaken by the firm. But I expect he told *you* that, too.'

'Quite probably, but I can't remember. There was so much stuff to go through, you know.'

'Wouldn't it be extraordinary if that grape turned out to be pure gold. It's soft, you know—real gold, I mean. Perhaps that's why it fell off. Would it not be wonderful if all of the grapes and leaves were made of gold? You would be fabulously wealthy!'

'Oh, Lady B!' He burst out laughing. 'You have a wonderful imagination. You think the first Lord Hargreaves built his famous fortune into his staircase?'

Rosalie pouted. 'I don't see why not.' She drained the last of her coffee. 'I must be going. Beth!' she called to her daughter. 'Gather your things. The trap will be here any minute.'

As Hargreaves bowed over Rosalie's hand, he could barely resist the temptation to take her in his arms. But of course he had to resist, not only now—but always.

He went to see his sister in the drawing room, where her red nose was deep into *La Belle Assemblée*. She looked up. 'You know, Charles, I do believe skirts are going to get even wider this season!'

'Really? Lady B sends her good wishes for your speedy recovery.'

'She's a lovely lady. You like her very much, don't you, Charles? Why don't you ask her to be your wife?'

'Emily! Don't be ridiculous. How could I possibly support a wife? This place takes every penny I have. I'm just thankful Nicky's education is safely in a trust. And before you say anything, you already contribute more than your fair share of the housekeeping.' He wandered over to the French doors and looked into the conservatory at the huge vine, just showing fat green buds and thought, *Selling real grapes would be far more use than gilded metal ones.*

That evening, seated in his favourite chair, enjoying the occasional pleasure of smoking a clay pipe, Hargreaves was idly turning over the pages of the large book Matthew had given him. He reached the page devoted to Coverdale Hall, and the paper marking the page slid onto his knee. It was about seven inches long and folded concertina style, making it about one inch wide, but a piece had been roughly torn from the bottom, leaving an uneven edge. Hargreaves unfolded it, but it was bare of writing, except that, just above the tear, were the handwritten words 'Lord Benedict St Maure.'

But it was the shape of the tear that reminded him of something—something recent. He carefully tapped out the pipe and racked his brains. The image became clear, as he remembered the piece of paper Lady B had given him after her dinner party to pass on to Matthew, but he'd forgotten. He sent for Royston to enquire.

'Yes, M'lord. I removed it from your pocket and placed it in your dressing table drawer.'

'Please fetch it for me.'

As soon as he had it in his hand, he decided to consult the fount of all wisdom and went in search of Emily.

'My dear, what do you make of these? They are from the book Matthew gave me.' He handed her both parts of the bookmark.

'Can I have a look at the book, too, please?'

Hargreaves went to get it and returned to see his sister examining the smaller piece. 'What does this sign mean, Charles?' She had turned it over and looked at the back—something none of them had done on that first day at Mairsford.

Faint but clearly written in pencil was '\$7.23.'

'It is the sign Americans use for the dollar. It would mean seven dollars and twenty-three cents.'

'It's in Matthew's hand,' said Emily. 'He's left-handed, you know, and the figures slope backwards. The writing on the bigger piece is in a different hand.'

'There's an inscription in the front of the book.' Hargreaves placed the volume on Emily's lap and put his finger on the writing inside the front cover.

Emily looked at it closely and then announced, 'They're the same. Matthew's mother must have written them both!'

'What does that tell us, then?'

'Don't be so obtuse, Charles. Don't you see?'

'No.'

Emily heaved a sigh. 'It means that she wrote, "Lord Benedict St Maure, Mairsford, Kent," on the paper; folded it up; and used it as a bookmark.'

'Quite possibly. But that doesn't explain why Matthew was holding it when Nicky nearly ran him over, does it?'

'It could do. Let me think.' Emily creased her brow.

While she was pondering, her brother rang for Parsons to bring some wine. When he had done so, Hargreaves pored a glass for his sister and handed it to her. Well?' he enquired.

Emily took a sip of her wine. 'I think it could have gone something like this, Charles. Imagine if Matthew was looking at the book. He did say he must have packed it because he was coming to England, and it might be of interest.'

Hargreaves nodded. 'Yes. I recall that.'

'Now just suppose that, while he was doing so, he remembered he owed someone seven dollars and twenty-three cents, or they owed it to him. It would be quite natural to use the nearest piece of paper to jot it down. So he tore the bottom off the bookmark and put it in his waistcoat pocket. Then all those terrible things happened to him, and that little scrap of paper with "Mairsford, Kent" written on it was the only thing he had left!' Emily finished triumphantly, convinced she had solved the problem.

Hargreaves looked at his sister, shrewdly, before saying slowly, his lawyer's caution to the fore. 'Yes, I suppose it *could* have happened like that, but there's no proof.'

'The proof is the fact that he was looking at the paper, while standing by that signpost. Despite near starvation, and terrible injuries to his feet, he had almost reached his destination—even if he didn't know why.'

After a little thought, Hargreaves said, 'You know Emily. Perhaps I should let Lady B, know about this discovery.'

'Why, Charles?'

'Well. Matthew did end up at Mairsford Manor. And her late husband's name is on the bookmark, written by his mother.'

'I don't think that is a good idea,' replied Emily, quite firmly. Before her brother could reply, she went on. 'It might upset her. And I'm sure you don't want to do that, now do you?'

'What about the Coverdales then?' said Hargreaves. 'I feel someone ought to know, and Matthew certainly can't tell them, although I'm sure he would, if he could. But I will give it some thought.'

'Yes, Charles. You do that.'

A little while later, he found Emily in the conservatory and came straight to the point. 'About what we were discussing earlier.'

'You've decided what to do?'

'Yes, I've decided what *you* should do. You should write to Lady Coverdale and tell her all you have told me and enclose the bookmark and the torn off piece. She will undoubtedly discuss it with her husband, and I believe they have a right to know everything about Matthew, as their daughter is practically engaged to him.'

'Very well, Charles. I will do it right away, but I do not think for one moment that Matthew is involved in any kind of duplicity, and no one will convince me otherwise.'

Hargreaves smiled, 'I agree with you, Emily. But that is not the point. I will take the letter with me when I go to London in a few days' time.'

Chapter 47

That night, Hargreaves tossed and turned in bed, before finally falling asleep, and dreaming that he was dancing the waltz, something he hadn't done for years, with Lady B in his arms. Her skirt was so wide he kept tripping over it and saying sorry. She said it wasn't his fault, because her head was very heavy; the grapes in her head-dress were all made of real gold. He woke with a start as Royston pulled back the bed curtains, to place his tea on the bedside table. But the dream made him decide to examine the staircase more closely.

Parsons was quite surprised to find his master halfway up the stairs, apparently trying to pull off one of the gilded leaves. 'May I be of assistance, My Lord?'

'Oh, Parsons, yes. You remember Mr Matthew inadvertently dislodged one of the grapes, and no one could find it?'

'Yes, M'lord,' said the butler impassively.

'Mr Matthew found it in Bedford's bed after the dog died and returned it to me. But I was wondering if anything else was loose—a leaf, perhaps. You take the other side and just give each one a little tug.'

'Certainly, M'lord,' said the butler, managing to convey compliance and disapproval simultaneously. It was not long before he announced that he had found a loose one, as requested.

Hargreaves gave it a wiggle, and the leaf came away in his hand. 'Thank you, Parsons. That'll be all for now, but I suppose they should all be checked. They've been there for a long time.'

He returned to his study, holding the leaf and the grape—one in either hand, trying to put all the facts he had gleaned together. There was the underground room that might have been used as a forge; the Indian servant who had visited the blacksmith; the little book with the dates and probable payments: The rumoured fabulous wealth, which apparently had not descended through the family; and finally, the elaborate designs for the staircase, that had not been executed by the firm that had drawn them up.

Hargreaves considered his next move but was determined to say nothing until he had proof, one way or the other. He was due in the House of Lords for the last vote before the Easter recess and decided to take the gold with him to London—where he was sure an assayer would be easy to find. He also took with him the letter for Lady Coverdale, penned by Emily.

Justin and Amanda entered the drawing room of the Dower House, the residence they preferred to Coverdale Hall when they were not entertaining. The evening sun of early spring washed the pale yellow walls, and an open window admitted the shrieks and laughter of their children playing a raucous game of cricket on the newly scythed grass. Justin walked over and closed it. 'Well, Amanda, my dear, what do you make of Emily Hargreaves's letter?'

His wife, who was holding it, said, 'I think she may very well be right, Justin.'

'And that doesn't worry you?'

'Not in the least. Should it?'

Justin took the armchair opposite to her. 'You don't think it has all been a ploy by Matthew to ingratiate himself with the family ...'

His voice trailed off as he saw the look on Amanda's face, before she gave a hoot of laughter. 'That, my darling, is utterly ridiculous, and you know it.'

Justin looked a little abashed. 'I suppose so, but I have to think of Julia.'

'Of course. We both have to think of our daughter, but my thoughts have been running in a different direction.'

'Oh, really?'

'Yes. Now don't you laugh, because I'm deadly serious, and Emily's letter sort of backs it up.'

'Backs what up, my dear?'

'That Matthew could be Benedict's son.'

'What?!' Justin exploded.

'I knew you'd react like that. But *it is possible,* you know,' Amanda continued quickly, before her husband could interrupt. 'You told me categorically that Matthew's Tunbridge Ware box once belonged to Benedict. and how you were so overcome when you saw it again. So there has to be a connection. We also know that Matthew's father was seventy-two when he died. The War Office told you. So he must have been sixty-two when Matthew was born—'

Finally, Justin interrupted. 'You're saying that Benedict had an affair with the garrison commander's wife in the middle of the war.'

'It wasn't the middle. It was the beginning. And he and his battery were unable to move for weeks. The sergeant told me …Yes, Justin, I went down to Longacre farm this morning, and—'

'Asked him if my brother had an affair with Mrs Stuart.' Justin raised his voice angrily.

'No, of course not. I took some preserves for his wife and mentioned that we had met someone from Canada, and what was it like? And he told me about the guns being bogged down and having to remain in York.. So I then asked him about the living quarters and the people. In all honesty, he didn't know much, only that Benedict had stayed with the commanding officer and his wife. I promise you, Justin; it was quite casual and chatty.'

Despite being rather cross with his wife, the marquis was also curious. 'Did he say anything about Colonel Stuart's wife?'

'He said he only saw her once, when he was talking to Benedict, and she came out to tell him that dinner was ready. I asked him what she was like, and he said she was a fine-looking woman and much younger than her husband.'

'But Benedict wouldn't—'

'No, perhaps not, but *she* might. A beautiful childless woman with an elderly husband and a young, handsome officer, three thousand miles from home, nervous about his first campaign. He could be ripe for seduction, don't you think?'

Justin got up; walked up and down the room several times, scratching his head; and then went to a side table where a decanter of wine and glasses were displayed on a silver tray. 'I need a drink. Do you want one?'

Drinks in hand, he offered one to Amanda. Justin sat down again and drew deeply on the wine. 'It's all a bit far-fetched, you know. But I suppose it is possible—if not probable.'

'It would have made everyone happy, you know. Mrs Stuart would have the child she always wanted. Colonel Stuart would have a son to carry on the name—all men want that; you should know. And Benedict would either be killed in battle or return home completely unaware. And there's my feeling,' Amanda added.

'What feeling?' said Justin ominously.

''Well, it was right at the beginning, when I went to stay with Rosalie, and Matthew was so very ill, and no one knew who he was. He was lying in bed, so thin his body hardly made a ripple in the coverlet. His head was bandaged and his face bearded. But for a moment, I thought it was Benedict, lying there. Then he opened those lovely navy blue eyes, and the moment was over. Perhaps someone was trying to tell me something, but I've never forgotten that feeling.'

Justin drew in a dep breath. 'You know, Amanda. We shall never know the truth. But if you're "feelings" are right, and he is Benedict's son, it makes him Julia's first cousin.'

'Does that *really* matter, Justin? Matthew has all the attributes that would make Benedict proud of him. And besides, there is every reason to believe that Queen Victoria will marry her first cousin, Prince Albert of Saxe Coburg Gotha. And surely what is good enough for the queen is good enough for our daughter.'

Justin refilled both their glasses. 'As I said, my dear, all this is just speculation. And whatever we think, we should keep it to ourselves.'

'You don't think we should tell Rosalie? She might be pleased to think—'

'No. She might be very upset. It's best we forget we ever had this conversation. Everyone will be much happier if we do.'

Hargreaves returned to Staplewood Park in the knowledge that he was potentially a very rich man, and could barely get the words out when he told Emily what had happened.

'What are you waiting for, then? Go and tell— I mean go and ask her. You've wanted to long enough.'

'I'll ride over to Mairsford right away.'

'No, Charles, you will not. You will call Royston and have a wash and a shave and change into your best clothes, while I get Hampton to bring round the carriage. Looking like you do now is no way to propose to the lady you love,' Emily said severely, but her face was wreathed in smiles.

Hargreaves could hardly wait for Soames to announce him. 'You were right, Lady B. You were right!' he said, rushing across the room to bow over lady B's hand. 'The grape has been tested by Johnson Matthey. They are the assayers to the Bank of England. It's all pure gold.' Hargreaves was quite breathless with excitement.

'I think you had better sit down, My Lord, before you explode all over my carpet!' Rosalie laughed. 'But it's wonderful news. If the whole staircase is all made of gold, you are a rich man indeed, I will call for some wine to celebrate. But what an strange thing for the first lord to do – hide his wealth from his entire family.'

'I don't suppose we will ever know, and quite frankly I don't care. It will give me the freedom to do all the things I want to do—modernise Staplewood, improve the estate, rebuild the lodge, start the adult reading classes. And I owe it all to you, Lady B.'

'Is that all?' Rosalie said, the corners of her mouth turning down. 'I thought you had something much more important to do—something I have been waiting for you to ask me for some time!'

'I cannot think what you mean, Lady B,' said Hargreaves gravely, but the look in his eyes betrayed him.

'And I think you do, Charles, my dear. Isn't it about time you started to call me Rosalie and ask me a very important question?'

He did.

'Yes.' said Rosalie

Soames opened the door and then quickly closed it again when he saw his mistress and Lord Hargreaves clasped in each other's arms.

The wedding took place in St Saviour's, Upper Mairsford, on a sun-drenched April morning. The church was filled with spring flowers, the colours echoed in Rosalie's cream satin dress, trimmed with embroidered forget-me-nots. Bethany, dressed in pale blue muslin, with a circlet of primroses in her hair, was the proud bridesmaid. Nicky acted as best man to his father, and Sir Piers Abbot, Rosalie's brother, gave her away. Neither family had many close relatives, but Harriet Hargreaves and the Ascourts and Emily and Matthew supported the groom, and the Coverdales, along with Mrs Sylvia and Lady Sophia Abbot were on the bride's side.

However, the church was far from empty. All the ground staff and household employees from both houses filled the rear pews and formed an arch of flowers as the newlyweds left the church to take the long way back, through Lower Mairsford and Staplewood to the park, where the wedding breakfast was to take place.

The long table was dressed with flowers and all the silverware Parsons could muster. The guests were standing behind their chairs, awaiting the arrival of the bride and groom. The sound of the carriage was heard, and Rosalie's maid, Jenny, was in the hall, ready to see that Rosalie's dress was not crumpled. George opened the dining room door wide; the newlyweds stood framed in the doorway, while applause echoed round the room.

Soames announced in solemn tones, 'Lord and Lady Hargreaves.'

Charles and Rosalie looked at each other and smiled delightedly. Then Hargreaves pointed at the table. 'Oh, my God!' he exclaimed. 'Look, Rosalie. That must be the Hargreaves ship!'

And it was. Appearing to sail majestically along the table, on a sea of blue-green silk, was a magnificent silver galleon in full sail. The couple took their places at the head of the table. Grace was said, and the meal began. Parsons was standing behind his master's chair, Hargreaves beckoned his butler forward and pointed to the ship. 'How did this happen, Parsons? Where did it come from? Where was it found?'

'I was commissioned to find it, M'lord.'

'By whom?'

Parsons gave one of his rare smiles. 'I am afraid I am not at liberty to say, M'lord.' But the butler's gaze travelled down the table and fixed a meaningful look on Matthew, who gave a resigned smile and nodded.

'It was Mr Matthew, M'lord. He asked if I could discover the ship's whereabouts.'

'Was that difficult?' asked Rosalie.

'Not really, M'lady. I have many contacts in London.'

'You must tell us all about it one day, Parsons. I'm sure it must have been very exciting.'

'It will be my pleasure, M'lady.'

'Rosalie squeezed her husband's hand gently, and her smiling blue eyes looked into his. 'Matthew did it for you, Charles.'

'No, my darling. I think he did it for both of us.'

THE END.....but,

If you would like to read about Amanda, Justin, Rosalie and Benedict, ypu will find their story in : "THE YELLOW DIAMOND.

Acknowledgements

Writers work mostly alone, but the encouragement, information, and helpful comments of others: friends, fellow writers and those with technical know how, are invaluable. For this reason I would like to convey my warmest thanks to: Joyce Rawlings; Roger Woodward and Margaret Thuegood for their time and patience, and also to my dear late husband for his knowledge of metalwork. Finally to my publishers: AuthorHouse, for keeping calm when all about me seemed chaotic!